# PRAISE FOR PETER DAVID

"David is a genuine master of the tie-in novel, and provides smart handling of *Star Trek*® elements and a brisk story, enhanced by well-done action scenes and the ability to give the *Star Trek* universe a lived-in feel."

—*Publishers Weekly*

"Peter David's writing has always been the epitome of *Star Trek* fiction; written by a fan, for fans. [*New Frontier*] is easily his most ambitious project since *Imzadi*."

—*DreamWatch*

"An established *Trek* novelist whose name is a . . . guarantee of quality."

—*SFX magazine*

# STAR TREK®
# NEW FRONTIER™
## EXCALIBUR

# RESTORATION

**Peter David**

**Based on *Star Trek: The Next Generation*
created by Gene Roddenberry**

**POCKET BOOKS**
New York   London   Toronto   Sydney   Singapore

*This one is for my mom, Dalia*

---

For information regarding special discounts for bulk purchases,
please contact Simon & Schuster Special Sales at 1-800-456-6798
or business@simonandschuster.com

POCKET BOOKS, a division of Simon & Schuster, Inc.
1230 Avenue of the Americas, New York, NY 10020

Originally published in hardcover in 2000 by Pocket Books

This book is published by Pocket Books, a division of
Simon & Schuster, Inc., under exclusive license from
Paramount Pictures.

ISBN: 0-7434-1064-5

First Pocket Books paperback printing November 2001

10 9 8 7 6 5 4 3 2 1

Printed in the U.S.A.

# RHEELA

SHE KNEW HE WAS COMING before she even saw him.

It wasn't unusual for her to feel that he was approaching. Truth be known, most days she would get a cold feeling in the base of her spine. At those times, wherever she was—whether it be doing chores in her run-down abode or standing on the cracked and arid plain that constituted what she laughingly referred to as her property—she would stop what she was doing and wait to see if some sign of him appeared on the horizon.

Most times, it did not. On such occasions, the feeling would pass, and she would return to whatever it was that she had been doing. In short order, she would forget that she had felt any sense of dread at all.

This time, however, when she *did* see him making his approach, all those false alarms were naturally forgotten. Instead, all Rheela could think was, *I knew it. I can always tell when he's coming.* A gentle breeze was wafting across the plain, which was an unusual enough event in and of itself. She straightened the strands of green hair that were blowing in her face and turned back to the house. "House" might have been far too generous a term; it was not much more than a hut, although it was built of sturdy enough materials that it managed to keep the interior remarkably cool, despite the crushing heat. Just to provide a bit of style, she had even constructed a small porch on the front of the hut. She now sat on the edge of the porch, arranging her hands neatly in her lap and staring out at the emptiness of her land. Every so often, she would glance down at her hands, turning them over and studying them as if she was looking at someone else's hands. They were leathery and weather-beaten. When she had been a little girl, her skin had been so fair, so pale; but now it was such a dark brown that it seemed as if the sun had baked her as thoroughly as it had the land around her.

It was amazing, though, that the vegetation—her crops—was still fighting resiliently for life. They poked up through the cracks, green and brown cacti-like plants that seemed determined to ignore the untenable nature of their respective situations. They were going to need water, though, and very soon. It wasn't just her crop, either; she'd been hearing as much from other steaders as well. They spoke to her, as always, with that telltale look of annoyance and resentment, even as they talked wistfully of the rain that was needed in order to salvage their crops.

She looked to the sky, trying to feel the moisture in the air, in her bones. Nothing was forthcoming. But she could have sworn that the intensity of the heat was growing, rolling in waves off the land. Not for the first time, she felt a sense of vague despair. She didn't simply reside on the world of Yakaba. She fought it. She struggled with it every single day, the way that a germ cell would battle the white blood cells that strove to kill it. It wasn't her favorite analogy, though, because that, in essence, made her the infection, and she didn't fancy thinking of herself in that way. But perhaps that was how the planet thought of her.

The wind was picking up, and she heard a distant rolling. Although she continued to sit on the porch, still she shielded her eyes with one leathery hand while studying the horizon line. Ironically, she knew what she was going to see before she actually saw it. Sure enough, there he was: Tapinza.

Tapinza's skin was not a golden bronze color despite the sun.

Instead, much of the paleness that was typical for those of the Yakaban race was still present. Not unusual, then, that Tapinza was clad appropriately, with a wide-brimmed hat and long coat that flapped in the steady breeze as he sped toward Rheela's stead. He was clutching the rigging of his customized sailskipper, guiding it with an expert hand. Rheela had to give him that much: When it came to sailskippers and similar desert transportation, Tapinza was second to none.

What did surprise her, however, was the smaller form that was also clutching the main mast of the sailskipper. She blinked and rubbed her eyes, not quite believing what her eyes were informing her she was seeing. "Moke," she called cautiously toward the house behind her, and when there was no immediate answer, she repeated, louder this time, *"Moke!"* Still no reply. She got up and went into the house to look around for herself, and, to her utter shock, found that Moke was, in fact, not there. She had been absolutely positive that her son had been indoors napping, and the fact that he was not was, to say the least, disconcerting. What brought it several levels *above* disconcerting was that it meant her eyes had not deceived her. It was unquestionably Moke clutching the sailskipper, the increasing breeze driving the skipper along faster and faster. And even from this distance, she could now hear the child's voice calling, "Maaaa! Look, Maaaaa!" across the broken plains.

"Hold tightly, boy," Tapinza warned him, "we have quite a few solid gusts propelling us toward your mother." Then he laughed quite heartily. Rheela had never liked the sound of his laughter. It sounded . . . cultivated. As if he had stood in front of a mirror for hours on end and practiced delivering a confident-yet-unthreatening laugh of which he could be proud. Everything about him seemed manufactured. For a woman whose very existence depended on nature, someone as "fabricated" as Tapinza could not help but set off all manner of mental warnings within her.

Tapinza had a fierce scar that ran from the top of his forehead to just under his nose. How he had acquired it was something of a mystery; in all the years he had resided on Yakaba, he had never once hinted at the mishap that apparently had laid open part of his face. His brow was a bit sloped, his eyebrows thick and green, and the overall effect was to give him the air of a primitive.

Rheela's impulse was to take issue—very loudly and very intently—with the fact that Tapinza had been reckless with her son's safety. Ultimately, however, she decided to try and tone down her ire, because it was so rare that Moke looked as happy as he did at that moment. She actually heard that rarest of commodities on Yakaba—rarer even than water—namely, her son's laughter, echoing across the plains. As opposed to the "manufactured" sound of Tapinza, Moke laughed with pure childhood abandon. There was such joy in it that Rheela felt a tightening in the pit of her stomach. She almost felt grateful to Tapinza, and she had to remind herself that such sentiments could prove disastrous if left unchecked.

Moke looked like a miniature version of his mother, so much so that she derived some amusement from it. She had yet to cut his hair; it hung in ragged braids, framing his face when he was at rest (which was seldom). As it was now, it fairly flew behind him as he whipped along across the desert, holding on for dear life while simultaneously celebrating a life most dear.

For a moment Rheela was convinced that the sailskipper was going to crash into the side of the house, and then Tapinza whipped it around. The wheels scudded across the plain, chewing up dirt and sending a small cloud scattering. Moke jumped off the sailskipper and ran excitedly to his mother. "You should ride it, Ma!" he said without preamble. "Maester Tapinza said he would take you!"

"Titles are never necessary among friends. A simple 'Tapinza' will do," Tapinza said to him. But as he spoke, his gaze was not upon the son, but instead upon the mother. The comment was obviously being delivered to her, and the small child was, of course, unaware of the subtleties of what was happening around him.

"Quite expertly guided, Maester Tapinza," said Rheela; continuing the use of the title, she was sending a message so clear that a blind man could have read it from ten feet away. "However, considering I was under the impression that my son was indoors, I am

4

most curious as to what he was doing sailing around the desert with you."

"You're asking the wrong person, Rheela," he replied. "I was simply out and about, minding my own business. I happened upon young Moke, wandering about on his own. I thought that it would be only appropriate to return him to you." Just to be extra dashing, Tapinza removed his hat and bowed deeply, sweeping the hat across the arid ground. The gesture kicked up a bit of dust.

Rheela shifted her gaze to her son, who had suddenly developed a great fascination with the tops of his own feet. "Moke," Rheela said very slowly, very distinctly, "what were you doing out? It's the hottest part of the day. You should know better."

Moke shrugged.

"Moke, what would you have done if Maester Tapinza hadn't picked you up?"

He shrugged again. Much of his vocabulary seemed shaped by shrugs.

She should have let it pass. But instead, Rheela felt—as unreasonable as it sounded—as if the boy was showing her up somehow. Being defiant of her while in the presence of a man in front of whom she did not wish to be defied. This time, she resolved, shrugs would not be sufficient. She took Moke firmly by the shoulders and asked once more, "Why were you out?" trying to make it clear by her tone of voice that an articulated response would be the only acceptable one.

Moke took a deep breath, and then looked her squarely in the eyes. "Looking for Dad," he said.

*Well, you deserved that,* thought Rheela. She didn't release the boy so much as her fingers simply slipped loose of him. He didn't step away from her, though, but just stood there and eyed her with curiosity.

"I didn't find him," Moke added, almost as an afterthought . . . and then he looked curiously at Tapinza and back to his mother. "Did I?"

"No," she said tonelessly. "No . . . I'd wager you didn't."

" 'Cause I thought maybe Maester Tapin—"

*"No."* This time she spoke much more quickly, and with far greater force. It was so loud, in fact, that Moke jumped slightly. "No . . . Maester Tapinza is not Daddy."

"Are you sure?" He sounded a bit regretful.

"Yes . . . quite sure."

"How do you know?"

Rheela didn't quite have an answer ready for that one. Surprisingly, it was Tapinza who stepped in and said firmly, "Because if I *was* your father, Moke . . . I would never have left."

Much to Rheela's relief, the response seemed to satisfy the boy. Feeling drained of any energy to continue conversation along these lines, Rheela ruffled the hair on his head and said, "Go in now. You're overheated as it is. I want you to keep cool . . . at least, as cool as you can." Moke nodded, then impulsively hugged his mother before darting into the house.

"My home is considerably cooler," Tapinza observed. "I have a cooling system now. You are welcome any time."

"Yes. I am well aware of that, Maester," she said, with a laugh that was equal parts amusement and bitterness. "It is difficult to be unaware of that which goes on in your home. It is . . . quite impressive."

"Thank you."

She rose from kneeling, dusting herself off as she did so. "It was not intended as a compliment. However, you did bring my boy home . . . and I was not even aware that he was missing. For that, I do owe you my thanks. So, I suppose it all evens out."

"The boy," Tapinza said slowly, *"does* deserve a father, you know."

"Very little in this life has anything to do with what is deserved, Maester. If I have learned anything in my time in this sphere, it is that. If you'll excuse me . . ."

She turned to head back into the house, but then realized that Tapinza didn't seem to be showing any intention of departing. She turned back to face him, one eyebrow cocked in curiosity. "Something else, Maester . . . ?"

"Is it really so necessary that you address me formally?"

"I do very little in this world that I don't deem necessary, Maester."

Tapinza gestured toward the house. "At the very least—even if you have little regard for what is deserved—the child should be entitled to know who his father is."

"That is between Moke and me."

"And me."

Her temper flared, and she took a step down from the porch. "What do you mean by that?"

"I asked him if he knew. He said he did not." Tapinza idly moved his hat from one hand to the other. "I asked him, if he did not know who his father was, how he would recognize his father if he did meet him. He said that he hoped that, instead, his father would recognize him. It was somewhat sweet, actually."

"Perhaps it was, but I will thank you not to discuss such matters with him. Ultimately, they can only serve to upset him."

"I would not do that for all the world."

"Maester," and she came down the last step, standing eye to eye with him, "I think there is very little you would not do for all the world."

"Who is his father? I know beyond a doubt that it is not I," and he smiled mirthlessly, "having never had the pleasure of—"

"Shut up," she said sharply, and then inwardly cursed herself for allowing him to rattle her so easily.

"The people of Narrin are likewise curious."

She shook her head. "The people of Narrin must have very little of true import on their minds, to worry about matters that are none of their affair."

"You fascinate them, Rheela. Fascinate them and frighten them, because they depend on you so, yet they know little about you. People fear that which they do not know."

"I do not see the good people of Narrin flocking to my door to try and learn more of me," she replied. "If they are so over-whelmed with curiosity, let them ask. Otherwise, they—and you—are cordially invited to attend to your own business and leave me to mine." She paused, and then said in exasperation, "What do you want of me?"

"You know what I want, Rheela. We have discussed it innumerable times."

"No. We've 'discussed' nothing. You've spoken of it, and I have turned you down. That does not fit any definition of 'discussion' that I know."

He sighed heavily. "You provide a service, Rheela. A service for which you charge nothing. That is foolishness."

"Is it?" She was only half-listening to him now. Instead, she was starting to detect the first bits of moisture. They were meager and spare, but it was enough to work with. She could almost sense the desperation in her crops. The juices that were nurtured inside the plants were still there, but they would not last much longer if some sustenance was not provided, and soon. She licked her dry lips and looked to the skies, reaching out, gathering strength.

Tapinza was clearly oblivious to what she was up to. "Part of the reason people fear you is because you act in an altruistic manner. The average person does not understand altruism."

"But you are not an average person. You are the most successful businessman in Narrin Province . . . possibly in all of Yakaba. So you would be far more likely to understand it, yes?"

"Oh, yes. *Likely* to understand. That does not mean that I endorse it, however, or think it to be anything other than foolishness. And you seem like such a bright woman, Rheela. . . ."

"Do I? If I am so bright, then why did I allow Moke's father—whoever he is—to get away?"

"Even bright women have their lapses. For they remain women, after all."

"Your sympathy is appreciated," she said with rich sarcasm.

"You seek to help people out of the goodness of your heart. In that way, you hope to raise them up to your level. But people do not like to be raised, Rheela. It is much too much effort. They would far prefer to drag you down than to be lifted up themselves. When you treat people with such compassion, they are reminded of their own shortcomings. That will not endear you to them, no matter how much you would wish it otherwise. Now, commerce, trade, self-involvement, self-benefit . . . these are things they can appreciate and respond to. Since you do not charge them for the gifts you give them, they ascribe no value to them. If you charged them . . ." He smiled broadly. "They would come to love you."

"Perhaps, Maester, I care more about being loved by myself than I do about being loved by others." She took a deep breath to steady herself, channeling the effort. The skies began to darken slightly.

"I would not want you to do anything that would be at odds with your conscience," said Tapinza. "That is why, as always, I would be happy to serve as your agent in the matter."

"My agent."

"For a reasonable commission, I would broker your services to the residents of Narrin Province. They would pay handsomely, willingly. Plus, I am greatly respected in these parts, as you know."

"Respect and fear are not the same thing."

"They are when they need to be. In any event, people would view you in a different light by dint of your association with me. Of course . . . there are other associations that could accord you even greater respect and esteem in the eyes of others. . . ."

"I have my own eyes, Maester, which serve me quite well. I do not feel a need to concern myself with the eyes of others." She spoke in a very distant voice, as if Tapinza were no longer there— or, at the very least, of no real consequence to her. The wind was now whipping up in a most satisfactory manner, and small dust devils were already whirring across the plain . . . a sure sign that matters were progressing nicely.

Tapinza, for his part, didn't seem to be paying attention. He was much too caught up in his own words, his own vision of things. "We have spoken of this oftentimes before, Rheela, but talk becomes tiresome. It saddens me to see you so stubborn, needlessly inconveniencing yourself. I do not know what is in your eye when you look around you, but allow me to tell you what I see. I see a woman who made an error with some unknown man . . . A woman who came to this province with barely enough money to start her own homestead, a child in her belly, and a talent that could take her so far that it would be beyond her imagination. You have no long-term goal, Rheela. You have no plan, no great vision. I have none of your natural talent or ability, Rheela, but vision I have in abundance. I saw myself in a position of power, and now look at me. I have that power. I was able to reshape myself. Reshape my reality into something that more suited my desires. I can do that for you . . . provide you with a better home, better opportunities for yourself, for Moke. You have no reason not to take advantage of that which I'm offering you."

"No reason except that I do not trust you, and therefore would not join you in business . . . and I do not love you, and therefore would not join you in bed. As for what I have to offer the people of Narrin . . . my talents are as much from nature as anything else is. I will not charge them for that with which I was fortunate enough to be blessed. You are correct about one thing, Tapinza. I do have a conscience. It can be something of an annoyance at times, but I have learned to live with it. And if the people of Narrin have to live with it as well . . . then so be it."

Tapinza was about to reply when the first crack of thunder startled him. He looked up and around, and noticed the darkening of the skies for the first time. The wind was coming up even more fiercely than before. Then there was a noisy, scraping sound, and Tapinza saw that his sailskipper was starting to roll, the fierce winds having caught up the sails and started propelling the vehicle away. Even as he bolted for it, large droplets of water began to fall from the sky, first individually and then in clusters, and finally in great waves.

By that point, Tapinza was clutching the sailskipper, having given up any hope of actually managing to steer it. The sail vessel was not designed to handle easily in such fearsome winds. All

Tapinza could do now was hang on for the ride. And the winds were more than happy to give him that ride, shoving him back across the plains over which he'd come. As for Rheela, for the first time in quite a while, she felt the urge to laugh without question or restraint. For a moment, all her concerns, her murky future, and the suspicion in which all those who dwelt in the province held her . . . all of that didn't matter. All she cared about was the glorious moisture falling upon her, and being eagerly soaked up by the living things near her. The flora did not care in the least about her past, or Moke's father, or anything except what she could provide for them.

The rain came down even harder, and still she remained outside, allowing it to soak her through.

"Ma!" came Moke's voice. She turned to him, standing on the edge of the porch, and gestured for him to come down to her. He vaulted off the edge, ran to her, clasping her hands in his small ones, and they danced with one another in delirious circles of joy as the rain pelted them with moisture and life. The rain would not last long; not even her abilities could completely overcome the tendency toward drought that gripped Narrin Province. But, at the moment, it was enough, and after all this time, Rheela had learned to live for the moment.

In doing that, she didn't have to give a moment's thought to the threat that was implicit in Tapinza's tone, if not his words. For it was very clear to her that, as far as Tapinza was concerned, if she was not with him, then she was against him. It wasn't true, but if that was his perception, well, there was nothing she could do about that. And, of course, if he decided that she was against him . . . then he might very well take combative action. She could do nothing about that, either. That was for another moment . . . and she stubbornly refused to budge from the one that she was in.

She and Moke kicked off their shoes, skidded in the newly formed mud, and continued to dance in the soggy moment that was theirs.

\* \* \*

The rain was coming down just as fiercely in the city of Narrin (as opposed to the province), and Maestress Cawfiel was not impressed.

She watched through her window with disgust as, all through the streets of the small town, people were running about as quickly as they could, turning and somersaulting. Many had already stripped down to their undergarments (and, in the case of a couple of drunken revelers, even less) and were dancing about like mindless heathens. In the meantime, the water collectors were doing their job; the structures were turned up toward the sky, catching as much of the precipitation as possible in their funnels, to be stored for future use. A full fifty had been built over the past year around the perimeter of Narrin, and the town budget called for at least ten more. All of them fed into the underground reservoir from which the residents of Narrin, as well as the farmers in the outlying regions, got their supply of $H_2O$.

The reservoir had, in recent years, dropped lower and lower, to the point where there had been discussion as to whether Narrin could possibly survive. But then had come Rheela, and everything had been different.

However, the Maestress knew better than anyone that different was not always better. She continued to watch out her window, did Maestress Cawfiel, until she could endure it no longer. She bolted out the front door and into the street. Her feet sunk partway into the mud, and as she slogged her way through there was a distinct *thwuk* noise every time she managed to pull a foot out.

The revelers did not see her at first, but then someone noticed, and, very quickly, the word spread. Maestress Cawfiel was not one to mindlessly join in the celebrations of others. That was neither her place nor her function. So the celebrants knew that if the Maestress had entered the street in the midst of the cavorting, it was certainly not for the purpose of endorsing it, or even—heaven forbid—joining in.

She did not speak immediately. Instead, she just stood there, not even trying to move her feet anymore, because to do so was clumsy and not particularly dignified. She waited, for she had more patience than did anyone else in the city. ("City" might have been something of a misnomer, since Narrin had exactly one main street, and she was standing on it. The street itself was no more paved than any other part of Narrin Province; none of the buildings were higher than two stories, and were—for the most part—rather ramshackle. The place ran about two miles from end to end. In short, impressive it was most definitely not. But it was the only thing resembling civilization for miles around, so the inhabitants thought of it as a city, and there was none around to gainsay them.)

The patience of Maestress Cawfiel came as a result of her age, and that she had likewise in abundance. The Maestress was said to be older than dirt, and considering the amount of dirt they had in Narrin, that was pretty damned old. She was half a head shorter than the shortest adult in town, and yet, through the sheer force of her personality, she loomed large over it all. Her skin was so light as to be almost translucent, a sign of how rarely she came outside. The rain plastered her short, sensible green hair to the sides of her face, and water dribbled into her eyes, but she made no move to wipe it away. Instead, she just continued to stare, her head swiveling back and forth on her scrawny neck like the top of a short conning tower.

Bit by bit, the noises of celebration ceased, until all attention was focused on her. Once it had reached that point, she afforded a glance upward and smirked to herself. Just as she had expected . . . the clouds were already beginning to dissipate.

"Look at yourselves," she said in disgust.

Many of them could not bring themselves to do so, but a few of them did. Whether they were truly appalled at their sodden condition didn't really matter. If the Maestress felt they had reason to be, then they were.

"Look," she repeated. "Dancing about in the rain. Gallivanting around like imbeciles. Giving her exactly what she wants: your dependence."

There was some uneasiness among the erstwhile revelers, and then a man stepped forward. He was an older gentleman, and Cawfiel knew him instantly, of course. He was, after all, Praestor

Milos, the town's political leader. Duly elected for ten years in a row. Everyone was more than happy with the job he was doing, which didn't surprise Cawfiel in the least. Praestor Milos excelled, above all, at being beloved. But even Milos knew enough to stay out of Cawfiel's way if matters became truly difficult. He was, after all, concerned with their political life and the survival of their bodies. It was Cawfiel who had to attend to the survival and growth of their morality. Of the two, she had by far the harder job, and she never missed an opportunity to let Milos know it.

"Maestress," Milos said, making a visible effort to choose each word carefully. "The people are merely celebrating. Celebration is good for the soul . . . is it not?"

"Not when that celebration stems from obvious efforts to corrupt morality," shot back Cawfiel. "And we all aware of the immorality that poisons the woman called Rheela."

"We don't know for certain that Rheela was responsible for this rain," said Milos. It was an unconvincing statement, and everyone there knew it. No rain had been sighted, no storm fronts had been moving in of their own accord. Any storm that was this abrupt, and this encompassing, almost *had* to originate with Rheela, whether the Praestor wanted to admit it or not.

"Do not waste my time with such foolish comments," replied Cawfiel. She surveyed the people once more, looking with unveiled disgust at the sheer bits of clothing that were sticking, drenched, to their bodies. "Look at you. *Look at you!* You should be ashamed. Ashamed, I tell you! I see these sorts of displays, and I wonder about the future of our people. I wonder where it will all lead." The rain had tapered off to almost nothing. "I am a Maestress, by birthright, by training, by tradition. Am I to stand by and watch you make fools of yourselves, in celebration of a woman who is not entitled to such worship? To *any* worship? You know the evil of her . . . you all do. There is a darkness about her, which you are all willing to overlook because it suits you to do so. Her and that . . . that child of hers. And her powers that can only come from darkness."

"How do we know?" The question had come from someone in the crowd, but it wasn't clear who.

"How do we know her powers come from darkness?" The Maestress could scarcely believe the question, since the answer was so clear. "Isn't it obvious? We are, all of us in this town, Kolk'r-fearing, good people. If beings such as us were meant to have such powers . . . why wouldn't right-thinking, upstanding, morally straight people be given them? Why not me? Or the Praestor, with whom I may have my share of disagreements, but who still seems to me a good and right-thinking man when all is said and done."

"High praise indeed, Maestress," said Milos, bowing deeply. Water dripped off the top of his head when he bowed, and, self-consciously, he brushed it away.

"Isn't it obvious," she continued, "that the very fact that *she* has this ability and *we* do not means that it is inherently evil?"

There were murmurs of acquiescence. There was certainly no denying that logic.

"Do not," the Maestress continued, "let yourselves be caught up in her obvious chicanery." Her voice turned soft and sympathetic. "I know how difficult it is. I know how tempting it is to embrace the convenient. My lips know the same thirst, my throat the same parched sensation as your own. If we suffer, we suffer together. But we should not allow the temptations of one woman sway us into thinking, even for a moment, that Kolk'r above would support such . . . such abominations. And have you not considered the fact that, since Rheela came here, the rainfall has been even less than usual? Who is to say that she herself is not causing the extreme conditions? After all, if she is capable of bringing us rain . . . why is it so difficult to believe that she can also deprive us of it? I tell you that if you continue to embrace that which she provides you, it will end in death and destruction for this entire town."

As the rain tapered off and her words sunk in, the citizens clearly began to feel some degree of embarrassment. They covered themselves, picking up fallen pieces of clothing now caked with mud.

"Go to your homes," said Cawfiel. "Get cleaned up. Go about your business."

"And forget any of this happened," added the Praestor.

But to his obvious surprise, Cawfiel immediately countermanded him. "No. Do not forget this. Not even for a moment. Burn this into your memories for all time, as firsthand evidence of how those wielding powers of darkness can convince anyone—no matter how pure and good-hearted—to revel in evil. Only by remembering the mistakes of the past can you avoid them in the future."

There were nods and grunts of affirmation, and the people of Narrin headed for their homes. The Maestress did not move but, instead, simply stood there and watched them go. She knew them. She knew them all too well. Oh, they would make noises of repentance and claim that they felt badly for what had transpired. But the truth was that they were willing to tolerate Rheela, and this was just the latest evidence of that forbearance. At the times that Rheela came into town, some would look away or give her a wide berth. But there were others who greeted her civilly, if stiffly. And no one gave the slightest thought to forcing her to pack up her farm and get out of the Province. The Maestress knew exactly why that was. Despite whatever claims to the contrary they might make, the people had grown horribly dependent upon her in a depressingly short amount of time. Cawfiel felt as if she had let her people down on that score. And she knew that the time would come when she would have to do something about it.

She had simply not yet made up her mind precisely what that something would be. But when she did . . . that would definitely be the last that anyone heard of the weather witch who called herself Rheela.

"Pathetic little witch," she murmured. "Who could possibly help you now?"

# SHELBY

". . . Mackenzie Calhoun."

Elizabeth Paula Shelby, newly installed commander of the *Exeter,* looked up while maintaining a carefully neutral expression. "Pardon?" she said slowly.

The woman seated across the desk from her had come extremely highly recommended. Slim, bordering on diminutive, she nevertheless possessed an air of quiet authority. Her hair was long but knotted in an efficient bun, and her chin came to a point that was perpetually upthrust ever so slightly, as if she was leading with it.

"Mackenzie Calhoun," she repeated. "I was asking what he was really like. If everything people said about him was true."

Shelby had been studying her file on the computer screen, but now she turned it away on its pivot and looked squarely at the woman she was interviewing. "Tell me, Commander Garbeck . . . do you think my views on Mackenzie Calhoun are remotely relevant to this interview?"

"No, Captain," Commander Alexandra Garbeck acknowledged easily. "However, since you're going to be appointing me as your first officer, I did not feel it would be a breach of protocol if I inquired about the man. He was . . . a most interesting study."

"He was more than a study, Commander," said Shelby, choosing her words as if they were live hand grenades. "He was a fine man and a fine officer. And, frankly, I find your utter confidence over receiving this post to be—premature, shall we say?"

"That may be," Garbeck replied. "But I look at it this way, Captain. If I am, indeed, made your first officer, as I am hoping will be the case, then my confidence is not misplaced. If, on the other hand, I am wrong, then this is the only opportunity I will have to see you. Given that circumstance, does it not make sense to strike while the opportunity presents itself? I wish to learn more about Captain Calhoun . . . and, in particular, the circumstances involving the destruction of the *Excalibur.*"

"Why?"

"Because there are gaps," she said flatly. "I've read the transcripts of the hearings, the discussions . . . and there seem to be things missing. I don't know if that's the case because certain things are inexplicable, or because the people conducting the hearing didn't think to ask the right questions. Plus, Captain, I am hoping to lead a long and successful career in Starfleet. If something occurred that was preventable, I want to know how to prevent it, so that my ship and crew does not fall victim to the same fate."

Damn her, it seemed a reasonable request. That might have been the most annoying aspect of all.

"Are you familiar," she said slowly, "with the file known as the 'Double Helix' incident?"

"Of course," Garbeck said with such certainty that one would have thought Shelby had asked her if she knew that space was an airless vacuum. "A techno-virus designed to essentially collapse every computer base in the entire Federation, sending it spiraling into chaos."

"A very 'decorative' way of putting it, Commander," Shelby said, allowing a small smile. Then she became serious once more. "The *Excalibur,* as it so happens, was squarely in the middle of it . . . and, at one point, was rendered inoperative due to an early version of that very virus." She paused, waiting for some reason for Garbeck to prompt her with "And . . . ?" But Garbeck simply sat there and waited patiently, hands folded tidily in her lap.

So Shelby went on. "Unfortunately, even though we managed to deal with that situation when it happened, we didn't realize that there was a secondary virus also implanted within the computer, which was not detected. Over a period of time, it insinuated itself into all aspects of the ship's operation."

"And no diagnostics picked it up?" Garbeck sounded dumbfounded. "I mean, with all respect, your chief engineer sounds like he or she—"

"S/he, actually."

"Oh. A Hermat." Garbeck let out a sigh of very faint exasperation that gave Shelby the immediate impression Garbeck had her own war stories about dealing with Hermats. Shelby felt herself warming to her. "It sounds like s/he dropped the ball on this one."

"That was, indeed, one of the avenues that Starfleet pursued in its investigation. However, Burgoyne's track record on performing such diagnostics was flawless. The problem is—"

"The problem is," Garbeck said, and then immediately stopped herself. "I'm sorry. I shouldn't have interrupted, Captain. My apologies. Sometimes I get a bit ahead of myself."

"No, it's all right. Go ahead," said Shelby. "I know all about me, after all. This is for me to find out about you."

"Yes, well . . . the problem is that, for all the advancements made in everything from cybernetic response time to A.I., computers are still only as good as the information we feed into them. A diagnostic program can only look for that which it is programmed to look for. And if there is a new and unique virus, with a specially designed 'chameleon' factor that enables it to hide itself no matter what sort of search program is being instituted—"

"Exactly. Exactly right," Shelby said, nodding in approval. "In this instance, what Burgoyne postulated had happened was that the virus created a sort of internal null field around itself. So, any attempts to spot it resulted in those attempts reflecting back upon themselves. To put it in the parlance of old-time magicians: They did it with mirrors."

"So, what happened?"

*Ah, now she's asking,* Shelby thought with grim amusement. "Well, eventually the virus revealed itself, all right. Except that, by that point, it was too late. Essentially, once it had—over time—thoroughly ingrained itself into every aspect of the *Excalibur*'s system, it triggered a self-destruct sequence, setting the warp core to overload. And there was absolutely no way to shut it down. Don't think we didn't try."

"The saucer section—?"

But Shelby shook her head. "Locked it in. We couldn't activate the separation protocol."

Garbeck's eyes widened. It was obvious to Shelby that Garbeck was wondering—given the circumstances—what Shelby was even doing sitting there. All things being equal, there was no way she should have survived. Then her eyebrows puckered slightly in thought, and she said, comprehending, "The lifepods."

"Yes."

"Let me guess: The auto-eject sequences on the lifepods were also shut down." Before Shelby could confirm it, Garbeck was continuing, "Which would have meant that the only way to do it would be to employ the extreme option of individual manual override on each of the pods."

"Right," said Shelby. "We started loading crewmen into the lifepods and ejecting them as fast as we could. The problem is—"

She stopped. She was surprised at herself that she couldn't get it out. Considering the number of times that she had discussed it already, one would have thought that it would be easy for her by now. Except she found the recounting of the incident sticking in her throat, like a thing alive, refusing to emerge for the retelling.

And Garbeck seemed to understand. She said nothing at first, giving Shelby the opportunity to continue, but when she didn't, Garbeck said slowly, "The problem is that manual ejection of the lifepods—in an *Ambassador*-class ship such as the *Excalibur*—

has to be done from within the ship itself, at the lifepod stations. There wasn't an in-pod manual release. It was a design flaw that was corrected in subsequent starship models, including this one."

" 'Design flaw.' Is that what they're calling it?" Shelby said with grim sarcasm. "Nice of them to finally attend to that. Now, if I could just sit down with the genius who thinks that it's a good idea putting the bridge at the very top of the saucer section with a dome, making it an easy target, instead of hiding it in the interior of the ship for maximum protection . . ."

"If you'd like, I can send a memo to Central Design."

"I've sent three. Go argue with tradition." She shrugged. "In any event, the crew acted smoothly together, I'll give them that. Helping each other into pods, ejecting them from the ship to a safe distance. Eventually, though, it came down to the captain and me. Naturally, he . . ."

She stopped.

She couldn't keep going.

Silently, she cursed herself for what she felt was weakness on her part. It had happened, she had discussed it endlessly, and this simply shouldn't have been that difficult, dammit.

Alexandra Garbeck didn't say anything at first. Then, very softly, she said, "I'm sorry for your loss."

Shelby nodded.

"There is, however, something I don't quite understand," Garbeck said after a moment's more consideration. "The standard period of time between the realization of a warp core breach and the subsequent detonation of the ship is, at most, five minutes, eleven seconds."

"Something like that."

"Captain, with all respect, I feel as if something is still missing. I mean . . . five minutes." She shook her head, as if she was having trouble wrapping herself around the concept. "Five minutes to get the crew . . . the *entire crew* . . . into lifepods? To eject them, get them clear? That's . . . well, I don't know, it's just hard to believe."

"You would be amazed, Commander, how fear of imminent death can lend wings to one's feet."

"That may be, Captain, but even so—"

Shelby shrugged. "I don't know what else to tell you, Commander, except that we're here. I know that. We weren't all blown to pieces and replaced by a thousand or so impostors or clones. Whatever the reality of what should be, I can only tell you about the reality of what *was*. And what was . . . was that we survived, no matter how much the time frame seems to have been against us."

Her tone of voice suddenly shifted, became all business. "Now, then . . . enough of me . . . let's talk about you." She looked back to the computer file she had been perusing earlier. "Fast-track for promotion . . . double majored at the Academy in both science and tactics . . . four star approval ratings from three commanders you've served under . . ." She smiled and looked at Garbeck. "You're too perfect. What's wrong with you?"

"Nothing. It's a curse. I've learned to live with it," Garbeck deadpanned.

Shelby laughed at that. She found herself liking Garbeck even more.

Garbeck leaned forward and said earnestly, "Captain . . . it's very simple. I come from a long line of Starfleet officers. There was never a moment in my life when I didn't know what I was going to do with that life. It was a given. I freely admit, there has been no mystery, no great journey of self-discovery in my existence. I've reserved the voyage of discovery for my activities once I get out into space. That is my true home, and that's where I'm supposed to be. I know every regulation backward and forward. I know the case history of every major first-encounter situation that every Starfleet captain has ever had. I know the—"

Shelby interrupted. "General Order eighteen, subsection three."

*"Although all efforts are to be made to accommodate local traditions and customs whenever representing Starfleet and the Federation on member worlds, commanding officer will not designate away-team leadership responsibilities to any officer who voices*

22

*personal inability to cooperate with said traditions and customs,"*
Garbeck said crisply. *"Such lack of designation will be done without prejudice and not be reflected negatively on the officer's
record. This will include, but not be limited to, matters of personal
attire, specific dietary restrictions . . ."*

"All right, all right," Shelby laughed, putting up her hands to
admit defeat. "Very good. I'm officially impressed, particularly considering that you had that down word for word. No paraphrasing."

"You knew that because you likewise know them word for
word," Garbeck said.

Shelby nodded. "I've prided myself on that for a very long
time, Commander. Familiarity with rules, regulations. Knowing
precisely how everything can and should be done."

"Captain Calhoun didn't . . . well, I have no wish to speak ill of
the dead, Captain, particularly considering the circumstances,
but—"

"No need to speak ill, Commander, if what you're saying is a
truth that Captain Calhoun himself would have freely acknowledged. He had only passing interest in regs. He saw them as more
of a challenge than a guideline, as if . . . as if he took pride in finding ways around them." She was surprised to hear herself speak in
a tone of such gentle amusement. When Calhoun had been
around, and she had served under him, she'd found his attitude to
be nothing less than relentlessly aggravating. But now that he was
gone, there was a nostalgic haze surrounding the recollection.

"With no disrespect to the late captain—whose valor remains un-
questioned in any event—I believe very strongly in the importance
of regulations and procedure," Garbeck said firmly. "Starship captains have tremendous power at their disposal. Any time any one of
them feels that he or she is entitled to live or act outside the laws of
Starfleet as set down by the regs, there is going to be a temptation to
abuse that power. Power, after all, tends to corrupt—"

" 'And absolute power corrupts absolutely,' " Shelby finished
the quote. "Well, Commander, I don't know that the crew of the
*Excalibur* would necessarily have agreed with you. They were

a . . . rather eclectic group, to be certain. A captain, after all, tends to surround himself with those who suit his command style."

"If I may ask, Captain—and if the question is too personal, I withdraw it—considering your record of adherence to regs, and . . . not to be indelicate, but I learned that you had a personal relationship with Mackenzie Calhoun which ended badly . . ."

"Why did he make me his Number One?" She laughed softly. "You know, he never actually told me in so many words . . . but, knowing the way his mind works, I think it came down to the concept that he needed someone whom he could tolerate . . . and who could, in turn, tolerate him. You know, I still have—" She stopped herself.

"Still have what, Captain?"

"Nothing. It doesn't matter," Shelby said, abruptly all business.

"Very well," Garbeck said, responding in kind. "Let me assure you of this, Captain. I'm putting in a very serious bid to become first officer of this ship. I'm quite familiar with your career, and— if I may say so—admire you greatly as an officer."

"You have my belated permission to say so."

"I believe that you and I share similar views, and give similar priority to Starfleet regulations. To me, that ensures that, as captain and first officer, we will interact smoothly as a team. Furthermore—"

"Garbeck," said Shelby, cutting her off but not in a way that seemed hostile. "Tell you what: I'll save you time. If this is you putting in a bid, then this is me saying, going, going, gone. Sold. Congratulations." And she stood behind her desk, extending a hand. "Welcome aboard the *Exeter.*"

Garbeck had maintained a veneer of utter reserve, but that veneer slipped ever so slightly as her genuine excitement made itself evident. "Really?" she said, and obviously immediately regretted her "gosh-wow" attitude.

"Really," laughed Shelby, confident that she had made the right decision.

*I'm not going to do it tonight,* Shelby told herself.

She lay on her bed, fingers interlaced behind her head, gazing up at the ceiling. The *Exeter* would not be departing drydock for another week, but Shelby was already living full-time in her quarters. Why not? She really didn't feel as if she had anywhere else to go or anything else to do. Her parents lived on a far-off colony world; she had only one sibling, whom she almost never saw.

She had been working on crew rosters and material relating to the *Exeter*'s launch until the late hours. Her eyes had become sore with fatigue, and that was usually a good indicator for her that it was time to call it a night. But once she was reclining, she felt her fatigue evaporating as she replayed in her head, once again, those events in the final moments of *Excalibur.*

She hadn't wanted to. There was no purpose to it, nothing to gain. And yet, no matter how many times she thought about it, she kept wondering . . . what if there'd been something she'd overlooked? What if there'd been a way to save the ship, to save . . . him? Questioning and second-guessing, over and over, and finally it was no wonder that she wasn't able to sleep. With everything tumbling about in her mind, what person *could* have slept?

Before she could even give it any further thought, she heard her own voice say, "Computer. Play entry from personal log."

"Specify," came the automatic voice of the computer.

*Stop this, stop this right now,* her inner voice fairly shouted at her, but she ignored it. Instead, she called up the log entries that she had begun while in the lifepod, hanging in space outside the *Excalibur,* watching in bleak futility, as she knew that there was nothing, absolutely nothing, that she could do.

As if speaking from a chasm of a great many years, her voice came to her over the cabin's speaker system. She couldn't believe the tone of it, no matter how many times she had listened, because it didn't sound like her. Didn't sound like someone who was leaving the kind of log entry that could possibly be useful to scholars and historians who might study such documentation later. These were . . . well, there was no putting a positive face on it. These were the stream-of-consciousness comments of someone who still thought that she was, conceivably, going to die.

*If the ship could feel . . . speak . . . what would it be doing right now? Would it be crying, begging for its life? Would it be ranting over the unfairness of it all? And what could it possibly say about "unfairness" that I haven't already figured out.*

Mac and I moved with such efficiency, such speed, up and down the hallways, launching the lifepods into space. According to my chronometer, we'd gotten all the pods launched in one minute, thirty-seven seconds. That should have been impossible. But I wasn't thinking about anything like that at that moment.

All the lifepods were launched but two. One for the second-in-command, one for the captain. Except someone needed to stay behind and provide the manual launch . . . which would not leave that someone the opportunity to get off the ship in a lifepod. A shuttle might provide a possible escape, but there was simply no time to get down to the shuttlebay. I couldn't quite believe that we'd managed to get as many people off the ship in so brief a time as we had. It was one of those instances, I suppose, where things become so focused that it seems as if time has slowed to a crawl. Sort of an emergency scenario not dissimilar to the approach to light speed: the faster you travel, the more time seems to slow down around you. I suppose that's what was happening on the Excalibur. As the time we had left before the ship blew up dwindled, the time we spent in trying to escape the calamity lengthened.

But it wasn't going to, couldn't possibly, lengthen enough.

It had come down to us two. A computer voice was echoing over the ship, giving a calm countdown. We had just over a minute. I wanted to scream at the computer, as insane as that sounds. I wanted to ask it why, if it was so damned smart, it was going to allow the ship to blow itself to kingdom come instead of lifting one digitized finger to stop it.

Even as I spoke, even as I said the words, I knew he was never going to allow it. But I said them anyway: "I'm not leaving."

"Now, Eppy. That's an order."

"The captain is too valuable a commodity to lose. Starfleet has too much invested in you." In retrospect . . . I think I was being self-

*ish. As crazy as it sounds, at that instant I felt as if I would rather die than have to live, thinking of what his last moments had been like.*

*"The captain goes down with his ship," he said.*

*"There's no up or down in space."*

*And suddenly, just like that, he was kissing me. His lips were so hard against mine, and it roused a hunger in me so fierce that I started to wonder what it would be like to be making love to him just as the ship went up. To perish in an explosion of white light at that moment of passion that the French refer to as "the little death."*

*He lifted me up in his arms. I had been about to argue with him more, but I couldn't remember what I was about to say.*

*And the son of a bitch threw me into the lifepod. As I landed, he lobbed something gently in my direction. It clattered on the floor, and I looked down and realized that it was his short sword. He'd been carrying it with him the entire time; it represented a direct link to his youth on Xenex, and he wasn't about to let it go up or down with the ship. It was as if it was the only tangible aspect of him that was of any importance, and if it managed to outlast him, then, in some way, he would live on.*

*I started to lunge for him, but he slid the door shut and, instinctively, I yanked my hands back before the closing portal could sever my fingers. The last view I had of him, just before the door closed him off from view, was Mac, mouthing two words to me.*

*I threw myself against the door of the lifepod, trying to will it open, trying to get back to him. I look back upon my behavior and can only feel relief that no one else saw it. It was not remotely appropriate for a Starfleet officer. I should have handled it far better. I have been in life and death situations, after all. I am not anxious to die, I do not embrace it . . . but I am not terrified of it, either. It's simply something that happens, sooner or later.*

*But, at that moment, if I was going to die, I wanted to die with him. And if one of us was going to live, I wanted it to be him. I had placed his welfare above mine. On some level, I can argue that that was exactly the right attitude to have, because part of a first officer's job is to protect the captain under any and all circum-*

stances. But there was more to it than that, and I can admit it to myself now that he's gone. He has to be gone, because there was no doubt that the ship was destroyed. I know, because I saw that momentary flash of white, and then came the impact of the shock waves. Odd. They taught us that shock waves don't travel in space. Well, these certainly did, sending my pod tumbling end over end.

At that moment, though, I didn't care whether I survived. In retrospect, of course, I'm glad I did, but right then, it mattered very little to me.

Because I had come to a self-realization, you see.

I loved him. It was something that I had tried to ignore, tried to fight against during all our time together. But I had a good, long time to come to terms with it. Floating there in the lifepod, waiting for the rescue beacon that was sent out to Starfleet to bring a ship to retrieve us from the depths of space.

And who should it be but, naturally—naturally—the Enterprise. It took some time for the great flagship of the fleet to arrive, but when it did, it brought us all aboard with its usual efficiency. I debriefed Captain Picard on what had happened—the first of many times that I would tell the tale of the Excalibur's final moments.

Picard looked tremendously saddened. He kept it in, of course, with that customary reserve that he has perfected. But I could tell that he was upset. And why shouldn't he have been? After all, he was the one who had first discovered a young warrior named M'k'n'zy of Calhoun and convinced him that he had a place in Starfleet. For that matter, it was Picard who had tracked down Mac and convinced him to return to Starfleet after he had resigned years earlier over the Grissom incident.

"I am sorry for your loss, Commander," Picard told me after I had lapsed into silence.

"And I, for yours," I replied, acknowledging his long-standing bond with Calhoun.

I had mentioned to Picard that Mac had mouthed something to me just before the door closed. It was a fact that I would never *mention to anyone else, because Picard asked me about it specifically, and I realized that others would do the same. So I didn't repeat it to anyone else, because it wasn't germane to the ship's destruction . . . but I told Picard, because he asked.*

*"He said, 'I love you,' " I told him.*

*"Indeed." Despite the seriousness of the moment, Picard nevertheless smiled slightly at that. "Well, that's typical of Mac, isn't it? Master of the well-timed bon mot."*

*"I suppose he didn't want to risk hearing my not saying it back," I said.*

*Picard considered that for a moment, and then suggested, "Or else . . . he wanted to give himself incentive to come back and hear you say it."*

*I decided I liked Picard's interpretation better than mine.*

Shelby listened to the entire entry once through, and then a second time. It was the second time that she lost it, the tears streaming down her face, sobs racking her body. She was furious with herself for what she perceived as weakness, and furious with Calhoun for going off and getting himself killed and leaving her behind.

She reached under the bed. She hadn't been able to bring herself to keep it out on open display in her cabin. She didn't want to have to explain it to anyone who might ask. But now, from its secure place beneath her bunk, she pulled out the short sword that was the last remaining artifact—aside from her heart—that marked the passage through the world of Mackenzie Calhoun. Tears fell on the blade, intermingling with the slight discoloration of dried blood that still remained, no matter how many times he had polished it.

"Damn you," she muttered, although it wasn't clear—even to herself—just who she was cursing. Herself . . . or the deceased captain known as Mackenzie Calhoun.

# MOKE

MOKE WAS FEELING RATHER PROUD of himself. He had managed to slip out of the house yet again without his mother noticing, and considered that to be nothing short of a personal triumph. There were days when the boy felt as if he was suffocating under his mother's watchful eye. It was more than watchful; it was practically omnipresent. It seemed that she was obsessed with being protective of him, and that was fine, as far as it went. But certainly he should be entitled to some latitude. He was getting bigger, after all, not smaller; older, not younger. It just wasn't fair that his ma kept such close tabs on him. It wasn't as if they lived somewhere with wild beasts waiting to assault him around every turn.

Moke had a most impressive sense of direction. He could walk and keep on walking until his home was little more than a speck in the distance, and still find his way back with absolutely certainty. He was embarking on just such an excursion now, his hands tucked serenely in his pockets, his lips puckered in an aimless whistle. The sun was beating down on him, just as it did everyone else, but Moke wasn't remotely as bothered by it as others were. From the boy's attitude and generally relaxed demeanor, it was clear that he was feeling utterly at ease in the infernally dry and overheated afternoon.

A few days ago, he'd been watching his mother speaking with

the sailskipper man . . . what had his name been? Oh, yes. Tapinza. He seemed nice enough, but Moke's mother didn't seem to like him. Moke couldn't help but wonder why. He had asked his mother about it. First, she had scolded him gently for spying on her, and then she had simply said, "Sometimes adults just don't get on well with one another." Clearly she expected that to be the end of the discussion, and Moke had not been able to find a good way to get her to continue it. So he had let it drop, albeit reluctantly.

Was Tapinza his father? Moke didn't think so. There was something about the way that his mother looked at him that made it seem as if they were strangers somehow. Moke was still a bit fuzzy on where babies came from, or how mothers and fathers produced them, but he couldn't shake the feeling that—at the very least—they had to be familiar with each other on some level. Tapinza came across to Moke like someone that his mother had kept at arm's length for—well, forever.

He had recurring dreams about having a father. In those dreams, his dad was always tall and straight and proud, and he had eyes like storms and a smile as gleaming as the morning sun. When he laughed, it was deep and from the belly, like thunder rolling across the plains. Moke liked him instantly, and knew that they would always, always be together. It would be Moke and his ma and dad, and everyone would like them. They'd go into town whenever they wanted, and people would not give him those odd looks that people always did.

There was an oasis nearby, although, from an actual water point of view, it wasn't much of an oasis. Most of the plant life was brown and unappealing. However, there were a few rock formations that Moke enjoyed climbing, so it was one of his favorite places to go. One of his secret places, which he never even told his mother about, because a guy is entitled to keep *some* things private.

He got to the oasis and, even as he started to clamber up one of the rock formations, he wondered why it was that people always seemed to be muttering about his mother and him. What had they ever done to anybody? His mom made water for them, after all. Or at least she encouraged it to rain, and the clouds seemed to listen, for the most part, although sometimes she was luckier than other times. The problem was that she usually could only make it rain for a short while, and the effort cost her mightily. She would take long naps, although she showed an almost supernatural ability to rouse herself to wakefulness any time that Moke made the slightest attempt to depart the domicile. But this most recent endeavor appeared to have taken more out of her than usual, perhaps because there had been so little raw weather material to work with. Because she had been sleeping so soundly, Moke had been able to follow his own instincts and set off on his own little adventure.

He had toyed with the notion of going into town and asking people directly why they had a problem with his mom and him. Whenever he showed an interest in doing so, his mother would tell him not to try and start trouble. Except that he didn't see it as trying to start it so much as he was trying to forestall future problems. He couldn't get his mother to see it that way, though. He had mentioned that frustration to Maester Tapinza during their time together, clinging to the sailskipper as the wind carried them across the plains. The Maester had told him that his mother was simply a woman, and all women were flawed, but that eventually the Maester would make it better. He didn't say how or when; he just said he would. Moke just wished that it would be sooner rather than later.

And that was when Moke let out an alarmed scream.

A firm hand had grabbed him by the back of his shirt and hauled him off the rock he had been climbing so fiercely that he had scraped himself up as he went. Moke's feet pinwheeled in midair, and then he was whirled around, still in the air, and slammed up against the nearest rock. He let out a choked sob and looked into a twisted and furious face that was the single most frightening he'd ever seen.

The man had a scar, the way Tapinza did, except it ran down the right side of his face. It was partly obscured by beard stubble, but it was still quite evident. His face was dark-skinned, blistered and red and bruised, and his hair was black and matted with dirt. His lower lip looked swollen, and the upper lip had dried blood on it . . . perhaps from a nosebleed. It was his eyes that were the most striking to Moke. They were deep purple, and there was a crazed anger in them. But the anger was diluted slightly by confusion, and even a touch of fright. Immediately the fear began to ebb from Moke, to be replaced by pity. This man now seemed more scared than scary to him.

*"Where . . . am I . . . ?"* the man growled. His voice was barely above a whisper. He sounded very thirsty, as if he hadn't had anything to drink for days.

Moke didn't know what to say. "H-here," he managed to get out.

*"What . . . planet is this . . . ?"*

The question made no sense to Moke at all. "This one . . ."

The man was starting to tremble. For a moment, it seemed as if his legs were going to buckle, but then he found new strength and kept his firm grip on Moke. *"Stop . . . playing games . . ."*

Moke was still having trouble mentally processing the man's presence. He was like no one else Moke had ever seen in this world. Possibly like no one else that anyone had ever seen.

Was it . . . possible . . . ?

"Dad?" whispered Moke.

The man froze, his face right up against Moke's, and his gaze darted furiously about before his eyes remembered to focus on Moke once more. "Xyon . . . ?" he whispered.

Moke shook his head. "Moke," he said.

But the man didn't seem to hear him. Instead, he let out a yelp of joy and croaked, *"You're alive!"* Instantly all the anger, all the fury that had been seizing the man seemed to evaporate, and he embraced Moke with every bit of strength he could muster . . . which Moke quickly realized was not a lot. Nevertheless, he returned the embrace.

*"You're alive! You're alive!"* Over and over he repeated it, and Moke had the distinct impression that the man thought Moke was

someone else. His son, presumably, who had apparently perished. Clearly the man was very upset about it. And if it gave him pleasure and comfort to think that Moke was his son, why . . . Moke didn't really see anything wrong with that. Besides, who knew? Maybe the man was right. Maybe Moke really *was* his son. The only one who would know for sure was his mother.

"Let me take you home to Mom," suggested Moke. "She'll want to see you."

The man gaped at him. "Your . . . your mother's here, too? Alive? Am I . . ." Then confusion passed through his eyes. "Am I . . . dead? That's it, isn't it? I'm dead. That's why you're here . . . and her . . . I'm dead . . ."

"You're not dead," Moke said with certainty. He was not a terribly learned young man, and didn't profess to know much, but he certainly had an idea of what was alive and what was dead. And he was quite positive that he and his mother fell into the former category. "You're just . . ." He paused, and then decided. "You're just confused."

"Confused . . . ?" He licked his cracked lips with his thickening tongue. "Confused?"

"Let me take you to Mom," he suggested again.

This time the words seemed to get through. The man relaxed his grip on Moke's shirtfront, and the boy slid to the ground easily enough. He stepped to one side and stared up at the man. He was a very strange individual. He wore clothes such as Moke had never seen. They seemed very fancy, extremely well-made, although a bit torn-up. Moke reached up and fingered the fabric with curiosity. The man didn't even seem to be aware of it.

"To Mom," he said a third time.

"I'm . . . tired, Xyon. So very tired," the man said. "Everyone . . . clear? Did everyone get clear? I think . . . but it's hard to know."

Deciding to guess at a response that would probably make him happy, Moke said firmly, "Yeah . . . everyone got clear. It's all okay."

The man sagged with obvious relief. "It's okay . . . they got clear," he said, with a tone of voice that made it sound as if he was informing Moke of that which Moke had just told him. "They got clear . . . thought they might . . . hoped they might . . . *grozit* . . . they must think I'm dead by now. Got to get back . . . tell them I'm okay . . . that you're okay . . . Xyon . . ."

"Lemme take you home."

"Do you have . . . subspace transmitter . . . or beacon . . . at home?" asked the man. He seemed to be making a tremendous effort to focus on what he was saying.

Moke thought about the large illuminating lamp that his mother kept in one of the kitchen cupboards for emergencies. She referred to that as a beacon. "Yeah. We do," he said firmly.

"Okay . . . good . . . good boy, Xyon . . ." Whatever menace there had been about the man was gone now. But his eyes still looked glazed, and sweat was pouring down his face in rivulets. He was hot to Moke's touch, and Moke was no longer wondering whether the man was in bad shape, but instead just how bad a shape he was in.

The man took a deep breath and pushed himself away from the rocks, trying to walk. Then his legs started to buckle once more, and Moke ran over to him to lend him support. It was not an easy matter, because the man was, naturally, much taller than Moke, and his weight caused the boy to grunt rather loudly. For a moment it seemed as if both of them were going to fall, and then the man managed to haul himself to standing again. He took a deep breath, wiped the sweat from his eyes, blinked furiously against the stinging of the perspiration, and then took several tentative steps. His legs were still wobbling, and Moke was ready to catch him should he start to stumble once more. But the man did not fall. Instead, each step seemed a bit stronger than the one before. It was as if, now that he had a genuine purpose, nothing was going to stop him from getting where he wanted to go.

Moke came up next to him, and the man steadied himself by putting a hand on Moke's shoulder. This time, though, he wasn't resting the entirety of his weight on the boy, and Moke was able to support him with no trouble.

"How . . . far . . . ?" the man rasped out.

Moke decided that this was a case where a lie might serve better than the truth. "Not far at all," he said, and hoped that the man would not be keeping track of the ground they were covering. The man simply nodded upon hearing this, and they started to move across the plains.

It took a horrifically long time. Despite the fact that he was moving on his own, he was still going rather slowly. One foot slowly, deliberately, in front of the other, and it seemed to Moke that the man was gradually getting hotter as they went. But the man wasn't complaining, so that was a benefit, at least. Every so often he would pat Moke on the shoulder and call him "Xyon" again, which Moke didn't even begin to understand. And he would mutter things; incoherent babbling that Moke couldn't follow no matter how hard he tried. Stuff about "the ship" and "blowing up" and "pods" and "Eppy." None of it made the least bit of sense. But at least the man was moving, and that was all that mattered.

Moke wondered what his mother would say. Would she demand to know why her son had brought this stranger home? Or would she take one look at him and blurt out his name in surprise, before admitting to Moke that this was indeed his dad, returned home ill and feverish from some great adventure and needing help? He had no idea what to expect, really, but there was some excitement to that in and of itself. For a little while, at least, Moke could fantasize what it would be like to be with his dad. And that was the greatest adventure of all.

Deciding that it would be better to bring his mom to the man rather than the man to his mom, Moke brought the man to the small shed where they kept an assortment of their supplies . . . including the luukab, which was actually an animal. But they didn't have a real barn, and so the luukab stayed in the shed. They used the luukab when they were going to be riding long distances. Not much more than a large, hairy, four-legged *thing,* with rocklike skin beneath the hair and a large tusk that was handy for a rider to hold on to, the luukab required little in the way of nourishment, and seemed to thrive on the cacti that grew on and around their property. The one disadvantage was that the luukab wasn't much for hot days—which Yakaba had in abundance—and preferred to stay inside during the hotter periods. Consequently, if Rheela was going to go anywhere that was not within easy walking distance, and intended to ride the luukab there, she either had to go early in the morning or late in the day, because otherwise the stupid creature was going to leave her stranded.

The sun had begun to descend, cooling things off slightly, although far from completely. All during the slow trip back, the man had continued his muttering and contributed nothing else to the discussion. That was fine with Moke. Just being with this mysterious man was more than enough to make him happy, for he represented a future that Moke found just a bit less lonely.

"Here. You wait here," he said as he eased the man into the coolness of the shed.

"Is this home?" asked the man. He looked around, but didn't seem to be seeing anything. The luukab regarded him with vague disinterest before returning to its contented chewing on cacti needles.

"Kind of. Yes. You get some rest here. I'll get Mom."

"Mom?" His attention seemed to be slipping away. He appeared to be getting a bit more agitated, although not dangerously so. "Who is . . . Mom? Who are you? I don't . . . I . . ." If anything, his voice was sounding more scratchy and parched than before. His eyes were so clouded that it seemed as if he wasn't seeing anything anymore.

*Oh, Kolk'r, he's going to die . . . my dad's going to die,* thought Moke bleakly, even as he said, "Just . . . just lie down! Lie down!"

And he said it with such force and certainty that the man did exactly as he was told. It was as if, having no clear idea of what he should be doing, he accepted whatever suggestion was tossed out to him. He flopped onto the floor and just lay there, glassy-eyed.

He was starting to shiver, which made no sense to Moke. Why should he be shivering if he's so hot?

Realizing that simply standing around and chatting with the mysterious man wasn't going to accomplish anything, Moke shut the door behind him and raced toward his house. He bolted into the house, looked around frantically for some sign of his mother . . . and didn't see any.

"Mom!" he called urgently, panic starting to well up within him. What if the man died before his mother could help him? What if all of Moke's efforts in this area failed? Even worse . . . what if this man were indeed his father, and he died . . . and his mother somehow blamed Moke for it? He could just hear her. *You found your father and you let him die? How could you!* It was an appalling thought. On how many levels could he possibly fail?

It was at that point that he suddenly heard his mother's scream, and came to the frightening conclusion that he was about to find out.

Rheela was becoming frantic with worry.

She had looked all over the house, all over the immediate area, and there was no sign of Moke. She was beginning to think that perhaps she should install a tracer of some sort in him, so that she could locate him when she needed to.

Having no idea which direction to strike out in looking for him, she chose east at random and started walking, calling his name. Her trip had turned up nothing, and so she decided to head back the way she'd come. This took a terribly long time, and all during her walk she conjured up all the horrible things that might have happened to Moke. She tried to tell herself that she was being overly protective, and that Moke was most likely perfectly fine. Indeed, she knew on some level that she should stop nattering at the boy, stop being so frantic. Be willing to trust him, somewhat, to look after himself. For all that, though, she still couldn't help but be concerned, and the longer he was gone, the more worried she became.

She noticed, however, that it was starting to get cooler. Which meant that the luukab would be far more willing to come out of its nice cool shed and provide her with a means of locomotion far more efficient and ground-consuming than her own legs. So, upon her return, she went straight to the shed and threw open the door, with the intent of getting the luukab and mounting up immediately.

Instead, she stopped dead in her tracks, frozen in the doorway, gaping at the man who was lying on the floor.

"Wh-who are you?" she stammered.

Slowly he sat up, and she immediately saw the differences in him from any other man she'd ever met. His skin color, his hair, were both wrong. He had to be some sort of . . . of genetic freak, capable of who knew what? Even more daunting was the way in which he got to his feet. It was with an economy of movement, as if he wanted to give an opponent no clue of just how fast or strong he might be. . . .

Opponent . . . ?

This naturally brought her to the disconcerting realization that he was eyeing her as if she were some sort of enemy. There was a crazed look in his eyes, feral and ugly. For a moment, he had seemed to have trouble discerning just where she was, but now that he'd locked on to her whereabouts, there was clearly no question or hesitation for him. A low, raspy growl sounded from deep in his throat.

"Now, just . . . just . . . stay where you are," she said, trying to gather her wits. She was still holding the door open.

"Danteri slime," he snarled. "You killed my father. . . ."

"I . . . did what? I'm . . . listen . . . there's a . . . a mistake . . ." He took a step closer, into the light filtering through behind her, and she came to a realization as she saw him more clearly. "You're not well. You're sick."

"Sick . . . yes . . . sick of Danteri monsters like you. . . ." His legs wobbled slightly, and then he steadied them.

"I'm . . . not a monster . . . I . . ."

And suddenly he leaped right for her.

Rheela let out a shriek and belatedly tried to slam the door, with the hope of locking him in. But she had no chance. Her attacker smashed into it, knocking the door open with such force that it sent her tumbling back, her ankles going high over her head before she rolled to a stop. Before she could get up, the man was upon her.

She had never seen a more terrifying look in someone's eyes before. He seemed to be looking right through her, perhaps at the ground, or perhaps at someone long gone. She slapped at his face, at his chest, but he didn't even seem to feel it. For one crazed moment, she thought he was going to rape her, and then when his hands clamped down on her throat, she realized that he meant nothing less than to kill her.

He kept raging about "Danteri," and she had no idea what in the world he could possibly be talking about. *How pathetic,* she thought, *to die in ignorance.* And then she thought of her son coming home and finding this madman, who would most certainly do to her son what he was doing to her. This thought was enough to give her renewed energy, and she fought with everything she had. Unfortunately, that still didn't amount to much. Not in the face of such a demented attack by a much stronger opponent.

She couldn't get air into her lungs, and her panic caused her to throw herself around in a desperate attempt to dislodge him. But it still was as nothing against his attack.

"Mom!" She heard Moke's panicked voice coming from what sounded like a very great distance, and then he was right there, shoving at the man, trying to get him off her. The crazy man barely gave him a look, and instead swung his arm around, knocking Moke off his feet and sending him rolling. This, of course, caused him to release his grip on her, and Rheela tried to push him completely off. Her hand grabbed up some loose dirt and dust and she threw it in his face. The man let out a roar of fury, clutching at his eyes, reaching about at thin air, momentarily blinded. She lashed out with one foot, knocking him off her, and she clambered to her feet with every intention of getting away from him. She only got a short distance, though, and then he was back upon her. This time he landed on her from behind, slamming her to the ground. She cried out in despair, feeling that her one opportunity to survive this deranged encounter had just slipped away from her because she was too slow. She was going to die, and her boy was going to die, and there wasn't a damned thing she could do about it. All this went through her mind even as his fingers clamped upon her throat once more. The world started to gray-out around her.

And then there was the distinctive grunt of the luukab, and suddenly—just like that—the man was off her. She sat up, her eyes wide, and if her throat hadn't been in such agony, she would have laughed.

The luukab was heading away from the scene at a fairly brisk gallop, and attached to the creature's tusk was one end of a rope. The other end was secured around the man's ankle, and he was howling in fury as the creature hauled him around. Were the situation not quite so serious, it would actually have been funny.

Moke ran to her, and his words were tumbling out so fast that Rheela had trouble understanding everything he was telling her. It seemed that he was saying he was responsible for bringing the man here, and he was sorry, and the man wasn't so bad when he wasn't trying to kill you, and maybe he was Moke's father, and wouldn't it be okay if he stayed because he'd probably be much nicer if he wasn't sick . . .

Then Rheela rewound part of the conversation in her head. "Your father . . . ?" she managed to gasp out, rubbing her throat and hoping that he hadn't broken something in her during his assault.

That was when the luukab trotted up to them, looking at them in a rather blasé manner. The luukab's burden was not in any condition to complain about the treatment it was getting, for the man was clearly unconscious. His clothes were now shredded, his face and upper body bruised. His breathing was shallow, but steady.

A hundred questions tumbled through Rheela's mind, but finally she managed to say, "We have to get the Majister."

"The Majister! But he'll put him in gaol!"

"He *belongs* in gaol, Moke!" Rheela told him. She pointed at her throat. "Listen to how I'm talking! Listen to how raspy! *He did this to me!* If you hadn't thought so fast and tied him to the luukab, I'd be dead by now!"

"He's just sick, is all, Ma!"

"We don't know how he'll be when he isn't sick, Moke!" Quickly she went to the shed and came back out with a long knife. She cut the rope off the luukab's tusk, and then took the rope and proceeded to bind the man as securely as she could. "We'll get him all tied up," she said, as much to herself as to Moke, "and then we'll ride the luukab into town, get the Majister, have him put this . . . this crazy man into gaol, and that will be that. That's the Majister's job, after all. It's his job to attend to hurtful people like this . . . not . . . not our job to fight them off."

"He's not hurtful! I know it! I—"

She turned to Moke and said, with irritation, "He's not your father, Moke! All right? So stop talking about it!"

"He's not?" The disappointment from the boy was palpable. "Are you sure?"

The naïveté of the child was almost touching, in its way. It almost made her laugh. Almost. "Yes. I'm sure."

"Oh." He sighed. "Okay."

As soon as the man was tied up, Rheela dragged him over into the shed, secured the door, and locked it for good measure. Then she and Moke mounted up on the luukab and headed toward town as fast as they could.

And as they did so, the man with the purple eyes and fearsome scar dreamed of exploding ships. . . .

# SHELBY

IT WAS . . .

   . . . so . . .

   . . . quiet.

Shelby could scarcely believe it. She sat in her command chair, the steady flow of activity all around her, and she was reveling in it.

And it was . . .

   . . . so . . .

   . . . quiet.

It had seemed, back on the bridge of the *Excalibur,* that there was always someone chattering or going on about something that had nothing to do with anything. There would be Lefler, reciting one of her many "laws" about something or other that Shelby always suspected Lefler made up on the spot. Or McHenry, snoring—*snoring!*—at his post.

Then there was the time Soleta became obsessed with understanding the formulaic humor inherent in "knock-knock" jokes. After tracing "knock-knock" jokes back to a sequence in the Shakespeare drama habitually referred to (by superstitious humans, apparently, who considered the show jinxed) as "the Scottish play," Soleta had tried out a series of knock-knock jokes on assorted crewmembers until everyone was sick of them, and pretty much of her as well.

Steady chatter, jokes, laughter, odd incidents, all manner of strangeness aboard the *Excalibur*, with Calhoun coming across less like a CO and more like a patient den mother. He bore up under the give-and-take with equanimity, and nothing ever seemed to bother him. In fact, he actually seemed to enjoy the oddities that were his crew's hallmark.

And it was never quiet. Always there were odd moments, or strange statements, or arguments over matters of trivial importance. Always there was something going on. There had been times when Shelby felt as if she was never going to fit in with the rest of the crew. As if she was always going to be an outsider on a vessel that served as both her permanent place of work and play. It was a lonely way to be, but she couldn't change her essence. She couldn't find any sort of sympathy or preference for the way that Calhoun chose to do things.

But here, on the *Exeter* . . . it was so very . . .

. . . very . . .

. . . very . . . quiet.

The crew, handpicked by Shelby, went about its business with calm, certain efficiency. There was not a wasted word or moment. Everything her crew said or did directly related either to the current state of the *Exeter*, or to updates on the ship's position while the powerful vessel continued en route to the planet Makkus.

"Her crew." There was something about that phrase—"her crew"—that brought deep and abiding satisfaction to her. Yes, the *Excalibur* had been something of a family to her—but oftentimes it seemed a family to her in the same way that Alice considered the residents of Wonderland a family. In Wonderland, it was as if there was some sort of great, massive joke that everyone else was in on . . . except Alice. That was how Shelby felt. She was Alice at the Mad Hatter's tea party, and oddball residents like McHenry and Kebron were at either end shouting, "No room! No room!" while Calhoun sat serenely on a large mushroom, observing all the insanity around him with aplomb. She readily admitted to herself that she might be exaggerating her recollections. But if she was, it certainly wasn't by much.

Now, this group, on the other hand, was far more her speed.

Alexandra Garbeck—whom Shelby had taken to calling "Alex," but only when they were together privately—was studying several recent communiqués from Starfleet, wanting to keep herself abreast of the latest decisions and thoughts of her higher-ups. At the science station, Lieutenant Commander Chris Tulley was preparing a report on the atmosphere of Makkus, to make certain that the away team would not run into any trouble on the planet. Tulley, slim and waspish, was the youngest person on the bridge—understandable when one is so bright that he graduates from the Academy two years ahead of schedule.

At conn and ops were the two officers who had come to operate so smoothly together that many speculated they had been separated at birth. At conn was Matthew MacGibbon, tall and well-muscled, with thick, red hair. He had a ready smile and went about his duty with ruthless efficiency. Next to him, at ops was Lieutenant Althea McMurrian. She likewise had red hair, which matched MacGibbon's in shade, but in contrast to MacGibbon, she rarely smiled, her mouth perpetually drawn into a tight pucker that seemed to convey constant concentration. If there was anything going on having to do with any part of the ship's systems, MacGibbon not only knew about it, but solved it before having to report word one about it to Shelby. McMurrian and MacGibbon had worked together on two previous commands and, despite their basic differences in temperament, had developed such a seamless working relationship that they were occasionally referred to by the combined name of McMac. Amazingly, they actually responded to it. In times of emergency, Shelby could snap out orders by saying, "McMac, plot an emergency course out of here and signal all hands to battle stations." It saved time, and there was never any hesitation as to who was to do what.

Situated directly behind Shelby, normally, was Lieutenant Naomi Basner, head of security. But Basner was undergoing some physical therapy after a shooting incident on Zeron III, so filling in for her was the next in line for the job, Lieutenant Karen Kahn. Shelby couldn't help comparing Kahn to Zak Kebron, and couldn't be more struck by the differences. Kebron was a massive Brikar, invulnerable to virtually anything thrown at him. He moved fairly slowly, but considering that he was a walking tank, he didn't have much need for speed. Kahn, by contrast, was of mixed Native American ancestry, and was absolute lightning in a variety of martial arts. Shelby had watched computer video of Kahn doing a workout, and her hand and leg movements had been so fast that Shelby hadn't even been able to track them. She'd needed the computer to give her a frame-by-frame playback, and even then she didn't dare blink lest she miss something.

Her crew. Her people. Handpicked, carefully studied. Shelby knew that the composition of her command staff was absolutely vital, because a captain was only as good as the people she had directly supporting her. And if there was one thing that Shelby was convinced of at this point, it was that she had done as good a job as anyone could do in assembling her team. They were efficient, professional, knowledgeable . . . everything that she could possibly have asked for.

And . . .

. . . so . . .

. . . quiet.

Tulley broke the silence as he turned from his post and said, "Captain, atmosphere survey complete. Makkus's air is a bit thinner than Earth standard, but should not present a problem."

"Good," Shelby said.

Garbeck turned in her seat to face Shelby. "Will you be handling the away team yourself, Captain?"

"I had intended to. Does that pose a problem for you, Number One?" Shelby had decided she liked that term. Picard had referred to Riker in that way, and it had a good sound to it.

"No problem, Captain," replied Garbeck. "It is usually preferable for the first officer to lead such endeavors, but the captain does, naturally, have the option. And this does not seem to have a good deal of potential for personal danger. So I don't see the harm."

"I appreciate the permission, Number One," Shelby said wryly.

Garbeck looked at her blankly. "I wasn't offering permission, Captain. That wouldn't be appropriate to my station. I was simply offering an observation."

"I understand that, Garbeck. I was simply . . ." Shelby gave a small shrug. ". . . I was simply making a small joke."

"Oh," said Garbeck. That was it. That was all. No "I see," or "Very funny, Captain," or even "Not very amusing, Captain." Just "Oh."

Shelby glanced out the corner of her eye to see if anyone was reacting to the conversation she was having with Garbeck. No one was. They all seemed engrossed in their individual duties. Shelby decided that it would probably be a good point to let the discussion go, and she did.

Makkus . . . she was going to Makkus . . .

It wasn't what she had been planning.

Somehow, Shelby had just assumed that, with the loss of the *Excalibur,* she would be assigned back to Sector 221-G—formerly known as Thallonian space. The *Excalibur* had been assigned there—a lifetime ago, it felt like—to try and offer humanitarian aid, and to stitch back together the fabric of an assortment of worlds that were operating independently for the first time in their collective history. With that mighty ship gone, there was no one to oversee things in Thallonian space.

But that had not occurred. Instead, upon receiving command of the *Exeter,* she had been assigned another section of space entirely. Sector 47-B, a territory that wasn't quite as "wild and woolly" as Sector 221-G. Oh, it had its challenges, of course. No area of space was fully known, no matter how thoroughly it had been charted and explored. Those who allowed themselves to become complacent in their knowledge of an area were generally the same people who allowed themselves to become dead. And that was a group to which Shelby had no intention of allowing herself to belong.

Still, she had raised a mild protest—more of an inquiry, really—with Admiral Jellico, stating that she felt there was still more to do in Thallonian space.

"You may very well be correct, Captain," Jellico had said. "However, these things are done in rotation. The *Exeter* has been assigned to Sector 47-B, and was slated for that territory before you came aboard as captain. We're not going to reconfigure our assignment list just to accommodate a single officer, even if she is the CO." It was exactly the kind of hard-nosed attitude she had expected from Jellico. So she'd been surprised when he added, "We are very likely going to be christening a new vessel as *Excalibur.* That one will probably go back into Thallonian space."

"Very well," she had said.

And as surprised as she'd been before, she'd been nearly dumbfounded when Jellico had actually said to her—in a tone that sounded more like a concerned uncle than his usual clipped, vaguely impatient air—"Besides . . . it probably wouldn't do you much good to throw yourself right back into the section of space where you lost Calhoun. Might make you too tentative, or too aggressive. Either way, it'd be best if you allowed some time for your associations with Thallonian space to cool. All right?" He seemed genuinely interested as to whether it was "all right" with her. She nodded, and he seemed satisfied with that. Shelby told herself that everyone, even an inveterate pain in the butt such as Jellico, was capable of surprising you every now and then.

Thus far, aside from the shooting incident by a jumpy native on Zeron III, which had injured Basner's leg, things had gone fairly smoothly during her first command. She was certainly hoping that Makkus would fall into that same category.

Makkus was a world on the outer edge of Sector 47-B. The natives had undergone tremendous scientific progress in the last hundred years or so, not too dissimilar from the dazzling burst of advancement that had seized the latter half of the twentieth century on earth. The Federation had established first contact with Makkus some years back, and by all reports the Makkusians had taken firsthand proof of life on other worlds somewhat in stride. That shouldn't have been a surprise; such worlds were generally investigated very thoroughly to make sure that they were, in fact, prepared to handle such revelations without it being damaging to the world's society as a whole.

It was now felt, however, that the people of Makkus had advanced to a sufficient degree that they were ready to be given the opportunity to join the Federation. It was an exciting prospect for Shelby, being sent to handle the invitation personally. Who knew, really, the future that any world might realize in their development? If Shelby's invitation got Makkus to join the UFP, who knew where the world might end up in terms of its involvement with, and relation to, other worlds? And their success would be, in some small measure, Shelby's success.

But she didn't want to start thinking that way; it came across to her as self-centered and self-aggrandizing. The planet's welfare was to be considered first and foremost, and any contributions she made to it would be a distant second.

However, she also felt a brief bit of amusement over Garbeck reminding her of the first officer's obligation to afford protection to the captain whenever possible. Shelby had a reasonably high opinion of herself, but the thought of her providing protection to Mackenzie Calhoun . . . well, somehow it just seemed laughable. Putting aside the harsh truth that, since he was dead, she hadn't done much of a job protecting him, there was also the matter that Calhoun had never lost—as he put it—the need to lead.

When they were young, he had spoken to her with derision about the Starfleet mandate that captains should minimize their time with away teams, and certainly never expose themselves to danger. Mackenzie Calhoun, back when he was the young M'k'n'zy, had carved himself a bloody path to no less a post than Warlord of his native Xenex. Once he had acquired that title, he had not then positioned himself to the rear of the ranks in any given situation. Instead, he had been in the thick of things, carving with his great sword, slicing away at his enemies, blood spattering his muscled frame and howling war cries ripped from his lips. "Protect the captain from danger?" young Calhoun had sniffed. "What sort of troops respect a leader who is willing to shove them into hazardous situations, but not himself? A leader leads. People follow a leader; they don't precede him to shield him."

"And if the leader is killed?"

"Then he is killed. No one person should ever be indispensable. If a leader can drive any one lesson into the heads of his people, it's that one. No movement should fall apart just because one man goes down. There must always be another to step in to fill the void, and another, and still another, each as capable as the one before. That, Eppy, is how you win wars."

Eppy.

God, how she had hated that nickname.

God, how she missed it.

"Captain—?"

She realized with ever-so-brief embarrassment that she had been thinking about other matters and paying no attention to the immediate matters at hand. She turned to Garbeck and said, "Yes, Number One."

"In regards to the away team: Might I suggest Lieutenant Augustine? She served a residency in xeno-studies as part of the NOT assigned to this world ten years ago, so she's well familiar with them."

Shelby nodded. She was, in fact, familiar with Toreen Augustine. The NonObservable Team, or NOTs, as they were usually referred to, were a standard part of the procedure for determining a planet's development, and whether they were ready to be approached for Federation membership. Either they watched the natives from a hidden outpost, or else actually disguised themselves as residents of the world and mingled to get a reading on how advanced they were. However, Shelby had no desire to undercut Garbeck's industry by saying she had already opted to make use of Augustine, so she simply nodded and said, "Good thinking, Number One. Inform her of—"

There was a sharp whistle over the comm unit. "Kosa to bridge," came the voice of CMO Daniel Kosa.

"Bridge; go ahead, Doctor," Shelby said. There was something in his voice that informed her this was not exactly a simple, "Hi, how you doing?" contact.

"We've had an incident down in holodeck two. I think you'd better get down here," said Kosa in his normal, gravelly tone.

"On my way." She didn't even bother to ask what had happened. If Kosa was faced with an emergency and he wanted her down there, then she was going down, and that was pretty much that. Still, as the turbolift whisked her to the deck where holodeck two was situated, she couldn't help but wonder what could possibly have happened there that would require medical attention. After all, the holodeck was equipped with safety protocols. No matter how hazardous the situation a participant might conjure up, there was no risk of injury—outside of, possibly, something along the lines of a sprained ankle. But Kosa had not sounded particularly happy. Then again, that was Kosa's typical tone of voice. He had little patience for illness, which was part of what made him such an excellent doctor. He seemed to take such things as sickness or injuries personally, as if they had occurred specifically to annoy him and challenge him. "No respect," he would be heard to mutter every so often during an examination, and it was never clear to anyone precisely what Kosa meant by that. Did he mean that germs were showing him disrespect by treading on his territory? Or did he mean that the patient was displaying no respect for their own body because they were allowing these things to happen? Unfortunately, no one on the ship—including Shelby—quite had the nerve to ask Kosa to define his notorious "No respect" comment. By a sort of unspoken agreement, it was probably better that way.

When Shelby got to the holodeck, she walked briskly through the door . . . and stopped in her tracks. She couldn't quite believe what she was seeing.

The landscape around her was a centuries-old cityscape that had recently been the scene of some kind of bizarre combat scenario. Oddly costumed holographic warriors—most apparently human, but some questionable—were held fast by the holodeck in the midst of their conflict.

The warriors seemed to be lacking the kind of weaponry that could account for the destruction surrounding them, but it seemed clear they were responsible in some way for it. One was frozen in the midst of attempting to lift what seemed to be a very heavy ground vehicle many times his size. His plan seemed to be to hurl the vehicle at his enemies, where it would join the crushed pile of other such vehicles that he had apparently already thrown.

Standing in the midst of it all, looking around with a distasteful eye, was Doctor Kosa. A pure-blooded Sioux, Kosa was jowly and gray-haired, and seemed to like it that way. Twin-sister med techs Patty and Sali Wynants were on either side of the body on the floor, surveying the scene with clear befuddlement.

"I wanted you to see this for yourself," rumbled Kosa, "so that when my report came through, you wouldn't call down to me and say, 'What the hell are you talking about?' "

Security chief Naomi Basner was flat on the floor, with her head crushed.

Shelby was aghast. For one wild moment she was starting to wonder if maybe, somehow . . . it was her. That the oddities on the *Excalibur* had stemmed not from Calhoun, but from her presence. Because she had seen some bizarre things during her stint on *Excalibur,* but never anything quite like this. She tried to find the words, her mouth forming an *"O,"* but nothing emerging at first. Kosa waited patiently. "How—?" she finally managed to say.

"According to the twins here," said Kosa, indicating the Wynants, "Chief Basner had a fondness for this particular holodeck scenario, which she created from scratch. Apparently, it was based on an old Earth entertainment form called . . ." He frowned, trying to remember.

"Comic books," chorused Sali and Patty. They tended to do

that: speak in sync. Shelby had heard it privately mused that they were not actually twins, but that one was, in fact, a clone of the other.

"Thank you," Kosa said, without actually sounding particularly grateful for the help. "It seems she considered the type of combat engaged in in that medium to be the ultimate challenge for a security chief, in terms of reacting to sudden and unexpected circumstances."

"She always said she never—" began Sali.

"—knew where to look first," finished Patty.

*I'm back in Wonderland,* Shelby thought incredulously. She gestured toward Basner. "So what happened to her?"

"As far as we can tell," Doctor Kosa replied, "she was hit by a hammer thrown by—" Kosa pointed at one of the frozen warriors, one with long blond hair and the costume of a still more ancient era, "—that guy."

"But this shouldn't have happened!" For a moment she feared that this was the first hint of yet another computer virus eating away at yet another ship. But then the realization dawned on her. "She removed the safety protocols."

Sali and Patty nodded in unison.

"The only people damned fool enough to do something like that are security people," said Kosa, shaking his head as if he couldn't believe it. "Apparently, they feel they can't train properly if there isn't real danger involved."

"I won't have it," Shelby said, fury mounting in her. It was insane to be angry with someone who was dead, but she was. "I won't have my people putting their lives at risk for some damned training stunt in a holodeck simulation!" She hit her combadge. "Shelby to engineering!"

"Engineering. Dunn here," came the voice of the chief engineer.

"Commander," she said forcefully, the use of the rank underscoring the fact that she was not in a good mood. "We've had a fatality in holodeck two."

"Impossible," returned Dunn's voice, "unless someone made the mistake of—"

"Yes, that's exactly what they did," Shelby cut him off.

Dunn whistled. "As mistakes go, that's a lulu, all right."

"I want you to—"

"Go through the computers and eliminate all options to remove safety protocols, so that no one can ever have the ability to override the safety features again."

"Exactly," she said.

"Done and Dunn," said Dunn, which was his favorite turn of phrase. A bit self-congratulatory as far as Shelby was concerned, but she'd made no comment on it. Dunn might be slightly colorful in the way he handled his duties, but he was as hyperefficient as everyone else was. And besides, he added a splash of color to the steely black and white of the rest of the command staff. And a little color never hurt.

She glanced around. A lot of color, on the other hand, could be absolutely, overpoweringly deadly. She prepared to head back up to the bridge and inform Karen Kahn that she was the new head of security, now that the old head *had* no head. And she couldn't help but consider the fact that, if a hammer had slammed into the skull of Zak Kebron, it would have gone quite badly for the hammer and likely had little to no impact on Kebron himself.

"End program," Shelby said, having seen quite enough. The program vanished.

"No respect," muttered Dr. Kosa as he prepared to take Basner's remains to sickbay. Shelby still had no clear idea what that meant, but she had the strangest feeling that—whatever it did mean—she'd very likely be in full agreement.

# MAJISTER FAIRAX

MAJISTER FAIRAX HAD BEEN in charge of enforcing the law in the city of Narrin for three years, nine months, and one day. The Majister was looking forward with great eagerness to the moment the current year of his contract expired, for four years was as much as he had committed to, and he had not developed a great deal of fondness for the residents therein. For the most part, he found them provincial, quick to anger, quick to judge, and slow to extend compassion. On the other hand, they were valuable guides, for all he had to do was embrace the opposite of their attitudes, and he was reasonably sure that he would wind up a decent enough fellow.

The only one in the area that he found particularly tolerable was that woman . . . Rheela. The one who had a little place by the outskirts. Rheela . . . the rainmaker. She was an odd one, she and her boy, there was no denying that, and on some level he could understand why a number of the townspeople didn't trust her. On the other hand, she had never done anything to harm anyone. Quite the opposite, as a matter of fact. She had been helpful to the point of craziness, bringing rain cascading down in torrents for the benefit of the people. She had given them freely of this amazing ability she possessed, and in return they had given her suspicion and scowls.

"Why do you do it?" he had once asked her. It had been during a holiday festival, and the town had been alive with celebration. Half the population was already drunk, and the other half was well on its way, so obviously no one was giving the young woman any trouble about her presence. It was one of the few times that he'd been able to hold a conversation with her without people giving them dirty looks.

"Do what?" she had replied. She was keeping a wary eye on her son, who was gallivanting around with the other celebrants.

The Majister had scratched his grizzled chin and looked her up and down. Were he a younger man, he might very well have made some serious endeavors in her direction. But he was old enough, wary enough, to know just how ridiculous a man of his age would look if he was courting such a fine young woman. At least, ridiculous in his own mind, and that was all that mattered. "Stay around these parts," he had asked. "There's been very little done in the way of making you feel at home. If you packed up and left tomorrow, these folks wouldn't be the least bit sorry to see you gone. And I know I'm not hurting your feelings when I say that, because I sure ain't telling you anything you don't already know."

"That's as may be, Majister," she had replied, indeed, not sounding the least bit put out. "But they would miss the water I bring to them. So, in that way, they'd miss me."

"Meaning to them, you're a means to an end. They're using you."

"Everyone uses everyone, Majister," she said with a shrug. "That's the way of the world. Sometimes the use is for individual benefit, sometimes for the benefit of many. Ultimately, though, what makes one happy is what matters."

"And staying here where people don't like you makes you happy."

"Whether they like me or not doesn't matter."

"Then what does?"

"Whether I like them," she said with a laugh.

"And you do?"

"I think they have . . ." She thought for a moment. "Potential."

"Potential." He shook his head, looking distinctly unimpressed by the notion. "I don't know that I agree with you."

"Really. That is an odd sentiment, coming from someone whose job it is to protect them."

This time it was the Majister who laughed, a deep and gravelly noise. "Well, that's the key to it, Rheela. It is, in the final analysis, a job. Once hired to do this job, I will do it, and protect everyone in this town to the best of my ability."

"Because you feel you have a certain skill that will benefit them." She nodded, seeming to understand. "Well, Majister . . . I feel the same way. The only difference is, I don't get paid for it."

"Why don't you?"

For a moment she seemed to withdraw, as if she was suspicious of him suddenly. "Why do you ask that?"

"It just seemed a reasonable question. If you find it offensive—"

"No . . . no," she said quickly, briskly recovering her good spirits. "I . . . suppose it *is* reasonable. Perhaps, Majister, it's because this way . . . I know that I'm being sincere. I help because I want to, not because I'm obliged to. It helps me remain true to myself." She seemed to consider her words, and did not appear pleased with them. "Does that make any sense?"

"Yes. Yes, actually, it makes perfect sense."

"I think, Majister, you're being kind."

"As it so happens," he said nobly, "being kind is also in my job description."

She laughed at that, and they spoke no more of it. Ultimately, though, he felt closer to her as a result of the conversation. And, since that time, he had made it his particular province to keep a special eye out for her, since she struck him as a special kind of woman.

So, when she had contacted Majister Fairax about the strange man whom Moke had taken it upon himself to bring home, naturally the Majister attended to it as quickly as possible. In no time at all, he had ridden out to Rheela's homestead and gathered the mysterious stranger who was unconscious and tied up in her shed. Fairax needed to take no more than a single look at the man to know that he was not—to put it mildly—from around there. His skin, his hair—everything was simply wrong. He did not dwell on it, though, because that was not his job. Nor did he worry too much about the fact that the man—at least, that was what he appeared to be—was clearly ill, for that also was not his job. His job was to protect, and the best way to protect others from this newcomer was to make certain that he was put where he could do no harm to anyone.

That, of course, meant gaol. Which was exactly where he put him.

The newcomer made no protest, offered no resistance on the trip back into town. He simply lay slumped over the Majister's own luukab (a larger, hardier version of the one that resided in Rheela's shed) for the length of the journey, at most offering some muttered comments that resulted more from matters flittering through his dreams than anything having to do with the real world. Once he got the man back to the gaol house—which was also where the Majister had his office—he tossed him into a gaol cell and slammed the door securely shut. It clanged with that sort of definitive finality that the Majister always found most appealing.

From that point on, the Majister simply waited for the newcomer to die. He wasn't hoping for it, or encouraging it. But he was not a medman, and the medman was not due back in the area for some weeks yet. Nor were any of the ladies who customarily served as interim nurses and healers interested in turning out to try and attend to him, since his different hue and generally unYakaban appearance made him an instant source of suspicion and fear in the town. So the newcomer lay unattended and feverish, still tossing about on the narrow platform that served as a bed in the cell. After a short time, the Majister became accustomed to the moaning that arose from the cell and developed the ability to turn a deaf ear to it.

Unfortunately, Kusack was having a bit more difficulty than the Majister when it came to ignoring the newcomer.

Kusack was in a cell near to the newcomer, and he made it quite clear to the Majister that he was not appreciating the new setup one bit. Kusack was broadly built, with a wild mane of hair and irregular teeth that resulted from his odd habit of chewing on rock to sharpen them. The Majister had put Kusack in gaol when Kusack had been foolish enough to kill a man named Turkin over a game of cards, while in the Majister's presence. Kusack had claimed that the killing was justified, since Turkin was alleged to have been caught cheating at cards. It wasn't the killing of Turkin that annoyed Fairax so much. The truth was that Turkin had been caught cheating. Caught red-handed, in fact. And, considering that the Majister had lost a significant amount of money to Turkin just the previous week, the revelation was not a happy one as far as Fairax was concerned. Nevertheless, the law tended to frown on killing another person over a game, and considering that Kusack had displayed the monumentally poor taste to engage in the homicidal activity in the Majister's presence, Fairax had simply had no choice but to arrest the stupid sod.

As a result, whenever the newcomer would rant or shout, Kusack would complain loudly. "How am I supposed to sleep, Majister?" he demanded one time.

"Deal with it as best you can," the Majister advised.

"Deal with it? I shouldn't have to deal with it! I shouldn't be here in the first place!" Kusack's beefy hands were each wrapped around one of the bars on the cell door, and they twisted and flexed as if threatening to tear the bars from their mooring. "When my brothers catch wind of this—"

"When they do, they'd be best advised to leave bad enough alone and not make it worse," the Majister said. It was, as far as he was concerned, sound advice, and he could only hope that Kusack's brothers actually followed it.

Late one evening, not long after Fairax had incarcerated the newcomer, he was sitting in his office, minding his own business, when he heard a slamming against the cell door from inside. Pulling his plaser from its holster, he rose and stepped through the door to the adjacent area where the cells were. There he saw the newcomer, his eyes wide and wild, clutching the door bars and looking around as if he was some sort of caged animal.

"May I help you?" asked the Majister patiently, with the forced air of someone who had absolutely no real interest in helping the party he was asking after.

"The pods are all gone," whispered the newcomer. The Majister glanced over to the corner of the cell and saw that, once again, the newcomer had eaten virtually nothing save for the water. And it was fairly obvious where the water had gone, for his entire body appeared matted with perspiration.

"The pods are all gone?" the Majister repeated. He tried to sound sympathetic about it. "Where did they all go?"

"Crew. Crew is in them. All of them." He was talking so fast that it was difficult for the Majister to know what the hell he was talking about. Then again, even if he'd been speaking slowly, it was unlikely that Fairax would have been able to garner the slightest clue of what he was saying. "Had to send them on their way. Only way. All the automatic systems . . . off-line. Had to be done manually."

"That sounds like a shame," said Fairax, trying to sound sympathetic.

"Shuttlebay . . . only hope . . ." With astounding force, he threw himself against the gated door and bounced back off the bars. He hit the ground, rolled, and came up under the platform that was his bed. "Got to get to shuttlebay . . ."

From the cell next door, Kusack moaned, "Dear Kolk'r, shut him up."

"You shut up, Kusack," shot back the Majister. There was something about what the newcomer was saying, the certainty and conviction with which he was speaking—as if he knew something that the Majister couldn't possibly know—that Fairax found extremely fascinating. "You've got to get to the shuttlebay . . ."

"Got . . . to get . . ." His face was flushed, and he was squeezing his fists so tight his knuckles were turning white.

And then, on a hunch, the Majister took a step forward and said, "You're at the shuttlebay."

"Shuttlebay! Made it! Moved . . . so fast. Don't know how I moved so fast . . . but I did," said the sick man, with unmistakable triumph.

"What are you doing now?" prompted Fairax.

From his cell, Kusack was watching the exchange with confusion and quite a bit of suspicion. "What sort of stupid game is th—"

"I said, shut up!" he hissed at Kusack before turning back to the newcomer in the cell. "You're in the shuttlebay," he repeated.

"Whole ship is trembling. Going to blow any minute. I'm in my shuttlecraft." It was as if his gaze was turned inward, seeing a scenario that was clear in his mind and incomprehensible to anyone else.

"Are you leaving the ship?" inquired the Majister. There was unfeigned interest in his voice. Most of his time was spent sitting around, so anything that served as a diversion was enough to catch his fancy.

The newcomer shook his head so fiercely it threatened to topple off his neck. "Trapped . . . bay doors not responding . . ." His hands were moving in what looked like a vague pattern, as if they were operating invisible controls. "Make it . . . make it work . . . got to . . . onboard weaponry . . . blow it open . . ."

"You have onboard weaponry?"

"Blow it open . . ." He was shaking. "Ship . . . going up . . . did it . . . doors are gone . . . go! *Go! Go!*" And suddenly the scar-faced man threw himself against the gaol door with such force that, just for a moment, Fairax thought that he might actually smash the door down in his delusions. The door shook violently, but held firm. He banged into it again and again, and each time he did so he yelled, "Go!" as if trying to drive the imaginary shuttle-craft as far and as fast as he could.

Suddenly he threw his arms around his head and cried out, *"Look out!"* He did it so convincingly that, in the next cell, Kusack automatically hit the dirt to get out of the way of whatever it was that was ostensibly going to provide a threat. If the Majister hadn't been so caught up in the odd drama of the moment, he would have found the whole thing funny. *"The ship's going!"* he continued. "Shockwave . . . taking a pounding . . . shielding holding up, but barely . . ." His words, which had slowed down before, were coming faster and faster again. His breath was ragged in his chest. "Shields gone . . . navigation out . . . comm out . . . barely holding it together . . . force of explosion . . . propelled . . . no idea where . . . no idea . . . lost . . . can't get my bearings . . . planet ahead . . . don't know it . . . trying to hold it together . . . fighting to get retros on-line . . . slow it down . . . I'll burn up . . . burn up if I don't . . . slow down . . . got it . . . like flying a brick . . . hit . . . hitting atmosphere . . . on fire . . ."

And that was when something jogged in the Majister's memory. A few days ago, he'd been sitting out at sunset, looking at the night sky . . . and seen something that bore a resemblance to a shooting star. It had streaked across the horizon, flared out, and then seemed to disappear. He'd thought of it as a simple astronomical phenomenon, pretty to look at, but of no deep or lasting consequence. Was it possible that he had been wrong? That, in fact, he had never been *more* wrong? That what this man was saying . . . rather than being the ravings of an ill and delusional genetic oddity . . . was the Kolk'r's honest truth? Was he some . . . some sort of outer-space creature?

As quickly as the thought crossed the Majister's mind, he shook it off. He was a rational man, a down-to-Yakaba man. He dealt with, and excelled in, the real and the now. He was simply not given to flights of fancy. And he had no intention of starting to embark upon them now.

"Keep her up . . . keep her up . . ." The newcomer's voice was starting to trail off. He seemed to be running out of energy. "Keep . . . nose up . . . coming in fast . . . too fast . . . tearing up . . . *grozit* . . . hold on . . . hold on . . ."

That was when he toppled over.

The Majister was far too smart to enter a cell when a prisoner was putting forward a pretense of illness. Instead, he simply stood outside and watched as the newcomer lay on the floor, arms splayed.

Kusack, who had been trying to peer through the bars at the next cell, looked to the Majister and asked, "Is he dead?"

The Majister shook his head as he watched the unsteady rise and fall of the man's chest. "Nope. Don't appear to be."

"What if he dies?"

"Then we bury him and move on."

He did not, however, die. The Majister went to bed in the small room that served as his home whenever there were prisoners in gaol, since there was no one except him to keep an eye on them, and he didn't like to leave them unattended. What with the Majister's knack for sleeping lightly, any attempt to escape from the jail would awaken him instantly. He had no idea whether the rather curious individual in the cell would be alive when he awoke the next morning. He hoped that he would, but wasn't really holding out much hope.

So, it was with some surprise that, when he walked into the gaol area the next morning, not only did he see his strange prisoner alive, but awake and sitting up and—other than his odd coloring—looking fairly normal.

The first thing that struck the Majister was how the gaze of the purple eyes seemed to pierce him. He saw in the man an almost disquieting intelligence. In a way, it almost seemed to the Majister that he was the prisoner, and this strange man the gaoler.

"Good morning," said the Majister carefully.

The purple-eyed man blinked very slowly, shutting his eyes and then opening them again over a period of several seconds. It seemed that there was even greater clarity in his eyes at that point than before. "Is it?" he said.

"It seems so, yes. How are you feeling?"

"Damp," he said. He pulled at the tattered clothes that were stuck to his sodden body. "I appear to have sweated through everything I have on."

"I can get you something else to wear."

"That would be appreciated. As would some water. I'm feeling a bit . . . dehydrated."

Water, as always, was not in abundant supply, but the Majister didn't see how he could reasonably turn down the request. Kusack was being obliging enough to remain asleep, so he didn't have to worry about yowling from the other inmate, or complaints about preferential treatment. Within a few minutes he returned with both a small amount of water and some extra clothes from the back. He walked up to the gaol door and said, "Step back."

He waited for the prisoner to ask, "Why?" But the purple eyes flickered over the Majister, and then, without a word, the man stepped away from the bars. He leaned against the far wall, folding his arms and watching the Majister with what seemed a combination of assessment and amusement. Fairax pushed the cup of water and the clothes through the bars, placing them on the floor, never taking his eyes off the prisoner. The man didn't make the slightest threatening move, or any move of any kind. Indeed, he was so motionless that he might well have been carved from rock. The Majister moved away, and only then did the prisoner pick up the glass and sip from its contents.

"Figured you'd just drink it down. Afraid I put something in it?" inquired the Majister.

"No. Just don't know when the next will be coming." He picked up the rough-hewn clothes, inspected them closely, and sniffed them. Then he looked up at the Majister and said, "Death."

"Pardon?"

"I smell death. On these clothes. Someone died while wearing them."

The Majister blinked in surprise. "Yes. That's right. A man was stabbed in them. But the hole from the knife was sewn up, the blood cleaned off."

The man said nothing, but instead simply started stripping off the tattered clothes he was wearing and proceeded to pull on the new ones.

"It does not bother you," the Majister said with interest, "to wear the clothes of a dead man?"

"Only if he were wearing them at the same time I was."

The Majister laughed brusquely at that. "You're a cold-blooded bastard, I'll give you that. So you are fully recovered, I take it."

"I believe so. I still feel a bit weak in the legs. That should pass." He glanced around. "Where am I?"

The way he spoke, it sounded less like a question than it did a command that he be informed of his whereabouts. Something about this man indicated to the Majister that he was not only accustomed to giving orders, but also to being obeyed. "You're on the planet Yakaba. In the city of Narrin." He paused, and then added, almost as an afterthought, "In my gaol."

"Yes, I can see that." His fists gripped the bars, and although he did nothing overt, the Majister noted the flexing of the tendons beneath his skin. The man was testing the strength of the bars. Well, he would not be disappointed in that regard. "A customary habitat for criminals, I assume."

"Correct."

"Which would seem to indicate, in your eyes, that I am a criminal."

"Correct again."

"I see. And what might I have done to warrant such low status?"

"You attacked a woman. Tried to kill her."

That seemed to startle him. It only did so for a moment, though, and then he drew an invisible mask over his face, to cloak whatever might be going through his mind. He did so with a most impressive ease.

"That is . . . unfortunate," he said finally. "I was . . . not myself."

"Really. And may I ask who you yourself are?"

"Calhoun. Mackenzie Calhoun. And you?"

"Majister Fairax."

" 'Majister' being some sort of title, I imagine, from the way you said it. In charge of law enforcement, I surmise."

"You surmise correctly."

"Majister Fairax . . . I'm . . . not supposed to be here."

"Just passing through, are you?"

"In a manner of speaking, yes."

"Well, Mackenzie Calhoun," said the Majister, leaning back in his chair and tilting slightly on the legs. "It would seem that you're not going to be passing through as quickly as you previously supposed."

"You do not need to keep me in here," Calhoun told him. "I'm not a threat to anyone."

"And I know that . . . how? It's not as if you've exactly had the chance to refrain from hurting anyone while you've been in there, right? For all I know, I let you out of that cell, and you'll go on a rampage."

"I won't go on a rampage. I assure you. Let me talk to the woman. Explain things to her. I'm certain I can get her to drop charges."

"Perhaps you can, perhaps you can't. Thing is, Mackenzie Calhoun, that's not up to either you or her or even me."

"And who," he asked patiently, "is it up to?"

"The Circuit Judiciary. You see, Calhoun, you're guilty of trespass and assault. Only the Circuit Judiciary can set those changes aside."

"I'm guilty of nothing," Calhoun told him firmly. "I was injured, feverish . . . possibly even concussed."

"And might I ask how you came to be in such a state?"

"It's . . ." Calhoun sighed. "It's a long story." He glanced around at his surroundings, as if trying to make some judgments about the world itself based upon what he could discern right here. "One that I don't think it really appropriate to tell."

"Have something to do with your crashing shuttle?"

That obviously caught him off guard. Calhoun looked at the Majister with surprise, and even a bit of respect.

"We may seem a bit backward to you," Fairax said, allowing himself to be a bit smug about it, "but we have our moments every now and then."

"The point is," Calhoun went on, apparently not wanting to let himself be pulled into a discussion of his arrival at his current happenstance, "I'm being held for no reason. But I can see that your mind is made up regarding this Circuit Judiciary business."

"It's not a matter of 'made up.' It's simply my job."

"All right," Calhoun sighed, resigned. "When can we talk to this Circuit Judiciary?"

"When he comes through this way on his circuit."

"And that will be . . . ?"

"About five months."

If the Majister was expecting an extreme reaction from Calhoun, he was greatly disappointed. Calhoun simply processed the information and then announced, "That is unacceptable."

"I'm afraid it's not for you to accept or reject. The CJ came through just last month. Small scuffles, disputes and such, these are things that I can attend to. But assault is a serious matter; assault on a woman even more so."

"I told you, I wasn't in my right mind."

The Majister considered that for a moment. Finally he said, "I have this funny feeling, Mackenzie Calhoun, that you're not unfamiliar with being in the position of having to worry about peoples' welfare. So put yourself in my place. Imagine some stranger blows into town, nearly strangles a woman to death, and then later says that he feels kinda bad about it and he's just passing through and won't cause no more trouble. Would your immediate instinct be to trust him? Or to be suspicious?"

"Suspicious to start out. But my inclination would be to hear him out."

"Except hearing you out isn't my job, it's the—"

"Circuit Judiciary's, yes, so you've said," sighed Calhoun. After a moment, he turned and sat on the bench, which doubled as a bed. "So you're saying that I've no choice but to wait."

"Yes. Said it several times, as a matter of fact."

"That is . . . unfortunate."

"I'm sorry that you're inconvenienced."

"I meant, unfortunate for you."

The Majister found this a most intriguing statement. "Are you threatening me, Mackenzie Calhoun?"

"Not at all, Majister Fairax. However, others have attempted to imprison me."

"Really? So you've broken the law elsewhere, have you?"

"Actually, it usually happened while I was busy enforcing . . . other laws. The point is, Majister . . . all such attempts have ended badly for those who were making the endeavor. You seem a decent enough man. I would not like things to end badly for you."

"Your consideration for my welfare is truly heartening, Calhoun. But if it is all the same to you . . . I'll take my chances and keep you locked up until the CJ can process your case in the approved manner."

"As you wish," Calhoun said with a small shrug. "I can tell you one thing with certainty, though—I'm not going to be sitting here for five months."

"How do you know that?"

"Because, Majister, not even in infancy did I ever spend five consecutive months in relative peace. Believe it or not, I almost wouldn't mind the time off. But I've never been that fortunate. Fate always has something else in store."

"I am not a great believer in fate, Mackenzie Calhoun."

"I've known quite a few people who agreed with you, Majister."

"Perhaps," smiled the Majister, "they will come and visit you."

"I doubt it," Calhoun replied evenly. "They're all dead."

The Majister's smile began to fade under the unyielding gaze of Mackenzie Calhoun. "Who," he said, looking for a more comprehensive answer than he'd gotten before, "are you?"

"Mackenzie Calhoun. And I'm just passing through."

"Well, Mackenzie Calhoun who's just passing through . . . you'll have five months to change your mind."

"Perhaps I will," Calhoun said, sounding a bit sad, "but I've got this very depressing feeling . . . that you won't."

The Majister's smile evaporated completely, and he didn't look directly at Calhoun for the rest of the day.

# MAESTRESS CAWFIEL

THE MAJISTER HAD A FEELING that the day wasn't going to be going well when he emerged from his simple bunk in the back room to discover the frosty visage of Maestress Cawfiel waiting for him. Even worse, the rest of her was attached to the visage.

"Good morning, Maestress," said the Majister with a slight bow as he walked over to his desk. He cast a glance in Calhoun's direction. Calhoun was awake; unsurprising, since the Majister didn't have the faintest idea when the man slept. When the Majister went to bed, no matter how late it was, Calhoun watched him go. When the Majister arose to start the day, no matter how early, there again was Calhoun. This had been going on for the last week, and although the Majister found it extremely disconcerting, he was certainly not going to let Calhoun know that it bothered him. He could not help but think, though, that the next five months promised to be very, very long.

He had even started toying with the idea of riding out and tracking down the Circuit Judiciary. Plead with him to make a special swing back to Narrin, so that he could attend to Calhoun. Furthermore, he could always approach Praestor Milo and ask *him* to make a ruling about Calhoun. But he didn't want to give the impression to anyone that something as simple as a jailed prisoner could give him pause. So he had kept his peace, and hoped that matters would get better . . . or perhaps Calhoun would simply keel over and die, or something equally convenient.

"Good morning, Majister," replied the Maestress, returning the bow. There was nothing in her eyes, though, that gave the slightest indication she was at all happy to be there, or pleased to see the Majister. Her gaze traveled over to Calhoun, and she took him in with one silent, contemptuous stare. "So, this is it," she said after a lengthy quiet.

"This is what, Maestress?" inquired Fairax.

"This . . . individual," and she pointed one claw-like finger at Calhoun, "is the creature that assaulted Rheela."

"That would seem to be the case," agreed the Majister.

She approached the cell thoughtfully. The Majister's immediate impulse was to tell her to keep her distance, but then he reasoned to himself that the worst-case scenario would involve her lifeless body sinking to the floor, thanks to a neck snapped by the muscular-looking Calhoun. So he kept his peace.

The Maestress drew just within range of Calhoun, but the Majister was slightly saddened to see that Calhoun made no move against her. Only slightly saddened, because the truth was that—no matter what his personal feelings about her—he would have felt compelled to come to her aid. Which he would have drawn no satisfaction from, but one had to do the job one had agreed to undertake.

"He's very odd-looking," Cawfiel announced after a time.

Calhoun tilted his head slightly in acknowledgment, as if he was appreciating a compliment given him. He did not make the obvious observation that the Maestress was not exactly a raving beauty.

"Even somewhat ugly," she added after further consideration. She turned back to the Majister, her face darkening. "But, then again, what would one expect from someone who would consort with Rheela?"

"I wouldn't know, Maestress," said Fairax neutrally. He sat behind his desk. "Is there something that I can help you with?"

"Yes." She moved over to a chair but, curiously, did not sit in it.

Instead, she stood next to it and rested a hand lightly on the back. "You can tell me why you would give priority to a woman like that . . . and display so little respect for a woman such as myself."

"So little respect, Maestress?" He looked at her blankly. "I haven't the faintest idea what you mean."

She didn't respond at first, but merely glared at him. Finally, apparently deciding that she had made him "suffer" long enough, she said, "Last week . . . when I was lecturing in the streets, and I spoke of the darkness within that woman . . . a voice called from the crowd, asking how I could know that there was a stain on her soul. I did not recognize the voice at first. But, having had time to dwell on it—thinking upon the voice that spoke up, the tone and attitude—I have little doubt now that it was you."

"Me?" His eyebrows almost puckered in a curious question mark.

She frowned even more. "Do not," she warned him, "embarrass yourself, or me, by claiming anything otherwise. I pay attention to such things, Majister. As a matter of fact . . . I pay attention to *everything*. There is nothing that occurs in this town that escapes my notice."

"That's very comforting to know, Maestress. Perhaps you'd like to sign on as my assistant, to aid me in keeping the peace."

"I do not consider that funny, Majister."

"That's all right, Maestress. I didn't consider it much of a joke."

She glowered at him, but he returned none of the enmity. He seemed quite bland, almost bored by her.

"I hope you are not intending to cross me, Majister," she said at last. "I hope you have not forgotten who truly cares about this town . . . who truly . . ."

"Who truly holds the power? Is that what you were going to say? Going to impress me with how one withered woman can keep so many people in her sway?" He laughed when his words were rewarded with a slight, indignant purpling of her face. "Maestress . . . believe it or not . . . I'm not your enemy. Because, in a few months, I'm going to be leaving here, voluntarily. So, you see, struggling with you for the hearts and minds of the residents of this city is the last thing on my mind. My intention is to do my job to the best of my ability, keep people from hurting each other as much as I can, and—when my contract is up—move on. Now . . . is any of that in contradiction to your own hopes or desires for Narrin?"

"No," she said tersely, her normal color beginning to return.

"Good. Then I certainly think we'll be able to coexist with a minimum of effort, if that's all the same to—"

The door to the gaol house abruptly banged inward. The Majister looked up, his face carefully neutral.

One at a time, three men entered. Each of them was half a head taller than the Majister, and although they had three different faces, they shared one expression: surly. Their very manner exuded confidence, as if they knew everything that was going to happen and were simply fulfilling their roles in the proceedings. Large plasers—crude and heavy, but no less deadly—hung from their hips. The Majister felt the weight of his own plaser on his hip, and drew some comfort from it.

Two of them held back as the third stepped forward. He was apparently the oldest of the three, with a drooping mustache and shaggy hair. He looked the Majister up and down, and was clearly unimpressed by what he saw.

"Morning," said the Majister carefully. "Can I help you folks?"

"You the Majister?" His voice was gravelly and distant, as if uninterested in the answer to the question.

"Yes. And you would be?"

"Hey, Temo." It was Kusack who had spoken up from his cell. He seemed rather chipper. "How you doing?"

"Better than you," said the one who'd been addressed as Temo. "What the hell kind of fix you gotten yourself into, Kus'?"

"Kusack is in gaol for murder," Majister Fairax said neutrally.

"Really."

"Yes, really."

"Well . . . I'm his brother. And these two gentlemen here," and he indicated the men standing on either side of him, "are also his brothers. And I think you should know . . . that we frown on murder. Kus' . . . I thought you knew better than that. Hang your head in shame, Kus'."

Kusack promptly hung his head in shame.

Temo swung his baleful glare back to the Majister. "There. You see? Clearly, he's ashamed. Our family has certain standards, and it upsets us deeply—*deeply*—to see that our brother has violated them. Do you know what we're going to do, Majister?"

"Why don't you tell me?"

"We are going to bring him home and discipline him severely. That's how our family operates, you see. We're big believers in personal responsibility."

The Maestress stepped forward and said firmly, "And we are big believers in the law."

"Maestress, I can handle this. Perhaps you should leave," the Majister said slowly. He did not like the way this seemed to be shaping up.

"Perhaps she should," agreed Temo. But then one of the brothers took a couple of steps to the right, squarely blocking the door. "Then again, perhaps she shouldn't."

Something changed in the air; something electrical seemed to shift polarity. Calhoun was now up behind his cell door, his face absolutely inscrutable. "Majister," he said softly, "perhaps you'd better—"

"I'm not looking for advice from a beater of women, Calhoun," the Majister told him curtly. He shifted his focus back to Temo and the other two. "Your dedication to family and your high ethics are duly noted," he deadpanned. "However, my first duty is to the law and to the citizens of this city. The law says that your brother is going to have to wait for the Circuit Judiciary. And that's what he's going to do. Now, I suggest that you gentlemen accept that reality, turn around, and depart. If you want to discuss it further . . . then let the Maestress go on her way, and we can continue—"

Temo gave no warning whatsoever. One moment his hand was

hanging relaxed at his side, and the next, the plaser was in his hand.

Even as he moved for his own weapon, the Majister knew that he was too slow and too late. Temo fired once, and once was all it took. The plaser bolt slammed Fairax squarely in the chest, knocking him off his feet and sending him smashing against the cell in which Calhoun was imprisoned. He hit it hard and then slid to the ground, a massive scorch mark across his chest. His head lolled to the right, and his hand slumped away from the butt of his plaser. He had never even managed to get it clear of the holster.

The Maestress did not let out a shriek, as another might have done. Instead, regardless of her own safety, she pointed straight at Temo and snarled, "You . . . murderer!"

Ignoring her, Temo said to one of his brothers, "Get him out," and nodded toward Kusack. The brother strode forward, pulling his plaser as he went. The third continued to block the door.

With one quick screech of a plaser bolt, the door lock was blasted away. Kusack let out a whoop of triumph and shoved the door open. "Qinos!" he said joyfully, clapping the brother who'd just freed him on the shoulder. "Shadrak! And Temo . . ." His arms were open as he approached the brother who'd led them. "How can I thank you for—"

Temo slapped him, hard. Kusack staggered, putting a hand to his face. "Wha—what did you—?"

"Idiot. Letting yourself get dragged into gaol by this piece of . . ." He couldn't bring himself to finish the sentence. Instead, somewhat annoyed, he kicked the unmoving body of the Majister. "What in hell were you thinking?"

"I was drunk . . . he . . . he tricked me, snuck up on me . . . I was—"

Temo slapped Kusack again, and then steadied himself. "You know what, Kus'? I don't want to hear it. I don't want to hear anything about this entire misbegotten incident anymore."

"Well, you're going to!" It was the Maestress who had spoken.

"This will not end here! I swear, you're going to pay for what you've done! You're going to pay!"

"Why haven't we killed her?" growled Qinos.

And that was when Calhoun spoke up. "Let me," he said.

Their attention swiveled to him. "Who is this?" Temo asked of Kusack. "For that matter . . . *what* is this?"

"His name's Calhoun."

"What'd the Majister call him? Oh, yes . . . beater of women." Temo's lips twitched upward. "Now, there was a ringing endorsement."

"He kept telling the Majister that he wasn't in his right mind when he beat 'em," Kusack offered.

Calhoun gave him a contemptuous look. "And you told your brothers you were drunk when the Majister arrested you. We all make excuses."

"And why do you want to kill her?" asked Temo. He was wearing a broad-brimmed hat, and he nudged it back slightly on his forehead as he studied Calhoun.

"She insulted me. She said I was ugly."

"You are."

"I'll kill you next," Calhoun told him.

This prompted Temo to let out a bark-like laugh. "I like this one. Push the woman over toward him so he can kill her." He reached to a scabbard that hung on the back of his belt and extracted a knife. While he did that, Shadrak grabbed the Maestress by the arms and pinned them back. This prompted her to let out an infuriated yelp. He started shoving her toward Calhoun as if she had no weight.

But when Temo proferred the knife to Calhoun, he shook his head. "She's not worth staining perfectly good steel for. Bare hands will do."

"I am impressed," Temo said approvingly.

"Let me out to do it."

This, however, prompted caution. "I think not," he said slowly.

Upon hearing that, Calhoun shrugged and moved to the back part of the cell. "Then forget it. I've no interest in having her corpse lying here and me stuck in this cell so that I can be immediately executed for her murder . . . and, who knows, perhaps they'll try to stick the Majister's death on me as well."

"Why should we let you out?" demanded Temo.

"Why shouldn't you?" Calhoun spread his hands. "I have no weapon. You're three armed men. Four, if you give your brother a weapon. Look . . . never mind. If you're that afraid of me . . ."

"Who said we were afraid of you?" Temo demanded.

Calhoun said nothing, but simply shrugged.

Temo looked suspiciously toward the Majister's plaser, but saw that it was securely in his holster. So Calhoun hadn't removed it and hidden it on his person as some sort of ambush.

"You're monsters! All of you, monsters!" Maestress Cawfiel said in thundering moral outrage.

This was more than enough for Temo. He aimed his plaser at the lock of the cell door that held Calhoun and fired once. The lock was instantly blown out, and the door swung open.

Calhoun rose and walked slowly out of the cell. He cast an appreciative glance at the fried lock and nodded approvingly. "Very nice," he said. "Very nice work."

"Shadrak," said Temo briskly, "give him the shrieking little harridan and let's be done with it."

"And once I've killed her, what then? You let me go on my way?"

"Why shouldn't we?" replied Temo. "As you yourself said . . . what do we have to be afraid of?"

At that, Calhoun smiled. If Temo had been looking very closely, he would have seen that none of that smile was reflected in Calhoun's eyes. But he wasn't. Instead, he simply stood there as Shadrak brought the Maestress over to him. The Maestress began to struggle, and Shadrak had to increase the pressure on her wrists to hold her steady.

"You're gripping her all wrong," Calhoun told him. "There's a convenient way to immobilize someone. Here, I'll show you."

He reached for Cawfiel's right arm . . . and then went right past it and gripped Shadrak's arm instead. The move was so quick, so subtle, that Shadrak didn't even realize it was happening.

And suddenly, just like that, Calhoun had spun Shadrak around, twisted his arm back and frozen him in place. Amazingly, he had done so with only one hand; with his free hand, he yanked Shadrak's plaser out of his holster.

Temo had never holstered his weapon, but it had all happened so fast that he'd been caught utterly flat-footed. His movement was instinctive, and he fired, but Shadrak was serving as a shield, and all he did was nail his brother in the chest. Shadrak let out a stunned shriek, and then his head slumped forward.

Calhoun lashed out with his right leg and knocked the Maestress flat to the floor. For a heartbeat, she thought it was an attack, and then she realized: he was shoving her to the floor to get her out of harm's way. He swung the plaser around and, from behind his shield, fired. The first blast hit Qinos in the arm, and he staggered back, clutching at the wound and howling. The second barely missed the fast-moving Temo, and blew his hat clean off his head.

*"Go! Go!"* screamed Temo, and he and Qinos backed up. Kusack started to follow, and Calhoun fired again. This blast nailed Kusack in the leg, and he went down, clutching at his upper thigh.

Temo ducked under another blast, fired again, but couldn't get past the dead mass of meat that had been his brother. He snagged Qinos by the wrist, and they charged out the door.

*"Come back!"* Kusack shouted pitifully, lying on the floor and clutching at his injured leg.

"Shut up," Calhoun said sharply. Still wielding Shadrak's body in front of him, he went to the door and looked out. Apparently he was satisfied with what he saw—namely, the two brothers bolting across the dirt streets of Narrin, trying to put as much distance between him and themselves as possible. He turned back to Kusack and, gesturing with the plaser, said, "Get back in your cell."

"I can't walk—!"

"Neither can he," Calhoun said tightly, indicating the Majister's corpse. "And unless you want to follow his example, you'll get in the cell now. *Now*."

Realizing that Calhoun wasn't exactly in the mood for discussion, Kusack dragged himself across the floor. As he hauled himself into the cell, Calhoun allowed Shadrak's body to slide to the floor. Then he looked down at the Maestress, who was still on the floor and looking up at him in wonderment.

"Get up," he said tersely, but made no effort to help her. The Maestress did so, dusting herself off and watching him cautiously. "There's no lock on the cell door anymore," he continued. "I'll wait here and make sure he doesn't go anywhere. You go get help."

"How do I—?" Then she caught the question before she completed it. Obviously, she had no reason to think that he was going to do anything other than what he had said he was going to. He could have killed her. He could have walked out after he'd shot Shadrak. Instead, he was standing there and telling her to bring someone else. It seemed extremely unlikely that he was going anywhere.

She had no idea why he was doing it. But she knew one thing beyond a doubt, one thing that was the only appropriate thing to say or do, given the circumstances.

"Thank you," she said.

He nodded slightly. "You're welcome," he replied. And then he sat on the edge of the desk. The last thing she saw of him as she ran for help was him immobile, seemingly almost bored . . . and perhaps just a bit sad . . . but, ultimately, comfortable in the sea of violence that surrounded him.

It was at that moment that she knew; he was her man.

# SHELBY

SHELBY TILTED HER HEAD BACK, looking up and up as she squinted against the Makkusian sun. It glinted off the astounding sculpture that towered so high, and no matter how hard she tried and how much she craned her neck, she still couldn't begin to make out the top.

"Most impressive . . . is it not?"

The tall man stepped into view, blocking out the sun. He was close to seven feet tall, with long, flowing brown hair, and an air of peace that hung about him like a warm blanket. Indeed, being with him was so relaxing that, every so often, Shelby had to fight the urge to nod off.

"Very impressive, Hauman," she admitted. Nearby, Toreen Augustine was nodding as well, even though it was not the first time she had seen it. Also with them was Lieutenant Glen Scott Wagner, newly promoted (due to the unexpected demise of Lieutenant Basner) to assistant chief of security. "And this entire structure . . . this whole thing—"

"Constructed from former weapons, yes," Hauman said. "Melted down, or pounded flat and reconfigured. A monument to the neutrality that has become the lifeblood—indeed, the true legacy—of Makkus."

They walked for some time around the base of the tower, and they did so in silence. Hauman, the Makkusian leader, had been most friendly upon the arrival of the *Exeter* team, and had insisted on showing them around his capital city personally. Shelby had been struck not only by his lack of pretensions, but also his lack of retainers. Helpers, naysayers, yes-men, and all manner of types who seemed to exist throughout the galaxy—although their forms might vary from world to world—customarily accompanied heads of state. But Hauman seemed to have no interest in such official trappings.

Nor, clearly, did he feel any need for bodyguards. He walked about in the city, nodding to citizens as he passed them, and they naturally returned the gesture. For someplace that was a capital city, she couldn't help but feel that it felt a bit . . . provincial. Not especially advanced for a potential member-world of the Federation. At least, that was the opinion Shelby had voiced during a prelanding conference, and Augustine had semiconfirmed it.

"I wouldn't say they're not advanced, Captain," Augustine had said. "Their spaceflight capabilities are on a par with any member of the Federation, and although their weaponry wasn't quite equal to ours, it was formidable—"

" 'Was'?"

"They don't use it anymore. I think they still have ships, but they employ them solely for immediate onplanet needs or humanitarian missions. They don't even journey into space anymore. It's not just that they're disinterested; they're disinterested with a passion. To them, science is a symbol of what went wrong on their world. They do not automatically rush headlong toward advancement, because they are painfully aware—from firsthand experience—just what a double-edged sword advancement can be."

Shelby was receiving confirmation of that attitude now, as Hauman continued to lead them in a slow circle around the monument. "Every one of the former weapons you see here, Captain," he said quietly, with almost hushed reverence, "was used to kill someone. Or to try and take a life. Here, it can do no harm. Instead, it all contributes . . . to a work of art."

Wagner was eyeing the monument skeptically, and Shelby couldn't blame him. It didn't look like any work of art to her, but rather like a . . . well, a big, tall metal thing, twisted in on itself in no discernible pattern, that just kept going up and up. Art, though, was definitely in the eye of the beholder, and she had no intention of possibly aggravating things by speaking ill of their remarkably beloved monument.

Hauman looked up at it a while longer, then let out a deep sigh. "I just wish it didn't look so damned ugly."

Shelby was instantly converted into a fan of Hauman. "It *does* look ugly, doesn't it?" she admitted.

"Oh, unquestionably. At the very least, it's ostentatious beyond imagining. Still," and he surveyed it proudly, "at least it stands for something. Means something to everyone who looks upon it. It says that we can rise above a base compulsion to destruction."

"That is certainly a message that the Federation shares, Hauman," Shelby said readily. "That is the linchpin upon which the UFP hinges, as a matter of fact. On that basis, I don't see why you wouldn't want to join—"

"You don't understand, Captain."

"No. I don't. So, if you would care to explain it to me. . . ."

Hauman looked at the monument, hands draped behind his back. He appeared wistful, even sad. "Captain . . . you are looking at a race that nearly depopulated itself. Our scientists were very, very imaginative when it came to the development of weapons of mass destruction. Weapons so horrific, we could have brought an end to ourselves, or to any that we might use them against. We have neighboring worlds, Captain, and they have no more desire for mutual destruction than we do ourselves. In short, we came to our senses . . . particularly thanks to the teachings of the Mage."

"The Mage?" Shelby fired a questioning look at Augustine, but she shrugged. Obviously this was something she hadn't heard before.

"The Mage," said Hauman with reverence. "She came to us generations ago . . . guided us, taught us. Helped us realize the error of our ways. One of the reasons we created the tower was as a testament to her."

"Is this 'Mage' still around?"

"Oh, no. No, she has long departed."

For one insane moment, Shelby thought of Morgan Primus, the mother of Robin Lefler. Morgan was, to put it mildly, long-lived, and had such a shrouded background that, if there was anything odd going on that involved a woman, Morgan was the first suspect that came to Shelby's mind. "The Mage . . . what did she look like?"

"Tall, willowy . . . a face that shone with the light of a thousand suns, hair like floating gossamer that—"

"You've met her?" asked Wagner. He sounded somewhat suspicious.

"Oh, no. Nor do any visual representations exist, for she allowed no likenesses of any kind to be made of her. But the poets have written of her extensively."

Well, the physical description didn't sound a damned thing like Morgan, so Shelby was inclined to dismiss that notion before it became implanted too deeply in her imagination.

"In any event," continued Hauman, "when we put aside our weapons and things of violence—in short, when we matured as a race—we came to realize that the only means through which we could avoid any temptation to take up such weapons again was to adopt a philosophy of strict neutrality."

"And we're not asking you to set aside that philosophy," Shelby told him. "The Federation respects all philosophies. Again, that's part of our credo. There's far more the Federation could offer you besides the opportunities to 'take sides' in matters of war. There's humanitarian aid, education, health programs for—"

"But war can sometimes come, whether you expect it or not, true?" Hauman very politely interrupted. When she nodded, he continued, "And at such times, would the UFP not look to us to join them in any such violent endeavors, since we would be part of the alliance?"

"There is every likelihood that you would be approached, yes," Shelby said slowly. "But no one would force you to fight if you felt strongly against it."

"If that were to be the case, why . . . then we would be most frustrating and annoying allies to have as part of the Federation, would we not?" Hauman asked with a gentle smile. "On the one hand, having no hesitation to avail ourselves of whatever benefits the UFP might have to offer, while, on the other, refusing to provide support in times of dire need. What's that Earth phrase used to describe such people . . . ?"

"Fair-weather friends," Wagner said. Shelby fired him a look that indicated she wasn't happy with him right then.

But Hauman smiled and nodded gratefully. "Yes. That is it. A very good term. We would only be friends when the weather was fair. When the clouds open up and the torrents descend, then we would not be found. Does that sound like someone with whom you would like to ally yourself, Captain?"

"All the UFP ever asks is that an ally do the best and most that it can for other member-worlds," she explained. "That should not sound unreasonable to you. Besides, the unfortunate truth is that there are hostile worlds out there. You need protection against them. We can provide that."

"I have no doubt that you can, Captain," replied Hauman. "Obviously, you care a great deal about providing protection, including for yourselves." He indicated the phaser that was attached to Shelby's uniform at the hip.

"Standard issue in away situations," Shelby said by way of explanation. "One can never be too prepared."

"Another philosophy of the Federation, no doubt," Hauman said, although he didn't sound sarcastic so much as mildly amused. "Again, though . . . I am inclined to wonder what we are providing in return."

PETER DAVID

It was Augustine who spoke up. "The pleasure of your company, Hauman. Sometimes . . . that is sufficient."

Hauman smiled at this, and laughed appreciatively. Shelby glanced at Augustine and gave an approving nod. Discussions weren't going as smoothly as she'd hoped, but they weren't crashing and burning either. Perhaps if she remained consistent enough, pushing gently toward the answer she wanted, she could—

Her combadge beeped. "Excuse me a moment," she said to Hauman, who nodded. She tapped it and said, "Shelby. Go."

"Captain, this is Tulley," came the voice of the science officer. "I've been scanning your immediate area, and I'm getting a life-form reading I can't say I like."

"Life-form? What sort of life-form?"

"Insectoid would be my best guess. A considerable swarm, in fact, and it is at this moment approaching the—"

And that was when a loud howl began to sound throughout the city. Hauman, so at ease only moments ago, suddenly was whipcord-tense. He was looking urgently to the skies, although he clearly didn't have an idea of which direction to check first. At that moment, a short woman with an urgent expression dashed up to them. "What is it, Brandi," asked Hauman, but there was no interrogation in his voice. He sounded like he knew what the answer was going to be before she gave it.

Very rapidly, she told him, "Bugs. Coming in from the Northwest. ETA, three minutes."

All the remaining pleasantness in Hauman's manner evaporated like tissue in water. "Come," he said with sudden urgency. "We have to go. Right now."

Shelby hesitated. The link was still open and she could call for a beam-out—but her gut said that would be wrong. "After you," Shelby said to Hauman.

"Captain!" said Wagner, sounding shocked. "We have to call for beam-out! My job is to—"

"Protect me, I know. I'll be fine. This is Hauman's planet and

I'll trust him to protect us. That's what the Federation is all about: Trust."

"But, Captain, the risk—"

Shelby quieted him with a look. Then she turned to Hauman and Brandi. "All right. Now what?"

"Come," he said, gripping her hand. "Pardon the overfamiliarity; I wouldn't want you to get separated in—"

"Don't worry about it," she said.

They dashed across the town square, and Shelby could faintly hear a distant buzzing. She looked off in the direction that Brandi had indicated, and saw a dark cloud appearing on the horizon. For one wild moment, she thought that the Black Mass was attacking. That, somehow, they had survived the encounter in Thallonian space and had returned to wreak more havoc. But then she brushed that off, knowing it not to be the case. Aside from the fact that Tulley would have recognized them as such, it was clear that Hauman had some sort of prior familiarity with whatever it was that was swooping down toward them. And if it had been the Black Mass, well . . . no one has familiarity with them, because once they show up, that's more or less it for the planet in question.

"Up ahead!" called Hauman. "There's a shelter!"

There was indeed: a steel doorway that seemed to rise up directly from the ground, obviously with stairs that angled it down to some sort of subterranean safe house. Hauman's long stride would have carried him there easily in a heartbeat, but he was slowing in order to make certain that Shelby kept up. Others who were in the streets were likewise dashing into the shelter. And all around Shelby could see people in their homes slamming shut large metal sills, covering over their windows to provide shielding from the new arrivals.

Suddenly an alarmed and pained screech came from behind her. She stopped, turned, and saw that Brandi had fallen, tearing up her knees. She was sobbing in hysterical fear, and Shelby immediately saw why. Whatever the creatures descending upon them were, a couple of them had managed to get ahead of the rest of the swarm and were dive-bombing toward Brandi. Shelby couldn't believe the size of them; she made them out to be at least six inches in length, perhaps more, but they were moving so quickly that she couldn't see much in terms of detail beyond that.

"Get to safety!" Hauman shouted at Shelby as he turned to help Brandi. But Wagner and Augustine were already helping her stagger to her feet, blood smearing her lower legs, and the bugs were almost upon them.

Shelby had absolutely no idea what the oversized insects would do once they made it to their prey, but she wasn't about to find out. She yanked out her phaser, thumbing it to wide-beam even as she brought it up, and she fired without even taking the time to aim. The blast intercepted the insects just before they could strike and knocked them out of the air. Shelby couldn't quite believe what she was then seeing, though. The phaser blasts should have been more than enough to stun a human into unconsciousness, even with the wider dispersion of the beam. In this case, the bugs were down, but most definitely not out. They were flipping around on the ground, thin legs clawing at the air, emitting outraged buzzing noises and obviously trying to reorient themselves so that they could make another pass.

Fortunately enough, no one was waiting for that to happen. Brandi was limping, but she was doing it very, very quickly, and with help they made it to the shelter. Other Makkusians were standing in the doorway, gesturing frantically for them to hurry. Wagner was supporting Brandi on one side, and Augustine was helping to keep her up on the other. They half-ran, half-stumbled into the shelter, and the door slammed resolutely shut behind them.

The shelter was nothing incredibly deluxe, but it was more than enough to serve the immediate need. There were foodstuffs lining the wall, obviously in case a lengthy stay was going to be required. And a monitor up on the wall was alight, giving them a view of the city itself.

The bugs were now descending from everywhere, more and more seeming to show up with every passing moment. The sound of the buzzing would have been deafening, had they been outside.

As it was, the walls of the shelter dampened it somewhat, but Shelby still had to speak loudly to be heard.

"What the hell *are* those things?" demanded Shelby.

"Bugs," he said tersely.

She was now getting a closer look at them, hurtling about or crawling on walls. She frowned. "I don't see any stingers on them."

"They don't have any."

"So what's the danger they provide? Disease?"

Brandi, whose sniffles had died down, nodded mutely. Hauman looked equally grim. "Their bite transmits an assortment of lethal diseases. It's a relatively recent problem, only within the last year or so. But it has become our number-one health and safety issue."

All around Shelby, other Makkusians—huddled together for warmth in the coolness of the shelter—watched the screen with morbid fascination as the bugs flitted this way and that. "They look for food, for nourishment. When they do not find it here, they will move on, although we cannot know when they'll return. They're bloodsuckers by nature," said Hauman. "They've always been an irritation. But they've never been deadly until, as I said, about a year ago. Have you ever experienced anything like this?"

"Personally? No. But my homeworld certainly has. We had diseases spread by insects called mosquitoes, for instance, capable of annihilating half a countryside."

"And what did you do?"

"At the time? Died, mostly. We didn't have the technology and ability to treat it. Over time, though, we developed the tools to combat them."

"Can you combat these?" It was Brandi who was asking, with tremendous urgency. Hauman tried to stop her from talking, but she wasn't listening to him. "Our scientists have tried. You saw; they resisted blasts from your weapon. Their exoskeletons are very formidable, protecting them from most force. We have tried to use insecticides to eliminate them, but they have adapted to them with terrifying ease. But, as advanced as our scientists are, they're nothing compared to yours. Everyone knows that."

"We don't know that at all," Hauman said, sounding a bit defensive. But then she looked at him in a way that said, *This is no time for foolish pride,* and Hauman sighed heavily. "I suppose there is some likelihood that your facilities could succeed where ours have failed. Can you . . ." He took a deep breath. "Can you help us?"

"I don't know," Shelby said honestly. "We'd have to examine the creatures, see what makes them tick, and then, maybe . . . but until then, I don't know."

"One chance is better than no chance."

She had to admit that that much was true. And when she saw the eager, hopeful faces around her, she realized she was looking forward to trying to help them. Unfortunately, she also realized that doing so might present some problems . . . and she was most definitely not looking forward to explaining why she might very well have to let them all die.

# TAPINZA

TAPINZA ARRIVED PRECISELY on time for the breakfast meeting he'd scheduled with Praestor Milos, and was not a little annoyed to discover that Milos was nowhere to be found. That was not at all how Tapinza liked to do things. To him, an appointment was an appointment, a breakfast a breakfast, and he did not like being made to wait for anyone . . . least of all an officious bureaucrat such as Milos.

He sat in Milos' receiving room for an unconscionable amount of time (ten minutes, in fact), being assured by Milos' staff that the Praestor would be along as soon as possible. That he was in an emergency meeting, and really, it wouldn't be long at all, not at all. This did not assuage Tapinza, however, and he was preparing to give Milos a serious piece of his mind when he suddenly heard raised and urgent voices from a room down the hall.

Tapinza, of course, knew no fear. Was he not a Maester, after all? There was nothing that daunted him, nothing that he had any reluctance to do if it suited his purposes, and that certainly included barging into meetings being held at a time when attention was to be paid to him. He rose from his chair and headed down the hall. Milos' agitated staffer tried to stop him, to get him to return to the waiting area, but Tapinza brushed him aside scornfully and strode into the room. The chatter abruptly stopped as Tapinza saw several confused faces looking up at him . . . and one face that was utterly calm.

There was Milos, and over there was that withered crone, Maestress Cawfiel. He recognized a couple of others from the town council . . . that preening, self-satisfied mortician, Howzer, and the annoyingly earnest Spangler, the fellow who ran the local newspaper. And there was another fellow, whom Tapinza made no pretense of doing anything other than staring at openly. Tapinza's stare was levelly returned by deep, purple eyes that seemed perfectly capable of boring straight into Tapinza's head and dissecting down to the smallest atom whatever it happened to find in there.

"Maester Tapinza," Milos said hurriedly, rearing to his feet. "I'm . . . I'm so sorry . . . we had an appointment, I know, but this matter, it . . ." He cleared his throat. "We had an emergency."

"The Majister was killed," Spangler said, in a dark voice laden with portent. "Just this morning." That was typical of Spangler; he thrived on being the first one with bad news.

"I'm sorry to hear that," said Tapinza, who wasn't. Fairax had always been a bit too full of himself, too annoyingly obsessed with the mechanics of the law, to suit Tapinza's tastes. He had not looked away from the purple-eyed man. "Is this the man who killed him?" It didn't seem likely, considering that he was simply sitting there and not looking particularly threatening. Then again, for all he knew, the council had hired this man to dispatch Fairax because they had likewise tired of him. He doubted that was the case, but a man like Tapinza didn't like to rule out any possibility, no matter how absurd on the face of it.

"This man? Kolk'r, no," Milos said quickly.

"This man saved me. Saved my life," the Maestress informed him. "Faced down by four brutes, and survived to tell the tale."

"And what a tale it was, I imagine," Tapinza said. "Congratulations."

"Thank you," said the purple-eyed man.

"I am Maester Tapinza."

"Mackenzie Calhoun." He rose slightly from his chair in what seemed to be an acknowledgment or greeting, but he didn't stand very tall, and there appeared to be deep distrust in his eyes. Well . . . good. That made him Tapinza's kind of man, since Tapinza trusted no one as well.

"You're not from around here," Tapinza observed.

"That's right."

"May I ask where you *are* from?"

Calhoun gave the matter a moment's thought, and then said, "Up north."

"Up north. Really. I've been up north," said Tapinza. "I have to say, I've never seen anyone who looks quite like you."

"Then I imagine I'm from further up north than you've been," Calhoun said evenly.

"We were just discussing," Howzer spoke up, not having made any contribution thus far—and not terribly likely to make one in the near future, even though he was now speaking—"the possibility of Calhoun here becoming Majister."

"Making a total stranger Majister?" Tapinza made no effort to hide his surprise. "A bit unprecedented, don't you think?"

"Not really. Who ever heard of Fairax before we took him on?" Milos pointed out. "We're more interested in someone who can do the job than someone with whom everyone in town has familiarity."

"And he can do the job," the Maestress said firmly. "I wouldn't be alive if he couldn't."

*And wouldn't that be a tragedy,* Tapinza thought sarcastically.

"But how will the people of the city take to the idea?" mused Spangler. "They might be suspicious of him."

"Good," said Howzer. "Let them be suspicious. Let them be unsure of him. He's supposed to be enforcing the law. He's supposed to be instilling fear in people. But people don't fear what they know too well. If they don't know much about him or what to make of him, they're that much more likely to stay in line."

Calhoun spoke up, with what sounded like a touch of amusement in his voice. "I hate to bring this up," he said slowly, "since you all seem to have made up your minds about it . . . but I haven't said I would take the position. I haven't even said I'm interested."

"But . . . you *have* to be," Milos nearly stammered. "You can't leave us in the lurch. . . ."

"I can't?" asked Calhoun, one eyebrow slightly raised. "You people stood by while I was thrown in your 'gaol.' And she," he indicated the Maestress, "said I was ugly. Pardon me if I don't feel as if I owe you anything."

"You said he was ugly?" Milos turned to the Maestress, looking stricken. "Did you say that?"

"I didn't know him then," Maestress Cawfiel replied tartly. "It took me a while to adjust to him, because he has unusual features." Defensively, she added, turning to Calhoun, "Well . . . you do. I apologize if I gave offense."

"Very well," said Calhoun diplomatically. But Tapinza was watching him carefully, and he was fully aware that Calhoun did not give a naked luukab's hindquarters what Cawfiel thought of his looks. He was simply yanking her around a bit, probably for his own amusement. It was an attitude that Tapinza could readily appreciate.

"Nevertheless, I don't know that I'm interested in any sort of law-enforcement job. I'm just passing through, you see."

"Really," said Tapinza. By this time he had taken a seat, even though none had been offered him. Tapinza was not on the town council, mostly because he saw no reason for it. Through his business dealings and power structure, he already had significant influence and control over these people's lives. Why waste time in pointless council meetings to reinforce that which he already possessed? "And where are you passing through to . . . precisely?"

"Depends. Where have you got?"

"You happen to be sitting in what passes for the height of civilization on Yakaba," Tapinza told him.

Calhoun looked around and saw uniformity of bobbing heads from the others. Spangler did break off from the others long enough to add, "Although I hear that, in Padulla province—about a hundred miles east of here—they're actually developing a machine capable of generating cooling air inside buildings. They've been testing it out."

"An air conditioner," Calhoun said slowly. "You're saying they've invented air-conditioning."

"I'm not sure what they call it," said Spangler.

"And this Padulla . . . what do they have in the way of communication facilities?" Calhoun asked. Tapinza instantly knew that it was a question of extreme significance to Calhoun.

This drew blank stares from the council. "What do you mean?" Milos said finally.

"Well . . . how do they communicate with one another?"

"They . . . move their mouths . . . and words come out." Maestress Cawfiel was speaking very delicately, as if addressing someone who was mentally deficient.

"I mean, what if long distances separate them?"

"Then they walk toward each other."

Calhoun rubbed the bridge of his nose as if he was suddenly in a good deal of pain. "What if you want to talk to someone in Padulla?"

This generated laughter from everyone in the room, with the exception of Tapinza, who was watching the exchange with great curiosity, and Calhoun, who did not share in the merriment his question had prompted. "Why," Milos asked when the laughter had subsided, "would we want to talk to someone in Padulla?"

"I don't know. Perhaps you'd want to acquire an air conditioner."

The notion immediately seized their collective fancy. "You know . . . that's not a bad idea," said Spangler.

"It would keep bodies cool," Howzer pointed out. "Certainly make my job easier."

The Maestress did not seem enthused by the notion. "Such things," she said, "can carry dire consequences. They are not natural."

"It was just an example," Calhoun said impatiently. "The point is—"

"Allow me." Tapinza cut in and turned to Calhoun, a benevolent and patient expression carefully crafted on his face. "Calhoun . . .

you don't quite seem to grasp the local mind-set. Clearly, you've spent a good deal of time on your own, and so you may have . . . forgotten . . . local mores."

"Perhaps," Calhoun said judiciously. "Why don't you enlighten me?"

"There is a great deal of territoriality in the Yakaban mind-set," Tapinza explained. "Cities tend to be fairly . . . insulated. Communication from town to town, city to city, is considered . . . rude. Intrusive. People tend to keep to themselves. It can be a convenient philosophy if one has . . . personal matters . . . one would rather not have discussed."

"I'm sure," said Calhoun, his voice emotionless.

"Unfortunately, it tends to limit personal growth, and diminishes the chances that this world will ever be united enough to achieve something of truly stellar proportions, such as . . . oh . . . I don't know . . ." And then, with great significance, he said, ". . . communicating with races from other worlds."

This drew a round of unrestrained laughter from the council. "There he goes again!" said Milos, his eyes twinkling with amusement, before he added, "My apologies, Maester. I did not intend to give offense. But we've had this discussion before, and, I admit, I always find it most entertaining."

"If I can lighten your day in any manner, it is my pleasure to do so," said Tapinza. But he was paying no attention to the others at all. Instead, he was focusing once more, entirely, on Calhoun.

Calhoun was looking right back at him, and even though his face was impassive, Tapinza could tell that his message had gotten through and been acknowledged. He knew Calhoun for what he was, even if these blind fools did not, and Calhoun knew that he knew.

"We've gotten significantly offtrack," the Maestress said archly, endeavoring to bring matters back into focus. "The question before us is—or should be—convincing Calhoun here to stay on as Majister."

Calhoun started to speak, but he was already shaking his

head, and that was when Tapinza said quickly, "Perhaps . . . I might be able to speak to Calhoun . . . in private? For a few minutes?"

The council members looked at each other in puzzlement. "Maester, I'm . . . not quite sure what you could say that could possibly—"

"I . . . have a way with people. That's all," said Tapinza. As if the matter was already settled, he rose and gestured to the door. "Calhoun? After you . . ."

Calhoun hesitated, but then shrugged again and rose. Without a word, he followed Tapinza out the door and into an adjoining hallway. He turned to face him, and simply waited there, his arms folded.

"I know what you are," Tapinza said briskly.

"Do you?"

He sighed. "Calhoun, the good residents of Yakaba are, at heart, decent . . . or at least have the potential for it. But their experiences, their knowledge, are provincial and limited."

"And yours aren't?"

"Mine? Certainly not. I am the most successful businessman in the three territories combined."

Calhoun nodded slowly, appearing to consider that. "Is that good?" he asked finally.

Tapinza chuckled. "Yes. That's very good. Of course, I'm sure that it's meaningless to someone like you. Someone who has walked the corridors of outer space and been to other worlds would certainly consider what transpires on this one little planet to be insignificant, indeed."

"You believe I'm from outer space. Odd. None of your associates seems to have drawn that conclusion."

Tapinza leaned against the wall and chuckled once more. "Calhoun . . . there is something you need to understand about my people. As a race, they have very little imagination. I do not know why that is. Call it a trait; call it something in the structure of the brain, an underdevelopment of some lobe or stem. I'm not a biologist; I've done no study. I'm simply saying that that is who we are. Base superstition, distrust of the unknown . . . these are things they can easily grasp. But to be able to look to the skies and wonder what dwells beyond . . ." He shook his head. "I am afraid that it is simply beyond them. They look at you and they literally do not know what they see. Oh, I suppose if you had extra arms flopping about, or came in with unknown weaponry and began destroying the city in flying war machines, they might begin to grasp that there is much that they have not yet begun to dream of. For the moment, however, such notions are beyond their range."

"But not beyond yours," noted Calhoun.

"No. Not beyond mine." He looked askance at Calhoun. "You have not volunteered the information. Why?"

"Caution. I wasn't quite sure how they would take it."

"That was wise. A revelation of that sort might very well be more than they could handle. Or they would not believe you. Or they might try to kill you. No matter what, it would not go well for you." He scratched his chin thoughtfully, and then said, "You wish to find a way back to the stars."

"That is my hope, yes."

"You arrived in a vessel. Crashed, I assume, else you would have simply climbed into it and taken off."

"I'll need to find it again, look it over. But the landing was very rough. It's extremely unlikely that it's spaceworthy, and I'm getting the distinct impression that I'm not going to find here what I would need to repair it. Unless, of course, I was interested in installing an air conditioner."

"That you are an alien and yet are fundamentally shaped like us . . . that, I accept. But I understand your words, and you mine. How is that?"

"Instantaneous translator. I'm just lucky it wasn't damaged in the crash, or we'd be standing here speaking gibberish at each other." Calhoun studied Tapinza thoughtfully. "You're going to suggest I take this position they're offering, aren't you?"

He nodded. "You are, to all intents and purposes, marooned

here. What you need is some sort of broadcast device that will enable you to contact your . . . peers. Let them know that you are here, so they can come back and rescue you."

"That was my thought, yes."

"As you might have surmised, such technology does not exist on our world . . ." He let the rest of the sentence hang.

Calhoun picked up on it. "Yet."

"Yet. That is correct."

"Let me guess: It's something that you are working on, trying to develop."

"Trying, but not being entirely successful. I have what passes for technicians working on such a thing, but progress has been slow. You, on the other hand, could help me tremendously in that pursuit. Show me where our research has gone wrong, teach us—"

Calhoun shook his head. "Would that I could. The thing is, I've never been a technician. I can use such devices if they already exist, but knowing how to build one? No. No, I'm afraid my expertise lies in other areas."

"Such as?"

He appeared to consider his assorted strengths and finally said, "I'm a hell of a dancer."

Tapinza smiled thinly at that. "That will certainly serve you well. Very well, Calhoun. I shall continue my research, pursue my own endeavors. My people inform me that they are quite certain they will have a working device . . . in a year or two." He watched Calhoun's expression carefully, but was rewarded by nothing. Calhoun's face was as inscrutable as ever, although there was brief amusement flickering in the purple eyes, as if he knew that Tapinza was trying unsuccessfully to read his mind. "Now, of course, I need not allow you to avail yourself of the device, if and when it should be operational. However . . ."

"If I take on the job of Majister, you will allow me use of it. And may I ask what your interest in all of this is?"

"Isn't that obvious?"

"Not readily, no."

"Why . . . I care about these people, Calhoun. Care about what happens to them. No matter that I may have a low opinion of them; they are still my people, and I can—and should—do whatever I can to aid them. Particularly because I am a man of vision. If those with vision do not provide leadership . . . who will? And besides, Calhoun—do you have anything better to do?"

"It . . . would seem not," Calhoun admitted.

"So, why not use your time constructively? To help others?"

"And possibly get myself killed."

"Odd. You do not strike me as a man who fears death."

"In that regard, sir . . . you're correct." He thought about it a moment more, but Tapinza knew he had him. He was positive of it.

"And there's one other thing that you haven't considered," Tapinza added.

"What might that be?"

"You've seen the low level of technology all around us. A low level that exists primarily because of lack of vision. You, sir, have vision. Why, the two of us together," Tapinza draped an arm around Calhoun's shoulder, "could bring new technology, new concepts to this city . . . improve the standard of living beyond anything that the people of limited sight here could possibly believe."

"You're a great believer in technology, I take it."

"I would think I've made that quite clear. And you are, as well."

Calhoun laughed softly to himself. "I'm not quite as sure about that as you are. Technology has its uses, certainly. And I'm dependent upon it to get out of here. But it's not the be-all and end-all that you seem to think it is. Once upon a time, I lived on a world that was very low in technology, indeed. In some ways . . ." he said wistfully, "I think those were the happiest times of my life. I didn't know or care what was beyond my little sphere."

"You lived in ignorance."

"No. I thrived in ignorance. And that, Maester Tapinza . . . is not always a bad thing."

Calhoun turned and headed back into the other room. The momentarily confused Tapinza followed him. When Calhoun entered, everyone in the room—with the exception of the Maestress—got to their feet. He gestured for them to sit and looked around at them for a long moment. Tapinza had the distinct feeling that Calhoun was dragging it out for his benefit.

"All right," he said finally. "I'll do it." There was an audible sigh of relief from those in the room, and then Calhoun continued. "But I'm not going to commit to any length of time. It has to be understood—I'm just passing through."

"Where are you passing through to?" inquired the Maestress.

"Wherever the road may lead," Calhoun said.

"Well," said the Praestor, "I'm hoping that our little town will grow on you, and you'll be willing to stay here indefinitely. But, in the meantime, I'll be more than happy to take whatever you're willing to give us. Welcome to Narrin, Majister Calhoun."

"I hope you don't get killed," Spangler said cheerily.

"That makes two of us," said Calhoun.

"Three," said the Praestor, and everyone else in the room chimed in, upping the number one by one until only Howzer the mortician had not offered an opinion.

He glanced at his watch. "My, look at the time," he said.

Calhoun looked at the others and commented, "Now there's a man who has his priorities in order."

Tapinza, however, had his own priorities in order as well. Calhoun's little lecture about the joys of living in a low-tech world gave him the uneasy feeling that Calhoun's priorities might be in conflict with his own. He hoped that would not be the case. He saw Calhoun as a potential ally. But if Calhoun were to become an enemy, well . . . Tapinza had had enemies before. They had all wound up in the same place, and Tapinza was still here. And Calhoun was unquestionably out of his territory. If it came to a conflict, there was no doubt who was going to come out on top.

# SHELBY

"CAPTAIN, WE CAN'T. It'd be a violation of regs."

It was all Shelby could do to stifle a laugh, despite the seriousness of the situation. She could not count the number of times she had said those exact words, in that exact tone, to Calhoun. She wondered if Calhoun had felt at those times what she was feeling now: annoyance. Impatience at being second-guessed. Perhaps a tinge of guilt, because the statement was absolutely true. Aggravated over being presented with a scenario where the compulsion was to help and the regulation was to withhold same.

By the same token, she knew precisely how she herself felt when issuing such pronouncements: frustrated at having to point out that which was so obvious. A sense of self-righteousness, because she was so certain that she invariably knew what was best. Perhaps a certainty that she would not be making these kinds of mistakes or decisions if it were she who was in charge.

They had been on her—although with all respect, of course—from the moment they had all sat down together, starting with Shelby's refusal to depart planetside. "I would have been within my rights to beam you up, Captain, whether you were inclined to go or not," Garbeck had pointed out.

Shelby's response was that she had been concerned over sending mixed messages about the UFP. To say to the Makkusians, on the one hand, how the UFP and Starfleet were going to be there for them when help was needed . . . and then the first time that some sort of jeopardy presents itself, they bolt? No, she'd felt it necessary to stay on the surface for the duration of the attack, for as long as she'd had to. It was, to her mind, the only way to show that she was acting in good faith. Still, it was an explanation that had not gone over well with her command staff. Then again, since when did she have to worry about what the command staff's opinion of her was?

Seated there were Garbeck, Science Officer Tulley, Security Head Kahn, Lieutenant Augustine, Doctor Kosa, and the ship's Counselor, Laura Ap'Boylan, a Betazoid with large, limpid eyes that had the remarkable knack of burrowing deep into one's soul, and a thick shock of startlingly bright blond hair that made her look as if her head was perpetually glowing. It had been Garbeck who had spoken, but clearly they were of one mind.

For some reason, this bugged the hell out of Shelby. Whenever such discussions had arisen on the *Excalibur,* there had been as many differing opinions as there were people in the room. Yet here . . .

*Stop complaining. You handpicked this crew. You didn't like the way things were on the* Excalibur. *So you don't get to whine about it now.*

"I'm aware of that," Shelby said carefully. "Technically—"

"There is no 'technically' involved, Captain," Garbeck told her firmly. "It either is or it isn't. In this case, your suggested action clearly is in violation. These insects are a natural outgrowth of the planet's environment—?" Although she was looking at Shelby, the question was obviously addressed to Tulley.

The science officer nodded briskly. "Yes. Absolutely. The captain was kind enough to bring us back a specimen or two," and he inclined his head toward Shelby in appreciation. "We've made a thorough study of them and they are definitely native to this world. There is . . . a curiosity about it."

"Curiosity?" growled Kosa. "Meaning, you found something and you're not sure what it is." Although Dr. Kosa was not particularly enamored of anyone on the ship, it seemed, he particularly wasn't wild about Tulley. Shelby suspected that he felt Tulley in some way infringed on his territory at those points—such as this one—where scientific investigation and medical research tended to overlap. Tulley was quite aware of this mild hostility on the doctor's part, and did not hesitate to give as good as he got. Shelby sighed inwardly and wondered if any other starship captain had ever had to deal with a chief medical officer and science officer who had serious antipathy toward one another.

With the sigh of one who carries the weight of the world upon his shoulders, Tulley said, "I'm simply saying that I've found something that requires further research, Doctor. Specifically, it's the disease this insect is carrying. It seems to have—for want of a better way to put it—come out of nowhere. I'm having difficulty tracking down the root virus that it may have mutated from, although I suspect that is basically what has happened."

"I'll put my people on it," Kosa said in preemptive fashion. "If it has to do with illness, it should be under my purview, anyway."

"Captain," Tulley protested, working to keep his annoyance in check. "This had been under the auspices of science."

"You'll work together," Shelby announced, feeling like King Solomon. Kosa and Tulley glanced at each other, Kosa looking darkly smug and Tulley clearly not too happy about the decision.

"The point is, Captain," continued Garbeck, "that this life-form is indigenous to this world. It's not as if the Makkusians are being attacked by, say, the neighboring world of Corinder. If the Corinderians were assaulting them, we could intercede. But, in this case, we're talking about a species that developed on this world, as did the Makkusians. In short, it has as much right to be there as the Makkusians themselves do. It wouldn't be appropriate for us to simply step in and wipe them out . . . essentially, destroy an entire species of animal, which is what the Makkusians would have us do."

"The Makkusian race has been decimated, and I mean that in the accurate sense of the word," said Shelby, "namely, reduced by a tenth. One out of every ten Makkusians has died because of the disease these creatures are transmitting. And preliminary tests on the virus itself, according to CMO Kosa here, is that the damned virus mutates so quickly that finding a cure for it is problematic and could take months."

"We'd nail it eventually," Kosa said, "but right now we don't even know how bugs get it, or how to cure them, let alone the people."

"I've no doubt we'll nail it. But how many people will die in the meantime? People versus insects, gentlemen and ladies. I don't think we can lose sight of that."

"Nor can we lose sight of the Prime Directive, Captain. I'm sure you know that, as does everyone here at this table," said Garbeck.

*And yet you felt the need to spell it out just in case,* Shelby thought. *My God . . . if I were in her position and Mac were in mine, which side would I be on?*

"I haven't lost sight of anything, Number One," said Shelby forcefully. "I am very much aware that the Prime Directive would frown upon—"

"Prohibit," Garbeck said.

Shelby paused just long enough for her annoyance at the interruption to register on Garbeck. Garbeck shifted uncomfortably in her chair, aware that she might very well have just overstepped herself.

"—prohibit," Shelby quietly amended, "the annihilation of the life-form that is causing this hardship. After all, who knows? In a couple of million years, the Makkusians may be nothing but a distant memory, and these insects could well be the dominant life-form on the planet. It's impossible to tell, and it's specifically because we don't want to have that kind of impact on worlds that we have the noninterference directive in the first place." There were more nods, this time approving of what she was saying. Her hand was near the computer console, but no one noticed.

"Captain," Ap'Boylan said, in her best conciliatory fashion. "I very much sense the conflict that you're going through. You want to do what you feel is best for these people. It is natural for you to elevate them in importance above the insects, but one must remember that the—"

The conference lounge was suddenly alive with a high-pitched buzzing.

Immediately, her voice loud with alarm, Shelby said, "Tulley! Your specimens must still be alive!"

Suddenly everyone but Shelby and the Betazoid ducked and someone shouted in alarm, "Get it!" Kahn was on her feet, her phaser out, trying to sight the creature and pick it off.

Garbeck, meantime, had hit her combadge and was barking orders, instructing the area to be sealed off and a gas lethal to insects readied to flood through the corridors. . . .

And then Garbeck noticed that Shelby hadn't budged from her spot. Instead, she was sitting there with a small, satisfied smile on her face. Without a word, Shelby turned the monitor around. An image of the insects swarmed and moved across the screen, their earsplitting whine filling the room, but otherwise offering no more hazard to life and limb than any other picture on a monitor would provide.

"Sentiment's a little different when you're the ones at risk, isn't it?" Shelby said quietly as she shut off the monitor. The noise promptly ceased.

Ap'Boylan still sat in her seat, having sensed what her captain was up to. Kahn holstered her phaser sheepishly. Garbeck looked extremely unamused. "That was not necessary to make your point, Captain, in my opinion."

"In my opinion, it was, and as it so happens, my opinion outranks yours," Shelby told her.

But Garbeck wasn't particularly cowed. "Captain," she said firmly, "I have nothing but the greatest respect for you . . . but this is not the frontier. Starfleet captains have a great deal of discretionary power, certainly, but not enough to unilaterally toss aside the Prime Directive as they see fit."

"I am aware of that, Number One," said Shelby. "However . . . there are options."

The officers all looked at one another. "Options, Captain?" asked Kahn.

"First, can we incapacitate these bugs in some gentle way?"

Tulley said, "Not without a lot of study."

"Then could we get rid of these things if we had to? Worldwide, I mean."

All eyes went again to Tulley. He gave it some thought, and then said, "Actually . . . yes. Yes, it wouldn't be that difficult at all. Captain, would you mind putting on that buzzing again?"

Shelby didn't quite understand, but she complied. A moment later, the buzzing was again filling the room. Tulley was concentrating on it, pursing his lips and humming along. His actions drew confused looks from the others, but they were respectfully silent. Finally he said, "All right, thank you, Captain." Shelby shut it down, and they all waited while Tulley continued to hum.

"Lieutenant Commander . . . ?" prompted Shelby.

"All right. It'll take a few passes, but it should work. Basically, we'll use the deflector dish to generate a harmonic beam to a specific section of the planet's surface . . . devoid of Makkusians, of course. We'll key the beam to exactly imitate the buzzing sound that the insects produce, and, theoretically, they will swarm toward it, joining others of their own kind."

"Use it as a decoy to bring them together," Kahn said, nodding.

"All right, I'm with you so far," said Shelby. "Once we have them all together . . . then what? Phasers?"

Tulley shook his head. "Too imprecise. Simplest thing would be to, basically, beam them into space."

"Transport millions of insects?" Shelby looked incredulous.

"Theoretically, it should work."

"Theoretically." Less than convinced, Shelby tapped her combadge. "Shelby to engineering."

"Engineering, Dunn here," came the brisk reply.

"C.J., we have a question. Can you use the transporter to transport, say, a million or so insects at one time?"

There was dead silence for a moment. "You're kidding, right?"

"Do I sound like I'm kidding?"

Another silence, although, remarkably, this one "sounded" more thoughtful somehow. "Are you talking about beaming them aboard the ship?" he said doubtfully. He sounded less than enthused by the idea.

"Lord, no. Surface-to-space."

"Oh!" His voice audibly brightened. "So . . . you don't care if, when they rematerialize, they're in working order or not."

"Could not care less. I doubt deep space would be conducive to their long-term health in any event."

"All right." He was obviously thinking out loud. "I'd probably have to rig all the transporters to simultaneous run, and remove all the pattern dampers. It wouldn't be necessary to store the molecular patterns for reintegration, because, essentially, you're just . . . you know, Captain . . . you wouldn't have to send them into deep space. I could just demolecularize—no, wait. That might not be a good idea. I mean, nothing might happen as a result . . . but on the other hand, it could cause an explosion that would tear a hole in the atmosphere the size of a small moon, so that won't help matters. Yeah, yeah, deep space would be safer. We'd simply reduce them to molecules, redirect the beams into deep space, and release them. Not even bother to reintegrate them. That would solve—"

"C.J.!" Shelby cut him off. "Yes or no?"

"Yes."

"Good. You'll be coordinating with Lieutenant Commander Tulley."

"Done and Dunn."

She rolled her eyes as she cut the transmission.

"Captain," Garbeck said patiently, "as I recall, the question before us was not whether it *can* be done . . . but whether it *should* be done."

Shelby turned to face her first officer. "If Makkus agrees to join the Federation," she said, "then, as Federation members, they may ask for humanitarian aid. The captain then has the prerogative to grant it, if she sees fit. The Makkusians do not have transporter technology, so this solution is beyond them. Using our technology, we can step in and attend to their problem. Augustine, you know these people best: Do you think they'll join the UFP if, in exchange, we dispense with these insects for them?"

"I do not see how they could say no, under the circumstances, but—"

But Shelby was already tapping her combadge. "Shelby to bridge. McMurrian . . ."

"Here, Captain."

"Get me Hauman of the Makkusians on screen."

"Aye, Captain."

"Captain!" Garbeck said. "You're talking about blackmailing them into agreeing to joining the UFP. My understanding is that they are philosophically opposed to it."

"Absolutely true, Number One." Shelby leaned forward, fingers interlaced. "However, I strongly suspect that they are also philosophically opposed to dying. We'll just have to see which one has the greater priority."

"Captain, it's a bit more involved than that."

"Really?" She cocked an eyebrow. "How so?"

"Well," said Garbeck reasonably, "even if the Makkusians agree to apply for Federation membership, there are still procedures to be followed. There is a review process, and a vote is required."

"At which point they'll be accepted. You're not going to tell me that the process you're describing is anything other than pro forma."

"That's certainly true enough, Captain," Ap'Boylan agreed. "An invitation to join the UFP wouldn't really be extended if there was not every intention of then welcoming that world in."

"See, that's the problem in the thinking here," Shelby said. Her gaze took in everyone in the room. "We're not talking about a world. The world is inanimate; the world is of no particular interest. It's the people *on* the world I'm concerned about. Barring a catastrophe, the world will be there tomorrow, next week, next year, next century. Can we say the same, with all certainty, about those residing on it?" When a reply was not immediately forthcoming, Shelby prompted, "Well? Can we?"

"No, Captain," admitted Garbeck. And no one else seemed especially inclined to contradict her.

It didn't take long at all to get Hauman on the screen in the conference lounge. When Shelby laid out for him the possible solution to their problem, he brightened considerably . . . until she told him the condition upon which it hinged.

Her staff sat around her, stoic. She knew what they were thinking, since they had not stinted in letting their opinion be known. But she knew what she had to do . . . or, at least, she knew what she was *not* going to do. She was not going to stand by and let these people die. She was going to do whatever it took to save them.

*My God . . . I sound like Mac.* It was not the first time the thought had gone through her head, and she had the odd feeling it wasn't going to be the last. She had to wonder whether she would have been operating along the same lines as she was now if she hadn't spent so much time with him. Would she have done everything she could to rescue these people if she'd never had anything to do with Mackenzie Calhoun? If she had, in short, been like those who were sitting around the table, watching her with uncertainty or even thoughtful calculation? It was impossible for her to be sure.

"Although you are behaving as if you're presenting me with a choice," Hauman said slowly and thoughtfully, "you're not really, are you, Captain?"

"Not really, no," she readily agreed. There was no use dancing around it. "I'm giving you a way out, but there are—as we say on Earth—strings attached. And one of those strings ties you to the Federation."

"Even though we are philosophically opposed to it."

"Even so."

"You are asking us to compromise our—"

Shelby made an abrupt, cutting gesture. "Hauman," she said, a bit more brusquely than she would have liked, "I think we all know what I'm asking you to do. You can cloak it with as many expressions of irritation as you want, but the bottom line remains this: Do you want to save your people or don't you? It's not a very complicated question."

"Actually, it is."

"All right," she sighed, "perhaps it is. But the answer itself is not very complicated. It's one of two one-syllable words, and, depending upon which word you say, your people will live or die. It's up to you. But if I were you, I wouldn't lose sight of the fact that you have to consider the big picture."

"The big picture," he repeated blankly. He didn't seem to understand, but he didn't appear to care all that much, either. He let out a long, unsteady breath as if he was trying to exhale the weight of the world that was on him. "You are sure," he said finally, "that this process will rid us of them?"

That was when she knew she had him, of course. "Yes," she said, nodding vigorously. "It's actually very simple, really. We can institute the process almost immediately." Garbeck cleared her throat loudly, obviously wanting to say something, but Shelby ignored her. "Do you need to consult anyone, any governing board, before rendering a decision?"

"No, Captain. My people trust me, you see." He looked sad and a bit lost. "They trust me . . . and, in order to save them, I'm about to betray them. What sort of leader have I become?"

"I know you meant the question to be rhetorical, but—in my opinion—you're the best kind of leader there is," Shelby told him gently. "The kind who's willing to make the tough decisions that will save his people."

He didn't appear to be impressed by that, but he simply shook his head in response. Then, steeling himself, he said, "Very well, Captain. After due consideration, I am asking that my world, Makkus, be made a member of the United Federation of Planets."

"I will relay your acceptance of the offer to my superiors," Shelby assured him. "In the meantime, my people will get to work on ridding your world of your insect problem. I assure you, Hauman, you've made the right choice."

"I have made the only choice. Whether it is right or not . . . may not be for me to judge. I shall likely have to leave that to history to decide."

"Because of you," she reminded him, "your world is going to *have* a history. Shelby out." The moment his image had blinked out, she barked, "Shelby to engineering."

"Engineering; Dunn here."

"Captain," Garbeck started to say.

But Shelby steamrolled over her. "Dunn, you're going to work in tandem with Science Officer Tulley. You're going to institute that little deinfestation solution we were talking about before."

"Done and Dunn."

"*Captain,*" Garbeck said, a bit more forcefully than before, and this time Shelby focused her attention on her. "Captain, as I said before, there *are* review procedures. Pro forma or no, they're in place for a reason—"

"And Hauman agreed to his world becoming a member of the UFP for a reason as well," pointed out Shelby. "I am inclined to honor that reason."

"But—"

Shelby had had enough. "The only 'buts' I want to hear, Number One, are the sounds of your collective butts lifting out of these chairs and attending to the matter at hand. If you think I'm going to sit here in orbit and wait for more of these people to die, while the UFP council convenes and casts a vote on something that's already a foregone conclusion, then you have drastically failed to comprehend the situation. I asked them if they would join. They said they would. Good enough for me. Now, kill the damned insects. Any questions?"

There was a chorus of "no's," some louder than others, some crankier than others. But the result was the same.

It made Shelby feel good. Damned good. As she headed back to her ready room, she realized that Mac would very likely have been proud of her. The thing she couldn't quite figure out for herself was, if Mac would have been proud . . . then did that mean that the Shelby she had been would have been ashamed?

# *RHEELA*

RHEELA HAD A BAD FEELING about that evening's town meeting, and she had no idea why. Then again, truth be told, she always had an uneasy feeling about such meetings, so it really shouldn't have surprised her. Still . . . this feeling seemed stronger than usual, and she wished she had some idea why that might be.

She had just changed into the one truly decent outfit she owned. Unlike her normal clothes, there was a splash of color to this ensemble. Since she wore them less frequently, none of the threads were coming unwoven; no spots on it were obviously in need of repair. She studied herself in the mirror and nodded once in approval. From a large, overstuffed chair nearby—his long-time favorite piece of furniture—Moke watched her giving herself the once-over. "You look very pretty," he ventured.

"Thank you, honey," she said appreciatively.

"You really do."

"Thank you again."

There was a knock at the door. Rheela immediately looked at Moke in confusion, her face a question. Moke shrugged in response. Obviously he wasn't expecting anyone, and Rheela certainly knew that she wasn't. She headed to the front door and opened it . . . and let out an alarmed shriek.

Standing there was the purple-eyed man who had tried to strangle her.

Immediately she slammed the door in his face. Moke, who had not seen who was on the other side, struggled out of the chair. "Ma, what is it?" he said, picking up on her obvious consternation.

"It's him!"

"It is?!" Moke blinked. "Him who?"

Before she could reply, there was another knock at the door. There was no more urgency to it than before, and when he spoke from the other side, it was with a mixture of amusement and obvious regret. "It's all right," he called.

*"How is it all right?"* she demanded.

"I'm feeling much better now."

"Oh! So you're in much better shape to attack me again, is that it?"

"I'm sorry about that," he said, sounding genuinely regretful. But she had to keep reminding herself that just because he sounded a particular way didn't make it so. "If I'd been in my right mind, I'd never have hurt you. I was ill. But I'm not anymore."

"I think he means it, Ma," Moke suggested.

He certainly sounded like he meant it, but that didn't give Rheela the slightest compulsion to lower her guard. "I think you'd better go now!" she called. "If you don't, I'll . . . I'll tell Majister Fairax that you were harassing me!" She definitely liked the sound of that. She was taking a firm, no-nonsense position from strength, and not coming across as the least bit frightened. That was definitely the position to take under the circumstances.

So it sent a chill down her spine when she heard him say, "Majister Fairax is dead."

She had no immediate response to that. "Dead," she whispered. "Did . . . did you . . ."

"No, of course I didn't kill him."

"How do I know? How do I know that you didn't kill him and want to finish the job——?"

And then, to her shock, the door was suddenly shoved inward.

She let out a shriek and stumbled back. The purple-eyed man was standing there, his hand flat against the door. She'd had no lock on it . . . had never felt the need. The only thing that had been holding it closed against him was her own body weight and strength, and that had been as nothing to the frightening man who stood there, his gaze boring into her.

"Because," he said quietly, "if I wanted to kill you, I could."

With that, he closed the door, still on the outside. It clicked silently back into place. Rheela stared at it a moment, not quite believing what she had just seen. She picked herself up, dusted herself off. Moke was watching the entire sequence of events, apparently spellbound by them. "Wow," he said. "He's really strong."

Once more, a knocking. By that point, of course, the message was obvious to her. He could enter at will, could do whatever he wanted. Instead, he was leaving the option of keeping him out entirely up to her, showing respect for her concerns and fears. If he were really as frightening and terrifying a creature as she had previously thought him to be, well . . . she'd likely be dead by now anyway. The fact that she was still breathing—that alone should have been enough to make her realize that she had badly misjudged the situation.

As if reading her mind, he said, from the other side of the door, "Can't blame you, really. If I were you, I'd be terrified."

"I'm not terrified," she lied, but she was beginning to feel her concern subsiding.

"If not on my behalf, then certainly on the boy's."

That was certainly true enough. After all, if he attacked and murdered her, Moke would most certainly be next. Still . . .

"How did the Majister die?"

"Some thugs murdered him."

She shuddered. It wasn't fair. It just wasn't fair. A good, honest man, losing to creatures of evil. "Have they been brought to justice?" On some level, it was a pointless question. No amount of "justice" would bring the Majister back to life. At the moment, though, it was all she could concern herself about.

"One of them. The others will. I promise."

"You promise." What odd phrasing.

"Listen . . ." he continued, "I came to apologize. To tell you that you've nothing to fear from me. And I felt it would be better to tell you now, here, in the privacy of your home, rather than for you to see me in the streets of the city and run screaming, under the mistaken assumption that I'm going to hurt you again."

"Why would I see you in the streets?"

"Well . . . what with my being the new Majister . . ."

That, finally, prompted her to yank open the door and gape at him. Sure enough, pinned to his shirt was the burnished metal outline of a flame: the torch of justice emblem that was worn by anyone who had the title of "Majister."

"You can't be serious," she said tonelessly.

"Why? Just because a criminal tossed in gaol one day becomes the chief law enforcer the next day? Does that strike you as strange somehow?"

"Very," she said evenly. Nevertheless, for all her consternation and grief over the loss of Fairax, she couldn't help but note that this newcomer had a very pleasant smile. And yet, there was something in that smile, and in those eyes, that bespoke pain deeply felt.

He cleared his throat. "My name is Mackenzie Calhoun." He paused, and then added, "My friends call me Mac. I would like to think I can count you among them."

"Rheela," she said after the slightest hesitation. "And Moke." She indicated her son.

"Yes, I . . . vaguely remember him. Vaguely remember a lot of things."

"Including trying to kill me?"

"Yes." Had to give him credit: he faced it head on, with no prevarication. "I have already apologized. If you'd like, I'll apologize again. There's really only so much I can do about what's past. If you're unwilling to forgive me—"

"No, no, it's all right," she said. "I . . . forgive you."

"Thank you." He paused, and then said, "Well . . . I said what I came here to say. Good evening to you, then." There was a luukab, the one that Fairax used to use, standing nearby. Calhoun turned and started to head over to it.

And Rheela heard herself saying, much to her surprise, "Would you care to accompany me into town? For the meeting?"

He turned back and looked her up and down. "I'd be honored," he said. "Is Moke coming?"

"No . . . no, Moke is always bored at the—"

"I'll come." Moke was immediately at her side, looking up eagerly into Calhoun's eyes. "If it's okay."

"Of . . . course it's okay. I'm just surprised, Moke. You went once, and you said it was so boring that you never wanted to go again."

"I know. But Mac is going to be there. Right, Mac?"

Calhoun nodded readily. "I suppose I should be."

"See? And I bet, with Mac there, things are never boring!"

"I appreciate the vote of confidence, Moke."

Rheela shook her head. "I . . . don't know what to say, Calhoun. He's . . . not usually like this."

"Like this? You mean, an exuberant child?"

"Well . . . yes."

He laughed at that.

She decided he had a nice laugh.


The ride to Narrin on their respective luukabs went without incident. She was surprised to see how engaging and pleasant Calhoun was when he wasn't trying to kill her. She also noticed, however, that he was decidedly guarded whenever she would broach—however cautiously or in a roundabout manner—questions about his own background. "I'm from up north," was all he said. "No place you ever heard of."

"Really? What's it called?"

He looked at her with quiet amusement as the luukab's back swayed gently up and down. "Xenex," he said finally.

"You're right. I never heard of it," she said. Moke was seated behind her, his arms wrapped around her narrow waist. "Tell me, Calhoun . . . do all the men in Xenex have purple eyes?"

"No."

"Or scars?"

He sighed. "Only those few who were stupid enough to let it happen."

"A fight?"

He nodded.

"I'm sorry you fared so poorly," she said. "And the one who did it to you . . . ?"

"Fared even more poorly," Calhoun said. There was something in his voice that made it quite clear to her that further inquiries along this line might not yield any result she'd be comfortable with.

She wisely dropped the inquiries on that topic, and instead said, "Have you ever been a Majister before?"

"Not . . . exactly. I've done some jobs, though, that were somewhat along the same lines. They were just called something else. On that basis, I suppose I'm qualified to do this."

"And . . . do you have a woman?"

"Not . . . exactly," he said after a moment's thought.

She looked askance at him. "A man?"

He laughed. "No," he said with far more conviction. "And you?"

"And me what?"

"Do you have a man? What of Moke's father?"

She felt Moke tense up behind her, and she said quietly to Calhoun, "This . . . might not be the best time to discuss such matters."

Apparently he had realized as much even as he had spoken. "Yes. Of course. My apologies." They spoke no more of it. Instead, they chatted in simple, noninflammatory ways about simple matters of less-than-dire consequence.

She decided that she actually liked this man. She didn't trust him, of course. She trusted no one. She had no intention of allowing him into her life, any more than she would permit men such as Tapinza near her. There was no way to tell what anyone's true priority was, after all, or whether they intended good or ill for her and her son. All she knew was that she wanted to live her life, let Moke live his, and do whatever she could to help the people of Narrin. In a way, it had become a challenge for her. The more she was cold-shouldered by some, the more she felt compelled to try and make the remainder realize that she could only benefit them.

The city was now evident in the near distance. "I'm told you're a rainmaker," Calhoun said suddenly.

"I wouldn't say that. I have . . . influence. No one 'makes' the rain do anything."

"Then what exactly do you do?"

"I . . ." She smiled. "I ask nicely. Make requests of the weather, and it listens to me."

"How very considerate of it. Would it listen to me if I asked equally as nicely?"

"I don't think so," she admitted. "But I wouldn't take offense if I were you. The weather is, after all, just the weather. Most of the time, you can't change it. Not even so much as which way the wind blows."

"Very wise words. I'll keep that in mind," he said.

There was a good deal of activity outside the town meeting hall. Apparently it was going to be a fairly full house that evening. Then again, it was a full house most of the time. It wasn't as if there was all that much to do around town most nights.

"Do you get into town much?" asked Calhoun as they approached the meeting hall. They had both left their luukabs tied off at a nearby post. The creatures seemed more than content to just stand there and wait for someone to come back for them.

"No. Not all that much," she said.

"I'm surprised. A pretty woman such as yourself . . ."

She stopped in her tracks and turned to face Calhoun. Moke had gone on ahead, attracted by the lights from within and the general loud noise and discussion. "Majister Calhoun," she said, sounding quite formal, "let me be quite clear: I appreciate that you apologized to me. I appreciate that you took the time to accompany me here to the meeting. I freely admit that I misjudged you . . . albeit understandably, considering that misjudgment was based on your attempts to throttle me." He inclined his head slightly, acknowledging the comment, and she continued, "However, you can stop now."

"Stop? I wasn't aware I'd started."

"You are being overly solicitous, overly attentive . . ." She sighed heavily. "It's obvious, I'm afraid."

"Obvious?" His eyebrows knit. "If it's that obvious, would you mind explaining it to me?"

"You have your own motives, your own desires. You want something."

"I do?"

"Yes. You do."

"And might I ask what that is?"

She folded her arms and made an exasperated sound. "Are you going to compel me to spell it out for you?"

"Ah." The edges of his mouth turned upward. "I see. Is that what you think?"

"Majister, I don't know what to think, and to be perfectly honest, I don't want to have to worry about it one way or the other. I have too much to worry about: a farm—or what there is of a farm—to attend to, and a child to raise. I simply don't need any further complications in my life."

"I appreciate your honesty," he replied. "Now let me be equally candid: I'm simply passing through. I do not intend to be here for an inordinate period of time. And I need complications in my life even less than you need them in yours. All right?"

"All right," she said, suddenly feeling uncertain. She had the abrupt impression that she had offended him, and, in mentally reviewing her words, she realized that there was probably no way he could not have taken offense. She tried to say something to that effect, and perhaps even apologize, but he was already walking away.

Well . . . she needn't dwell on it, really. He seemed a sturdy enough individual to be able to handle even perceived insult. Still . . . it was a shame that he was obviously cross with her, because Moke certainly liked him . . .

Immediately she drove the thought out of her head. She couldn't think about what Moke liked and didn't like. He was a child, she was the adult, and it was up to her to watch out for his best interests. That was all there was to it.

She headed into the hall, and she noticed that there were a few nods of greeting. In times past, many people had been reluctant even to glance her way, but, slowly, some folks seemed to be thawing toward her. She held no illusions; it was probably because she had provided them with water not too long ago. As long as they felt there was a need for her, they would probably treat her decently. Well . . . there were certainly worse fates than being treated decently.

Once inside the hall, she took a seat at the end of one of the long rows of benches. She looked around, trying to catch sight of Moke, and finally spotted him halfway across the room. He seemed to be engaged in animated discussion with Tapinza. That was certainly something that she couldn't say she was happy to see. What was it about that boy that he seemed drawn to men who would ultimately be bad for him? She supposed that she shouldn't think of it that way. Moke was simply an outgoing child who got on with just about anybody. Indeed, if there was ever someone whom Moke *was* at odds with, Rheela would be well-advised to run in the other direction the moment that person drew anywhere near.

Rheela also cast a glance in Calhoun's direction. She saw that he wasn't talking with anyone, but merely walking along the edges of the room. He seemed to be surveying the area, looking for any possible trouble spots. Residents of the town were glancing toward him in a manner that they no doubt considered to be surreptitious. In point of fact, it was nothing of the kind, because if Rheela could see them engaging in such foolish behavior, Calhoun most likely could as well. However, he had a tendency—or perhaps the simple politeness—to look pointedly in the other direction from anyone who was looking at him. Thus did he give them the impression that they were spying on him with impunity when, in fact, he was fully aware of every moment that they were watching. It was almost like a game, and he played it extremely well.

There was a banging of a gavel from up front, and people scurried to their respective seats. The Praestor was gaveling the meeting to order. Moke, upon hearing the meeting getting ready to start, looked around for his mother, caught sight of her, and headed toward her. She smiled approvingly as he slid into the seat next to her. Tapinza kept his distance. This struck her as being a good thing.

"Fellow citizens," called Praestor Milos once all of the normal chatter had died down, "I thank you all for coming to our town meeting. These meetings are the single most vital part of keeping our town running smoothly and for the benefit of all—"

"—its citizens!" A number of voices were chiming in from all around, and this set off a round of good-natured laughter. The Praestor was renowned for saying, in essence, the same speech over and over again at the beginning of every town meeting. Even the Praestor laughed in mild self-rebuke. "I suppose I should really get a new opening statement, eh?" There were nods from throughout the room.

He rose from behind the table, and Rheela found her gaze drawn to the people sitting behind it. It was the usual town council—the Praestor, the Maestress, and the mortician and the newspaper editor. The fifth seat was empty, however. Previously, Majister Fairax had filled it, and the sad and vacant state of the chair was a silent reminder of the loss that had been thrust upon them. Rheela cursed herself for being so out of touch; services had already been held for Fairax, his body disposed of by fire, as was the custom. It wasn't as if she lived that far away, and yet it seemed as if a chasm separated her from the town.

She wondered if Calhoun was going to be installed as the fifth member of the council. It seemed extremely unlikely; Fairax had only taken the position after he'd been there for three years, upon the unexpected demise of Old Man Binner. Would the council really suggest installing Calhoun, who was such a new arrival to the city, and with a background that was—at best—a question mark?

"I am reluctant to begin our meeting on a somber note," said Milos, "but this is the first one we are having after the passing of our dear and wise Majister, Fairax. I think it would be respectful to have a moment of silence in memory of a good man who was cut down doing his job—defending the people of this community."

All heads were properly lowered, and a silence fell upon the meeting hall. After a brief time had passed, the Praestor said, "All right . . . that's the first thing. The second thing is, the town council, in emergency session, has decided to install a replacement for the late Fairax: Mackenzie Calhoun."

Now that subterfuge and hidden glances could be set aside, all eyes turned openly and unabashedly toward Calhoun. He nodded in acknowledgment of the scrutiny, even tipping his wide-brimmed hat slightly with a faintly amused air.

"What do we know about him?" asked the Widow Att from across the room. "We don't know anything. He could be anyone. He doesn't look like anyone from around here." There were a few nodding heads, but most people seemed to be playing their emotions close to the vest. They didn't seem inclined to openly commit their feelings on the matter.

"I'm from up north," Calhoun said.

"That doesn't tell us anything," the Widow Att pointed out.

"It tells you I'm not from down south."

There was some faint laughter, but the Widow Att simply scowled all the more fiercely.

"We respect your concerns, Att," Praestor Milos said smoothly. "However—"

"We had to make a decision, fast," Spangler, the newspaper editor, spoke up. "Naming Calhoun the new Majister was the decision we chose to make. Given the circumstances, it seemed the best one at the time. However, we are no longer faced with an emergency. This matter can now be put to the entirety of the town. We are, after all, only the town council, not the town dictator. The permanent installation is a matter for the entire town to decide. Calhoun . . . do you have anything to say?"

"Depends," Calhoun said slowly.

"On what?"

"If the vote is yes . . . then no, I've nothing to say. If the vote is no . . . then I'll say 'Good-bye.' "

There were uneasy looks around the room. "Is that your entire statement on the matter?" Howzer, the mortician, said with a touch of annoyance.

"Pretty much, except to say that whichever of you decides to take over the position, well," and he smiled broadly, "I hope you don't get shot."

Rheela put a hand to her mouth to cover her broad smile. She could see the suddenly nervous expressions of everyone around her. In short order, a simple hand vote indicated that an overwhelming majority of the people attending thought that keeping Calhoun employed as the Majister was just a terrific idea.

"So ordered. Majister Calhoun, welcome aboard. Do you have any opening or official statement you'd like to make to the good people of Narrin?"

He smiled, bobbed his head and said, "I'll do my best while I'm here . . . but I'm just passing through. Keep your heads down and, with any luck, none of you will get blasted. By me, at any rate."

Rheela bit her lip so as not to laugh out loud. The "good people of Narrin" looked at each other with clear uncertainty that they had done the right thing, but it was too late to go back now.

The meeting then proceeded, with discussion on a variety of other topics. There were times when Rheela found it difficult to stay awake, but she knew as a responsible citizen that it was her obligation, at the very least, to make a pretense of paying attention. She found her gaze drawn time and again to Calhoun, though. He had taken up a position in one corner of the room that seemed to suit him, and she realized that, from that one spot, he could see every corner of the place with equal facility. He was leaning back against the wall, looking very relaxed and apparently not expecting trouble at all. But she watched as his gaze swept the room, consistently and steadily. No, he might not have been expecting trouble . . . but he was anticipating it, so that he would not be caught unawares. It made her wonder if there was any reason to expect trouble at the meeting, but ultimately she decided that he was just being cautious. It was incredibly ironic. She still knew next to nothing about him, aside from the fact that he'd tried to kill her. And yet, inexplicably, she felt safer with him around than without him.

It was everything she could do to throw off such sentimentally nonsensical thoughts. The last thing she wanted to do was depend on someone else in order to feel safe. The only one she could count on not to abandon her or Moke was herself. And she could never, ever, lose sight of that fact.

"That," the Praestor announced eventually, "takes care of old business. Now . . . on to new business. Not to be too unfeeling on a painful subject, but it's obvious that we need to replace Majister Fairax on the town council. Now, we of the council have thought long and hard about this, trying to come up with an individual whom we feel has given a great deal to the community, and presumably has more to give in the future. And after developing a very short list of names, we would like to present to all of you the individual whom we feel would be the most appropriate to place on the council. This is subject, naturally, to your vote, but we are hoping that our recommendation will provide sufficient sway, or—at the very least—quell any concerns you might have."

"Who are we talking about here?' inquired Ronk, an impatient and perpetually cranky dirt farmer from the southern district.

"I am speaking of none other than the right honorable Maester Tapinza."

There was a round of genuinely enthusiastic applause in response to that, but Rheela shook her head in disbelief. Was everyone truly blind to the fact that there was something . . . unappetizing about him? Granted, he had never said or done anything truly threatening. She didn't like his point of view, trying to profit off the

Kolk'r-given ability she wielded. That alone, though, didn't automatically mean that there was something wrong with him.

Even so, though . . . even so . . . she felt nothing but great unease every time his name was mentioned. But all she was seeing around her were nods of approval.

Tapinza was standing, nodding and waving to the people. He cleared his throat and said, "My good friends . . . as much as I appreciate this warm ovation, there are rules for a reason. Things should be done according to those rules whenever possible. If those rules call for a vote, then I must insist that such a vote be held."

"Well said, Maester, well said," Milos beamed. "I think a simple show of hands will do. All those in favor of Maester Tapinza being appointed to the town council . . ."

Rheela saw hands all around her going into the air. With every fiber of her being, she wanted to sit on her own hands and send a statement—however futile it might be—that she still did not approve of the man. But then, much to her own annoyance, she raised her hand, falling into line with everyone else.

"There, then!" Milos said cheerfully, not even bothering to ask for "no" votes, since the show of hands had been overwhelmingly supportive of the question before them. "That's settled. Welcome to the council, Maester," and he shook hands warmly with Tapinza while another polite round of applause rippled through the meeting hall.

"Now, then," continued Milos, "is there any new business?"

And he looked straight at the Maestress.

This alone was enough to set off an alarm in Rheela's head. She had no idea why, but, nevertheless, she sensed that what was about to happen—whatever that might be—wasn't going to be good. Clearly, the Maestress had something very specific in mind, because the Praestor was apparently expecting it. She was getting the distinct impression that there was going to be some sort of ambush . . . and that there wasn't a thing she was going to be able to do about it.

Sure enough, the Maestress rose from behind the table. It seemed as if the others in the room visibly shrank when she did so. It was hard for Rheela to understand, even after all this time, the hold that Maestress Cawfiel seemed to have over so many of them. Then again, perhaps it wasn't that difficult to understand. Cawfiel had been part of the town for longer than anyone could remember. The general sentiment seemed to be that she had been there, literally, forever. She predated everyone, including Praestor Milos, who was one of the oldest men in the city. Virtually everyone in the meeting hall, when they had been children, had quaked in fear of the Maestress. One would have thought that, once they grew up, adulthood would have attended to childhood fears. But time had not lessened the strength of the influence she had upon them. If anything, it had graven it in stone.

When she spoke, it was with a low voice that was just above a whisper, so that everyone was forced to strain in order to hear her. From a psychological point of view, that was very clever on her part. In effect, it brought them to her. "As many of you know," she said, "I am very concerned over the behavior I saw in this city not all that long ago. The gallivanting, the mindless celebration. It does not bode well for the long-term health of our city. You *do* all see that, I hope."

Rheela didn't know firsthand what she was talking about, but she could certainly take a guess. The rain she had brought to the people a few days ago had been desperately needed, and there had probably been "gallivanting" in the streets when the skies had unleashed their liquid sustenance. She wished she could have been there, as it must have been quite a sight to see.

There was visible tension throughout the room. And then the Maestress . . . smiled. Rheela couldn't decide whether that was a good thing or not, although, if she had to guess, she would have opted for "not."

"But I have been giving the matter some thought . . . and I want you to know that I am not angry. I hold no grudges. I simply want what's best for you. As the spiritual mother of this community, I embrace each and every one of you," and she held her arms wide symbolically.

Immediately, relief swept through the crowd. The residents of Narrin reciprocated, likewise holding open their arms and symbolically welcoming her gesture. For her part, Rheela found herself looking toward Calhoun to see what his reaction was. His face remained inscrutable. There did seem to be, though, a hint of cold amusement in his eyes. Then again, Rheela couldn't be sure; she might have been imagining it.

The Maestress lowered her arms, and the others followed suit. Rheela saw, though, that the Praestor was making no effort to step in or act as if that was all the Maestress had to say on the matter. That being the case, the odds were that the Maestress was, in fact, going to say more. Rheela still felt uneasy.

"I think," the Maestress, predictably, continued, "that part of the problem is that I have not presented you with sufficient guidelines. As a result, I've constantly been in the position of having to scold you after the fact. But that is inefficient and—worse—unfair to you. So I think it would be much better for all concerned if the rules were made clear. Made clear . . . and accepted by all of you. A sort of contract, if you will, between us."

" 'Us' being what?" It was Ronk, once again, who had asked. He added, "And what kind of 'contract' are you talking about?"

" 'Us' refers to the people of this town . . . and the council, its appointed representatives and guides in all matters having to do with orderly life here in Narrin. And as for the contract, why . . . that's a very good question, Ronk, and one that is easily answered."

She turned and nodded to Spangler. He got up from behind the table, carrying the stack of papers that had been on his lap. He went along the rows of people, handing out stacks and indicating that they should be passed down. As he did so, Maestress Cawfiel explained, "We call it the Standards and Decency Act. I, of course, dislike such words as 'act.' But that's our way of letting you know that it is coming through the council, rather than at the whim or will of any one individual. Moreover, what makes it a contract is that it will be entered into willingly. Read it over. You will see that it is ultimately just and fair."

Rheela skimmed it over. She hated to admit it—it even frightened her slightly—but most of what she was reading didn't seem all that bad. It preached moderation in all things, respect for authority, treating others in the same manner that you yourself wished to be treated.

She was three-quarters of the way down the single page of the document when she stopped cold. The passage leaped out at her like a dagger.

"No people of questionable moral virtue shall be tolerated on or about or anywhere within proximity of the city, as they set a poor example and will lead others down the road to depravity. These types of people shall include, but not be limited to, abusers of children . . . abusive partners . . ." The list went on, and most of them seemed reasonable, except her eye had skipped to the end, ". . . and parents of children with questionable or unknown background."

She heard muttering, rumbling that sounded like voices of discontent. But, for the most part, she also heard comments of approval. The vast majority of those surrounding her seemed to appreciate having everything spelled out for them.

"You see?" the Maestress said. "It's not unreasonable. Certainly nothing that anyone who wants the best for this town would have any objections t—"

It took everything Rheela had to muster up her nerve, because she was quite certain of the response she was going to get. Nevertheless, she got to her feet and said, "Excuse me."

The Maestress hadn't been looking in her direction, but she did so now. Very slowly, her gaze fastened on Rheela, and her thin lips stretched across her face. But it was a smile that displayed utter confidence in herself and in the moment. "Yes, Rheela?"

"I have to believe, Maestress—with all respect—that one of the stipulations put forward here is aimed specifically at me."

"Not at all, Rheela," the Maestress replied coolly. "The 'stipulations,' as you call them, are designed only to provid a life of purity of spirit for all concerned. That is not aimed at you. It's aimed at providing what's best for all."

The Praestor spoke up, sounding vaguely patronizing. "I assure you, Rheela, that when the rules of decency were being drawn up, your name was not mentioned. Nor was anyone's. We took aim at no single lifestyle, but instead, what will simply be best for everyone."

Ronk reared to his feet. The fact that he was arguing came as no surprise; Ronk had a tendency to disagree with everyone about everything. It was what he enjoyed doing. Nevertheless, this time, his stated concerns actually had relevance to Rheela. "I know 'zactly what Rheela's referrin' to. It's this part here, about unknown children and such. How's it gonna be best for everyone if she's driven away because of that?"

Moke was now looking around in confusion, and Rheela was cursing herself that she had brought him along at all. What spectacularly bad timing and judgment she had displayed. He clearly didn't understand what was happening, but she wasn't going to be able to shield him from the realization for much longer. He had come close to her when she had risen to speak, and now he was clutching apprehensively at her leg.

"No one is driving her away," the Maestress said calmly. "We are speaking of demanding a single standard for those who reside in and around Narrin. That does not seem unreasonable to me. But this is not a dictatorship. This is a place," and she smiled ingratiatingly—or, at least, as close as she could come to being ingratiating—"where everyone has a say. I look to you for a vote on the Standards and Decency Act."

"Can we pick and choose?" Ronk asked. "Vote yes for some rules, no for others?"

The Widow Att now stood and spoke, voice dripping with disdain. "What a superb idea. By all means, let us accept without question those things that we find convenient and easy . . . and reject that which would challenge us." She snorted even as she held the paper over her head. "I tell you that this document is a masterful expression of the Narrin mind, and that it would border on sacrilege to accept it in any way other than in its entirety."

There were many nods of approval, and Rheela noticed that almost all of them were coming from the older residents of the town . . . of which there were many. The younger were much fewer, and even many of them were nodding. A few of them were looking regretfully or nervously at Rheela, but didn't have the fortitude to stand up in the face of such widespread disapproval.

"She brings us the rain!" Ronk protested.

"Rain came before Rheela arrived here," replied Howzer. "And it will continue to come long after she is gone. This town didn't spring up overnight, you know, or at Rheela's whim."

"But shouldn't we discuss—"

"There is nothing to discuss," Praestor Milos said forcefully . . . a little too forcefully, in fact. Clearly, he did not wish to cross the Maestress, and was doing everything he could to stay in her good graces by helping to railroad the Act through. "Something is either right or it is not. Discussing it isn't going to make it more or less right. I call for the vote."

For some reason, Rheela found herself looking over to Calhoun. He had not budged from the spot he had taken up before. He just stood there, arms folded, watching the proceedings with an unreadable expression. She looked over toward Tapinza . . . and saw that he was watching her with a certain degree of smugness on his face.

Then the Maestress began to speak again, and her voice soared with the righteousness of her indignation. "Has it occurred to any of you," she thundered, "that Kolk'r is testing us? That he withholds the rain because of what he sees as laxness in the way we live our lives? Notice that I say 'we.' I do not exempt myself. I have lived a life of purity and service, and yet not for a moment do I think that I don't share your fate. What affects one of us, affects all of us. I have had a vision—a vision, I say—of an improved quality of life for everyone in this city. But that depends on our ability to realize the truth and the way of things, and to follow the right path! A path that is being given to us, here and now. You must not let foolish fears stop you from doing what is right! What is just! What is best for everyone! The council is already solidly behind this Act. It is now left to you to decide whether you're going to follow our lead. This is one of those moments, my children, when one's future is on the line, and one has to decide in what direction one is going to take that future. I'm asking you all to make that choice now."

Ultimately, it wasn't even close. When Rheela watched the vast majority of hands accepting the Standards and Decency Act, she felt as if she was having an out-of-body experience. As if she was seeing the entire thing happen from someplace very far away. The few people who didn't vote in favor of it couldn't even bring themselves to look her in the eye. And even in their cases, she wondered whether it was because of any genuine affection and sense of fair play . . . or whether they were just afraid of losing a natural resource.

Even without looking, she felt Tapinza's gaze upon her. Every bit of her skin crawled. It was becoming more clear to her by the minute that he had something very definite in mind. She brought her gaze up to look him in the eyes, and sure enough, he was watching her. He hadn't looked away from her the entire time. It was becoming obvious: this was some sort of "punishment" that he had cooked up in conjunction with the Maestress. She had refused to cooperate with him, and, as a result, he was now going to drive her from her home.

Her heart hardened. Fine. Fine, let it be that way. She had done everything she could, operated out of some sort of misbegotten belief that she could improve their lives. They hadn't asked for her, but she had come just the same. But if that was how they were going to be, then she was more than happy to play it that way. She would just . . . just leave, that was all, exactly as the stupid Act required. She would leave it all behind—her farm, her dreams of stability—and she would just find somewhere else. And she wouldn't even let anyone know about the Kolk'r-given abilities she wielded. She wouldn't make the mistake of caring about what happened to people ever again.

Or . . . or better yet . . . she would stay. How would they like that? She would just sit there, remain on her farm exactly the way she had been. What were they going to do? Force her to move? Let them try. Let them see how much success they would have if—

She became aware that Moke was saying the same thing, over and over again. She looked down at him, and there were tears streaking down his face as he kept saying, clearly frightened, "I don't want to go! This is my home! I don't want to go!" He was looking fearfully at the people around him, trying to grasp why they would possibly despise him so.

She was stricken with grief on his behalf. She had never seen the boy look so vulnerable, so hurt. She wanted to take him up in her arms, to tell him that somehow, some way, everything was going to be all right. That he shouldn't let these peoples' ignorance or judgment weigh upon his conscience. He was a good boy, she was a good woman, and sometimes in life things simply happened that were unfair. But how does one possibly explain that to a child who is hurting?

And at that moment, Rheela—who had come to take her miraculous influence over the weather almost for granted—wished to Kolk'r for a small and simple miracle, any miracle, that would salvage the situation.

"Excuse me."

Calhoun had spoken. All eyes immediately were upon him. It was as impossible to get any sort of read of him as ever. "I think . . . it's time to be honest."

"Honest?" The Praestor looked somewhat confused. "About what, Majister?"

"About Rheela. And our son . . . Moke."

# SHELBY

ELIZABETH SHELBY WAS BEGINNING to wonder if she was losing track of herself. If she was becoming unclear on just what she believed, on what her philosophy was. Was she endeavoring to live up to Mac, simply because he was dead? Did she feel she "owed" it to him for some reason?

She had no idea . . . and was even less enthused when ship's counselor Laura Ap'Boylan took it upon herself to discuss the matter with her.

Ap'Boylan's heart was in the right place, Shelby was reasonably sure of that. Still, the relatively correct placement of her heart did not remotely prompt Shelby to want to talk with her. But Ap'Boylan didn't let such a trivial thing as reluctance on Shelby's part deter her.

"I admit to being a bit surprised that you're down here, Captain," she said, her dark eyes studying Shelby intently as she slid into the seat across from Shelby's desk. "Considering that we're in the process of ridding Makkus of its undesirable insect population, I'd think you'd want to be right in the middle of the bridge for it, rather than here in the ready room."

"I have every confidence in my people to handle this procedure," Shelby said coolly.

"That is good to hear," said Ap'Boylan. But then, with the

slightest flicker of hesitation, she added, "And do you believe . . . they have every confidence in you?"

"Have I a reason to think otherwise?" she replied.

"You answer a question with a question."

"Do I?"

Ap'Boylan's lips thinned, showing her lack of amusement at Shelby's response. "I am only here to help, Captain."

"I was unaware I needed any help," Shelby told her. She found, though, much to her annoyance, that she disliked taking a harsh tone with Ap'Boylan. The telepath really was harmless enough, and her face had such a look of innocence to it that being harsh with her was like clubbing a baby tribble. She laughed softly to herself over the image that prompted in her head, and then sighed. "Perhaps I do at that."

Ap'Boylan seemed positively buoyed by the admission. "Good. Good. Admitting one has a problem is the first step to solving it."

"I don't know for sure that I have a problem. I am sensing, though, a sort of . . . resistance . . . from the crew. Doubt, perhaps. Then again, I'm not the telepath. What are you picking up?"

"I'm not really here to discuss the crew, Captain, but you."

Shelby blinked at that. "I don't know that I personally need discussion."

For a moment, Ap'Boylan appeared to be considering the matter. "Captain," she said delicately, as if walking on very thin glass, "what is your philosophy of command?"

It was a fair enough question. "Actually," Shelby said, after a moment's consideration, "I'd say my philosophy would be pretty much in accord with the credo of the medical profession."

"Which credo would that be?"

" 'First . . . do no harm,' " Shelby quoted. She leaned forward on the desk, hands folded into each other; she displayed the determined jaw-outthrust attitude of someone who not only knew she was right, but dared someone to prove it otherwise. "I've been giving it a good deal of thought, and I think that's what it boils down to. The first priority of this vessel is to try and leave things better than we found them."

"And what of regulations?"

"Regulations are absolutely mandatory and necessary," she affirmed. "We cannot, and should not even try to conduct our business without them. However, regs are not a straitjacket to prevent us from doing things wrong. Instead, they're a guideline as to how to do things right. Does that seem reasonable?"

"You don't particularly care whether I think it is reasonable or not," Ap'Boylan said with quiet confidence. "It is simply how you feel."

"That's correct," admitted Shelby amiably. "One of the captain's prerogatives is that she gets to make up her mind and stick to it."

"And what prerogatives does the crew have?"

There was something in her tone—almost a warning sound to it—that got Shelby's hackles up ever so slightly. She forced herself to cool down. "What . . . do you mean by that, Counselor?"

"Nothing," said Ap'Boylan quickly.

"I rather think you meant something by it," Shelby said, "but we'll let it pass for the moment. Counselor, there is one thing upon which my resolve has not wavered in the slightest, and that is discipline. Discipline and obedience. If my crew wants to voice its feelings, and even register a protest, I am more than happy to listen to all sides for as long as is humanly possible. But it must never be forgotten that I'm the one in command, and no one else. Do you think any of my people are in danger of losing sight of that?"

"No," said Laura Ap'Boylan. But there was something in her tone that made the captain feel as if something significant was being left unsaid. Then she asked a question that caught Shelby flat-footed: "Do you think he's watching?"

"He?" Shelby stared at her, not understanding to whom the counselor was referring.

"He." She pointed at the bulkhead just to the left of Shelby's head. The sword of Mackenzie Calhoun was mounted there. "Calhoun."

"Oh." Suddenly Shelby felt as if her voice was terribly small, almost infinitesimal. "Do you mean, literally watching? Like a ghost of some sort?"

"No, not at all," she said quickly, but then seemed to feel as if she had spoken *too* quickly. "Well . . . perhaps just a bit, I suppose."

"I don't see him standing off to the side, his hands covered in blood while waving a skull at me, if that's what you mean. But, yes, I suppose that, to some degree, I feel as if he's keeping an eye on me. Is that so unusual?"

"No, not at all. It is very common to feel . . ." She seemed to search for the right word. ". . . to feel a desire for approval from someone who is gone. Especially if we were not able to get that approval in life."

"I don't know what you're talking about. Mac approved of me."

"You don't have to become defensive, Captain."

"I do when I'm being attacked."

"My apologies," Ap'Boylan said mildly. "I was unaware that you were perceiving my thoughts as an attack."

"It doesn't have to do with my perceptions, it's . . ." She made an impatient noise. "Never mind. This is exactly the type of situation that makes me reluctant to talk to counselors at all."

"You have difficulty discussing your emotions?"

"Discussing? No. Dissecting, yes." She leaned back in her chair, feeling in an expansive mood. "A captain, to a certain degree, has to fly by the seat of her pants. Do what she feels is right. Sometimes the regs are then brought in to justify a decision already made. But it's justification all the same. The bottom line is that the captain does what she feels is right."

"And you've always felt this way?"

*No.*

"Yes," she said firmly.

*No, you haven't; you're lying.*

Through gritted teeth, she said, "Shut up."

This drew an extremely surprised reaction from Ap'Boylan. "I'm sorry?"

135

"Nothing. It was nothing. I was . . ." She paused, knowing how it was going to sound, but seeing nothing else for it. "I was talking to myself," she admitted.

"Do you do that often?"

"No."

*Yes.*

She closed her eyes to force the inner voice to go away. "I . . . admit," she said slowly, "that my philosophies have . . . changed a bit. But it's natural that I would see things a bit differently now, isn't it? I believed that regulations were the beginning, middle and end of command. I think Mackenzie Calhoun represents . . ." She paused, and then, with effort, amended, "represented . . . a philosophy that was at the extreme other end. But if nothing else, it's made me realize that extremes of any sort are never a good thing. So it was probably appropriate for me to re-assess and realize that regs can be the beginning and middle of command, but the end requires something more. That's all I'm saying."

"And was that a difficult thing for you to conclude?"

"Why would it be?"

"Because," said Ap'Boylan, "it calls into question everything that you've believed up until that point."

Shelby laughed at that. "Counselor," she said, feeling more relaxed than she had in a while, "I happen to believe that any day that *doesn't* call into question everything I believe is a day that's been wasted. Truthfully, I'm not sure why more people don't feel the same way."

"I couldn't begin to tell you."

"Well, when you can, get back to me on it." She stood, and the counselor mirrored her action.

But the Betazoid couldn't quite let it go. "Captain," she said, sounding as if she was feeling her way, "despite the confidence with which you're speaking . . . I sense a degree of ambivalence from you. You're still not quite certain where you stand. You're feeling your way."

"You say that as if it's a bad thing. I happen to consider that a great positive," Shelby replied.

"Leaders," Ap'Boylan said, "don't feel their way. They can't. The one thing they can't afford is to be tentative."

"I never said I was tentative."

"You're becoming defensive again."

"That's because—" Shelby stopped and sighed, very loudly this time. "You know what? I've just made a very untentative decision: This discussion ends here."

"We can resume it at some other time if you'd like," offered the counselor.

Shelby smiled thinly. "I don't know that I'll be liking to anytime soon." With that, she walked briskly out onto the bridge.

"For a man who just had his world divested of a lethal form of insect life, you certainly don't seem particularly cheerful," noted Captain Shelby.

Hauman's image was on the screen of the bridge, and it was obvious to anyone that Shelby's assessment was exactly right. Hauman did not look the least bit cheered by the fact that his people were going to survive. He inclined his head slightly in acknowledgment and said, "Your observation is . . . not without its accuracy, Captain. If you desire, I shall endeavor to put on a happier face in the future."

"You don't have to do anything to accommodate me, Hauman."

"But I do," he replied, "since you have certainly gone out of your way to accommodate both me and my people. I must say that for you, Captain. You have done everything that you said you would. My scientists have swept the planet's surface since you completed your 'treatment' some hours ago. No trace of the offending creatures can be found."

"My people are very reliable," said Shelby. Out of the corner of her eye, she saw Tulley and Dunn—who had come up to the bridge specifically to witness this particular communiqué—look at each other with an approving nod. Even Garbeck had a relaxed air about her. That pleased Shelby. There were some officers who, if their opinion were overridden, would nurse a grudge or just sit there and steam over it. Certainly Shelby was familiar enough with the type, having been one of them herself for longer than she would have liked to admit. She'd outgrown it (or, at least, she liked to believe she had). But it had never been an admirable trait of hers, and she disliked seeing it in others as much as she did in herself. Fortunately enough, Garbeck appeared to have risen above that in her attitudes and comportment. If she was at all upset that rules had been bent and the Makkusians spared slow depopulation through a pernicious insect, she certainly wasn't letting on. Then again, who *would* want to make an attitude like that public?

"Yes, your people are obviously very reliable," Hauman commended her. "And you will find my people to be . . . equally so." But as he completed the sentence, there was an unmistakable air of wistfulness in his tone.

"Meaning . . . ?" said Shelby.

"Meaning that we will . . . honor our pledge to join your United Federation of Planets."

"Even though it compromises your pledge of neutrality." Shelby was leaning back in her command chair, drumming her fingers thoughtfully.

"Yes, Captain. Even though." He still did not sound remotely happy about it.

"Well . . . good. Good," Shelby was nodding approvingly. "I'm pleased that you're going to stick to the agreement. I mean, yes, I understand that it does violate your philosophy. But . . . hell," and she smiled lopsidedly, "it's not as if you were pressured into making the promise, right? I mean, no one held a metaphorical gun to your head and told you, 'You have to do such-and-such, or else . . .'" Forming her fingers into a gun, she mimed blowing her brains out.

"Captain . . ." Hauman said with obvious hesitation. "I . . . hate to bring this up . . . but, well . . . that is, in fact, what did happen."

"No!" Shelby spoke with what was clearly a sort of false

"shocked" voice. "Is it?" She sensed Garbeck stirring uneasily in the seat next to hers, but chose to ignore it. "You truly felt that you were forced into the pledge? That it was coerced from you, against your will?"

"Well . . . yes." Hauman sounded very uncertain, as if unclear as to why something that self-evident was even being discussed. "Yes, of course it was against our will. I made that abundantly clear to you, did I not?"

Looking rather huffy over the mere notion of it, Shelby sat up straight and smoothed the line of her jacket. "You did not, sir. You did not make it clear at all. And I certainly wish you had."

"But I thought—"

Ignoring his befuddled expression, Shelby pressed on, "Because we have a few philosophies and regulations back where I come from. And one of them states that any agreement entered into that is not completely mutual on the part of both parties is not an agreement at all."

"Captain," came a low, warning undertone from Garbeck.

"Not now, Commander," she whispered back, before continuing at her normal volume, "That's the entire purpose of entering into an agreement or contract. If someone compels you to do so, 'or else,' why . . . the very existence of the 'or else' negates any sort of good-faith dealing."

Hauman clearly understood where this was all going, but couldn't quite believe it. "Captain Shelby . . . are you insinuating that, if we wish to recant our agreement in this matter . . . there is a fundamental precept in your laws and philosophies that would allow such a thing to occur?"

"Of course."

*"Captain!"*

This time it was clear that Garbeck wasn't allowing herself to be ignored. "One moment, please," said Shelby as she turned to face Garbeck, the former's face a picture of innocence. "Problem, Commander?"

"Permission to speak privately, Captain?"

"Granted."

Garbeck had half-risen from her chair, heading toward the ready room, when Shelby cut the legs out from under her by saying curtly, "But later. Not now."

"Captain, I—"

"I said, not now, Commander. Was that confusing in some manner?"

For a long moment, Garbeck simply froze in place, and then, very slowly and very deliberately, she took her seat once again. She did not, however, look directly at Shelby.

"And what of the insects?" Hauman asked, suddenly cautious. "If I were to withdraw the agreement, would you—?"

"Put them back?" She laughed at the very idea. "No, not at all. Gone is gone, Hauman. Every one of those creatures—except for what's being held by my people for study—is nothing more than free-floating atoms."

"We have similar samples under investigation," said Hauman. "Thanks to you, we should be rid of the beasts forever. But, in the unlikely event that we're not rid of them, we can continue our research . . . this time without any help from the Federation."

Shelby heard McMac moan softly in their collective chests.

"So, what are you telling me, Hauman? That you are now pulling out of your commitment to the UFP?" She spoke so slowly and deliberately that her meaning could not possibly be lost.

A slow smile split Hauman's face. "Yes," he said, and then remembered to add an air of reluctant tragedy to his voice. "I'm afraid that's exactly what I'm saying."

"Well!" She sat back, shaking her head and looking discouraged. "I have to say, I'm obviously disappointed in your decision. It may indeed be in line with your world's philosophies, but I still feel the Federation has a great deal to offer you." She thought about it a moment, and then said, "I would like you to consider something, Hauman. I would like you to consider that it is because of the UFP that your world now stands safe from that which nature turned against you. And it is because of representatives of the UFP that you are under no obligation other than to live as good a life as possible. We are an organization that honors individual philosophies and ways of life, banding together out of no other motivation than mutual protection, and sharing in the wonders of each other's cultures. Have you considered the possibility that, by exposing other worlds to the way your people think, you might actually be serving to improve the existence of others, rather than simply diminishing the quality of your own lives?"

"We had not considered that, no," admitted Hauman. He appeared moved by what she was saying, and stroked his chin thoughtfully. "I cannot make any promises, Captain, but my associates and I will strongly consider what you have said . . . and what we have learned. Much of this is very new to us, but we are willing to admit that everything that we're doing . . . that, indeed, all of life . . . is a learning process. It is a foolish individual indeed who operates on the assumption that he knows everything there is to know. I may be many things, Captain, but I've never considered a fool to be one of them." He thought a moment longer and then added, "If it wouldn't be too inconvenient . . . would you be able to check back with us in, say, a month's time? There are individuals I need to discuss matters with, meetings to be held. As I've said, I cannot guarantee anything. But it is possible that, upon reflection, we may eventually be able to give you an answer more in line with your reason for coming here."

"All I have asked is fair consideration," Shelby said. *"Exeter* out." The screen blanked out, and she nodded approvingly to herself. Then she looked around at her crew—and saw, by and large, scowls or looks of disappointment. Very quietly, she said, "Does anyone have a problem?" When no immediate response came, she said, "It wouldn't be wise to make me ask again."

All eyes turned to Garbeck, who cleared her throat. "It's just that . . . it was our first mission, Captain. It would have been nice for it to be a one hundred percent success. Instead, it's something of a mixed bag."

"Life often is, Number One," Shelby said easily. "But ultimately, it is not our mission to browbeat reluctant races into joining us."

"They're ingrates," said Dunn. "After all the work we went to—"

"It was a task we undertook on our own initiative, Dunn," she reminded him. "We did it because it was the right thing to do . . . whatever the Prime Directive might have had to say on the matter. Just as not pressuring the Makkusians into joining was also the right thing to do. Two wrongs may not make a right, but two rights don't necessarily add up to a third right either."

"Actually," MacGibbon noted, "three rights generally gets you back to where you started in the first place."

This actually drew a mild laugh from others on the bridge. "Trust a conn officer to make note of that," said Shelby, amused. "If that's the case, MacGibbon, then I think we're ahead of the game. Because my suspicion is that, when we check back with them, they will indeed want to join the UFP. And our mission will have ended successfully after all. It will just have taken a bit longer than we originally thought."

"I hope you're right, Captain," Garbeck said diplomatically. But there was something in the way she said it that set off a small alarm in the back of Shelby's head.

# TAPINZA

"... AND OUR SON ... MOKE ..."

The uproar was instantaneous, but Tapinza didn't hear it at first because of the roaring in his ears. That roaring came from the blood that was pounding furiously through his head, as he watched his meticulously crafted plan fall apart.

Even as he watched the town meeting erupt into chaos, Tapinza's entire world telescoped down to two individuals: Calhoun and Rheela. She was staring at him, thunderstruck, his words just beginning to sink in. It was as if everything was happening in slow motion. Her mouth was moving, but no words were coming out. Moke was next to her, jumping up and down, his face incandescent with joy, pulling on her skirt and pointing to Calhoun while asking over and over again, *"Is he? Is he?"* Calhoun, inscrutable as always, was saying nothing. Instead, he actually seemed to be enjoying the chaos that his little announcement had caused. The Praestor was gaveling for order, but no one was paying attention yet.

*That bastard ... that bastard ...* Finally, words were creeping back into Tapinza's mind, fighting their way through the blanket of raw fury that had been draped over his head. How the hell had this happened? Where had this Calhoun come from, that he was stepping in and making a complete bungle of a simple and elegant plan?

In essence, Calhoun had beaten him to the punch.

Tapinza had been just about to stand up, just about to say virtually the same words as had emerged from Calhoun's mouth. He was going to claim paternity of Moke, give Rheela an out. Enable her to stay, to ally herself with, arguably, the most powerful man in town. Everyone was going to benefit from it, and if Rheela knew what was good for her, she would go along.

There was always the possibility that she would deny it, of course. If she did so, she would be tossing away a perfectly good gambit on his part, and that would be her decision to make. If she denied it, Tapinza would simply recant. "I was trying to help a woman so fallen that she seemed to need the help desperately," he would have said. This would naturally have gotten approval and support from everyone. It would have made him look generous, and her like the little ingrate that she was.

On the other hand, if she went along with his endeavor, then he would, in one stroke, have what he had been seeking to obtain. And then . . .

Then would come the possibilities.

For Tapinza, ever the man of vision, was seeing far beyond the relatively unimportant city of Narrin. He saw vast potential for great farms, massive growth areas producing food by the cartload, food readily generated thanks to the generous rainfall that Rheela would be able to provide him.

But even more than that . . . it would all be overseen by Tapinza, and doled out according to who was most willing to pay for it.

Ohhh . . . the possibilities, the endless possibilities.

Except that this . . . this *idiot* Calhoun had opened his big mouth.

Rheela had not yet erased the shocked look from her face. Calhoun, for his part, had stepped away from the wall and was coming toward her with slow, relaxed strides. "It's ridiculous to keep hiding it," he told her. "I want to do right by you . . . and by

Moke." The boy was looking up at him with eyes the size of saucers.

And still Rheela said nothing. "You—" was all she managed to get out.

He put his hands on her arms. "You want to do right by Moke . . . don't you?" he asked.

The babble of voices was tapering off into silence. Everyone was looking at Rheela, hanging on a silence that seemed endless.

Then she let out a sigh that sounded like an exhausted, yet relaxed, gust of relief. "Of course I do," she said. At which point, Calhoun took her in his arms and kissed her.

And that was more than enough to set off another chorus of cheers. There was also, Tapinza couldn't help but notice, a rather vocal minority expressing out and out disbelief, scoffing noises that indicated just how preposterous and absurdly timed was this claim by Calhoun.

Loudest of all, predictably, was the Maestress. "Come now!" she said. "Are we to believe that you are who you claim you are?"

Calhoun looked at her with a puzzled expression. "I was unaware, Maestress, that this town requires proof of parentage in all instances. Do you? Does every person in this room who purports to be the parent of a child who calls them father know, before Kolk'r and all, that they are unquestionably the *true* father?" He surveyed the room with a stare that was almost fearsome. "All cities have their secrets, things they would rather keep hidden. I would not suggest, Maestress, that you advocate pulling them all into the light. I do not know how much support you would muster for that endeavor."

The Maestress was about to reply, but then she saw the faces of those around her. The open nervousness, the clear evidence that no one wanted to even open that door, much less walk through it.

*Brilliant,* thought Tapinza grimly. *He plays upon their darkest fears like a master musician. The odds are that everyone here is exactly what they appear to be, no more and no less. But he has them so off balance that they don't know what to say, or even what to think.*

"In that case," said Calhoun, "I do not see where you have the right to single out Rheela or myself for close questioning. That field of examination is too dangerous to withstand evenhanded application . . . wouldn't you say, Praestor?" He deliberately ignored the Maestress, instead focusing on the nominal leader of the community.

Praestor Milo harrumphed loudly once, and then said in a strident voice, "Well . . . if the Majister has admitted to his . . . involvement . . . in the matter of Rheela and her son, then I hardly see where we have the right to say otherwise."

For one moment, Maester Tapinza thought that seeking Rheela's cooperation in the production of rain was going to be unnecessary, since the Maestress looked as if she was ready to summon a pure thunderstorm herself. She was about ready to eat thunder and excrete lightning, no question. But then Maestress Cawfiel reined herself in, and said nothing aside from, "Best of luck . . . to you both. To all three of you . . ."

"When did this happen?" Spangler suddenly asked. He was in full journalism mode. "How did it? How did the two of you meet?"

"That is no one's business," Calhoun told him.

"Yes, but the people want to know—"

"It's good to want things," Calhoun replied, smiling faintly.

"This has been a very busy meeting," the Praestor called out. "The time is getting late and, frankly, my friends, I'm exhausted. If there are no objections, I would like to call this meeting adjourned."

Tapinza wanted to voice half a dozen objections, starting with, *I hate Calhoun,* but, wisely, he kept his council. "This meeting is declared adjourned then," said the Praestor cheerfully, banging the gavel once.

Calhoun reached over and draped an arm around Rheela's shoulder. "Come, dear," he said gently. "Let's go to . . . home. We can speak more there." And he guided her out the door toward the street.

Naturally, Tapinza was out the back door and around to the front before anyone else had come close to exiting the hall. When he drew within range of Calhoun, he slowed, not wanting to run up to him like some sort of breathless fool. But he knew exactly what he was going to do. He was going to inform Calhoun that he had made a very serious blunder. Maester Tapinza was not someone that he desired to trifle with. He had thought, at the very least, that Calhoun would eventually be someone he would be able to deal with. But if Calhoun was determined to make their relationship an adversarial one, that was fine with Tapinza. Not for the first time did he consider the possibility of Calhoun as an enemy, and the conclusion he reached the second time was no different than the first: He could handle a dozen like Calhoun with no trouble.

"Calhoun," he said sharply as Calhoun, Rheela, and Moke walked out into the street. Two luukabs were tied to posts nearby, and that's where they were heading. Calhoun did not appear to hear him, or if he did, he didn't care. "Calhoun," he repeated, making it clear that he was not going to be ignored.

"He's my dad!" Moke said excitedly. He was holding Calhoun's hand so tightly that he was cutting the circulation off. "Did you hear? Did you hear, Maester?"

"Yes, I heard," he said with an oily pleasantness. "Calhoun, we need to talk—"

"I disagree," Calhoun said coolly.

"I am on the council, you are Majister, and you will answer to me." And, in saying that, he grabbed Calhoun by the wrist.

He didn't remember much after that.

All he knew was that time had abruptly passed, and he heard his name being murmured very distantly. Everything was extremely dark around him, and he wondered what had happened to the moonlight that had been flooding the town on this, a full moon night. Then he started to be able to sort out one voice from another, recognizing them individually, and finally he realized the reason it was so dark was because his eyes were closed. Slowly, he opened them, and discovered the missing moonlight, right where it was supposed to be. Concerned faces all around him were looking down.

"He's not dead!" said the Praestor, and there were relieved sighs from all around . . . except from Howzer the mortician, who seemed faintly disappointed. "Maester, we were very concerned about you! What happened?"

Several townspeople were already helping him off the ground. His legs were unsteady, and the world skewed around him at an odd angle as he tried to compose himself. "What . . . happened?" he echoed.

"We found you out here like this," said Spangler with great excitement, seeing a potential story for his newspaper. When one put out the news for a relatively small city such as Narrin, one tended to look for excitement wherever one could find it. "Who did this? Was it the new Majister?"

"Did what?" His thoughts were still swimming around . . . but then, slowly, they began to coalesce. What further sharpened his memory was the sudden stabbing pain originating from somewhere around his right jaw. He touched it, and moaned as he felt the lump that was most likely accompanied by an impressive black and blue mark. That was when Tapinza realized that he wasn't exactly ecstatic about the notion of being totally candid. He had his pride, after all. As near as he could tell, Calhoun had dropped him with precisely one punch, and that was not something Tapinza was especially anxious to broadcast. "Oh . . . this. No, no . . . this must have happened when I fell."

"Fell?" The people clustered around him in a small knot, looked collectively confused. "What caused you to fall, Maester?" asked Milos.

"I . . . don't know. A touch of illness, perhaps. I was feeling dizzy in the meeting hall. That's why I rushed out; I was hoping that some fresh air would do me good." He forced a ragged grin. "Apparently, not enough good. As for the Majister, why . . . I believe he had already ridden off by the time I came out." The last words were painful to get out, his jaw swelling up all the more.

"At least you're not hurt worse because of your . . . accident," said the Maestress. But it was abundantly clear, from her tone of voice, that she knew really what had occurred. She simply chose not to comment on it. For that, she had his undying appreciation, although he wished that their other little conspiracy had gone better. The truly ironic thing was, they had been working at cross-purposes, and she hadn't even known it. It had been Tapinza who had suggested the creation of the Standards and Decency Act, knowing that the Maestress would leap at the idea. Granted, she'd had no idea that he was then going to endeavor to step in and present himself as Moke's father, but that was all right. If she was angry at him, well . . .

No one lived forever. Not even Maestress Cawfiel.

But the entire matter had been rendered moot. Just thinking about it caused his stomach to churn in fury, even as the townspeople standing around helped him up. He thanked them, dusted himself off, and then abruptly had to lean on a few of them as a wave of dizziness swept over him. Yes, Calhoun had definitely done quite a job on him. And it was not something that Tapinza had any intention of forgetting, ever. There was no question in his mind that he was going to pay back Mackenzie Calhoun for this insulting, abusive treatment. Pay him back a hundredfold, no matter what it took. And if Rheela and Moke got in his way, well . . . they would have to pay as well.

# GARBECK

"DEUCES AND ONE-EYED JACKS WILD," said Garbeck. "A pair or better to open."

She glanced around the table with a grim look of satisfaction. As first officer, her influence over who was brought aboard the *Exeter* as part of the crew had been limited. She had, however, had sufficient influence to bring her favorite poker buddies along with her, and their weekly games had been the highlight of her term of service thus far.

Lieutenant Tim Lamb from geoscience made his customary face of disgust, the one he always made when Garbeck would announce some sort of flourish to a hand. "My God," he moaned, "can you just play poker like a man?"

"Sure. Can you?" Garbeck teased back without heat. Lamb stuck his tongue out at her.

Engineer's Mate First Class Kate Clark, on Garbeck's behalf, stuck her own tongue out right back at Lamb. "What's the matter? Too many rules to keep straight in that receding-hairline head of yours?"

"I'm not losing hair," he said archly. "I'm gaining face."

"Like we haven't heard *that* line a hundred times before," muttered Ensign Charles Carroll from special services. Next to him, weapons officer Kyle Jutkiewicz was studying his cards as if they contained clues to the whereabouts of the Holy Grail. "What's the matter, Lamb? Worried about being led to the slaughter?"

"Talk about lines heard a hundred times," Lamb riposted.

"Could we please remember why we're all here?" asked Garbeck.

"To enjoy the pleasure of each other's company?" Clark chirped in a cheerleaderish manner.

This drew guffaws and snorts of disbelief from the others. "I think the commander meant it was to play cards, not bicker," said Carroll.

"Right," said Jutkiewicz, still not taking his eyes off his cards. "If I wanted to bicker, I'd hang out with my girlfriend."

"That bodes well for *that* relationship," noted Lamb.

"Nobody asked you, Lambchop," retorted Jutkiewicz in a sufficiently cranky tone that Garbeck was led to believe Jutkiewicz hadn't been entirely kidding about the girlfriend reference.

Play proceeded briskly, with Garbeck raking in a fairly significant pot for the hand. In a few minutes, Lamb was shuffling the cards. "Okay," he said grimly. "Man's poker this time. None of this "Deuces wild" or "Jacks wild," or "All face cards painted in red except those with hearts on them are wild" stuff. Five card stud, straight up, down and dirty."

"Can something be both straight up *and* down and dirty?" wondered Clark.

This drew snickering from the card players up until the moment that Shelby burst in without ringing the chime or even knocking. The others, except for Garbeck, looked up at her in surprise. Garbeck's face remained impassive.

"Gentlemen, lady . . . if you'll excuse us," Shelby said tightly. "I'd like to have a few *private* words with Commander Garbeck."

The players didn't hesitate, since it was quite clear that Shelby was not in the mood to countenance any sort of back talk or questions. Within thirty seconds, Shelby and Garbeck were alone in the lounge.

"Can I help you, Captain?" asked Garbeck.

"I believe you can," replied Shelby. She began a slow circle of the room, her hands draped behind her. "You can explain to me the communiqué I received from Admiral Jellico today. Are you going to admit that you know what it's about? Or are we going to spend the next few minutes verbally fencing over it?"

"I was always taught in the Academy that one should not assume things," Garbeck said cautiously. "However, in this instance, I think it a safe assumption to conclude that it's in reference to the report I filed."

"That's exactly right. The report you filed." She stopped so that she was across the table from Garbeck, and she leaned forward, resting her knuckles on the tabletop. "There are a number of things I could say at the moment, Number One. One of them, obviously, would be that if you have a problem with me, then you come to me and we talk about it. Another would be that I would like to think you have some loyalty toward me as your commanding officer, and that I consider it a personal betrayal that you opted to file an unflattering description of my activities with the Makkusians with Admiral Jellico."

"My report was entirely within Starfleet protocol—" Garbeck began.

But Shelby raised a finger to her lips, silencing her. "But," she continued when Garbeck lapsed back into silence, "I'm not going to say any of those things. I don't have to. Because I can tell you exactly what happened. The Admiral brought you into his office. He told you how excellent you'd be for the post of first officer. He told you stories about Captain Calhoun, no doubt, and how unreliable he'd been . . . and how he'd no doubt had a very negative influence on me. That there was a danger I'd be unreliable as well, and, because of that, he'd want someone like you whom he could count on. Someone in the second chair who'd not only be able to keep me in line, but would be able to report back to him about everything that I had done that might be considered out of line with standard operating procedure.

"And if you were cooperative and helpful, then you could rest assured that Jellico would use his considerable influence to make certain you were duly rewarded. Perhaps you'd even be given your own captaincy, because you're bright enough and ambitious enough, and you're exactly the type of officer that Starfleet wants to see in the captain's chair. How am I doing so far, Number One? Am I close?"

Garbeck was not able to keep the surprise from her face. "Very much, yes. May I ask—?"

"How I knew?" She laughed curtly. "Because I had a very similar meeting with him before I started on with Calhoun. I was in your exact position, Garbeck. And you know what? I told the Admiral to go screw himself."

"Really. And how did he take to that?"

"He took to it so well that he took it upon himself to undermine the loyalties of my first officer."

Garbeck looked down and shook her head. "My loyalties are not in question in any way, Captain."

"Really? Considering you filed a report that stated my decisions were undercutting the morale of the command staff—"

"Might I note, Captain," Garbeck said stiffly, "that I was not alone in that opinion. The command staff signed off on that report."

"Yes, so I noticed. All of them . . . except Dr. Kosa."

Garbeck laughed softly to herself. "Yes, well . . . Dr. Kosa demurred. He just said something about 'no respect' and walked away." Then she looked back up at her commanding officer, standing there, her face a combination of rage, hurt, and annoyance. "Captain . . . my loyalty is to something bigger than any one person. It's to Starfleet. Look . . . to be honest—"

"A refreshing change."

Garbeck ignored the jibe. "Admiral Jellico is not my favorite officer, either, all right? But he is an admiral. He does outrank me. He raised issues in regards to you, and I felt it was necessary to listen to what he was saying and act in accordance with his wishes."

"So you thought it appropriate to spy on me."

Now Garbeck was starting to get angry. "I wasn't 'spying' on you, Captain. It was nothing like that, and you know it. I divulged no personal confidences, betrayed no trusts. I did nothing except report what you did, freely and in front of other crewmembers, and put forward my own opinions that what you were doing was outside the parameters of our mission, and the regs. Why shouldn't I say that? You said it yourself. You admitted to it. You even seemed to take a sort of . . . of perverse pride in finding a way around them so that you could do what you wanted to do. Frankly, you seemed to back up, with your actions, every concern that the admiral voiced about you. What would you have had me do? Ignore it? There's a *K-M* if I ever heard one."

"A *Kobayashi Maru,* you mean? A no-win scenario?"

"Right, exactly. If I keep my silence, say less than what's on my mind, then I'm in direct violation of an admiral's wishes. If I am honest and forthcoming, then I'm going to upset my C.O. As I said, a no-win. Well, you know what, Captain?" she said, standing up. "If I'm going to err, it's going to be on the side of truth and integrity. And if you feel that an accurate report of your actions puts you in a bad light, then perhaps you should consider questioning the actions rather than the person who reported them."

"What it makes me question, Number One, is how much of what we say gets pumped back to Admiral Jellico. How am I supposed to function if I feel that his proxy is in a room with me, questioning and second-guessing my every move?"

"There wouldn't *be* any second-guessing at all if the moves were solidly based in procedure and protocol," Garbeck reminded her. But then, in a slightly softer tone, she added, "However . . . I hope you do realize that anything you tell me in confidence remains that way. I wouldn't want you to think that I'm out to betray you or bring you down."

Shelby actually looked a bit regretful as she said, "Well, that's the problem, isn't it, Number One? It's rather impossible, isn't it, to control what someone thinks. Instead, you have to simply do what you feel is the best job you can, and deal with the consequences." She hesitated, and then said, "Tell me, Number One . . . do you feel *any* loyalty toward me at all?"

"You're my captain," Garbeck said immediately. "I have, and will continue to provide, all the loyalty and respect that the title entails."

"Alex," said Shelby, "don't you see that serving in Starfleet is about more than that? You shouldn't simply be loyal to titles. You have to be loyal to the people who hold those titles."

"As I said before, Captain . . . Starfleet is larger than any one person. It is that unity, that chain of command, that dedication to a single ideal, that makes us strong."

"Really." Shelby had turned and was heading for the door.

"Yes, Captain. Really."

Shelby paused in the now-open doorway, looked over her shoulder at Garbeck, and said sadly, "That's what the Borg say." And she walked out, leaving a thoughtful Garbeck behind.

# RHEELA

THE RIDE BACK TO THE FARM had been, paradoxically, both quiet and noisy. Noisy, in that Moke was talking a mile a minute, and quiet, because neither Calhoun nor Rheela was speaking.

"And that was something, the way you hit Tapinza!" burbled Moke.

"Moke, must you mention it again?" Rheela was no longer making the slightest effort to hide her annoyance with the topic. Why should she? The boy was making her crazy, and she definitely did not feel it an appropriate thing to talk about anyway. Unfortunately, Moke did not seem to agree.

"But it was one punch, Ma! One punch! One minute Tapinza was standing there, grabbing Calhoun's arm, and the next—"

"He could have simply told the Maester to release him," Rheela said primly, making sure to give a significant look of disapproval at Calhoun. Calhoun, riding his luukab, didn't appear to notice it, and instead looked resolutely forward.

But Moke wasn't having any of it. "Guys like dad don't tell people what to do! They *make* 'em do it—!"

"He's not your dad!" There. She'd said it. Moke wasn't going to be happy about it, but anything was preferable to allowing this . . . this charade to continue.

Upon being informed of this fact, Moke's entire response was to sniff disdainfully, as if the very notion that Calhoun wasn't who he said he was was inherently absurd. "That's silly. Why would he say it if it wasn't true?"

"You see?" Rheela said angrily to Calhoun. "You see what your interference has done?"

"It's enabled you to keep your home," Calhoun replied.

"It's led my son to believe that his mother lies to him! I don't want him to think such things! He's taking the word of a relative stranger over mine because he wants to believe so desperately—"

"Perhaps the reason he wants to believe," said Calhoun, "is because you've given him nothing else to believe in."

Frosting the air with her words, she said, "It's. None. Of. Your. Business."

Moke had no patience with any of the discussion back and forth. He had not taken his eyes off Calhoun, and now he said, "Are you my dad? Yes or no?"

At that simple, straightforward question, Calhoun reined up his luukab and looked, with a touch of sadness, at Moke. "Not to my knowledge . . . no."

At first there was no change at all in Moke's expression . . . and then his eyes started to tear up, and he looked with infinite tragedy at Calhoun. "Well, then . . . then why did you—?"

"Because I was trying to help."

"But we weren't asking for your help," said Rheela.

But before she could say more, to her astonishment, Moke turned on her. "*Why* didn't we?" he demanded, his childish voice rising in ire and timbre. "Why don't we? Why don't we ever ask for help?"

"Moke, that's not the poi—"

He acted as if she hadn't even spoken. "We help people! You keep telling me, we're here because you want to help! Because you gotta help! Because the whole reason you make rain is that you have to help other people! A whole town of people! And when one guy tries to help us, you get all mean at him and tell him not to! Why does everybody get help except us!"

"Moke . . . please . . . it's . . . it's difficult to understand, I know . . ."

"Lots of stuff is, Ma! But you can always explain it to me! So explain this! Please! I wanna understand, I really wanna. Can you explain it?"

Rheela, feeling utterly helpless, looked from Moke to Calhoun and back again. The three of them had come to a halt there on the plain, with the moon high in the sky. The farmhouse was not far off, and Rheela seemed to consider the situation for a long moment. Then, very quietly, she said, "Moke . . . the Majister and I need to talk. In private. Why don't you," and she slid off the luukab, "ride the rest of the way? When you get home, get into bed, and I'll come in and talk with you."

"Will Calhoun come and talk with me, too?"

She licked her lips, which suddenly felt quite dry. "I'm not sure. We'll see."

"I hate 'we'll see,' " he said stubbornly, but he did as his mother told him. Once she had dismounted, he dug his heels into the luukab's side, shouting, "Yah! Yah!" in that high, childish voice. His urging had zero impact on the luukab, which continued its slow, measured tread toward the homestead.

"He's a good kid," said Calhoun. "He deserves—"

"Don't start," Rheela said sharply, waving a finger at Calhoun. Then she hesitated, gathering her thoughts. She began to walk in a small circle, her arms draped behind her. Calhoun, who might have been carved from stone for all the emotion he was displaying, simply sat and watched her. "Don't act as if it had anything at all to do with Moke."

"It didn't?" He sounded politely confused. Apparently she had broached a concept that was utterly foreign to him.

"No. It didn't. This was entirely, and only, about you."

"It was?"

"Yes. You wanted to show how in control of the situation you were. Or that you could be in control if you wanted to. So you just shoved yourself into the middle of everything, and you only made it worse—"

"How did I make it worse?"

"You confused Moke!"

"He's a child. Life is confusing when you're a child," said Calhoun. Then he added, with a hint of a smile, "Of course, it's just as confusing when you're an adult. The problem is, as a child you can look to adults for answers. As an adult—"

"You can look to the gods," Rheela pointed out.

"That's something of a one-way conversation, I've found," Calhoun said.

"We're getting offtrack. You decided to stand up and thrust yourself into this situation out of a sense of self-aggrandizement. That's all."

"Why do you assume that?" he asked. "You don't know me well enough, I think, to decide on my motives."

"I do know you well enough. I know your type."

"Do you?" Amusement sparkled in his eyes. She noticed, not for the first time, that he actually looked slightly attractive when he regarded her that way. But then she quickly brushed the thought from her mind.

"Yes. I do. Swaggering would-be heroes who think they're capable of running people's lives for them. Never listening to what the people themselves have to say."

"I'm listening right now. You don't seem to be talking, beyond scolding me. That's all right, though. Believe it or not, I'm used to it."

"Don't you get it?" she demanded, her fists balled. "It's not fair!"

He appeared genuinely puzzled. "What's not?"

"You said it yourself! There you were, having barely gotten through telling me that you're just passing through . . . and suddenly you turn around and attach yourself to our lives!"

"I'm not attached," Calhoun said. For the first time he actually sounded a bit defensive. "Nothing I said has changed. I *am* just passing through. But when I do move on, at least the people of the town will 'know' who Moke's father is, and you'll—"

"Have respectability?"

"Yes."

"Wonderful. Respectability for something that isn't true! Don't you see, Calhoun? I've been here for years, helping these people, and I haven't earned an iota of the respect abruptly accorded me when you—a stranger—suddenly insert yourself into my life!"

"So it would appear that, to you, it's not about your son either. It's about your own ego."

"No! You're twisting it!" She waved her hands about in flustered motions. "You're taking everything that I say and turning it around!"

He sighed. "I hear that a lot. I think I know a woman you'd get along with quite well."

"If she ean stand to be around you for more than five minutes, she's a very impressive woman."

"I tend to agree."

She rubbed her eyes tiredly. "This is getting us nowhere. You refuse to acknowledge that you did anything wrong—"

"And you refuse to say 'thank you,' " he replied.

"I should thank you?"

"I think so, yes."

"Even though I feel what you did was completely wrong."

"Absolutely."

At that, she actually had to laugh. "Tell me, Calhoun . . . what color is the sky in your world?"

He got that far-distant look in his eyes again. "Depends. Red, most times. But it has been known to change, depending on atmospheric conditions."

They stood there, facing each other across a greater gulf than either of them could possibly cross with words. Then, with a weary shake of her head, she said, "Do you have anyplace else to stay?"

"There's a small room in the gaol."

"And you stay there to keep an eye on your prisoners?"

"The Praestor was good enough to appoint rotating guards to

the gaol, so I wouldn't have to do it single-handedly. Actually, I . . ." he shrugged slightly, "somewhat insisted that he do so."

"But otherwise, you have nothing."

"No. Nothing." He didn't sound especially sorry for himself. It was simply a statement of fact.

She shook her head. "I'm going to regret this, I know it . . . but no one should have to call a gaol home. We have a spare room in the house. I use it mostly for storage, but we can clean some of it out, make space for you."

"Thank you."

For some reason, she was annoyed by the fact that that was all he said. "Aren't you going to ask why?"

He shrugged. "No. Is that a problem?"

"Aren't you wondering?"

"I would question," he said thoughtfully, "why an enemy would do something for me. I would not wonder about the motivations of someone that I considered a friend. I don't quite see the point."

"And that's how you think I should view you."

"How you view me is your choice." He paused, and then added, "I wouldn't want you to have another chance to think I was controlling."

They had been walking toward the homestead, but she stopped and turned to face him. He waited patiently. There was something about him that seemed to say that, given the circumstances, he could wait forever for something to happen. For just a moment— the briefest of moments—she had a sudden mental picture of Calhoun, wild and free and savage in aspect, crouched and waiting in hiding for some animal to come near him. An animal that he was going to leap upon and bring down with his bare hands, teeth and possibly a knife, if he required it. And she could see him just waiting, for however long it took. Even when he was motionless, even when he was simply waiting for her to speak, he seemed to crackle with energy and a faint menace.

Which, for some utterly perverse reason, she found somewhat attractive.

She shook that last thought from her mind and said, "Tell me one thing, Calhoun. What's going to happen to Moke . . . when you leave?"

"Happen?" He frowned, not understanding.

"You've told him you're not his father. But that's not going to stop him from attaching himself to you. And when you leave, how difficult do you think it's going to be for him?"

"If that's what you're concerned about, why are you inviting me to stay with you?"

"Because if I don't, all he's going to do is ask about you. You've set things in motion, Calhoun, that neither of us can stop. In the end, all we can do is make the best decisions we can and pray we're making the right ones."

"You see?" he said. "We have something in common after all."

They rode the rest of the way in silence.

She lay in her bed, staring up at the ceiling.

Moke had been fairly bubbling over with excitement when she told him that Calhoun would be staying there. He had done as she told him and gone to bed, but upon learning the news he started bouncing around with such enthusiasm that she was worried he was going to break the bed. She tried to calm him, to no avail, and in involuntary desperation, she glanced at Calhoun.

"Lie down, Moke," Calhoun said in a voice of command.

Moke promptly lay down. She couldn't quite believe it. Rheela didn't know whether to feel relieved or angry, and decided to opt for the former, because it was going to make her life a lot easier at this time of night.

Calhoun had spent a few minutes helping her clear out the back room, and had thanked her for her efforts. In many ways, she still couldn't quite believe she was taking the risk. This man had once tried to strangle her while she was wide-awake. Who knew what he would do to her when she was asleep? *You're crazy, you're crazy,* she kept telling herself, but she knew that it was too late.

She'd made the choice, and now she was going to have to live with it. At least, she hoped she was going to live with it.

*You know nothing about him.* Her inner voice kept saying that, and yet she felt as if—when she looked him in the eyes—she knew everything about him. Everything . . . and nothing. She saw pain in those eyes, pain as endless as the skies, but also the strength to endure the circumstances that had inflicted that pain on him. His face was a literal roadmap of all that he had endured. The places he had been were not clear, but the paths getting there were certainly evident enough.

*He could kill you in your sleep . . . kill Moke . . . kill . . .*

She saw a shadow on the wall and sat up abruptly, the bedclothes falling away from her naked body. Quickly, she covered herself, squinting in the dim candlelight from the hall. He was standing there, in the open doorway. She cursed herself inwardly, having gotten into the habit of leaving the door open. It made for a more pleasant breeze, and it also meant that she could hear Moke if he cried out in the night.

Calhoun was standing there. He was barechested and barefoot, and the thin blanket that had been on his bed was wrapped around his middle. Rheela was positive that her heart had stopped.

She tried to whisper, "What do you want?" but her throat was constricted. She had never felt such fear.

"I've been thinking about what you said," Calhoun said softly. He hadn't moved from the door, had made no effort to enter the room. "There may be . . . an element of truth in it. But it really was about the boy. I . . . saw a child in pain. I had to help. I couldn't . . ." He shook his head. "I couldn't . . . not help."

"Let me guess," she said, fright edging sarcasm into her voice. "You had your own son, and you were never there for him. You feel guilty over him. And now you're trying to make up for it by being there for my son when you weren't for your own."

There was a long silence, and then, very softly, he said, "Something like that."

She felt instant remorse. Here she had made what was basically a flip remark, intended as no more than a cutting jibe . . . and had inadvertently zeroed in on what was apparently a very sore point with him. For one moment she wondered if he was fabricating his response in order to gain sympathy, or something like that. Even in the dim light, though, she could see a brief slip of an expression, which masked a world of hurt. And then, just like that, it was gone.

"In any event," he continued softly, "if I did it badly . . . I'm sorry. If you do not wish me to extend friendship to the boy, I won't. You're his mother, after all. And no, I cannot promise I'll stay around. In fact, I can promise that I won't. People come and go in life, Rheela. I've learned that much. No matter how much you want them to remain with you . . . you can lose them with no warning at all. There is much to be commended in long-term planning, but there is also something to be said for leaving yourself open to the vulnerabilities of the moment. I'm happy to offer the boy . . . and you . . . what I can. I hope that's going to be enough. If it's not . . . tell me now."

She knew, beyond any question, that he meant it. If she told him to depart right then and there, he would go, without a moment's hesitation. And wouldn't her life be ever so much simpler if that were to occur. She merely had to give the word . . .

"That . . . won't be necessary," she said.

He frowned. "What won't? Offering you what I can—?"

"No, no. Leaving, I mean. You don't . . ." She suddenly felt a slight choking in her voice. "You don't have to leave. If you don't want to. As long as you don't give Moke any more false impressions," she added quickly. "No more making him think that you're his father, even for an instant. All right?"

"All right," he said agreeably. "Anything else?"

"No. No, that . . . *ahem* . . . that covers it, I think."

"Good." He nodded and said again, "Good."

And as he turned to walk away, Rheela suddenly spoke up with urgency. "Calhoun . . ."

"Yes?" He didn't turn back to her.

In a voice so soft she herself could barely hear it, she whispered, "Thank you."

Even with his back to her, she could tell he was smiling. "See? That wasn't so difficult," he said, with a gently chiding tone.

She lay there in the bed and listened to his feet padding away, and this time when her inner voice spoke, it was saying with open admiration, *You know . . . he's not so bad . . . did you see that chest? Not huge muscles, but what there is is great quality. Sinewy.*

"Shut up!" she shouted at herself as she pulled the pillow over her head and fell into a very uncomfortable sleep.

# HAUMAN & SHELBY

THERE HAD NEVER BEEN A TIME in his life when he didn't know what he was supposed to do, supposed to be, and supposed to accomplish. The fact that there was no uncertainty in his life had become so normal for him that he had simply learned to take it for granted.

Leadership of the Makkusians was hereditary. Hauman had been born and groomed to become leader, much as his father before him, and grandmother before him. He had been schooled in the ways of peace and neutrality, been fully indoctrinated in the laws and history of his people. Leadership held no fear for him, because he was as comfortable with the concept itself as he was with his own body, his own breathing.

He had never questioned any decisions he had made, knowing that they were for the best. In his hands lay the future of his people, and he held that future comfortably and easily.

But now things were different. Very, very different.

"Base betrayers," he muttered to himself as he paced the gleaming floor of his inner sanctum with long, quick strides. His forebears had trod the same ground, but he was certain that they had never faced the sort of situation that was presenting itself to him. Their portraits lined the walls of his sanctum, and he could feel the weight of their eyes and criticism upon him, waiting to hear what decision he was going to render.

In truth, he had already rendered his decision. It was simply a matter of giving the orders. But when he had learned that the *Exeter* had returned to the area after a month's time, he considered that to be something of a sign. Before he headed down the final path, he knew that he had to inform Shelby of the circumstances that had brought them to it. It was not something that he was particularly looking forward to, but neither was he going to flinch from it.

It had been an uneasy time for Shelby.

The good thing was that the missions that they'd been encountering since their departure from Makkus had been relatively mundane. Star-charting, observation of assorted astronomical phenomena, an emergency transport of needed medical supplies to a colony in distress. In short, things that anyone could have handled. Hell, that guy who was the gardener at the Academy—what's his name, Boothby—could have been seated in the main chair and captained his way through it all with minimal training.

The bad thing was that she was feeling ill at ease. There had been no further blowups or difficulties comparable to the Makkus incident, but she still felt as if her own people were carefully scrutinizing her. She supposed, in a way, that it was the height of irony. After all, she had handpicked them for their fidelity to rules and regulations. But in so doing, she had created a sort of ad hoc board of judgment, so versed and certain of the essential rightness of all things regulatory, that they scrutinized all her efforts with scrupulous precision. Basically, she had been hoist on her own petard, a phrase that she had heard on occasion, and which had a certain resonance to it. It probably would have had even more had she ever bothered to find out what a "petard" was.

She kept telling herself that this was a positive thing, this dynamic between the crew and her. That it kept her "honest." Because (she reasoned) let's face it: The time that she had spent with

Calhoun might indeed have had much more of a negative impact on her than she would have possibly wanted to admit.

It might be (again she hated to admit it) that there was something to be said for the attitude of Garbeck and the others. And the fact was that Garbeck's approach to Jellico was really the more correct one. Shelby had allowed her reactions to be colored by the fact that she had a personal history with Calhoun, and had felt that relationship was being exploited by Jellico for the purpose of monitoring Calhoun, rather than her rightfully earning her place on the *Excalibur* by dint of accomplishment. Alexandra Garbeck, however, was under no such constraints, carried with her no such baggage. She was simply doing her duty as she saw fit. Once the hurt and anger had faded, Shelby could see that more clearly—and even wondered whether, given the same circumstances and minus the aspect of the personal relationship—she would wind up doing the exact same thing.

But still . . .

In her heart, she knew that what she had done in order to help the Makkusians was correct. She knew that Calhoun would have been the first to pat her on the back and say, "Nice job, Eppy." More than that, though . . . the old crew would have been nodding in approval. There would have been Lefler, grinning at Shelby's cleverness, and Soleta and Burgoyne would have teamed up to get the job done *without* signing off on a subsequent report chastising her, and Kebron—well, he wouldn't have said anything, really, he'd have just stood there, but even so—

And McHenry, why, he'd probably be dozing, but, at the same time, ready to come to full wakefulness at the slightest hint of trouble, in that way he had which bordered on the paranormal. At first it had driven her completely crazy, but now she had become accustomed to watching MacGibbon—one half of McMac—seated at conn, always alert, ever vigilant. It should have been comforting, reassuring. Instead it was . . . well, a little boring, really.

The crew of the *Excalibur* had driven her nuts. The day shift, and the night shift as well. They had shared their commanding officer's knack for eccentricity, and because of that, had gotten on

Shelby's nerves. At least, she'd thought they had. Now, though . . . dammit . . . she missed them.

She could practically hear Calhoun's voice in her head, saying, *Typical woman . . . never knowing what you want and don't want.* Taking umbrage, irrationally, at the comment she had manufactured for herself, she started to argue with the simulacrum of Calhoun that resided inside her head. She cut it short, though. She had enough problems.

The business on Makkus remained a major sore spot, and nothing would have suited Shelby better than to have it end in a positive manner. Her gut feeling was that Hauman was going to see the light and realize that he could have it all. That he and his people could be part of the Federation while, at the same time, maintaining the integrity of their personal philosophies. Why not? After all, if the Klingons could belong to the UFP and still be the aggressive, warlike race they'd always been, why would the Makkusians be poorly served in a similar alliance, simply because they believed in neutrality?

When they had made their initial approach to Makkus, however, and Shelby had desired to speak to him, he had seemed tense and distracted. As opposed to the first time she had encountered him, when he had posed what came across as a pleasant invitation, this time he practically ordered her to come down. It made her uneasy. It also made Garbeck uneasy. As a result, she volunteered to head planetside in lieu of Shelby in the event that there was trouble. Shelby, however, would not hear of it. "I'm the one who dealt with him before," she said, "and I'm going to see this through."

Garbeck nodded without protest, which was something of a relief to Shelby. However, the first officer insisted on increasing the security guards. So, when Shelby went down, with her was not only security head Kahn, but assistant chief Wagner and a third security officer named Allison Lee—a strapping young woman who looked like she could probably break both Wagner and Kahn in half without even trying.

Hauman's gaze flickered over the trio of guards, and there was grim amusement in his eyes. "More protection than before, Captain. Do you believe that we pose a threat?"

"Simply being cautious, Hauman. We live in hazardous times. Unfortunately, when we don't have official bonds of alliance, it's difficult to know whom we can trust."

"Sometimes, Captain, even such bonds do not provide us with that basis of trust. Sometimes . . . those we trust . . . can turn out to be our greatest betrayers."

Shelby did not like the sound of where this was going. Neither, obviously, did the security guards. She noticed that Wagner's hand was subtly poised over his holstered phaser. The women were not being quite that overt, but they looked ready for trouble just the same.

"Are you saying . . . that you feel we have betrayed you in some way?" Shelby asked cautiously, aware that the answer to that question might demand a quick, self-defensive reaction.

But Hauman simply frowned at them for a moment, clearly not understanding what she was referring to. Then his face cleared. "Ah. No wonder you have adopted this . . . this defensive posture," he said, indicating Shelby and those accompanying her. "You thought that my people had an issue with you. No . . . no, my friends," and he seemed almost relieved to clear it up. "No, you have done nothing to earn anything except our eternal gratitude for your aid."

"Then . . . what are you referring to, if I may ask?"

Hauman took a deep breath, as if readying himself to make a personally devastating confession. "Corinder," he said.

"Corinder." For a moment the name meant nothing to Shelby, but then it came back to her. "The next planet over in the system. Your neighbors."

"Yes. Corinder. But they have not been . . . 'neighborly.' "

"I'm not quite following you," she admitted.

He laughed bitterly. "I cannot say I blame you for not 'following.' I can scarcely believe it myself. After all this time . . ."

"All *what* time?" She exchanged looks with her guards, who were obviously as befuddled as she. "Hauman . . ."

But his anger was already swelling, as if the mere act of discussing it was enough to drive him to bubbling fury. "They underestimated us. They thought our scientists would not be able to figure it out. That we would not learn of their betrayal. You, who are relative strangers to us, saved us from a pernicious threat introduced by those whom we considered longtime allies."

"I'm still not—" Then she stopped, realizing, her eyes wide. "Wait . . . are you saying that the Corinderians were somehow responsible for—"

He nodded in affirmation. "The disease carried by the insects, yes. We discovered signs of actual genetic tampering in the specimens we managed to capture. Tampering that infected the insects with a disease that had ravaged Corinder more than two centuries ago. In the spirit of sharing, they decided to give the disease—in a more heavily mutated form—to us, with the insects acting as carriers."

"Are you certain?"

"Yes. And I have to tell you, Captain . . . we are incensed."

He was not simply spouting off. He was fairly trembling with barely suppressed rage. Shelby couldn't quite believe it. This was the man who had been the epitome of peace earlier, the advocate of neutrality. "Hauman," she said firmly, "I can tell you right now that choosing a course of action when you are this angry is never a good thing to do. You have to think rationally before you—"

But he wasn't even listening to her. Instead, he had started pacing again. His fists kept clenching and unclenching, as if he was envisioning what it would be like to have the collective throats of the Corinderians between his fingers. "We had thought that they were like-minded," he was saying, and it seemed as if he was speaking more to himself than to her. "We had thought that we shared philosophies, beliefs, a respect for a system of thought that guaranteed peaceful coexistence for all. Such, however, is clearly not the case. They tried to annihilate us, through dark and pernicious means. And you knew!"

"We did not know!" Shelby said immediately.

Again he shook his head. "My apologies. My anger makes me

choose my words poorly. I did not mean that you knew of their duplicity. I meant that you knew there were these types of people out there. People plotting our downfall, people who did not care in the least for promises or allegiances or commonality. People who want only what they want, when they want it, and do not care in the least whom they hurt or destroy or kill. That is the type of . . . of creature that inhabits Corinder."

"But why? Why would they do such a thing?"

"We can only surmise at this point, but we think we have a fairly reasonable idea. Corinder, you see, is massively over-crowded. You have not been there, have you?" When she shook her head, he smiled grimly. "You would be well-advised not to bother. You can barely turn around there, people are so packed in. Housing shortages, food shortages. They have no self-control, the Corinderians. They multiply like . . . what are those creatures? Small, furry . . ."

"Rabbits?"

"Tribbles," he corrected himself. "We have endeavored to pro-vide what you would call humanitarian aid. We have offered of our services what we can, but the people of Corinder have always been most prideful. They claimed they neither wanted nor needed our help, although they always did so in a polite manner." He laughed ruefully. "Obviously, they have chosen to be polite no longer. They have chosen instead to try and eliminate us. By wip-ing out our population, they would then be able to take up resi-dence on this world. That was what provided the beginnings of our suspicions about the insects, you see. We are very similar in biological makeup to the Corinderians, and yet our scientists dis-covered that the disease the insects were carrying would not have the slightest impact on Corinderian DNA. That made our scien-tists think that perhaps the illness was more manufactured than it was a natural outgrowth. One thing led to another in their find-ings, and ultimately we tracked the problem back to its source: those bastards on Corinder. Well," and he smiled in a way that was not reflected in any other part of his face, "if overpopulation is what the Corinderians are concerned about, then we will be more than happy to help them solve that problem."

"You . . . can't mean what I think you mean . . ."

"What else is there for it?" he demanded. "They tried to obliterate us. They came at us with a sword. What would you have us do?"

"Beat it into a plowshare, as you did with all your other weapons."

"Not all," he said darkly.

She did not like the sound of that. "You're saying . . . you're ready to go to war over this."

"Of course we are," he said matter-of-factly. "What other choice do we have? What other avenue is there for us to pursue? None. None at all. If they are inclined to try and destroy us, we have no choice but to do the same to them before they are able to do it to us."

"That's not true," spoke up Allison Lee, and then she immediately looked down. "I'm sorry, I spoke out of turn."

"No, it's all right, Lee. Say what's on your mind."

She looked up, encouraged by her captain's words. "Hauman, sir," she said, "my family goes way back in military history . . . all the way back to Richard Henry Lee of Virginia, one of the founders of my native country. And I can tell you that the alternative to war is always peace, and that peace is, more often than not, made. The only question is whether that peace comes before or after people spend years killing each other. But if more people respected and practiced the art of compromise *before* wars started rather than after, billions of lives lost throughout the centuries could have been spared."

"An excellent philosophy, Miss," said Hauman grimly. "We had an excellent philosophy, too. One that spoke of peace and neutrality. But we have learned that such philosophies pale in comparison to people who have the will and the dedication to annihilate their neighbors without cause, without pity, without mercy. That is the mentality that we are dealing with here. And we have you to thank, Captain," and he turned to Shelby, "for showing us the way."

"Me?" she said in surprise.

He nodded. "You have made us realize that one has to be willing to look beyond immediate philosophies. You have made us realize that we must consider . . . the big picture." She winced when he said that, but he continued. "I think it very likely that we will wind up joining your Federation, for the truth of just how dangerous a galaxy we live in has been underscored for us. But first . . . first we will dispatch our enemies."

"Hauman . . ."

"Please . . . Captain . . ." and he looked at her with an air of infinite tragedy. "Do not make this . . . any more difficult for us than it already is. Wish us well . . . and pray for us, to whatever gods you worship, that we shall come through this waking nightmare. For we must kill our neighbors now . . . and there are a great deal of preparations to be made for doing so."

Hauman stood alone for some time after that, the sound of the *Exeter*'s transporters still ringing in his ears. He felt the weight of the eyes of his ancestors still upon him.

"The big picture," he said again, with a certain degree of reverence. It was his new philosophy.

He missed the old one sorely. But every child, he reasoned, has to come of age sooner or later.

# CALHOUN

HE LIKED THE MOTHER. And the boy. Except he couldn't shake himself from thinking of them as "the mother" and "the boy," rather than by their names. He also knew precisely *why* he was having that difficulty; the reason he knew why was because Mackenzie Calhoun was forever cursed with the annoying ability to always know his own mind under any circumstance. Even when he had gone to Rheela after the fact and told her he'd been "thinking about" what she'd said, he really knew what his thought process had been. In fact, there had never been a time when he didn't know precisely why he did what he did. All the reasons, good or bad, moral or immoral. Every decision he made was pure and clear and made perfect sense.

At least, that was what he liked to tell himself. There were certainly others who would have debated that notion, but they weren't around.

Weren't around.

The days were turning into weeks on Yakaba, and Mackenzie Calhoun was slowly coming to the realization that his constant refrain of "passing through" might be serving as a nice, comforting personal mantra with very little relation to the reality of his situation. The truth was that he had absolutely no clue how long he was going to be marooned. That was really the word that summed up his present situation: He was marooned. For all the ability that he had to get off the damned planet, he might as well have landed on a desert island, with his only company being a couple of rocks and a palm tree.

Still . . .

. . . it wasn't so bad here. Really wasn't so bad.

In some ways, the frontier aspect of Yakaba reminded him more of his native Xenex than any place he had ever been. There was a distinct lack of sophistication among the populace, and there was something to be said for that. In some ways, Calhoun occasionally felt as if having too much knowledge was disastrous in the long term. This fairly simple life that had been presented him might wind up being a very unexpected gift.

The people of Narrin took to him as quickly and as easily as he in turn took to the job of Majister. Calhoun found the job had a certain amount of charm to it. The townspeople treated him with deference, bobbing their heads politely or, in other ways, making it clear that they had nothing but respect for his authority. It was both like and unlike being the captain of a starship—like, in that he was considered a central authority, unlike, in that these people weren't officially under his command.

Kusack, for his part, was not a happy individual. His leg had healed, and the door and lock had been repaired so that he was unable to go anywhere. He continued to make loud and threatening noises about what his brothers were going to do when they mustered the nerve to come back and face Calhoun once more. This didn't worry Calhoun himself especially, but he was concerned about others who might run into trouble as a result of the brothers' ire. Calhoun, after all, was not at the gaol all the time. The perpetually cranky Ronk was his main substitute when Calhoun was off duty. As near as Calhoun could determine, Ronk had taken on the job primarily so that he would have something to complain about. He complained when he arrived for his shift, he complained when he switched back off with Calhoun. But when Calhoun asked him why he was offering his services if he found it so personally inconvenient, Ronk would just give Calhoun a pitying look, as if he were the dumbest thing ever to set foot on Yakaba, and then go about his business.

Still, Kusack's continued imprisonment while the Circuit Judiciary was making his rounds was of concern to Calhoun, primarily because he didn't know what Kusack's still-at-liberty brothers were up to. So, at one point, Calhoun took it upon himself to organize a small group of men and head out to the last-known residence of Kusack's still-living brothers, Temo and Qinos. The problem was that he arrived there to find it deserted. Not only was it deserted, but he also discovered that certain key things were missing, such as toothbrushes and other scrubbing and bodily amenities.

"You don't possibly think," Howzer said, with obvious disdain and even a small bit of disbelief, "that creatures such as they care about such esoteric, social niceties as cleanliness." He stood in the middle of their ramshackle home, exuding obvious disgust.

"I wouldn't know about the one named Qinos," Calhoun said calmly, "but I was pretty up close to Temo. His clothes may have been shabby, but they were clean. His mouth, likewise, did not seem to emit any particular odor, and his teeth did not appear to be rotting. Instead, they seemed well cared for. His hair was washed and devoid of any insects. In short, he seemed to have quite a thorough grasp of personal hygiene. Based on that, I'd say that he cleared out of here and decided to take his implements for that with him."

There was active discussion then about the prospect of chasing them down. They were, after all, responsible for the death of the Majister. Calhoun was more than ready to attend to it, but the consensus of the council was that, since they had apparently departed Narrin Province, they were no longer of any concern. This did not sit well with Calhoun at all, for the thought of murderers running around unpunished was not a comfortable one for him. However, a point was made that he really couldn't refute: What if Temo and Qinos eventually doubled back to Narrin to cause trouble while Calhoun was out looking for them? Calhoun was, after all, just one man, and his primary function was to protect and serve the people of Narrin. He couldn't very well do that if he were chasing a couple of outlaws all over the place. Calhoun really had no response to that, and so he decided to stay put.

A lot of his time as Majister was spent attending to small squabbles and such in the city itself. He quickly discovered that his position was more than just strong-arming outlaws and such. Mostly, he served as an arbiter of assorted small disputes that he would either encounter in his rounds of the city, or people would come directly to him and ask him to settle. In such instances, Calhoun endeavored to settle the problems with as much fairness and evenhandedness as he could muster. He liked to think that, for the most part, he was successful. Certainly people weren't killing each other over minor arguments, which was a distinct plus.

He spent the rest of the time helping Rheela around the farm. She seemed appreciative of the help and, of course, Moke loved having him around.

He had one other endeavor that he embarked upon in his spare moments . . . and that was searching for the crash site. His personal shuttle had exploded on impact, the nature of his injuries made him reasonably sure of that. The problem was that he had been so dazed and confused during the crash that he had no clear idea of where he had actually come down. He hadn't calculated any landing coordinates; instead, he had ridden the equivalent of a falling rock down from the sky and just held on as best he could. Furthermore, he had no clue which direction he had gone once he had managed his "landing." North, south, east, west, and anything in between were all possibilities, and he couldn't even begin to guess which way to go first.

Nevertheless, "guess" he did. The fortunate thing was that he knew that he'd gone on foot. He didn't know how long he'd been walking, but he surmised that it couldn't have been for all that long. Hours, maybe a day or two at most. If he'd had some sort of air vehicle that would allow him to get an aerial view of the area, he would have been able to locate it in no time. As it was, he had to depend on his own two feet or, at best, the luukab to bring him around. He kept meticulous record of the areas he'd searched in, so as not to repeat himself. He also kept fighting the worry that someone had already located the crash site and had stripped it for whatever useful items might still be there. He especially didn't like the notion that Tapinza might have done so. He didn't want to think about what that bully and schemer might do with such objects if he got his hands on them.

At least Tapinza seemed to know enough to stay out of Calhoun's way. On those occasions when he would encounter him in town, Tapinza would nod and greet him, and even smile as if he was pleased to see him. No comment was ever made over the fact that Calhoun had knocked him cold with one punch that night. Perhaps the fact that it had, indeed, required only one punch was the reason for the unspoken agreement to say nothing about it. Still, Calhoun was not about to be foolish enough to let his guard down. He knew that Tapinza was bad news, and intended to keep a wary eye on him.

The problem was that Tapinza remained the only shot Calhoun had at getting off Yakaba. He had made a few inquiries of his own, subtly of course, and discovered that basically Tapinza had not been lying when he spoke of the stunted technological condition of this world. Not only was there almost no advancement in that realm, but there were still many who were suspicious of such things. Apparently it stemmed from a fundamental religious or social credo that went back many decades, perhaps even centuries. The philosophy was simple: That which their main god, Kolk'r, had intended them to have, he had put there for them. They had made some advancement, obviously; otherwise they'd all be naked (which certainly would have solved Calhoun's problems with concealed weapons). But there was still tremendous resistance to anything manufactured, as if it was . . . inappropriate somehow.

It was the origins of the plasers that Calhoun found the most disturbing. They had only started coming into use about ten years earlier, and no one had any real clue who had developed them. They became so popular, so quickly, that the homicide rate had skyrocketed. Indeed, it was because of the development of plasers, and their ready availability, that the position of "Majister" had come into being. Not only that, but the advent of plasers put a further crimp in the philosophies of the "techies," who still advocated that technology was the wave of the future for Yakaba. For the opponents of such thoughts—and there were many—were able to point to plasers as an example of how unfettered technology could lead a world down a path of total destruction.

Calhoun had his own suspicions about the origins of plasers, and all of them led him straight to Tapinza. But he couldn't prove it. Tapinza had interests throughout the continent, and if he was manufacturing weaponry and such, Calhoun had no way of pinning it down or researching it. The problem was that the various cities of Yakaba were relatively isolated. Transportation was limited to animals, and the distances between the cities made any crossing a challenge, at best. Calhoun made some subtle inquiries as to Tapinza's holdings, but the information he received was contradictory. He was certain that, if he devoted all his energy to it, somehow he could find a way to bring Tapinza down, in the long term.

The problem was that he lacked the facilities to do so. He never thought he would consider his battle to free Xenex, back in his teens, as something that was easy. But, comparatively speaking, it was. In that case, he was able to unite all his people, through his fire and passion, into a group with a single purpose in mind: Freedom from an oppressor. But Tapinza, damn him, was popular. It was impossible for Calhoun, the outsider, to foment rebellion among a populace against an individual they knew and trusted. Oh, sure, he could kill Tapinza. That was a nice, simple way to attend to the matter. But simply killing the man in cold blood didn't sit well with Calhoun. In self-defense, in battle, yes—then it was justifiable. That wasn't the case here, though. Tapinza was subtler than that, which meant that Calhoun had to be that way as well.

"Maester!"

Tapinza turned and was obviously startled as Calhoun approached him. The Majister did so with a ready smile and a calm, pleasant look in his eyes. People whom Calhoun passed on the street doffed their hats to him or greeted him by the title of his office, and he smiled in return and said hello even as he drew near Tapinza. "I have an offer to make you."

"Do you?"

Calhoun draped an arm around his shoulders. "I was thinking that I might indeed be able to help your researchers with their work on communications devices."

"Really. I thought you felt yourself to be not particularly useful in that regard," Tapinza said judiciously.

"Well, I've been remembering a few things . . ."

"Majister," Tapinza said, sounding a bit scolding. "Have you been holding out on me?"

"Perhaps. One has to be cautious in determining who one's friends are."

"And you think me your friend?"

"No," Calhoun replied. "But I think you are a potential ally."

"Really."

They were standing in the main street of the city, and Calhoun glanced around with unconcealed annoyance. "To be honest, Maester, I'm not entirely certain how you manage it. Manage to tolerate people who are clearly so backward. I considered it a pleasant change of pace for a time, but frankly . . ." He shook his head. "Well, let us just say that what charm there is tends to wear thin after a while."

"I fully understand," Tapinza said sympathetically. "However, I've been doing some thinking too, Majister. About you, about this 'situation,' as you would say."

"Oh, have you?"

"Yes, and to be equally as candid with you as you have been with me . . . I think that your presence here can only be of benefit to this city."

"Is that a fact?"

"That is very much a fact. I think, truthfully, that you should remain here a long time. A long . . . long time."

"Really. And here I thought you would have been anxious to get rid of me," Calhoun said.

"Well," laughed Tapinza heartily, patting Calhoun on the shoulder, "everyone's entitled to change their mind. I like the notion of watching you stay here . . . day after scorching day, night after endless night . . . looking to the stars that you came from and knowing that they're forever denied you. Yes, Calhoun . . . I like that notion quite a lot."

He chucked Calhoun under the chin.

Tapinza didn't remember much after that.

And as Calhoun walked away, leaving Tapinza's insensate body behind him, he chided himself that continuing to knock unconscious the one person who could be of benefit to him was, perhaps, not the smartest way to go.

That evening, as he rode back to the homestead, he was starting to wonder if perhaps he wasn't going about this the right way. Furthermore, he wondered about the reason that he might not be going about it the right way.

He always knew his mind. He liked to believe that. He held to that belief very, very dearly. Because to know one's mind means that one will not do anything for a harebrained reason, or trip oneself up because of uncertainty or second-guessing.

Yet when Moke bolted out of the house upon hearing the approach of the luukab, and Rheela followed right behind him, and Moke kept shouting his name over and over, waving his arms, it made him wonder whether he had been kidding himself or not.

Calhoun sat on the edge of the porch, staring up at the stars. He heard a soft footfall behind him, and didn't have to turn to know that it was Rheela. She rested a hand on his shoulder and said softly, "Thinking about how dry it is?"

"Yes," he lied.

"So was I. I'm sensing things as being . . . appropriate."

He craned his head and looked up at her. "Appropriate?"

"Even I can't fabricate something from nothing. Some elements have to be present for me to make it work."

He was struck, not for the first time, by the gentleness in her voice. The thought that he had tried to kill her at one time was repulsive to him, even though he hadn't been in his right mind when he had made the attempt. He felt as if that wasn't much of an excuse for having tried to hurt her. "And they're present now?"

"I think so, yes."

He looked up at the cloudless night sky. "Doesn't look that way from here. Looks pretty normal . . . which is to say, bone-dry."

"It has nothing to do with how things look. It's how they feel," and she tapped her breast, "here. And there." She gestured around her. She removed her shoes and stepped down into the dirt, which was still warm after the long day of having the sun pound down upon it. She closed her eyes and began to rock gently, swaying to a breeze that only she could feel. Speaking so softly that he had to strain to hear her, she said, "Oh, yes. Yes . . . this is going to be a large one."

"Is it?" he asked, one eyebrow cocked skeptically.

If she noticed the faint sarcasm in his voice, she didn't acknowledge it. Instead, she continued to sway back and forth, and suddenly Calhoun could feel the wind whipping up more fiercely than it had before. There was a repeated thumping, which he quickly realized was the front door of the house, and as he glanced at it, he saw Moke watching through one window with wide eyes and excited face.

There had been no clouds before, Calhoun would have sworn to it. They were sweeping in now, though, thick and dark, and he could swear that he even saw hints of electricity jumping around in some of them, lightning playing hide-and-seek with the thunder.

He had trouble believing what he was seeing. Granted, Calhoun was accustomed to seeing some very strange things, but even so, this was a new one on him. The wind whipped Rheela's simple dress around, and he couldn't help but notice that her legs were lean and muscular. As for Rheela, her eyes were closed, her head tilted back, her arms out to either side as if she was gathering in the random elements of the weather to herself. He tried to fathom how in the world she was doing it. There had to be some sort of scientific explanation. A person couldn't just command the weather through sheer force of will. It was more magic than science. . . .

Then again . . . what was extrasensory perception, or telekinesis, or empathy, except phenomena that would have once been ascribed to magic? On old Earth, they had burned anyone who displayed such tendencies, accusing them of being in league with dark or evil spirits. Scientists hadn't really managed to break down such talents into "nonmagic" terms, but instead had simply given them a different name and proclaimed—having done so—that they were now the province of science rather than sorcery. But just saying it didn't make it so. Perhaps science, in the final analysis, was simply magic with delusions of lack of grandeur.

Then large droplets of water fell on Calhoun's face. It was not angry rain but, instead, gentle, almost caressing. At first there were wide spaces in between the drops, but they closed up in fairly short order as the drops came down harder and faster.

Rheela laughed girlishly. It was clear that she was inordinately pleased with herself. She danced about, pirouetting in the rain. "Happy?" called Calhoun, shouting above thunder that was rumbling some miles away.

*"Ecstatic!"* she proclaimed.

"Why do you do it?! Why do you bestow this . . . this miracle on people who don't appreciate it!"

"Because I have to give it to somebody!" Her eyes still closed, she stuck her tongue out and tasted the drops as they ran down it and into her throat. "It might as well be to them! I'm hoping that they come around!"

"And if they never do?"

"I don't care!" she cried out with joy in her voice. Her cares and concerns were being washed away with the steady pounding of the rain. "If they never do, it's their loss! But if I stop trying, it's my loss! Better their loss than mine!"

The ground was becoming soaked, turning to mud beneath her

feet, which were becoming quite mud-stained. She grabbed Calhoun's hands and hauled him to his feet. She spun him about, and it was all Calhoun could do not to slip on the increasingly muddy ground. She continued to laugh, and then her feet did indeed go out from under her. Calhoun, thrown off balance, had nowhere to go but down. She hit the ground, he tumbled just to her right, and the laughter continued.

He rolled over, propping himself up on one elbow, looking at her as the rain cascaded down his face and into his eyes. She was looking at him as well. He felt the electricity between them, its undeniable presence, and when she rolled up against him and kissed him, it was almost a relief. He put his arms around her, returning the kiss with passion; he trailed his hand down her back and felt the curve of her spine. The storm increased in intensity, matching the depth of her desire and need.

They parted a moment, coming up for air, and he knew beyond question that he could have her. That she wanted him desperately, wanted to feel the warmth of him, to join with him. Her heart was thudding so furiously against her breast that he could feel it against his own.

And then . . . very slowly . . . he released her. Released her physically, released her from the spell that had momentarily seized him. "Calhoun . . . ?" she whispered, trying to understand what was happening.

"I think . . ." He cleared his throat. "I think . . . I'd better check on the luukab. In the shed . . ."

She was trying to hold on to the moment. "Do you . . . want me to come with—"

"No." He said it too curtly, too abruptly, but there was no calling back the tone of his voice. Still, he tried to soften it as he repeated, "No . . . Moke's inside. You'd . . . best tend to him. I think . . . that would be best for him. And you. And us. We . . . each have our responsibilities."

He rose and walked away from her as quickly as he could. He didn't glance behind himself even once, because he knew that she was still going to be there. And if he looked at her at that moment, he would be back to her and in her arms, and then there would be no going back . . . anywhere.

To anyone.

He stayed out in the shed for a long time . . . long enough, he hoped, for Rheela and Moke to go to sleep. He considered staying out in the shed, but felt that it would be unfair to Rheela if she happened to be sitting up, waiting for him. So, after a number of hours, he crept stealthily back into the house . . . and, sure enough, there she was, seated on a sofa, doing needlework. She had cleaned and dried herself up from the rain earlier, and was now looking at him with cool-eyed assessment. "I thought you were going to be staying out there all night."

"I thought about it," he said. He hesitated a moment, and then said, "Rheela . . ."

She waved it off quite casually. "No, no . . . you don't have to say anything, really. It's all right. I . . ." She chuckled lightly. "I let myself get carried away by the weather. That happens sometimes. I shouldn't let it." Her hands had still been moving in almost automatic fashion over the needlework, but now she set it aside as she continued to look at him. "She must be very fortunate."

"She who?" Calhoun said, puzzled.

"She, the other woman . . . whoever she is." She smiled gamely, although she looked a bit sad. "The one you saw when you were looking right through me."

"Was I?"

"Ohhhh, yes. Yes, you were." She sighed. "What a strange pair we are, Calhoun. Only weeks ago, I was terrified of you. Now, I'm practically attacking you . . . and being disappointed when you don't have similar feelings for me."

"I do. I do have similar feelings for you," he said slowly. "But I . . ."

"You what?"

He let out his breath, slow and steady. "I don't think . . . they're feelings born out of anything real . . . other than need. . . ."

"Need isn't real?"

"It's not enough. Not for . . . not for people like us. People with obligations. Rheela . . ." He looked down. It was a remarkable experience for him. He had faced down all manner of menaces, had taken down armies. But there was something about the simple, open nature of this woman that caused him to trip over his own sentiments. Or perhaps it was less her . . . than what she represented. "Rheela . . . I'm . . ."

"Just passing through."

"Yes." He nodded slowly. "Yes, I'm just passing through. And if you and I go in the direction that I think we were heading . . . I won't be able to pass through anymore. And that's not going to be good for you . . . or for Moke. Because, sooner or later, fairly or unfairly . . . I'm going to resent you for it."

She leaned forward and took his hand in hers. He was surprised by the roughness of her palm. "You've known women before, I assume . . ."

"On occasion."

"And did you always have difficulty attaching nothing less to passion and attraction than a long-term relationship?"

"No. Not at all." He laughed deep in his chest. "I had opportunities, and took advantage of them . . . and never felt a thing. In fact . . . I spent a long time . . . not feeling anything. I . . . shut myself off, because it was what I needed to do to function. To do what needed to be done . . ."

"What needed to be done, Calhoun?"

He couldn't think of how to answer that . . . and so he said, simply, "Everything."

"Everything. I see. And how do you know when you're finished?" There was a teasing tone to her voice, but also a certain degree of genuine interest.

He smiled sadly. "When you die."

"Oh," was all she said, very quietly. She looked at him for a time, and she felt her eyes tearing up, but quickly wiped them away. Finally, she said to him, "You know what? I'm still glad you're here. Whatever you can give me . . . and whatever I can give you . . . well . . . that'll be just fine."

He drew closer to her then, and put an arm around her shoulder, and stayed there until the sun rose in the morning.

# SHELBY

SHELBY, LOST IN THOUGHT as she sat in the ready room, didn't realize that Garbeck was standing in front of her until she heard the loud clearing of her throat. At that point, she wondered just how long the first officer had been standing there. Garbeck gave no indication of that, of course. She was too highly trained an officer for that, and wouldn't dream of intruding on her captain until such time that her presence was acknowledged.

"Contemplating suicide, Captain?" she inquired.

It seemed like an exceptionally bizarre question, until Shelby remembered that she was holding Calhoun's sword. She allowed a small smile. "That is the traditional remedy for failure, isn't it?" she asked. "Throwing oneself on one's sword. It's the ultimate way of taking responsibility now, isn't it?"

"Failure?" Garbeck looked genuinely puzzled. "You haven't failed, Captain. If anything . . ." She paused and then drew herself up straight. "If anything," she said firmly, "I'm the one who's failed."

Shelby stared up at her, flummoxed. "You, Number One? In what respect?"

"In what respect? Captain, the simple fact is . . . you were right."

"I was unaware the fact was as simple as all that." She gestured for Garbeck to take a seat, which she did, looking very stiff and formal as she did so.

"Captain . . . your instincts were correct. That's the harsh truth of it. My contention that we had no right to interfere with the situation on Makkus hinged on the concept that the indigenous life form—the bugs—had developed the disease they were carrying all on their own. But we now know that wasn't the case. And since it apparently involved attempts by another race to exterminate the Makkusians, that certainly would have fallen within the parameters of permissible involvement, even under the Prime Directive. But I was . . ." She cleared her throat. "I was bound by rules and regs, and didn't see that which was painfully obvious to you."

"There was nothing painfully obvious about it, Number One." Shelby shook her head. "I'd be lying if I told you that I had some great instinct that there was more to the infestation than I was admitting. All I knew was that I wanted to help those people. The regs didn't matter to me at that point . . . which was kind of astounding to me, considering how much they mattered to me when I was . . . well, when I was in your position. In any event, it doesn't matter. None of it matters anymore, I suppose."

"There's no reason to give up at this point, Captain," Garbeck told her.

"Actually, there is, and you know the reason as well as I. Hauman has informed me, in no uncertain terms, that he doesn't want our help."

"Well," sighed Garbeck, "that's that, I suppose."

"Yes. Yes, it should be."

There was silence for a moment, and then Garbeck said briskly, in an endeavor to return to business, "Just a reminder: Starfleet has informed us that we are expected at the reception on Nimbus II in three days, as part of the welcoming ceremony for their joining the Federation—"

"I thought we could leave a negotiating party," Shelby interrupted her. She wasn't even looking at her directly. She was sort of looking off into the distance, talking as much to herself as she was to Garbeck. "I mean, that seemed a logical thing to do. I knew that we had to head out to Nimbus shortly, so that our time here was going to be brief. But I thought that, if we left a negotiating team behind, perhaps something could be worked out between the two worlds. But Hauman looked at me as if I was this small," and she put her fingers to within a millimeter of each other, "and he said, 'How are you supposed to negotiate with someone who is trying to kill you? Do you say, "Stop trying to kill me, please?" ' And all I could think of to say was, 'It's a start.' " She shook her head, discouraged.

"Captain, if there's one thing they taught us at the Academy, it's that a Starfleet captain can do anything . . ."

". . . but not everything," finished Shelby ruefully. "Professor Tambor. I remember him all too well." She got up, and Garbeck reflexively started to do the same. But then she saw that Shelby was lost in thought, pacing the room, so she sat back down again. "There has to be something we can do. Something."

"There isn't, Captain. Nothing that occurs to me, and certainly nothing that's within regs. We have orders that say we have to be elsewhere, and we've no choice in that matter. Elsewhere is where we have to go. In fact, we're already running late on that, since Starfleet did not factor in our time in returning to Makkus. We should be able to make up that time rather easily by pushing the warp engines a bit—nothing drastic, just a bit. But we can't—"

"Garbeck . . . there's something you're going to have to learn about me, and the sooner you learn it, the better off we're both going to be."

"And what would that be?" asked Garbeck.

"I don't do well with 'can't.' "

"Captain, no one likes constraints. No one enjoys being told what they can and cannot do. But limits are just a part of reality, one that we all have to accept."

"He never did."

"He . . . ?" She rolled her eyes. "Of course. Calhoun. No, Captain, he never did. Did that, in your eyes, make him a good officer?"

"Once upon a time, I would have said 'no' so quickly it would make your head spin," said Shelby. "Now . . . now I just don't know."

"Captain . . ." And she lowered her voice in a confidential, even urgently friendly tone, "Elizabeth . . . you can be a far greater captain than Mackenzie Calhoun ever was. All you have to do is be a better officer."

"See, that's the thing, Alex. A better officer . . . isn't necessarily a greater one. I'm beginning to think that true greatness comes from somewhere outside the box, you know?"

"I know. I don't agree . . . but I know." She hesitated, and then said, "Shall I order best speed to Nimbus, Captain?"

She turned to face Garbeck. "A negotiating team might still be able to—"

"Captain . . . we can't," she said firmly. "You know that as well as I, so I should not even have to tell you. We simply can't, and there's no way to dodge the Prime Directive on this one. We've hit the limits of what we can do. And now it's time to move on." She hesitated and then added, "Isn't it?"

"Yes. Yes, I suppose it is." Shelby had stopped her pacing, and she picked up the sword that she had laid down on the desk. She replaced it in its mounting on the wall. "Inform McMac that they should take us out of orbit. Set course for Nimbus."

"Aye, Captain."

"And, Garbeck . . ."

"Yes, Captain?"

Shelby smiled ever so slightly. "I know you were trying, in your own way, to make me feel better. You didn't succeed . . . but I do appreciate the effort."

"Not a problem, Captain. I'm sure that, given the same circumstances, you'd have done the same for me." And she headed toward the door, leaving Shelby to ponder the fact that, if it had been Calhoun in the captain's chair, there would have been no need for easing of one's personal pain or frustration. Because Calhoun would have gotten the job done, dammit, and that would have been all there was to it. And there would have been Shelby, shouting at him about the rules that he'd bent or twisted or broken, while Calhoun just stood there with that confident smirk that used to drive her insane, but now she missed as much as if a piece of herself was missing.

Would she have done the same for Garbeck? Probably. But for Calhoun? He wouldn't have needed it. And if he didn't need it . . .

. . . why the hell did she?

For that, she had no answer.

"Captain . . . with all respect . . ." Garbeck was pausing at the door.

Shelby braced herself. Any sentence that started out with those words never came to any good. "Yesss . . . ?"

"You might want to try to get some sleep. You look exhausted."

Shelby laughed at that. "Kind of you to say so, Number One. I appreciate the concern." And the truth was that she *had* been sleeping fairly poorly lately. "I'll take it under advisement."

"Good. Wouldn't want you at less than full capacity if we find ourselves in the middle of a battle."

She didn't bother to tell Garbeck that some of her most inventive and daring exploits on the *Excalibur* had come when she was so looped that she hardly knew where she was. Somehow she didn't think that would add much to the luster of her reputation.

# RHEELA

*"MA! LOOK! LOOK!!"*

Rheela was feeling in a particularly good mood as she came in from having harvested some of the liquid crops. The plants had been especially generous, providing her with a goodly amount of juice that she would be able to bring to town and trade with. She had decided to get an early morning start on it, and was pleased that she had much of the rest of the day remaining to her to head into town. Not only that, but it was surprisingly cool, thanks to the strong and steady wind that was gusting off the plains. She could feel it in her bones; she would be able to produce rain again quite soon, perhaps even today.

"Look at what, Moke?" she said, trying to contain her laughter in the face of such uninhibited exuberance. He literally could not stand still as he bounced back and forth in front of her. "What do you want me to look at?"

"That!" he said, and he pointed to the shed. She saw where he was pointing and then gasped in amazement.

Calhoun had just emerged from the shed, and he was rolling a very familiar device in front of him. He was grinning lopsidedly, in a self-satisfied manner that was quite evocative of Moke.

"It's a sailskipper! We built it! Mac and me! We built it!" Moke kept saying the same thing over and over, apparently under the impression that Rheela was stone-deaf and wouldn't hear it the first fifty times.

"You built it!" she said, with that tone of approving wonder that came instinctively to mothers throughout the galaxy. "You and Mac? Together!"

"Together!" Moke said emphatically. "From spare parts of stuff we had lying around."

It certainly did appear cobbled together. It wasn't remotely as slick and of a piece as the sailskipper that she'd seen Tapinza piloting. But it was an impressive achievement, nevertheless.

"We're going to go out and ride it! The two of us! Mac said we could!"

She looked at him but he was already ahead of her. "No, Moke," he corrected gently. "I said that if it was okay with your mother, we could ride it, the two of us."

Naturally Moke didn't hesitate an instant. "Is it okay, Ma? Is it? Is it?"

Fortunately, Rheela knew better than to try and stem the tide of enthusiasm that was gushing from her son. "Yes, yes, fine. I was going to head into town, and I thought you might want to come along. But if you don't want to—"

"No! I wanna go with Mac!" said Moke, and then added "Pleeeease!" after Calhoun loudly cleared his throat to prompt the boy that something further should be said.

"I see that resistance is futile," she said with a laugh, and then caught an odd expression on Calhoun's face. "What's wrong? Is it something I said . . . ?"

He forced a smile. "No. No, not really. Just . . . your saying that reminded me of something, that's all. Nothing to concern yourself about. So!" He clapped his hands together and rubbed them briskly. "Shall we take a whirl at it, Moke?"

Moke needed no further urging. Encouraged by the steady wind, he ran to the sailskipper and clambered aboard. Calhoun did likewise, shoving the vehicle forward with a strong thrust of his leg. The vehicle creaked loudly, and for a moment Rheela thought the entire thing was going to be torn apart just from normal use, but it held together admirably. Within moments, Calhoun and Moke were zipping away, accompanied by a high-pitched howl of joy torn from her son's throat.

She shook her head. "Men," she said in amusement, deciding that the male of the species continued to be unfathomable at any age. Then she climbed aboard the luukab and headed into town.

She was actually surprised when her arrival was not only greeted positively, but enthusiastically. She had barely climbed down off the luukab when she suddenly found herself surrounded by eager townsfolk with looks of hope on their faces. More of them were assembling with each passing moment, looking almost relieved that she had shown up. "Is there a problem?" she asked, a bit confused.

It was Praestor Milos, master of extraordinary timing, who was heading across the street toward her and took the opportunity to reply to her query. "Not a problem, now that you're here, Rheela," he said cheerily. "How goes matters with you?"

She was about to reply, and then she saw Maestress Cawfiel in the crowd. The Maestress was saying nothing, but the glare from her seemed vicious enough to burn her alive, if that were possible. She forced herself to ignore the ferocity of the woman, and instead focused on Milos. "They go fine," she said cautiously. "I'm pleased that you are so concerned, and would you kindly tell me what's happening—?"

"Well, to be perfectly candid, it's been a while since our last rainfall . . ." He looked around as if seeking confirmation by the others, and heads bobbed up and down in agreement.

"Not . . . really," she said, a bit surprised. "I made rain just the other day . . ."

"For yourself," the Widow Att said. It was hard to believe that there was a woman in the city who was even more crotchety and dyspeptic than the Maestress, but the Widow Att had a genuine claim to that honor. "You made it for yourself."

"What are you talking about?" asked Rheela.

"We . . . saw that the skies had darkened in the general area of your homestead," Milos said by way of explanation, looking a bit chagrined even to have to discuss it. "Seemed pretty fierce, from the look of it. But there was a pretty steady wind around the town—"

"Almost like a barrier," the Maestress now spoke up, each word drowning in resentment.

"—and it appeared to keep the clouds at bay. We really didn't get much of anything," Milos continued. "And our reservoir is getting dangerously low . . ."

"Please help us," one of the younger people said. Always the younger people weren't too proud to say "please," Rheela had noticed long ago. The adults and seniors were busy conjuring all manner of sinister motives, but it was the youth that were not afraid to seek out succor wherever they could obtain it. "Please," one of them said again.

"Of course," Rheela said reassuringly, and she patted the young girl on the arm. The youth nodded gratefully. "As it so happens," continued Rheela, "your timing couldn't be better. The conditions are exactly right. I should be able to create an extremely significant storm for you."

Cheers went up from the crowd, a smattering of applause that got a bit louder as Rheela put down the bags she had been carrying and prepared herself. She felt the gaze of the Maestress upon her, challenging her, as if she was anxious for Rheela to fail. What a sad and pathetic way to be: If Rheela failed, it would be the residents of Narrin who suffered because of it. How could a woman who purportedly wanted the best for her people wish for something that would be to their detriment? Well . . . it didn't matter, really. Rheela had no intention of failing. She never had before, and she wasn't about to start now.

She walked out into the middle of the street, stepping away from the crowd that was rapidly beginning to gather. She placed her hands together, palm to palm, and closed her eyes. There was a steady murmur behind her, people whispering to one another, for most of them had never seen her actually summon the rains. She had never embarked on such an endeavor in the town; usually, when specific requests for her intervention came, it was the result of a small envoy that was sent to her homestead specifically to request it. They would see her engage in her weather influencing, and report back to the residents of the city what they had witnessed. She had little doubt that, as always happened with these things, the description of the process was embellished to the point of absurdity. Still, the thought that they would look up to her and even be a bit intimidated by her didn't seem such an unpleasant one to her.

She reached out with her heart, her mind. She could sense clouds wafting in, and she urged the breeze to push them toward her. She felt the heaviness of the rain contained within the clouds, and urged them to release, caressing them with her mind the way a lover would.

Everything felt normal. Everything felt right.

And then . . . and then . . .

Everything felt wrong.

She sensed the weather, bonded with the atmospheric conditions . . . in every way, felt attuned to the environment around her . . . but it wouldn't release the rain to her. The breezes whipped around her, but did not attend to her. She called to them, begged them, pleaded with them with every iota of her willpower, but still nothing happened.

Long minutes passed, and she heard rumbling. But it was not from thunder; instead, it was the annoyed rumbling of the crowd as they slowly began to realize that nothing much was happening in the way of precipitation. She heard muttered comments of "What's happening?" and "Why is it taking so long?" She had no response, though. Everything felt right, everything should have occurred in the way that it always did. And yet . . . there was nothing at all.

"Is there a problem, Rheela?" It was the Maestress who was asking, and there was something in her voice—the sneer, the pure contempt that she appeared to be dripping with—that prompted Rheela to turn and face her with barely contained anger.

"What did you do?" blurted out Rheela. Really, it was an absurd question. There was nothing that the Maestress could have done. Despite her demeanor, it wasn't as if she was some sort of witch, casting an evil spell that prevented Rheela from doing what needed to be done. She had spoken more out of frustration than any rational thought.

Unfortunately, the words were now out there, Rheela's impatience with herself prompting her, unwisely, to misdirect her anger. After all this time, it was exactly the sort of opening that the Maestress had been waiting for.

"Oh, is that the way of it?" demanded the Maestress. "You withhold your abilities when my people ask for them, and then try to blame it on me, making it seem as if I am acting to hurt them!"

"I'm not withholding anything!" Rheela protested. She saw the anger on the faces of the people around her. The skies above might not have been darkening, but the mood of the crowd was, and very rapidly. She gathered her patience, tried to reset the tone of the moment. "I'm sorry I snapped at you, it—"

But her apology was far too little, and a bit too late. It wasn't heard by those surrounding her as their ire rose with each passing moment. "You heard her! She tried to blame the Maestress!" "She didn't bring the rain!" "She's holding back on us!"

"I'm not holding back on anything!" Rheela said, unable to keep the desperation out of her voice. Even before she did it, she realized that she was backing up, as if she had something to hide. As if she was afraid . . .

Which she was.

Her luukab, tethered nearby, was sensing the mood of the crowd, and was clearly unhappy about it. The creature let out a loud, mournful howl of concern. Rheela couldn't blame it for doing so; she was feeling exactly the same way.

"Look," she said with growing urgency, "something just . . .

just didn't . . . I mean, this isn't an exact science! The conditions weren't right, the—"

"You said they felt *exactly* right!" Spangler accused her. He was taking notes for that damnable newspaper of his. She was getting the distinct feeling that she was going to be the lead item.

"I know, but—"

"Sounds to me," said the Widow Att, "as if you're still holding a grudge about the Decency Act, and want to get back at us!"

Of all people, the Maestress was the one who said, "I would like to think that such is not the case." But then, eyes flashing with a satisfaction that was nearly wicked, she added, "Unfortunately . . . we can only draw the conclusions that seem reasonable."

There was no mistaking it now: They were converging on her. Rheela found herself presented with two choices: Either she had to cut and run, or she was going to try to tough it out, stay there and convince them that they were simply wrong to think that, somehow, she was turning against them. And she had almost no time in which to make the decision.

She made the only one that seemed reasonable: She bolted. Without trying to offer any more words of defense, she turned and ran straight for the now nearly frantic luukab. *"Stop her!"* several of them shouted. She didn't hear which ones, but it didn't matter; it could have been any of them, for they were all thirsty and hot and angry, and she had let them down. She vaulted onto the back of the luukab, dropping the satchels of her crop as she did so. Realizing that stopping to reach for them would be tantamount to suicide, she slammed her heels into the creature's sides.

The luukab was normally a very placid creature, and any attempts to urge it to any sort of speed were generally rather futile. But, considering the mood of the situation that confronted it, the luukab was more than ready to bolt with a very uncharacteristic, but understandable, burst of speed. The crowd was converging from in front and behind, and the luukab reared up, its huge legs waving above the heads of those approaching. Considering the creature's weight, if it came down on anyone in front, it would not go well for those who ended up under its feet. Realizing this, they dropped back rather than risk death. Rheela, for her part, clutched the back of the creature for all she was worth.

The luukab barreled forward, grunting and howling its indignation as it went. It nearly, but not quite, drowned out the shouting and epithets that were being hurled by the townsfolk behind them. And that was not all that was being hurled, either. Rocks, shoes, pieces of wood . . . anything that they could get their hands on, they were throwing after Rheela as she fled.

*This can't be happening! This should not be happening!* she kept saying to herself. She felt as if she was trapped in some sort of insane dream, even as she crouched low to avoid the debris being tossed her way.

And then a rock nailed her squarely on the side of the head. Rheela cried out and almost lost her grip on the luukab. The thought of what would happen to Moke if she died in this way was all that kept her going as her hands dug in and she maintained her grip. The luukab, even more distraught by the missiles being lobbed in its direction, redoubled its efforts. As the world swam around Rheela, the luukab fairly galloped out of town, leaving the shouts and cries of anger swarming about in the air like angry insects.

Only when the luukab had put some distance between itself and the city did it slow down somewhat. The strain on the beast had not been a light one. Rheela literally could feel its heart—or was it hearts?—pounding against its sides, and its breath was heavy in its lungs, rasping and straining.

But there was only so much attention Rheela could pay to the animal's situation, because her own plight was no less dire. She could feel the massive lump already swelling on the side of her head. Not only that, but nausea swept over her in waves, and she knew she was in danger of losing consciousness. She reached over and dug her fingernails into her forearm, afraid that if she passed out, she would slip off the back of the luukab and tumble to the ground. If that happened, she had no confidence that the animal would stop or come back for her. It wasn't the brightest creature that Kolk'r had put on the planet's surface, and was just as likely to plod away home—or even trundle off into the desert if it didn't have her guidance, there to wander and possibly even die. Then again, the last thing she should be worrying about was the luukab's likelihood of survival, considering her own was somewhat in jeopardy.

She began to sing nonsensical songs to keep herself awake. When the effectiveness of that strategy wore thin, she started picturing Moke . . . Moke, and Calhoun. She pictured Calhoun's purple eyes taking her in, looking her up and down and appreciating her. Imagined his hands running over her body, carrying her off somewhere private and doing things to her that she hadn't experienced in ever so long. . . .

And then . . .

Then she started thinking about Moke's father. . . .

. . . about that evening . . . that one, insane evening, when he had come to her, like something from Kolk'r on high . . . the way he had smiled at her, and he'd had those flashing, mysterious eyes, and a voice as loud as thunder and soft as the caress of an errant breeze, both together. She had thought it more dream than reality, but not too long after, she had learned the reality of it. And she had never told anyone because, really, what was the point? Who would believe her? Who would think it anything other than a flight of fancy from a possibly demented mind?

She started to drift and fought herself awake, thrusting her body to one side with such violence that she threw herself right off the luukab. She hit the ground, and the jolt was more than enough to propel her to full wakefulness. She looked around, her body aching, her head throbbing, and then she realized that she was no more than ten feet from her own front door. The luukab had brought her safely home—although safety was a relative term.

Rheela hauled herself to her feet. The world spun around her once more before settling down. Taking a deep breath to steady herself, she lurched into the house while trying not to fall over once more, steadying herself by leaning against the doorframe before entering. She was pleased to see that the room wasn't spinning around as she went to the mirror on the wall and looked into it bleakly. There she saw a fair approximation of her face looking back at her, except that it was covered with dirt and grime and a trickle of blood from what she now realized was more a head wound than a lump. It was turning several different colors, none of them good-looking and all of them unfamiliar to her skin. She reached up hesitantly, and then decided at the last moment not to touch it. Certainly no good would come from doing so.

Instead, she used a small amount (always a small amount) of the household supply of water to clean her face. She dabbed at it hesitantly, looking at the way the dirt smeared, and wondering just what she could possibly say to the people of Narrin the next time she saw them. How could she possibly apologize . . . ?

*Apologize? To them? They hurt you! They did this to you! They should be coming on their hands and knees to apologize to you!*

She knew that to be true. She knew that she had been ill-used by people for whom she had displayed copious amounts of patience. She had every right to hate them for what they had done. But she could not bring herself to do so, no matter how righteous that anger would be. Call her anything from an eternal optimist to an unmitigated fool, but she still held out hope that, somehow, she and the people of Narrin City would be able to coexist. It had become a challenge to her. That was, of course, a foolish reason to pursue this potentially idiotic endeavor. Here she was, telling herself that she was acting on their behalf, when actually it seemed that she was being motivated by matters of pride more than anything. Surely if that was the case, she'd be bringing down on her own head anything that happened to her.

*Tired . . . so tired . . .*

Part of her mind was warning her that she should not go to sleep under any circumstance. But she was exhausted, and that exhaustion was overwhelming any other notions in her head. Deciding that a short nap really wouldn't be so bad . . . and it was getting to be late in the evening, after all, so naturally it was about time for her to go to sleep anyway . . . Rheela staggered over toward her bedroom. She flopped onto her simple bed without even bothering to remove any of her clothes, and within moments was fast asleep.

She had no idea what time it was when she awoke. The only thing she did know was that the room was filling up fast with smoke, and she could hear the crackling of flames as they licked hungrily at the outside of the house. At which point she fell back into a deep sleep. . . .

# SHELBY

SHE WALKED THROUGH THE FOREST, barefoot, the grass cool against her feet, and she tried to remember how she had come there. She was not wearing her uniform. Instead, she was wearing a pair of blue shorts and a cutoff shirt that left her midriff exposed. Oddly, her hair was longer than she was accustomed to keeping it. She wondered why that was for a moment, but then gave it no further thought.

Small animals ran past her, pausing momentarily to look up at her in curiosity. A rabbit sniffed at her feet, a robin landed on her shoulder. And Shelby couldn't help but notice how quiet they all were. Oh, the rabbit, sure, naturally that was quiet. How much noise do rabbits make, as a rule? But there was no flutter of the robin's wings, no chirping as it studied her. Not only that, but she now began to notice that, although the wind was steadily blowing the branches, the leaves were not rustling. She wondered for a moment if she was going deaf.

A hand gently touched her shoulder. She turned and gasped, and didn't hear herself do so.

Calhoun was standing there with a smile on his face.

She smacked him across the face as hard as she could. It made no noise.

"How dare you!" she choked out. "How dare you go and get

yourself killed and leave me alone! You had no business doing that, Mac, no business at all!"

She noticed, almost as an afterthought, that he was naked. An instant later, so was she. She gave that no further consideration.

"No business?" Calhoun laughed lightly at that. "Eppy, it's not as if I wanted to be a martyr . . ."

"Yes, it is! That's *exactly* what you wanted, Mac. It's what you've always wanted. Even when you were a teenager back on Xenex, running around, waving a sword and howling battle cries and fighting for your people, it was never about them! It was about you trying to be a martyr."

"How would you know that, Eppy? You weren't there."

"I didn't have to be, Mac. I know you better than you do yourself."

He turned and walked away from her. Despite the frustration she was feeling, despite all the anger, she still had to admit to herself that—damn, he had a fine backside. Then she pushed those thoughts as far away as her subconscious mind would allow them to go. "Well?" she called after him. "Aren't you going to deny it?"

He stopped and faced her. "Why should I? If you know me so well, then it's really pretty pointless to deny it."

"But . . . but I was expecting you to."

"Then I guess you don't know me as well as you think you do."

She growled in frustration at that. "Now you're just being arbitrary, Mac! Saying and doing things like this just to frustrate me."

"I guess I don't have a hope of fooling you," he admitted, looking downcast. But then that familiar smirk played across his lips, and at that point she was torn between an urge to kiss him and an urge to kill him. "If it's a vote, I vote for kiss," he said, reminding her in a rather unsubtle manner that her thoughts were open to him.

Shelby put her hands on her hips and gave him her patented I-don't-suffer-fools-gladly look. It had, unsurprisingly, no visible effect on him. Instead, he said to her, "All right, Eppy. Let's allow for the possibility that you know me better than I know myself. On that basis, I should know you better than you know yourself. Does that sound fair?"

He dove into the water, which surprised Shelby, since they hadn't been standing at the edge of a lake a moment before. But sure enough, there it was, big as life, and Calhoun was paddling around in it with abandon. She tried to call to him, but he didn't seem to hear her. With an annoyed sigh, she clambered into the water and started swimming. She noticed that the water felt neither hot nor cold. Curiouser and curiouser.

"I said," Calhoun called to her as she drew nearer, "does that sound—?"

"Fair, yes, yes, I know what you said." She shrugged under the water as she started to tread in place. She was impressing herself. Normally she wasn't that strong a swimmer, but this time she was keeping herself afloat effortlessly. "I suppose that sounds fair, yes, but I don't know if it's accurate."

"Let's say that it is," he told her. "And, that being the case, let's further say that you, Eppy, don't know what you want."

"And you do, I suppose."

"I absolutely do, yes."

"Well? Don't keep me waiting. You have all the answers."

"All right," Calhoun said amiably. "What you want is to be me, in the worst way. And you are."

"Thanks a lot. I don't have to listen to this," she said, and she started to swim away. Yet somehow he was suddenly ahead of her. She wondered how the hell he'd managed that.

"I don't see why you wouldn't want to, " he said. "After all, you're the one who wanted to discuss this with me."

"Me? Want to discuss my concerns with you? In your dreams."

"In yours, actually," Calhoun said with a laugh.

She continued to float in place. "What do you mean? 'In the worst way.' "

"Eppy . . . you might not have liked my style. You might not have liked the way I conducted myself, or the tone I set for the ship. You might not have liked the way I played fast and loose with the rules."

"Actually, the thing I disliked the most was the way you called me 'Eppy.' "

"The point is, Eppy," he said, as she knew he would, "the thing you *did* like was that I got things done. You didn't agree with the way I did it, but I did it all the same. And now, here you are, and you want to get things done . . ."

"I have. And I will."

"I believe you. But in the meantime, the Makkusians are going to get into a war that could end up depopulating their world as surely as the bugs you destroyed would have done. You want to stop it."

"I can't."

"Can't, or won't?"

"Same thing."

"Not to me," he said sharply. " 'Can't' means being faced with something so overwhelming that no amount of determination or willpower is going to accomplish the task at hand. 'Won't' is a matter of choice, short for 'will not.' " It's a conscious decision not to accomplish something. That's what you're doing here."

"Don't talk to me about what I'm doing! You're dead, and I'm . . ." She hesitated.

"Foundering?" he inquired.

For a moment her concentration started to sway, and she sank under the water. With a quick kick of her powerful legs, she bobbed to the top again. "Foundering?" he asked again as if she hadn't momentarily disappeared.

"Doing fine, thanks."

"I disagree. You think your crew despises you, and maybe some of them do. That's an occupational hazard. But nobody becomes a captain to be loved. You do it in order to get things done."

"And you get them done any way you can?" she asked sarcastically. "The ends justify the means?"

"Yes. Absolutely."

"I don't believe that."

"No, you don't. Neither does your first officer, or the rest of your command crew. But you know what the difference between you is?"

"What?"

"You *want* to believe it. You just aren't ready to."

"That's it? That's all you have to offer me? Mac . . . you think you know me, but you don't know me at all."

He swam toward her then. She wanted to move back in the water, angle away from him, but she remained right where she was.

He put his arms around her, and she felt as if she was melting against him. Still she felt no heat, no cold, no anything, but the hardness of his muscles pressing against her was unmistakable.

"I know you so well," he said, "that I knew you'd deny it. Just as I also know that you're going to kiss me now."

"You really are crazy, you know that?" she said, and then her lips were against his, her tongue seeking his out. They were sinking beneath the water, and she didn't care in the least. The water rippled around them as they drifted down, down, and she knew at that point that everything he'd said was absolutely right, whether she wanted to admit it or not.

Suddenly there was a high-pitched tone, rather like a comm link.

The lake, and Calhoun, and the entire moment dissolved around her. She sat up, blinking away the sleep from her eyes, and the beep sounded again. "Lights to half," she said groggily, and the lights of her cabin obediently came partway up. The beeping continued, waiting for acknowledgment. "Shelby here, go ahead."

"Captain, we're ten hours out from Nimbus," came the voice of Lieutenant Carroll, the special services officer who worked the nightside. "Technically, you're not on shift yet, but Starfleet wanted to know if we could arrive sooner than the scheduled ETA, since some of the ceremonies have been moved around. Naturally, I had to check with—"

"Turn us around." The words were out of her mouth before she knew she was going to say them. Once she had, however, she felt relieved.

Carroll, on the other hand, sounded completely confused. "I'm sorry, Captain, did you say—?"

"Turn us around, Mr. Carroll. Take us back to Makkus, warp nine."

"Warp nine, Captain?"

"Yes, Mr. Carroll. Warp nine."

"Captain, with all due re—"

"Mr. Carroll, so help me, if you're about to say, 'with all due respect,' I'm going to reach through this comm link and smack you. Is that clear?"

"Yes, Captain," said Carroll, sounding totally cowed. "But I . . . I will have to inform—"

"Inform Starfleet. Inform the Romulans if it suits your fancy, but carry out my order, and I mean yesterday. Is that clear?"

"Yes, Captain."

Whistling, Shelby proceeded to get dressed, and as she did so, she mentally started counting. She was just pulling on her boots when a chime came from her door. "Come," she said.

Garbeck entered, looking as if she'd been shot out of a cannon.

"Ninety-three," said Shelby.

That stopped Garbeck in her tracks. "Pardon?"

"Seconds. It took you ninety-three seconds to get down here. I'm surprised. I was expecting you to take under a minute."

"Captain . . ." she began, very formally.

"Ah, we're back to 'Captain,' are we? Two days ago, it was 'Elizabeth.' "

"Captain, I was just informed by Lieutenant Carroll—"

"That I ordered us to return to Makkus. Yes, that's correct. You should be pleased, Number One. It came as a result of your advice."

Garbeck paled slightly. *"My* advice, Captain?"

"Yes. You told me I should get some rest. It took me another day or so to give your advice some practical application, but once I did, things became a good deal clearer."

"Captain . . . Captain, I . . ."

Shelby was beginning to feel better and better about herself.

"It's nice to hear that you've got the hang of my rank, Number One."

"We're expected at Nimbus!"

"One of the first rules of command, Number One, is that you should always do the unexpected. If the choice I'm being given is to appear on a ceremonial basis at Nimbus, or have a chance to accomplish something back at Makkus, then I'm going to opt for the latter."

"Except that the Makkus situation is no longer an option for you, Captain. You said it yourself: They're not interested in having a negotiating team sent in."

"I'm not going to go back and negotiate. I'm going to go back and talk some sense into both of them. I'm going to force them to listen to reason, to make the Corinderians understand that you don't go around trying to obliterate your neighbors, and I'm going to make the Makkusians understand that endeavoring to return the favor isn't going to improve matters."

"Except that going in with all phasers blasting isn't going to improve matters, either."

"I'm not going to go in with all of them blasting, Number One. Perhaps one or two of them if necessary, but not all. Oh, and have Tulley meet me down in engineering. I have something I need Dunn and her to work on, and it's going to have to be done fairly quickly."

Garbeck looked as if there were a thousand different things she wanted to say, but she couldn't bring herself to say any of them. Finally, simply shaking her head, she started for the door.

Very softly, in as neutral a tone as she could muster, Shelby said, "I guess you're going to have an interesting report for Admiral Jellico, aren't you?"

Garbeck let out a low moan and turned back to Shelby. There was no anger in her eyes, but, instead, only a distant sadness. "Why would I do that, Captain? What possible purpose could it serve?"

"Well, isn't that what you're expected to do?"

"I hear tell that one of the first rules of command is to do the unexpected."

The answer surprised Shelby, although, upon reflection, she wasn't entirely sure why it had. "Are you angling for command, Garbeck?"

"When you were in my position, weren't you?"

Even more quietly than before, so quiet that it was barely above a whisper, Shelby asked, "Of this ship, perhaps?"

Garbeck sniffed disdainfully. "This ship? No."

"Something wrong with this ship, Number One?"

"Yes," Garbeck replied. "It's captained by someone with whom I suspect I disagree on a number of major principles. However, I want a career that I can be proud of, and I'll be damned if the way I get my first command is by stepping over the body of my C.O., whether that body deserves to be stepped over or not."

Shelby did nothing to hide her surprise. "Garbeck, every so often, you surprise me."

"You surprise me as well, Captain."

"How so?"

"It took you sixty-two hours to turn us around. I'd thought you'd have us heading back within ten." And she walked out of the room.

# CALHOUN

CALHOUN COULD SCARCELY BELIEVE IT.

He had been walking here, there, and everywhere throughout the area whenever he had moments free, trying to trace what direction he had come from. Seeking out, with what seemed growing futility, the crash site where his shuttle was piled up. And now he'd found it . . . thanks to the guidance of a small boy who had had no clue at all that Calhoun was looking for it. In short, thanks to Moke, he had lucked onto what he'd been searching for all this time.

"This way, Calhoun! Now that way, Calhoun!" Moke had been barking orders as Calhoun steered the sailskipper, trying to keep up with the vagaries of the wind while, at the same time, adhering to the rapid-fire directions Moke shouted out to him. Every time he'd angle the sailskipper this way or that way, Moke would howl with laughter. It was nice to see the boy enjoying himself.

And it forced him to dwell, however briefly—and unwillingly—on all the years he had missed in the growth of his own son, Xyon. The son that he had rediscovered, only to lose him shortly thereafter.

He chided himself mentally. There was simply no point to berating himself or dwelling in "might-have-beens." Such second-guessing had never been his style, and he certainly wasn't about to start now. Things were what they were, and second-guessing himself wasn't any way to live his life. He'd made his decisions, and he had lived with them.

Yet here was this boy . . . this boy . . .

He could make up for Xyon . . . maybe just a little . . . if he . . . If he what? Stayed? Denied what he was?

Except . . . what was he, really? Was he a Starfleet captain? Or was that merely a crafted façade that covered the fact that this life, wild and free and open, suited him far more? There was Rheela, whom he knew was attracted to him, and the boy, Moke . . . well, he was just hungry for a father figure. Any father figure, it seemed, which really wasn't all that flattering to Calhoun. Even so, what else could one expect of a child so young and desperate for attention?

Nevertheless, the sensation of the bridge beneath his feet, the hissing of the door from the captain's ready room when he strode out to his post, the array of stars that hurtled by a starship cruising the spaceways . . .

And Shelby. Elizabeth Paula Shelby. At night, when his keen hearing told him that Rheela was right down the hall, breathing steadily and very likely amenable to whatever he might fancy, there would be Shelby in his mind's eye. If Xyon was the son who had slipped through his fingers, so, too, had Shelby been the fiancée who had eluded him. Or he had eluded her. It had been more of a mutual elusiveness, it seemed, neither of them ready, neither of them willing to give of themselves in the way that marriage truly required.

But she haunted his waking moments, even as the relative simplicity of life on Yakaba called to him.

"What's that?"

Moke was pointing ahead of them, pointing up at a ridge at the top of a small bluff. Calhoun, stirred from his reverie even as he automatically guided the sailskipper with ease, looked where Moke was indicating.

He nearly fell off the sailskipper.

He recognized the debris almost immediately, even as he guided the sailskipper over toward it. "What is it, Mac?" Moke asked again, not having received an answer.

"It's . . . I'm not sure," Calhoun said quickly. He glided the sailskipper over to the foot of the bluff and hopped off it. "I'm . . . going to check it out."

"Let me come with y—"

Calhoun wasn't listening to him. Instead, he clambered up the side, easily finding toeholds and handholds on the rocky surface. "Mac, wait!" called Moke, huffing as he tried to follow Calhoun's lead, but failed. The starship captain was simply too fast.

Calhoun reached the summit and hauled himself up. He dusted off his trouser legs as he stood and studied the crash site. The top of the bluff went off for some six hundred feet. Even so, it had been nothing short of miraculous that Calhoun had managed to prevent the vehicle from tumbling to the edge of the ridge and over. It was even more miraculous that Calhoun was alive at all, because now that he was there, he could see the horrendous amount of damage that had been inflicted upon the noble conveyance. Pieces of various sizes were spread behind and around it, many of them half-buried in the hardened sand all around. Even someone who was familiar with such a vehicle would be hard-pressed to figure out what in the world the thing had been previously. At this point, it looked like the remains of an undersized house. The nacelles, along with an entire side of the vessel, had been torn away in the crash. Pieces of shipboard equipment were strewn all over the place. The shipboard control console was in one piece. It had been bent in half, and the controls themselves were smashed, but it was in one piece.

Calhoun heard a crumbling of rock behind him, and some gasping, and he realized that he had completely forgotten about Moke. He turned just in time to see the boy hauling himself just to the top of the ridge and suddenly starting to lose his grip. Moving quickly, Calhoun snagged Moke's wrist just before he slid down and off, and hauled him up onto the plateau alongside him. Moke was scraped up, and the left shoulder of his shirt was torn. His mother was not going to be pleased. "How did you . . . get up here . . . so fast?" the boy gasped out.

"Practice," said Calhoun as he slowly walked the perimeter of the crash site. The boy literally followed in his footsteps.

"What do you think it is, Mac?" Moke asked, his building excitement managing to overcome his momentary exhaustion.

"I think . . . I don't know," Calhoun said. He disliked lying to the boy, but he wasn't enthused about explaining the details of where he hailed from. He proceeded, bit by bit, to look over the entire crash site, to try and determine just what, if anything, was salvageable.

Even though he knew he was wasting his time, the first thing he looked over was the comm system. Very quickly, he confirmed that there was nothing remotely usable in this ghastly mess. He could sit there and try to fix it from now to doomsday, and still never hear anything except for the sound of his own voice (which, he remembered with a rueful smile, was what Shelby had always claimed was his favorite sound anyway).

The problem was that, the last time he'd taken the shuttle out, it had been rigged for scientific investigation. If he'd been taking it into battle, it would have been replete with weapons. As it was, he managed to find the equipment box, but it had also been damaged upon impact. There were a couple of phasers in it, but they had also been damaged in the crash and the energy had leaked out of them. If he'd found them earlier on, he might have been able to find a way to shut down the leak. As it was, the uncharged phasers would only be functional as weapons if someone happened to wander close enough to him so that he could bash their brains in with the barrel.

He did, however, find the mines, and he couldn't quite believe that they had not only survived the crash, but had survived it with their functionality intact. Thermo-mines, activated by means of a remote control, used primarily for excavation. Two of the bombs had made it through the crash, along with the remote that activated them. Which was terrific, if Calhoun had any intention of going on a dig.

It was hard for him to believe that that was all he was going to find that was of any use, but such was the case. And as he continued to search the area, Moke's enthusiasm was unabated. "What do you think it is, Mac? Where did it come from?" Over and over, he asked more or less the same questions, and Calhoun kept having to say, "I don't know . . . I'm not sure." Only once did he need to scold the boy, when Moke tried to pick up one particularly large metal shard that—if he'd held it the wrong way—could probably have sliced his fingers off. When Calhoun snapped at him to put it down, he did so immediately, and didn't seem the least bit put off by the severity of Calhoun's tone.

Calhoun had, by this point, pocketed the mines. They weren't especially big, no larger than his palm. He had managed to find a working tricorder as well, and this he stuck into the loose shirt he was wearing, which was tucked securely into his waistband. He certainly wouldn't have minded finding a working phaser. The plaser weapons that existed on Yakaba were certainly lethal enough, but they were clumsy and hard to aim. They were adequate in close quarters, but trying to hit a target at any significant distance with the plasers was going to be the equivalent of trying to perform a ballet while wearing swim fins. He wished there was some way he could transfer energy from the plasers into the phasers, but they operated on totally different systems. Phasers were mostly energy-based, while the plasers seemed to be some sort of plasma discharge, projected along a coherent light stream.

"Calhoun," the boy said abruptly, and there was great seriousness in his voice. "Do you think it came from . . ." He stopped.

In spite of himself, Calhoun prompted, "From where?"

"From . . . up there." He pointed heavenward.

"What," Calhoun said cautiously, "makes you think it came from there?"

"Maybe my dad sent it," he whispered. "Mom told me once that he came from up there. Or that he was up there. Something like that."

Calhoun smiled sadly. He knew immediately what the boy meant. Obviously Rheela had been alluding to the concept that the boy's father was dead . . . dead and gone to "heaven." And Moke was simply too naïve to realize that was what she'd been saying. The thought saddened him. There was no point in leading the boy on by allowing him to believe that the crashed shuttle was some sort of . . . of posthumous greeting card from Moke's unknown dad. Then again . . . what was the harm in humoring him, really?

"Maybe he did send it," Calhoun said thoughtfully.

"Wow," the boy whispered. "Do you really think so?"

"Anything is a possibility, when you get down to it," said Calhoun. He turned his back to Moke, as if wanting to get a final look at the thing. As he did so, he removed the tricorder from where he'd stashed it and used it to get a quick geographic lock on his present location. With that stored in the tricorder's memory, he would be able to return to the crash site whenever he wanted . . . although he couldn't think of any reason he might conceivably want to do so.

"Wait until we tell Ma!" Moke said excitedly.

Calhoun turned and knelt in front of him. "Moke," he said very softly, "what would you say if I suggested . . . that maybe, just maybe . . . we ought to keep this to ourselves for a while. Just you and me . . ."

"You mean, like a secret!"

"Just like."

"Wow!" Then he frowned. "Why?"

"Well," Calhoun said, his mind racing, "what if you're right? What if your dad really did send it down to you? If that's the case, then he intended it for you and only you. Other people find out about it, they might try and take it away from you. And that would make your dad really sad, wherever he is." Calhoun hated to play on the boy's adoration for his departed father, but he really had no desire to have the natives crawling all over the remains of his vessel. He didn't think he'd missed anything, but he had a feeling that, with his luck, within ten seconds of examining the wreckage, one of the residents of Yakaba would discover a working phaser that Calhoun had overlooked and blow his bloody fool head off.

"Ohhhh," Moke said sadly. "I wouldn't want to do that. Not ever."

"Good boy," Calhoun said approvingly, patting him on the

shoulder. He looked at the lengthening shadows and said, "Probably be good if we headed back now. If your mom gets back home before us, we wouldn't want her wondering what had happened to us, right?"

"Right!" said Moke in a cheerful voice. All of this had become one great adventure to him. In a way, Calhoun envied him.

The journey back in the sailskipper was one long recitation from Moke about how excited he was. Calhoun let him natter on. There was no harm to it, particularly since no one was around to hear. As for Calhoun . . .

He didn't know what to think. He'd been holding out some hope that, upon discovering the wreckage, he'd find something he could use to call for help. But nothing had been forthcoming. Even the homing beacon, standard issue in such vehicles, had been smashed beyond repair in the crash. Once again Calhoun was struck by the fact that he had survived.

Maybe he hadn't survived. Maybe he was dead. Maybe this place was actually populated entirely by people who were dead and simply didn't know it, had not been willing to come to terms with their demise. Then he shook the notion off as quickly as it had come upon him. That way lay madness, and he had no intention of taking part in such foolishness.

A convenient crosswind caught up the sailskipper's sail, propelling them toward the homestead. Calhoun kept a steady hand on the vehicle's sail, guiding it with confidence. He thought he heard Moke say his own name, and frowned. Why would the boy be shouting "Moke" over and over again . . . ?

Then he saw it. Saw that the boy was pointing frantically at the distant point where his home was situated. There, spiraling toward the sky, was a fearsome plume of thick black and gray smoke.

It was at that point, naturally—naturally—that the wind chose to die out on them completely.

"No!" Moke screamed, kicking furiously at the ground, trying to get the sailskipper to continue on its path. But it was to no avail; the sail vehicle was relatively useless if there wasn't enough wind to keep it going. It was designed for entertainment and leisure, not a device intended for genuinely getting you where you wanted to go.

Calhoun did not hesitate. Rather than wrestle with the sailskipper, he jumped off and started toward the house. Then he paused, spun, and, with one quick movement, ripped the sail clean off the sailskipper. Moke let out a yelp of protest, not because of the damage done to his precious sailskipper, but because he perceived it as the final blow to getting to the house in time. Calhoun had no idea whether Rheela was in there or not, but he was not about to take any chances.

He ran toward the house, his legs scissoring, the sail rolled up and tucked under his arm. He kept telling himself that everything was going to be all right, that he was going to get there in time. Hell, she probably wasn't even there. But even to Calhoun, there was a distinct lack of conviction. It was as if he knew it couldn't be that simple.

The luukab was there. He was wandering back and forth outside the house, making a cry that sounded so mournful he almost sounded like a child bemoaning the loss of a parent. That, however, was not an image that Calhoun wanted to carry with him. Not for a heartbeat.

He got to the front, and walls of flame were licking hungrily at it. The heat was so intense it was like a physical thing, shoving him back. He bunched the cloth from the sail and held it in front of his face, breathing in and out of it. He searched for a break in the firewall, found it, and shoved his way through.

Amazingly, the fire had less force inside. No . . . not so amazing, he realized grimly. It had obviously been set, from the outside. Rheela had managed to make someone quite angry. Or perhaps it was Calhoun himself who had been targeted. After all, he had made some rather unfortunate enemies since he'd gotten there, and since it was known that he was residing at Rheela's home, it was possible this was aimed at him. In any event, there was no time to stand around and wonder about it.

"Rheela!" he shouted, looking around. The reasonable place to try first was her bedroom, and he ran to it just in time to get a glimpse of her lying on her bed. Smoke was pouring in everywhere, and Rheela was just starting to sit up, looking dazed and bewildered. He spotted a bruise on her forehead and then, as he started toward her, a flaming piece of the roof crashed through the ceiling, cutting them off.

He heard a shriek from within, and Calhoun did not hesitate. He leaped through the flames that had sprung up between Rheela and him, muttering a quick prayer without being entirely too sure that anyone was listening. He landed in the bedroom and saw to his horror that Rheela was on fire. Some of the flame had leaped to her blouse, and the back was going up.

Calhoun whipped around the cloth from the erstwhile sail and practically tackled Rheela with it, smothering the flame while watching to make sure that they didn't land in another hotspot. Unfortunately, the entire area was developing into one big hotspot, with nowhere to go. He turned to retrace his steps, but he was blocked. There was a window to his right, but there was likewise a wall of flame there, providing further obstruction. Unfortunately, he didn't see any other way out: He was going to have to chance it, hoping that he didn't incinerate Rheela and himself when he went through.

He heard another loud crack, and for just a moment he thought the entire roof was coming down on them. But then he realized that it was thunder; as if to make its presence absolutely unquestionable, lightning ripped across the sky, with the thunder accompanying it like the door of hell slamming shut. And then rain began to pour. This was no simple shower. This was a deluge—huge, torrential buckets, cascading down. Just for a few moments, the raging fire outside flickered, backing down before the wet assault, and those were the only moments that Calhoun needed. He charged the window and crashed through it, clutching Rheela tight to him. He felt searing pain and then, at almost the same time, the cold, healing touch of the pouring rain. He hit the ground, banging his knees up fiercely, before staggering to his feet and shoving Rheela and himself away from the conflagration.

He looked up, and it seemed as if the clouds were converging around the house like things alive. Moke was screaming for his mother as he ran toward her, and, injured as she was, lungs coughing out smoke the entire time, she still found more than enough strength to wrap her arms around her son and sob her relief that she was seeing him again. Meantime, the flames flickered and, in short order, died as the rain pounded them into nonexistence.

She looked raggedly up at Calhoun. Her face was almost solid black from soot; her eyes peering out from the filthy mask she now wore. But streaks were already occurring, trails of water left behind by the raindrops as they ran down her face. Amazingly, she was almost laughing. "Better late than never, huh, Calhoun?" she rasped out.

"Did you see who did this?" he asked.

She shook her head, but then she told him what had happened in the city. The failed attempt at rain, the way the crowd had turned on her, the injury she had sustained in fleeing. It became harder and harder for her to speak, her voice a scratchy and terrible thing.

But when it came to terrible things, her voice was nothing compared to the rage that was pulsing through Calhoun's veins. Then he asked a question, and he hoped with all the world that the answer would be "No."

"Do you want to stay?" he asked. He wanted her to say "no" because he knew, in his heart, that these people didn't deserve her. That she was operating out of some insanely misplaced sense of Samaritanism. Or maybe it was just pure pride that was keeping her there, preventing her from simply getting when the getting was good. In any event, it certainly wasn't any motivation that was a positive one. She should just get out and leave while she was still able to. He tried to impart all this to her through means best described as telepathic.

She nodded her head. "Yes." And then, as if to make sure there was no miscommunication or confusion, she added, "I want to stay. This is my home. I can still help them, if they'll let me."

His jaw twitched slightly. It was the only indication of the disappointment he felt . . . and the vague dread that she was making a horrible mistake that could come back and cost her dearly. But all he said was, "I'll take care of it."

He then proceeded to do just that.

# HAUMAN

HAUMAN KNEW THAT, somehow, it was going to come down to him and the Ferghut.

He had never particularly liked the Ferghut—the traditional leader of the Corinderians—but he had tolerated him, as was consistent with the philosophy that he had (until recently) espoused. There had always been something—well—slimy about the Ferghut. He would say one thing, and seem to be quite a good friend while saying it, but Hauman always had the feeling that he might wind up with a knife in his back if he wasn't careful. And how many times had he chastised himself for having that philosophy? How many times had he said to himself, "Shame on you, Hauman, for having such a low opinion of someone, with nothing to base it on except your instincts. What would your ancestors say? What would your priests say? How they would scold you for being so uncharitable."

All those times he had blamed himself for being a poor student of their philosophies . . . and now this had happened. This. And there was no ignoring the fact that he, Hauman, was partly responsible for it. He had come to realize that his sin had not been being suspicious, but rather not being suspicious enough.

Well, it was a mistake he had no intention of repeating.

The battlefleet had been mustered. Even Hauman had to admit

that it was not necessarily the most impressive of endeavors. Their warp-speed capability was minimal at best. Their weaponry, while effective for their own needs, was not remotely on a par with something like, say, that of the *Exeter*. . . .

*Exeter* . . .

Even as he walked the bridge of his command vessel, Hauman's thoughts turned to that magnificent ship. He had never thought about the *Exeter* in terms of its firepower and defensive capabilities, but instead only in terms of the people that constituted its crew. He had come to the conclusion that they were good and decent people. They had meant only the best, and he had learned a good deal from them. In the event that he survived this encounter, he would hopefully learn more.

Still, he had doubts about the likelihood that he would survive it. After all, he was the first Hauman in the memory of his bloodline to thrust himself into war. His was a peace-loving race, and he had never thought that he would wind up making his mark upon Makkusian history by being the first to toss himself into the crucible of battle. But Shelby had been correct: the big picture was what was necessary here. And in the big picture, it was clearly drawn that the Makkusians were going to have to strike back at the Corinderians and their leader, the Ferghut.

He had no idea of the Ferghut's real name. That was part of Corinderian tradition. They were as antithetical to Makkusian tradition as possible, and that alone should have tipped him off. In retrospect, he could only curse the blindness that had settled upon him and made him think that somehow, in some way, the Corinderians could be trusted.

In the case of the Ferghut, the Corinderians actually believed that the key to a leader's effectiveness was anonymity. Appointment to Ferghut was a lifetime position, and a planetary computer base would choose the person who was considered the most able, most capable individual. Once that choice was made, everything about the new Ferghut's background was expunged. The identities of friends, family, all of it was deleted. The Ferghut became a blank slate, onto which the future of the Corinderians could be written. It was felt to be the best way to handle it, since that way pressure could not be put upon family members, nor would they be at risk while the new Ferghut served his life term.

The position of Ferghut had changed exactly one time during Hauman's tenure as leader, and what had struck Hauman was that the relatively new Ferghut (he'd only been in the position for two years) was strikingly similar in attitude to the previous one. Obviously the computer strove for, and achieved, consistency. Then again, legend had it that the parameters within which the computer searched had been crafted by the very first person to hold the title of Ferghut, so essentially they were seeing a leader perpetuating himself.

*Look what I have gotten us into, ancestors,* he thought bleakly. But he had no choice, none at all. He remembered the last time he had seen Ferghut, how complimentary the Ferghut had been over the Makkusian advancements. He had flattered Hauman endlessly, and Hauman had wondered if the Ferghut was sincere, or if he was simply trying to put him off guard for some reason. Obviously it was the latter. But never in his wildest imaginings would Hauman have guessed the immensity of the Ferghut's plans. He wasn't just being laudatory to Hauman for the purpose of achieving some short-term goal, no, no. His goal was much more sinister: to put Hauman and the rest of the Makkusians off the scent while they endeavored to exterminate their race, so that they would have somewhere to move to. The immensity of the scheme was so appalling, that—even as he led a fleet into battle in order to eliminate whatever further threat the Corinderians might pose—Hauman could still barely wrap himself around it.

The Makkusians did not have a large number of ships that were capable of making an assault. But, with any luck, it was not going to be necessary. The Corinderians were no more scientifically advanced than the Makkusians; as a matter of fact, when it came to space travel, they lagged a bit. So an attack on the homeworld of Corinder should have, theoretically, been a fairly easy thing. But nothing was ever certain, and Hauman wasn't kidding himself. They were embarking on a hazardous and risky proposition, and anything could happen.

The bridge around him was humming with activity. The men and women who were monitoring the instruments were, for the most part, younger than Hauman, and he was impressed—and, admittedly, also a bit appalled—by the eagerness that they were displaying for the upcoming battle. Whereas Hauman had been fully cognizant of the tragedy surrounding Corinder's betrayal of their mutual live-and-let-live philosophies, the young Makkusians saw nothing except an opportunity to show a neighboring world that Makkus was nobody's target.

Hauman regarded his crew thoughtfully. No one carried any sort of rank, for the Makkusians had no such thing as a standing army. These people had simply been recruited as being the best and brightest that the Makkusians had to offer. First and foremost of the crew was a young man named Bibbyte. His eyes were alive with a fiery determination to drive home to the Corinderians just how foolish their plan had been. Derailing himself from his grim train of thought, Hauman turned and said, "Bibbyte . . . estimated time of arrival?"

"We will be within firing range of Corinder in," and he consulted a chronometer, "just under fifteen minutes. Have you chosen our preliminary targets, Hauman?"

Expectant looks came from all around the bridge. Hauman took a deep breath. "I suspect," he said, "that our first targets will be the Corinder defensive fleet."

"What fleet?" asked Bibbyte.

"The one that they will inevitably send against us. What . . . you did not seriously expect, Bibbyte, that they would simply allow us to open fire on them with impunity? They must know that we're coming by now; their long-range scanners would most certainly have detected it. And I'm sure that they can surmise we are not approaching out of any spirit of conciliation. They will defend themselves."

"They will lose. They certainly have to know that they will—"

"Hauman!" called Lio, who had been put in charge of sensor scans. "Incoming fleet of Corinderian vessels!"

"How many?" asked Hauman quietly. His own fleet numbered no more than a dozen vessels of varying size.

"Eight," replied Lio. This generated a laugh from the even-more confident Makkusians, until Lio added, "but initial scans indicate that their weaponry carries a charge roughly twenty-seven percent in excess of the greatest destructive force our own cannons can generate. Also, their armor seems capable of withstanding forty-seven percent more damage than our own."

There was silence on the bridge for a moment as the crew took this in. Hauman, who had been standing, slowly sat in the central chair. Then, very coolly, he said, "Bibbyte . . . let me speak to our fleet, please."

Bibbyte, who was looking a bit less confident than he had been earlier, but nevertheless determined to do his job, did so within moments.

"My fellow Makkusians," announced Hauman, "as you are all no doubt aware, our enemy has moved to engage us. Battle will likely be joined within . . ." He looked to Bibbyte, who held up two fingers. ". . . approximately two minutes. We outnumber them, but their weaponry appears superior to ours. However," he added, and there was a determined smile on his face that he hoped translated to confidence in his voice, "we are in the right. They have transgressed against us, and we will not suffer that transgression to stand. We will triumph over them. There is nothing more definitely written in the future history of our race than that. But even though our victory is assured, do not take that as leave to be overconfident; from such overconfidence does a humiliating fall extend. Be brave . . . be cautious . . . and, upon my command, engage the enemy at will. Hauman out."

There were approving nods from around the bridge. "Well-spoken, Hauman," said Bibbyte, apparently on behalf of the crew. "We will follow you into the gates of hell itself."

"Let's hope that you won't have to do so anytime soo—"

"Hauman!" Lio suddenly called out, and there was definite alarm in his voice, so much so that Hauman felt a wrenching shock to his gut. "Hauman, I—"

Hauman was out of his chair, coming around to Lio's station, almost afraid of what he was going to see. Hauman was no battle-hardened veteran, and wasn't exactly prepared for whatever unexpected shocks combat might throw at him. But he was determined to put as positive a face on it as possible. Lio's inexperience in combat situations was palpable, but he was putting up a good front, and Hauman was determined to do everything he could to help Lio maintain it. "Steady, son," he said. "Tell me what you see . . ."

"A vessel . . . huge. I think . . . I think it's a Starfleet vessel. Dropping out of warp!"

"Starfleet!" It was Bibbyte who had spoken, and he didn't sound any too happy. "Is it possible they're here to aid the Corinderians?"

"If they are, we're finished!" said Lio, looking ashen. "We . . . we can't stand up to the might of a starship! Perhaps, if we had spent years developing our weaponry, instead of . . . of thinking that it would never be necessary, then, yes, we could accomplish something against them! As it is—!"

"Do not panic, Lio," Hauman cautioned him, putting a steadying hand on the crewman's shoulder. He looked around at the rest of his crew, who all appeared to be a bit daunted by the prospect of battling a starship. "None of you panic. I know this 'Starfleet.' They will not interfere in a battle between—"

"They've targeted us, sir," Lio said hollowly.

Hauman couldn't quite believe what he'd just heard. *"What?"* He leaned forward and surveyed Lio's instrumentation. There was no mistaking it. The starship had indeed focused its armed might on the Makkusians . . .

". . . and on the Corinderians!" Hauman suddenly noted. Lio looked and saw that Hauman was correct. "They have both of us in their sights!"

"What sort of game is this? What are they playing at?" Bibbyte demanded . . . although he did so in a very low voice, as if the starship could hear them through the void of space.

"Hauman . . . I believe that this vessel is the same one that came to Makkus some time ago!"

"The *Exeter*. Captain Shelby's vessel. Somehow, I am not entirely surprised," murmured Hauman. "And if I've made an accurate assessment of Shelby's character . . ." His voice trailed off.

"If you have, sir—?" prompted Bibbyte.

"If I have, why, then, Bibbyte," and Hauman smiled mirthlessly, "then in just a few seconds, the *Exeter* is going to be—"

"Right in front of us!" Lio announced.

And it was absolutely true. The starship, having dropped out of warp and moving at high speed as a result, had inserted itself directly between the two fleets that were converging on one another. The only way the two groups of ships were going to be able to fire upon one another was if they literally went through the *Exeter* . . . and if that occurred, it was more than likely that the starship would have something to say about that in response.

"Shall I attempt to raise her via ship-to-ship?" asked Lio.

"Not necessary, I think," Hauman guessed. "I suspect that we will be hearing from them in relatively short ord—"

"An incoming signal from the *Exeter,* Hauman!" said Lio.

This, of course, came as no surprise whatsoever. "Put it on screen, Lio," Hauman said, not allowing any of the turmoil he was feeling within him to bubble to the surface.

A moment later, Shelby's face appeared on the screen. But the screen itself was split, indicating a dual transmission. There was another image on the screen next to Shelby, and Hauman recognized him immediately. Amazingly, his face had an open and "honest" appearance to it, as if he not only had nothing to hide, but wouldn't know where to stash it even if he did.

"Hello, Hauman," said Shelby, but her words barely registered on him at first. Instead, his attention was focused entirely on the Ferghut. The Ferghut, for his part, had his face carefully neutral, even inscrutable. Hauman made a mental note not to engage the

Ferghut in a game of bluffing, because he suspected the Ferghut would win effortlessly. It was impossible to tell whether the Ferghut was happy or sad, pained or relaxed.

"Captain," and he nodded his head slightly. He did not even bother to acknowledge the Ferghut at first, but then he came to the realization that the background behind the Ferghut was of the planet's surface. "So . . . Ferghut," he noted, "I see you didn't find it within yourself to come up here and face me."

"I certainly feel no need to do something so foolish as to put myself at risk," the Ferghut retorted. He did not sound defensive or angry. Instead, he sounded mildly amused. His tone of voice enraged Hauman even further.

But Shelby did not give that answer a chance to build. Instead, she said briskly, "By this point, you've no doubt noticed that my vessel is between your fleets, which are converging upon one another."

"Captain, as I told you moments ago," the Ferghut said, in a voice laced with tragedy, "they are converging upon us. We are simply trying to defend ourselves from this unwarranted attack. You make it sound as if this desire for conflict is mutual . . ."

"How dare you act as if you've no idea what this is about!" said Hauman, outraged at the sheer gall of the creature. "You know why we are here! You know what you have done!"

"Do I?" asked the Ferghut, the picture of innocence.

"Captain, in the face of such perfidy—"

"Again he insults us. Captain, surely you see that—"

"Quiet, the both of you!" said Shelby in a voice that indicated she was not going to put up with much more of this. "Hauman . . . the Ferghut here claims that he has no idea why you are attacking. Have you sent him a formal declaration of war, outlining his transgressions?"

"Why in the world should I outline that which he already knows?" demanded Hauman. There was nodding from all around him. He felt a degree of confidence growing from that; at least his own people were not being the least bit taken in by this nonsense.

"Indulge me," replied the Ferghut.

Shelby was looking at Hauman expectantly. Hauman knew that this was a waste of time. He also knew that the *Exeter* would not fire upon him . . . Except, he *thought* he knew that, but he wasn't sure he knew that, and therein lay the shred of doubt that prompted him to carry this dance of denial forward to its conclusion.

And so he proceeded to lay out, in fast, broad strokes, the nature of their grievance against Corinder. As the Ferghut listened, his full face grew darker and more serious as he appeared to weigh every word. Once he even muttered, "Oh, dear," as if receiving some piece of particularly shocking news.

"—and so you see why we have been left with no choice!" Hauman concluded. "These . . . creatures . . . endeavored to practice nothing less than genocide! Our future security . . . our future as a race . . . depends upon our exacting revenge upon the Corinderians and letting them know that nothing like this must *ever* happen again! They must know that their actions carry with them dire consequences! And you, Captain, are taking it upon yourself to forestall our war! To prevent the Corinderians from dealing with those very consequences! Are you endorsing their attempt to—?"

"I'm endorsing nothing except the path of peace," Shelby shot back, "a path that you previously walked with as much confidence and certainty as anyone I've ever seen. I'm trying to return you to that path before a destructive conflict diverts you from it forever. Ferghut," she continued quickly, before Hauman could interrupt her, "you've heard the concerns, the charges, leveled by Hauman on behalf of the people of Makkus. Do you have any response?"

"What possible response *could* I have?" replied the Ferghut. "I am shocked . . . *shocked!* . . . at the nature of these accusations. We do not desire war with our good neighbors. These studies that they claim to have made, connecting this insect infestation and the disease it carries, to us, are—"

"One hundred percent accurate," Shelby interrupted him. "I've had my own people make their investigations on these creatures. You see, we demolecularized them. We certainly didn't store the DNA records of all of them in our transporter pattern buffers, but my chief engineer and my science officer were able to put together enough to verify the Makkusian's findings. It is quite clear that, in some way, the Corinderians were responsible for—and there is no way to put a positive face on this—attempted genocide."

The Ferghut looked even more stunned, as if he'd been hit between the eyes by a large rock. "This is . . . this is extraordinary news, surely. Horrific. I have no intention of doubting your word, Captain, since the honesty and integrity of Starfleet and its representatives is common knowledge, but still . . . would it be possible for you to transmit—"

"A copy of the report prepared by my people? Absolutely," Shelby said. Her voice hardened. "But I'm telling you right know, Ferghut, that this is only going to buy you a short amount of time."

"We have not guaranteed it will 'buy' them any time," Hauman declared.

But Shelby fired him a look that, even through the conveyance of a viewscreen rather than in person, was sharp enough to quiet him. "I wish to give the Ferghut my personal guarantee that the Makkusians will not do anything while he is investigating this situation."

Hauman considered this. He felt the eyes of his people upon him, but did not look at them so he would not be influenced. "One hour," he said finally.

"One hour!" said the Ferghut, sounding aggrieved. "Captain, honestly, this is—"

"One hour sounds sufficient to me," Shelby interrupted him. "The test results you have requested have just been transmitted to you. And let me underscore the seriousness of this, Ferghut. You can deny personal knowledge of this all you want—"

"He must have known, Captain, surely you see that!" Hauman cried out.

Shelby kept talking. "—but the bottom line is that it doesn't matter whether you deny it or not. The Makkusians demand vengeance, and frankly, I don't blame them. But I want to avoid a war that could wind up with both planets as little more than floating cinders. Because I'm reasonably certain that this fleet represents only the first wave. As of this moment, the Makkusians are doubtless preparing even more vessels to attack, as are you, and a continued conflict is going to have terminal consequences for all involved. I don't think anyone wants or needs that."

The Ferghut looked very grave. "One hour then," he said tersely. "And, Captain . . . whatever happens . . . thank you for your endeavor to stave off a conflict," and he stressed the final words, "that no one wants."

His image then blanked out, and Shelby's filled up the entirety of the screen. "I can count on you, Hauman, to hold your position and keep your fleet in check?"

"Peace is always desirable, Captain," Hauman said carefully. "We have not moved so far away from our beliefs that we have forgotten that. But survival is important as well. We have not lost sight of that. We trust that you haven't either."

"I've lost sight of nothing," Shelby assured him. "And in an hour's time, we shall see . . . what we shall see. Shelby out."

The screen blanked, a star field returning to replace it. There was a long moment of silence . . .

. . . and then, as one, the bridge crew stood and applauded their commander, Hauman, for his bravery and his refusal to back down in his pursuit of justice for the Makkusians.

He simply hoped that he was worthy of that continued confidence, for he had no idea what he was going to do if he had to go up against the *Exeter*. The battle against the Corinderians was daunting enough. Against the starship as well? He didn't like those odds at all.

# TAPINZA & CALHOUN

WHEN THE MAESTER SAW CALHOUN come riding into town that morning, he made a beeline for him. Something in the way that Calhoun looked at him, however, stopped him dead in his tracks. For a moment—just one moment—Tapinza thought that Calhoun was going to pull out his plaser and shoot him down on the spot. But then he rallied, reminding himself that he, Tapinza, had dealt with far more formidable foes than Calhoun. Besides, amazingly, this was one instance where his conscience was utterly clear.

"I heard. Is she all right?" he asked, and the concern in his voice was by no means manufactured.

Calhoun looked at him as if he were some sort of bacteria. "Are you saying you weren't part of it?"

"Part of it? I was nowhere near! I wouldn't be a party to such things," he sniffed indignantly. "Ask anyone. I was nowhere near here when the . . . unpleasantness . . . occurred."

"How convenient for you," Calhoun said sarcastically. "How many people do you have covering for you?"

Tapinza squared his shoulders, facing off against Calhoun. "Look, Majister, I know that, if you're so inclined, you can knock me flat. You did it before, you can very likely do it again. But before you do, let me tell you that—as much as you're reluctant to believe it—I actually have feelings for Rheela. I care about her, and want what's best for her. Despite our 'differences,' I want you to believe that if I *had* been here, I would have done everything within my power to prevent the awful situation yesterday from happening. They had no business attacking her that way when she was in town. And the burning of her farm . . ." He shook his head, his face a convincing portrait of concern. "Unconscionable. Was any of it saved?"

"Some." Calhoun didn't seem as if he was letting down his guard, or his anger, in the least.

"Is there any way I can help—?"

Calhoun studied him carefully, thoughtfully. "It needs to be rebuilt."

"Naturally," said Tapinza flatly. "I can provide her with whatever raw materials are needed to make the repairs. Manpower might be a bit more problematic. I have interests in a variety of—"

"Don't worry about manpower. I've got that covered."

Tapinza watched with interest as, without another word, Calhoun turned and headed for the saloon. Consumed with curiosity, Tapinza followed him. He didn't have the slightest idea what Calhoun was going to do, but he suspected that whatever it was, it was going to be unpleasant for someone. For once, he had every reason to believe that he was not going to be the someone for whom it was to be unpleasant.

Calhoun strode into the saloon as if he owned the place. Tapinza did the same thing, although in his case it was warranted, since he really did own the place. But he was a silent partner with the Praestor, and preferred to remain that way. Tapinza took a seat at the edge of the bar and watched the Majister with interest. There had been much noise, chatter, hubbub, just before the Majister had entered. But as the first people noticed that he was there, and as word quickly spread, the loud voices dwindled to urgent whispers, and finally to silence. Tapinza had to admit that Calhoun's sheer presence was nothing short of remarkable.

Calhoun had not moved so much as an inch, had not made the slightest threatening gesture. It seemed as if he was capable of fixing the entire crowd in the saloon with his stare. And quite a crowd it was. Breakfast was being served in the saloon, so it was fairly packed, as was usually the case. Tapinza saw that almost every prominent citizen—and most of the useless ones—was there.

Letting the silence hang for what seemed an unconscionably long time, Calhoun seemed in no hurry to move things along. Finally the Praestor stood, cleared his throat in an imperious *harrumph* manner, and said loudly, "Um . . . may we help you, Majister?"

Calhoun didn't reply at first. Instead, he seemed to be sizing up the crowd. Finally, he pointed at one man. It might well have been utterly at random, but he did so with considerable authority, nonetheless.

The man he pointed to, as it so happened, was Hodgkis. Calling Hodgkis a man was like calling a drought a little dry spell. Hodgkis was the biggest, most physically intimidating man in town. Hodgkis kept mostly to himself. When he appeared at town meetings, he was generally silent. He didn't *try* to intimidate anyone; he didn't have to. Still, Hodgkis tended to be present at any major town-related activity and/or incident. Calhoun was positive that Hodgkis had been present when the assault began. Whether Hodgkis had actually thrown anything was irrelevant to Calhoun. The point was, he could have stopped it, or at least deterred it. As far as Calhoun was concerned, anyone who simply stood by and let the assault occur was as responsible as those who actively supported it. As for the torched farmhouse, why . . . he might have done it. Might not have. At that point, Calhoun didn't know for sure and—what was more—he didn't especially care.

He pointed at Hodgkis. "You," he said.

Hodgkis seemed to take a moment to focus on the fact that Calhoun was addressing him, even though he was standing only a few feet away and pointing right at him. "Me?"

"You," Calhoun told him, "are going to help rebuild her house."

Hodgkis stared at him as if Calhoun had announced that he was about to start flapping his arms for the purpose of achieving flight. "Really," he said skeptically. He stepped off the barstool he'd been perched on and looked down at Calhoun, who was at least a head shorter than he. "Really," he said again, which might very well have required a full tenth of his existing vocabulary.

"Yes. Really."

"And if I don't?"

"I'll hurt you."

It was hard to believe that it could become quieter than the dead silence that already existed, but that was indeed what happened. Hodgkis looked at Calhoun with dead eyes. "Takes a lot for an armed man to threaten an unarmed one."

"Put your hands up."

Hodgkis stared blankly.

"Put. Your. Hands. Up."

Hodgkis did as he was told. At that moment, every person in the bar figured that Calhoun was about to shoot down Hodgkis. It was hard to believe that he would do something as boneheaded as that. Just up and murder a man, with all these witnesses around. Then again, Calhoun was a hard one to get a read off. One never knew what to expect from him.

Without a word, Calhoun unbuckled the belt that held plasers hanging from either side. "Keep them raised," he said. Everyone watched in utter astonishment as Calhoun strapped the belt around Hodgkis' waist. Hodgkis stared in mute shock at the weapons that now adorned him.

As if recapping what had just been said, Calhoun told him, "You are going to help rebuild her house, or I am going to hurt you."

Hodgkis didn't even hesitate. With both hands, he went for the guns.

Calhoun snagged both arms at the wrists and stopped them dead, bare inches from the holsters. For a long moment they simply stood there, the trembling of Hodgkis' arms the only outward indication that there was some sort of strained fight going on. Calhoun, for his part, didn't seem to be putting any effort into maintaining his grip. His mouth was set in a grim smile, and his eyes looked very far away, as if he was drawing something from far away into himself. Hodgkis grunted, and then switched tactics, apparently hoping to catch Calhoun off guard. Instead he tried to whip his arms up and around and lunge at Calhoun.

No chance.

Instead, Calhoun twisted around, shoving his hip against Hodgkis, thrust with one leg and lifted the bigger man into the air. He held him there for probably a moment longer than he had to, Hodgkis kicking and flailing about, helpless as any mewling infant. Calhoun still didn't exhibit any exertion, which meant to Tapinza that either Calhoun was incredibly strong or incredibly controlled, or some of both.

Calhoun, never having loosened his grip on Hodgkis' wrists, slammed him down onto a nearby table, scattering the men who'd been sitting at it, sending drinks flying. The table crashed to the floor under Hodgkis' weight and the impact of his body. Hodgkis lay there, stunned, apparently still not believing that he had been so easily manhandled.

Reaching down to the belt buckle, Calhoun undid it and removed the holsters from around Hodgkis' waist. He did not bother to buckle the weapons on again, instead holding them almost casually in one hand. "You," he said to Hodgkis, "are going to help rebuild her house."

Hodgkis managed a nod. At that moment, it was about all he could do in the way of movement.

Calhoun then looked around at the others standing nearby. He picked half a dozen men, seemingly at random, and to each of them he said the same thing: "You are going to help rebuild her house." Each of them nodded in turn, not offering the slightest objection.

At that moment, Maestress Cawfiel barreled into the tavern. Apparently, word somehow had gotten to her about what was going on, because she looked daggers at Calhoun, and said in a voice that was grave and portentous, "Majister . . . are you threatening these people?" she demanded.

"No," he said quietly.

She pointed a quivering finger at Hodgkis, who was only then getting up off the floor, brushing himself off and looking somewhat chagrined over the whole business. "Did you say you would hurt him unless he 'offered' his services in rebuilding Rheela's home?"

"Yes," he said, with exactly the same tone as he had used a moment earlier.

"So you lied!" she said, with something akin to triumph.

"No. I threatened *a* person. Singular. The rest agreed to the restoration without threats."

"And are you going to insist on my aiding in this 'project'?" she said with unveiled disgust.

"I have enough volunteers." He glanced at the 'volunteers' and they, knowing what was good for them, nodded in unison.

But the Maestress wasn't backing down. "And if I have you removed as Majister?"

"The house will still be rebuilt, because it's the right thing to do. Majister, or not, it's of no relevance to me. I'm just passing through."

"I will stop you from forcing our citizens to aid that woman!" Cawfiel told him angrily. "Or are you going to threaten me, also?"

Calhoun shrugged. "Do you want me to?"

"Is this some sort of game to you?" Her voice sounded like a screech.

"No. No, this is very real. Rheela almost died, that was real. Somebody, or bodies, was responsible for that. That was real. I expect that the town will unite in silence on the subject. I could arrest the town. Or I can force reparations to be made. Or I can just start killing people," he added as an afterthought. "Would that please you?"

"Try that, and you'll have to start with me!" the Maestress said defiantly.

"All right," Calhoun replied, calm as could be, and his hand speared toward her throat.

The Maestress let out the most soul-shattering shriek of alarm that anyone had ever heard. It wasn't dignified or imperious or any of the things that people had come to associate with her. Instead it was the pure, unbridled terror of an ancient and withered woman who abruptly realized, at the last moment, that she had gone too far.

Calhoun's hand stopped short about a centimeter from her throat. She gasped, flinching, expecting that air was about to be cut off, her throat crushed, and not quite believing it when she found that such was not the case. Instead Calhoun snapped his fingers in irritation, as if he'd just remembered something.

"Oh, that's right," he said, scolding himself. "I already killed my quota of little old ladies this year. Sorry." He took a step back and doffed his hat to her. "Maybe next year."

And there was a guffaw.

From Hodgkis.

It was purely spontaneous, for Hodgkis certainly had no reason to be the least enamored of Calhoun or anything he said or did. But nevertheless, Hodgkis let out a snorting laugh. Whether it was because of what Calhoun had said, or the look on Cawfiel's face, it was impossible to tell. Laugh, though, he did. This, in turn, touched off a chain reaction, as others snorted or giggled in amusement as well. Never had anyone acted in such a flip, offhanded manner with the Maestress, at least not in Tapinza's recollection.

The Maestress was clearly shocked at the response. Calhoun's face was a neutral deadpan, but she scowled at everyone around her. Out of habit, they tried to wipe the amusement off their faces, but only with partial success. Her body trembling with raw indignation, the Maestress turned on her heel and strode out of the bar with as much dignity as she could muster. More guffaws and snickers accompanied her departure, and although it was impossible to tell whether or not she heard, Tapinza had the distinct impression that she did.

Tapinza had never seen her more livid.

*"Where were you?!"* howled the Maestress. She was stalking

his elaborately furnished living room. "You saw what he did to me there! You saw!"

"Calm down, Maestress," Tapinza started to say.

But she steamrolled right over him, shouting, "Don't you tell me to calm down!" before he'd even gotten the words out. "That man humiliated me in front of the town! And no one shouted him down! No one stood up to him!"

"One man did, and Calhoun beat him up without any effort."

"Is that all that men respect? Someone who can beat them up?"

"No, but it comes fairly high on the list."

She whirled on him, like a small, angry dynamo. "I am a Maestress. You are a Maester. We have both come by our titles honestly, with hard work and dedication to a vision of what this city can and should be. Calhoun is obviously becoming a threat to that! His threat extends from that presented by Rheela! I knew that no good would come from her, I warned them all! I warned you! You and your foolish interest in her. You said that you would be able to control her! That she would come around to your way of thinking!"

"And you said that Calhoun would be more easy to control once he became Majister, because he would fall under the auspices of the council!" retorted Tapinza. "I warned you, did I not? I told you that you were underestimating him and overestimating yourselves. I know the kind of man Calhoun is. I've dealt with his kind before. Tough, resolute, impossible to control . . ."

"That hasn't stopped you from your own failed efforts."

"True," he admitted. "It just goes to show that people don't necessarily learn from experience. Still, that doesn't mean we can't change things for the future."

Her eyes narrowed as she looked at him suspiciously. "What are you saying? What do you mean?"

"I am saying, Maestress," he said coolly, "that you needn't worry. I am attending to it."

"How?" There was genuine interest in her eyes now, a hint of excitement. Clearly she was intrigued, even delighted by the notion that Calhoun was going to be 'attended to' in some way.

"Ah, Maestress . . . that would be telling."

She smiled at that, a broad, toothy smile. Then she laughed with what she undoubtedly figured was a girlish tone. It was a somewhat disturbing noise to hear, issuing from that far-from-girlish throat.

And then, to Tapinza's shock and distaste, she got up on her toes and kissed him. Her lips were papery and rasped across his, and when she shoved her tongue into his mouth, it was like leather. As he pushed away from her, he managed to rein himself in just sufficiently so that his reaction didn't come across as the pure revulsion that it was.

She took a step back and looked at him, and for just a second he saw a hint of vulnerability in her eyes. "Once," she said slowly, "men would have killed for even that taste. Believe it or not. But I knew my life's destiny, even then. And I restrained myself. And I denied myself. And where did it get me? *Where?*" The sudden outpouring of self loathing fury stunned him and then, just as quickly as it had surfaced, the storm passed, and the Maestress was the same untouchable, unknowable, self-depriving and withered creature that she had always been.

"Get . . . Calhoun," she rasped.

"Yes, Maestress," he said, bowing, and knowing that if the alternatives were making an attempt on the life of a man who could break his neck like a twig, or feeling the Maestress' tasteless tongue being shoved down his throat, he'd submit his neck to Calhoun and tell him to twist away.

The Maestress turned on her heel and bustled out of Tapinza's home, which certainly wasn't soon enough to suit Tapinza. Even as he drew a sleeve across his mouth to try and eliminate the foul taste from his lips, he heard a snickering chortle from behind him. "Who would have thought the old creature had that much juice in her?" came the contemptuous voice.

He turned and saw Temo and Qinos emerging from the adjoining room. They had arrived only moments before the Maestress, and taken refuge in there at Tapinza's insistence. And he truly had had to be insistent, because their inclination was simply to pull out their weapons and blast the old woman to bits, instead of hiding out so that she could come and go as she pleased.

Tapinza took two quick strides toward them and swung his hand around. It connected with Temo's jaw, knocking him off his feet. Temo stared up at him in mute astonishment, and then his face clouded as obvious thoughts of murder flittered across his mind. Qinos just looked from one to the other with surprise.

"Shut up," Tapinza said furiously. "You're lucky you're still alive. You're lucky I'm letting you live."

"You're letting *us* live?" Temo slowly got to his feet, a look of quiet fury on his face. "You listen to me, 'Maester.' Just because you employ us doesn't mean—"

"Whatever you think it means or doesn't mean is of absolutely no consequence to me," shot back Tapinza. He stood there for a moment, studying them, his eyes glittering, and his gaze traveled to the plaser in Temo's holster. Very softly, he said, "You want to pull that thing and shoot at me? Is that it? Go ahead, Temo. Be my guest."

If he'd had any illusion that Temo would bluff or in some other way hesitate to utilize deadly force, he was quickly disillusioned, as Temo, in one quick motion, pulled the plaser from his holster and squeezed the trigger at point-blank range.

Nothing happened.

Temo stared stupidly at the plaser, then swung it up and fired again as if a repeat would somehow have better luck. Still the weapon did nothing except sit in his hand like a large, useless piece of metal. Qinos did not even bother to draw his own weapon, but simply stared at Temo's lack of success. Qinos was a bit more reluctant to pull his gun these days anyway, since the arm in which he'd been shot continued to remain sore. Any sudden movement was agonizing for him, so he preferred to let Temo do the work . . . and, for that matter, the thinking whenever possible.

"Idiot," Tapinza said in a voice that dripped contempt. "Did you seriously think that the individual who is the source of all plasers on this world would leave himself vulnerable to that selfsame weapon?"

He reached into a pouch in his belt and pulled out another version of the plaser, smaller but no less deadly. He aimed it squarely at Temo, who froze in place, his eyes wide. Tapinza cherished the cretin's expression at that moment. It took all his willpower not to gun him down. "Now, whereas the dampener I employed is enough to put your plaser out of commission," he continued with the same disdainful sneer, "mine is fully operative. Would you care for a demonstration?"

"I believe you," Temo said. He had lowered his own weapon and tucked it back in its holster.

"How gratifying to hear that. And when I told you that you were to check to make certain that Rheela wasn't home before you torched her house, did you believe that, too?"

Temo looked desperately to Qinos, apparently hoping that his brother would provide some sort of backup. "We . . . we checked," Qinos said, except he sounded very halfhearted when he said it.

"Odd. I don't believe you."

"We didn't see her there," Temo said defensively. "We didn't."

"And even if you had, you'd still have done it. Because you felt you wanted to teach Calhoun a lesson," Tapinza surmised.

The brothers didn't say anything. They didn't even look at one another.

"I wanted to teach him a lesson as well," Tapinza spat out at them. "And I wanted to show Rheela the hazards of not having me as a protector and ally. Instead, you idiots afforded Calhoun the opportunity to go running into a flaming building and pull her to safety . . . and then to strong-arm the citizenry into rebuilding the house. What possible need is she going to have for me when she's got Calhoun there to solve her every problem?"

"I don't know," Qinos said, as if it were a quiz.

"We want to go after Calhoun," Temo told him. He looked as if he were fairly bristling with anger. "You're the one who instructed us to stay out of the city."

"Of course I instructed you to do that. Calhoun recruited several deputy Majisters to provide round-the-clock protection for the city. They're all instructed to shoot you on sight. Your going in to shoot or be shot is a pointless exercise, especially considering that the last time you gentlemen went up against Calhoun, you were four-to-one against him, and you were lucky to come out with your skin."

"He tricked us," said Qinos dully.

"Yes, I'm sure he did. I know Calhoun's type. He'll trick you again, like as not. Now, listen carefully," and he waved his plaser about for emphasis. "I don't care about you. I don't care about your idiot brother, Kusack. I care about building up Narrin, and I care about Rheela and her son. That's it. That's all. But I'm not going to send you in there in some sort of half-assed fashion. I don't trust you in a one-to-one battle with Calhoun, because I can tell you right now, he's going to outthink you in ways you haven't even thought of."

"How do you know?"

"Because I haven't thought of them yet, Temo, and I'm far smarter than you. Right now, you're in my employ. You'll get your chance at Calhoun, but it will be under my terms and at the time that I dictate."

"And when will that be?" Temo seemed most anxious to get started on that score.

Tapinza smiled mirthlessly.

"When Krut comes," he said.

Temo and Qinos looked at one another in silent confusion, and then back to him. "Who's that? Krut? Is he someone local?" asked Temo.

"No," and Tapinza's lips drew back slightly, showing his white and slightly pointed teeth. "He's from . . . out of town. And if anyone can help us dispose of Calhoun, it's Krut. Because it takes one out-of-towner to kill another. And believe me . . . Krut's about as out-of-town as you can get."

And at that moment, Krut's space vehicle angled down toward the planet's surface, in preparation for his showdown with Mackenzie Calhoun. . . .

# SHELBY

HAUMAN DID NOT DWARF the conference lounge in the same way that Zak Kebron used to, but, nevertheless, his considerable height made everything around him seem rather small. He was not seated, unlike everyone else in the room. Garbeck was the picture of calm, as was security head Karen Kahn. Also seated was Brandi, Hauman's associate, whom Shelby remembered from the alarm over the insect invasion back on Makkus.

"He will not come," Hauman said for what seemed the hundredth time.

Garbeck cast a look of mild frustration in Shelby's direction, and Shelby certainly understood it. This was not the first time that Shelby had been present when efforts were being made to avert a war, and if there was one thing that she knew beyond question, it was that tensions on the part of planetary heads rarely made for healthy negotiating. It was necessary for everyone to have a clear head and some degree of emotional distance. It was clear that Hauman, at this point, was whipcord tense. That alone might be enough to spell disaster. Shelby felt as if she could sense the guns of the ships on either side of the *Exeter* upon them.

It had taken some doing to convince Hauman to come to her ship at all. Although it seemed the logical choice, since it represented neutral territory, Hauman was still concerned that some sort of trick might be involved. It had taken a good deal of talking on Shelby's part, and a considerable leap of faith on Hauman's, to get him to come there and await the arrival of the Ferghut as well.

"Hauman," Shelby said firmly, "as I've told you before, the Ferghut has been in contact with us . . . and well before the one hour we gave him was up. He said that he has every intention of addressing the issues and problems that you have brought forward. He says he doesn't want war any more than you do."

Although Hauman looked at her balefully, it was Brandi who spoke. "What the Ferghut says is of very little consequence, Captain. It is his actions that will carry the day now."

"Because actions speak louder than words?"

Brandi blinked at her owlishly. "That's very good. Yes. A very good phrase. Did you just make that up now? Because I like that a great deal. Can I quote you?"

"I've never heard anyone say it before," Garbeck said quickly, and Shelby saw to her surprise that there was actually merriment twinkling in her first officer's eyes. Who would have thought that Garbeck had a slightly wicked sense of humor?

Playing along, Shelby said generously, "Feel free to quote me, yes. In fact, you can even pretend you came up with it."

"Oh, no," said Brandi as she made note of the phrase. "That would be dishonest."

Shelby rolled her eyes and was about to confess to the mild joke when her combadge beeped. "Shelby; go ahead," she said upon tapping it.

"A transport vessel is moving through the lines, Captain," came the voice of Althea McMurrian. "Requesting permission to approach and dock."

"Have you—?"

"Scanned them? Yes, Captain, that's standard procedure," said McMurrian with such a flat tone that it almost made Shelby feel like a dope for even asking. "I'm reading five life-forms, all Corinderian. No sign of any incendiary or explosive devices of any kind. I can tell you to a certainty that it's nothing more than what it appears to be: a transport vessel, bringing Corinderians here."

"Give them clearance to dock in the shuttlebay," said Shelby. "Kahn . . . send an escort down to bring them here."

"On it, Captain," said Kahn as she rose from her seat. Clearly, she had every intention of attending to this personally, and Shelby wasn't about to stop her. As Kahn headed out, Hauman turned to Shelby.

"Now what?"

"Now? We wait," said Shelby, "and we keep our fingers crossed."

Hauman and Brandi looked at each other blankly for a moment and then, clearly wanting to be accommodating, placed their index fingers from each hand so that they crossed one another. Shelby didn't bother to say anything about it, figuring that it probably wasn't worth the effort. Besides, for all she knew, she had just contributed something else to the Makkusian vernacular.

It certainly seemed as if Hauman's prediction was holding up, because none of the five Corinderians who filed into the conference lounge were the Ferghut. One of them bore a passing resemblance to that august individual, but for the most part they were a slim and somewhat fragile-looking group. They bore very serious expressions, and Shelby couldn't help but notice that they were regarding every inch of the conference lounge as if hoping to learn something from it.

Before Shelby could say anything, Hauman said sharply, "Where is the Ferghut?" This annoyed the hell out of Shelby, but she realized that all she could do was tell Hauman to be quiet and then, basically, repeat the question he'd just asked. That would look and sound rather stupid, so she kept her peace and settled for merely firing Hauman a look that—she hoped—conveyed her desire that he keep his mouth shut.

One of the Corinderians stepped forward, the one who looked

slightly like the Ferghut. "He did not feel his presence was required. I am Shuffer, head of the science council—"

"Not required?" Shelby said, before Hauman could get a word out. "Shuffer, I think the Ferghut doesn't seem to realize the severity of the situation. Your worlds are on the brink of war."

"Believe me," said Shuffer archly, "he understands all too well. Unfortunately, he also understands that there are those in this universe who practice deceit and treachery. As much as he would like to trust you, Captain, he must still exhibit caution. He is, after all, Ferghut."

"Then, may I ask what his purpose is in sending you?"

"We, his science council, are here at his service," said Shuffer, and the others nodded their heads in agreement. "As his messengers, you might say."

"And what would his message be?" Garbeck spoke up.

"We do not know."

Everyone else in the room looked at each other. "Then . . . what are you doing here?" asked Shelby.

"They're trying to delay!" Hauman declared. "Trying to stall for—"

"We are trying no such thing," said Shuffer mildly. "We have come bearing a message directly from him." He held up a computer card. "We believe that this is the proper technology for you to interface with?"

"Our computer can handle it, yes," Shelby assured them, taking the card.

"This is a waste of time," said Hauman, still not sitting. Brandi rested a hand on his arm, trying to calm him.

Shelby inserted the card into the proper slot in the computer. There was a slight flicker . . . and then the Ferghut's image appeared on the screen. He looked genuinely apologetic, which Shelby took to be a good sign. She knew that simple apologies weren't going to accomplish anything, but at least it was a start.

"My good and historically supportive Makkusian friends," began the Ferghut, "and my new and equally respected acquaintances of the Federation . . . this is quite possibly one of the most difficult things I have ever had to do."

"So difficult he couldn't do it in person, like a real leader," muttered Hauman. Brandi shushed him before Shelby could.

"The material that you sent me is—quite frankly—incontrovertible. It prompted me to launch an investigation into the matter . . . an investigation that, as I'm sure you can determine by my speedy response to this situation . . . did not take long at all. This is one of those instances where the truth made itself as clear as a beacon in the darkness.

"It is clear that your conclusions were correct. This vicious attempt against the entire Makkusian race did, in fact, have its origins with the Corinderians."

Shelby noted with silent satisfaction that Hauman looked surprised that the Ferghut had admitted to culpability. The question was: Now what?

But the Ferghut had not finished. "In the course of my investigation, I quickly discerned the origins of the plot . . . indeed, the only place from which it could have originated: my science council."

Up until that moment, the five Corinderians were watching the screen with what could only be described as polite interest. But when the Ferghut named them as culpable in the attempt against the Makkusians, their expressions gave way to utter shock. They all started talking at once, most of them firing questions at Shuffer, who had no answers but, instead, looked as befuddled as they. "Shut up, shut up!" he kept saying, shouting them down.

Throughout the pandemonium, the Ferghut continued to speak. The computer, sensing the raised volume in the room, increased the sound to compensate. "Naturally, I was distraught to discover that this base attempt against our neighbors was the result of a plan—no, a *conspiracy*—launched by people whom I had trusted. I was as appalled as you would be, were a similar happenstance to occur with those in whom *you* had invested faith. My original thought had been to put the villains on trial here on Corinder, but

I have decided that, since their crime was against the Makkusians, then it is to you that I must give them over. I turn them over to you, to suffer whatever punishment you deem worthy." He bowed slightly and his image disappeared.

The scientists looked mad with fear. "This can't be true! It can't be happening!" one of them was saying, clutching at Shuffer's robes and looking in stark terror at Hauman and Brandi.

Hauman's face looked as if a storm cloud had passed over it. "So . . . your own leader gives you up."

"He knew! He knew everything!" Shuffer was practically screaming. "It was his idea! He endorsed it! He . . . he ordered us to do it! We had no choice! None at all!"

*They were following orders,* Shelby thought with bleak amusement.

"He's denying it now to escape responsibility! To distance himself!" continued Shuffer.

"That may very well be," Brandi said thoughtfully. "However, you admit to your duplicity. . . ."

"I admit to nothing!" Shuffer said quickly.

"Actually, you just did," Garbeck quietly reminded him.

Shuffer opened his mouth, then closed it without saying anything. He looked at the other scientists, who had expressions of pure terror in their eyes. "This . . . cannot be happening. This cannot be . . ."

Hauman rose, and the very weight of his presence drew all focus to him. He did not speak immediately, as if considering all his options. "I expected the Ferghut to do anything rather than offer himself up to Makkusian justice," he said finally. "However, I would consider his offering you up to be . . . acceptable. I have no true desire to send my people into a battle that may very well cost them more lives. They believe in me. They . . . trust me," he said with what sounded like faint amusement. "If I inform them that these scientists acted alone, they will accept that, and be satisfied upon the execution of—"

"You cannot execute us for doing as we were commanded!"

Shuffer cried out. The other scientists were wailing in fear. "I do not believe this! It cannot be happening!"

"He keeps saying that," observed Brandi, who seemed grimly amused by it.

"But the Ferghut would not do this to me!"

There was something about the way he said that that caught Shelby's attention. "Why not? Why would the Ferghut consider you deserving of special consid—"

"He's my brother!"

There was a gasp from the other scientists, almost with one voice, and they took several steps back from him, as if distancing themselves from something unclean.

Shelby couldn't understand the reaction of the others, and apparently Hauman saw the confusion on her face. "Shuffer has committed something of a breach of protocol. He who is the Ferghut remains anonymous, you see. All family members are to keep their identities unrevealed to the public. It is . . . an odd custom, but a longstanding one. And, as I'm sure you know, a custom of long standing becomes sacred, no matter how stupid it may be."

The scientists ignored the casual slam to their tradition, still caught up in the shock of the revelation. Shuffer, in the meantime, was saying, "I have to contact the Ferghut. He couldn't have meant to do this . . . not to me . . . not after everything we've . . ."

"I doubt he'll be wanting to speak with you, considering what you've just done. In any event . . . you're no longer of use to him, Shuffer, " Hauman told him. There was an extremely nasty look in his eyes. "You can, however, be of use to me."

Shuffer took a step back, and then, with desperation in his face, he turned to Shelby and drew himself up with as much dignity as he could muster. "I demand political asylum, Captain. We are aboard a Federation starship. We ask for asylum. You cannot refuse us."

Cocking an eyebrow, Shelby said, "I can't?" She turned to Garbeck. "Is he correct, Number One?"

Garbeck seemed surprised that Shelby was asking. But Shelby simply looked at her blandly, and, slowly, Garbeck said, "Technically, Captain . . . you actually not only *can* refuse him . . . but you are *obliged* to do so."

"What?" It didn't seem possible that Shuffer's voice could have gone any higher, but it did. "How can she conceivably be *obliged* to do so?"

"Tell him, Number One."

Garbeck looked from one to the other, looked at the terrified faces of the scientists. "According to the Prime Directive, we cannot interfere with interplanetary politics—"

"Cannot interfere! You put your starship in between our fleets to stop a war!"

"That is true. But . . ." She paused and looked to Shelby, who was not interrupting her. "But the captain has broad discretionary powers. And Starfleet tends to be . . . elastic . . . when it comes to a captain exercising that discretion in favor of saving lives."

"Then save *our* lives!"

"If I save your lives," Shelby said implacably, "then millions will likely be lost. Because if I give you asylum . . . then nothing will be able to forestall a war. And that war will be fought either between your respective races . . . or between this vessel and the Makkusians. Neither of those options are acceptable."

"And sending us off with them . . . ?" His hand trembled as he pointed at Hauman. "That is acceptable?"

"I've found, in my experience, Shuffer, that often command is less about doing what's right . . . than it is about doing what's the least wrong."

Shuffer was shaking his head vigorously. It was as if he was disconnected from what was happening. "You can't do this . . . you can't . . ."

Shelby shrugged. "There are worse things I could do." Then she tapped her combadge. "Shelby to transporter."

"Transporter room. Mankowski here."

"Mr. Mankowski, prepare to beam—"

"No!" Shuffer suddenly screamed, and lunged straight toward Shelby.

Shelby didn't budge from the spot. Kahn, however, was on the other side of the room, unable to physically intercede. She went for her phaser to take down Shuffer . . .

. . . and at that moment, Garbeck stepped in between them, her jaw set and her fist cocked. She swung a fast right cross and caught Shuffer squarely on the side of the head. Shuffer went down, loud and hard. Even as he lay on the floor, dizzy and unable to move, he kept saying, "Can't be happening . . . can't be . . ."

"Are you all right, Number One?" Shelby asked solicitously as she saw Garbeck shaking out her fist. Garbeck winced, but nodded. Kahn, meantime, was already hauling the stunned and confused Shuffer to his feet. Shuffer was continuing to shake his head in disbelief. The other scientists didn't appear to be in much better shape, emotionally.

"Number One, would you be so kind as to escort Hauman, Brandi, and then . . . prisoners . . . to the transporter room, so they will be able to return to their vessel," asked Shelby.

Garbeck nodded and turned to the scientists. They were clustering together, as if hoping to be able to draw strength from one another. "Talk to her!" one of them said to Garbeck. "Ask the captain to spare us!" The others took up the cry, and they started pawing at Garbeck, as if hoping she could heal their critical situation with her touch. She worked to push them away, and it took Kahn's summoning other security personnel to manage the escorting of the scientists down to the transporter room. Surrounded as they were by *Exeter* security guards, it didn't stop them from pleading with Garbeck, asking her to do something, anything, since clearly the captain wasn't going to lift a finger to aid them.

"It's regulations," Garbeck kept saying to them, and she cast a stricken look at Shelby.

And Shelby saw it right there, saw it in her eyes. Saw a silent pleading for Shelby to come up with some alternative, to think of something, so that these pleading, pathetic specimens would not be sent off to certain death on a world that they had tried to destroy. But Shelby held firm, shaking her head. "Commander Garbeck is quite correct. It's regulations. And we can't go around breaking them whenever we feel like it, can we, Commander?"

"No, Captain. We can't," she said tonelessly as she led the shrieking scientists away.

Hauman nodded approvingly to Shelby. "Well done, Captain. I'm sure that wasn't easy for you. But we all have to make compromises, don't we? After all . . . we must never forget the big picture. And please inform your United Federation . . . that we would be honored to join."

"That's wonderful to hear," said Shelby, as a piece of herself died within every time she replayed, mentally, the cries of the scientists. She remained in the conference lounge long after everyone had left, not especially wanting to emerge.

# MOKE

"ARE YOU GOING to marry my mother?"

Calhoun had been sitting tilted back in his seat, looking quite at ease. Over in his cell, the semipermanent resident of the jail, Kusnok, sat up with interest.

Moke had wandered in during what was a pleasantly slow day. A number of citizens of the town were out at his home, endeavoring to rebuild the place and doing a respectable job of it. The thing that was most remarkable about it was the way in which his mother seemed to be reacting to the whole business. They had, after all, been responsible (or at least some of them had, apparently) for causing the house to burn down in the first place. But you'd never have known it from the way Rheela was handling it all. She was going around and offering people water from her private stores, or little cakes that she had baked, or juice that had been freshly harvested. These offerings had been greeted very guardedly at first, but slowly they had warmed to the notion that Rheela was a generous woman who—astoundingly enough—wasn't holding any grudges. Moke had even heard her saying something to Calhoun about "this being the thing that finally got through to them." Moke wasn't entirely certain what she meant by that, and considering that Calhoun simply grunted in response, it seemed as if he wasn't entirely convinced of it. Still, what mattered to Moke was that the house was getting rebuilt, and he and his mother would be able to stop sleeping in a tent (while Calhoun chose to sleep under the stars).

What also mattered to Moke was how his mother seemed to dwell on Calhoun. She never discussed it with him, of course. But, one night, his mother's tossing and turning had awoken Moke, and he sat up, confused and blinking in the darkness. He heard her saying something about "Mac," over and over.

He said nothing of his being aware of the dream to his mother, because he felt oddly as if he had been eavesdropping or somehow invading her privacy, even though he'd had no reasonable way of avoiding doing so. It did, however, give him cause to ponder what he had overheard, and, in doing so, coming to the decision that Calhoun's presence clearly made his mother very happy.

Naturally, Moke himself was rather taken with the notion of having a father around as well. But, really, his first and foremost concern was his mother's happiness, and if Mackenzie Calhoun possessed the power to do something to make that happiness permanent, then Moke felt obliged to do something about it.

So Moke had asked his mother's permission to ride into town while she supervised the work at the house. She'd hesitated at first, for Moke had never gone off on his own into the city before. But he'd assured her that he was going in to spend time with Calhoun, and this alleviated his mother's concerns somewhat. So off he'd gone, and now he was standing in the Majister's office, posing the question without even offering a "hello" first.

Calhoun didn't move from his position behind the desk. Kusack snorted in amusement from his cell, but didn't offer any commentary. "Where did this come from?" Calhoun inquired after a moment's consideration.

"This what?"

"This question."

"Oh. From me," said Moke.

"No, I mean . . ." He sat forward so that the front chair legs, tilted back before, were now resting on the ground. ". . . what prompted you to ask about that?"

"Because you make my mom happy. And she makes you happy." Moke hesitated. "Doesn't she?" he asked in a very small voice.

Calhoun smiled, and Moke instantly relaxed. "Yes. She makes me happy," Calhoun told him.

"So, are you going to marry her?"

"Yeah, are ya?" called Kusack.

Calhoun didn't even bother to look at him. Instead, he remained focused on Moke. "It's . . . not as simple as that, Moke."

"Why not?"

"Well, for one thing—"

"Your mother is lousy between the sheets!"

This last comment of Kusack's so amused the outlaw that he practically fell over laughing. Calhoun bobbed his head slightly to Moke and said, "Give me a moment." Then he walked over to Kusack. Moke never clearly saw Calhoun's hand move. One moment it was relaxed, at his side, and the next it was a blur, and then Kusack was laid out on the floor. His eyes were open, but he didn't appear to be seeing anything through them, and a large bruise was already appearing on his jaw. Calhoun turned back and returned to his seat, regarding Moke thoughtfully before continuing to speak. "Now . . . as I was saying . . ."

"What did he mean about sheets?"

Without missing a beat, Calhoun said, "He was saying your mom doesn't make the bed very well."

"Yes, she does!" Moke protested. "She gets the sheets nice and clean and flat!"

"That's why people like him are in gaol," Calhoun pointed out. "Now, Moke . . . you see, the problem is . . . I'm just passing through."

"What does that mean?"

"It means I'm only going to be here for a short while."

"My ma says that everyone is only here for a short while."

Calhoun smiled at that, the edges of his eyes crinkling as he did. "That's true enough," he said. "But what I mean is that I'm not going to be staying around here forever."

"How do you know?"

Calhoun seemed ready to give a quick answer, but then he closed his mouth and thought about it. "Truth is . . . I don't," he admitted. "I might be here . . . a lot longer than I'd intended. But, sooner or later, Moke, the odds are I'd be moving on."

"Then you can take us with you."

"No. I can't," said Calhoun.

"Why not?"

"It's complicated."

"I thought grown-ups could uncomplicate and explain anything to kids."

"Well," Calhoun sighed, "there's some people who say I'm more kid than grown-up."

"*I* think you should marry her," Moke said, a bit sullen. "I think you should marry her and stay here with us forever."

"That would be nice, Moke."

"Then do it."

Calhoun smiled once more and shook his head. "You don't let up, do you, Moke? You'd make a good—" Then he stopped.

"A good what? What were you going to say?"

"Majister," Calhoun told him.

Moke had the oddest feeling that that wasn't what Calhoun had been about to say, but before he could press the matter further, the door of the office suddenly burst open.

Once again Calhoun's hand was a blur, and he was on his feet with the plaser pointed straight at the door. His face was set, his eyes steely and focused. The relaxed man that Moke had been speaking to an instant before was gone, replaced by a taut and prepared warrior.

It was, however, unnecessary, at least for the moment. Standing in the doorframe was Spangler, and the newspaper editor seemed—to say the least—agitated.

"Majister!" he cried out, apparently oblivious to the fact that there was a gun pointed at him. "You'd better come quick!"

Calhoun had glided the gun back into his holster with such ease that the movement had not caught Spangler's attention. But his readiness for trouble did not let up at all. "What's the matter?" he said, although it didn't sound like a question when he said it.

"There's a . . . I think it's a man! A green man! Over in the tavern! Calling for you!"

"A . . . green man," Calhoun said slowly.

"That's right! He's like . . ." Spangler looked completely flustered. ". . . like nothing I ever seen before! I mean, hell, Majister, we've had the occasional mutant through here before . . ."

"Including you," Moke pointed out helpfully to Calhoun.

"Thank you, Moke. And this mutant . . . is nothing like me?" Calhoun asked Spangler. "He's green, you said?"

"Yes."

"Any antennae?"

Spangler stared at him blankly. "Any what?"

"Like these. Sticking out of his forehead." Calhoun extended his index fingers from his forehead and waggled them.

"No, he didn't have no fingers sticking out of his head," said Spangler.

Calhoun closed his eyes briefly in what appeared to be a moment of pain, and then he opened them again. "Nothing at all unusual sticking out of his head?"

"No."

"Eyes set in his face like mine? Were his ears pointed?"

"Yes to the eyes, no to the ears."

"I assume he had two arms, two legs, five fingers on each."

"Don't know if he had fingers on his legs, Majister."

"*Grozit*," moaned Calhoun. "On his hands. Five fing—never mind." He waved him off impatiently. "He's over in the tavern, you said?" Spangler nodded. Calhoun turned to Moke and said firmly, "Stay here."

He and Spangler headed out for the tavern.

Moke waited ten seconds and followed.

\* \* \*

When Moke had passed by the tavern earlier, he'd been impressed by the amount of noise that was generated by such a relatively small place. But now the quiet impressed him even more. He might not have noticed it if he'd just been passing by, but it provided such a stark contrast to what he'd been hearing from there before that it couldn't help but snag his interest.

Carefully, Moke peered through the large swinging double doors that allowed entrance into the tavern, and he couldn't quite believe—or even understand—what he was seeing.

There was Mackenzie Calhoun, the Majister, staring up at the single most impressive, and most intimidating, individual that Moke had ever seen. His head was shaved, his skin was a dusky green, and he carried so much hatred in his body that it seemed as if his frame was unable to contain it all. In the way that he studied Calhoun, he seemed to be evaluating everything the Majister had ever done in his entire life, and endeavoring to determine whether Calhoun was, in fact, worth his time.

The two of them were standing and facing each other from opposite sides of the tavern. Moke, still looking in from around the edge of the doorframe, his breath caught in his throat, watched goggle-eyed. Their hands were at their sides in what appeared to be a relaxed, even leisurely manner. But both of them were obviously whipcord tense.

"So," the green man said after a time. The patrons were looking from the green man to Calhoun and back again. No one seemed inclined to leap to the aid or defense of the Majister. "You are the Majister. The 'Mackenzie Calhoun' people in these parts seem to talk about with such . . . enthusiasm."

Calhoun said nothing. He seemed to know that this odd green man was going to talk whether Calhoun spoke or not, and so Calhoun kept silent. Moke instantly intuited why. The more he allowed the green man to talk, the more the green man might say something that Calhoun could use against him.

Why against him?

Because the green man was an enemy. If Moke had ever been

sure of anything, he was sure of that. This strange green man was going to try and hurt Calhoun.

"You," Calhoun finally said, "are obviously not from around 'these parts.' Why are you here?"

"My own reasons."

"And what would your 'own reasons' be?" asked Calhoun.

"My own. They need not concern you."

"I can guess," Calhoun said, with slight irony in his voice. "What is your name?"

"Krut," said the green man.

"Krut . . . I suspect you are here because of some sort of reward being offered. Some promise of remuneration. May I safely assume that you came here in a . . ." He paused, glanced at the wide eyes of the people around him, and then said cautiously, ". . . a vehicle."

There seemed to be something akin to amusement in Krut's eyes. "A safe assumption."

"Whatever you are being paid or offered . . . I can promise to pay you a great deal more, if you give me transport in your vehicle."

"Would, for you, that it were that simple. Mackenzie Calhoun. Mac," the green man continued. "Finally, a full name to put to the shortened one . . . and the scar. Oh, she told me all about the scar."

"She?" Calhoun's single-word utterance was in a carefully neutral tone.

"Tell me . . . does the name 'Zina' sound at all familiar to you?" he asked.

Calhoun frowned slightly. Clearly, he recalled it, but he couldn't quite recollect from where. Then it obviously came back to him.

"Yesssss," said the green man approvingly. "I see that it does. She spoke of the Xenexian named 'Mac.' The one with the scar that ran the length of one side of his face. The man who killed Krassus. You remember Krassus, too, I take it."

Calhoun nodded ever so slightly.

"I'm sure you thought nothing of killing him. Just another Orion. Just another victim for a mad-dog killer."

"If I were a mad-dog killer, Zina would not have been alive to spread my name and description," Calhoun pointed out quietly. It did not seem as if he really thought what he said was going to make any difference, but, nevertheless, he obviously felt constrained to point it out. "And you came here because of me?"

"I came here for my own reasons. Discovering you were who you were was simply a bonus."

At which point, Praestor Milos—who had apparently witnessed the entire exchange—asked what was easily the most unnecessary question of the day. "Majister . . . do you two know each other?" It was such an absurd query that neither Calhoun nor the green man deigned to answer it.

"What was Krassus to you?" asked Calhoun.

"He was like unto a brother to me. He was a business partner . . . a scholar . . . a great man . . . his one drawback being a less-than-deft handling of fiscal resources."

"He died owing you money," Calhoun guessed.

"Exactly so." Krut sounded slightly mournful over the admission. "A sizable sum. He was on his way to meet me and make restitution . . . except he became caught up in a card game with you. A card game at which you cheated. When he discovered your duplicity, you killed him."

"If I say that's not what happened, will it make any difference?"

"None."

Calhoun gave a small shrug. Clearly that answered that question.

"You have cost me money and inconvenience, Calhoun. Restitution must be made. If that is paid for in your blood, so be it. You might indeed have been able to buy me off . . . but no longer. This is a personal matter. So," and he smiled in what he probably imagined was an amiable fashion. It merely served to make chills run up and down Moke's spine. "Tell me, Calhoun . . . what do you think is worse? The moment of death . . . or the anticipation of the moment of death?"

"I've never given it much thought," said Calhoun.

"Well, you are in luck," Krut said, "because I'm going to give you the opportunity to anticipate it."

And just like that, just that quickly, Krut's hand was in motion, moving toward the large-handled weapon he had hanging from his hip.

Calhoun reflexively moved for his own gun, and there were shrieks from the patrons of the tavern, who threw themselves this way and that in order to try and get out of range. But before anyone managed to do so, Krut's gun was already in his hand and leveled right at Calhoun's chest. Calhoun's weapon had not even cleared the holster, was not even fully drawn.

Krut's gun didn't waver so much as a centimeter as utter quiet draped over the tavern like a funeral shroud. "Fingers off your gun, Majister," he said calmly, and Calhoun did exactly as he was told. It was obvious to everyone in the tavern that Mackenzie Calhoun was staring death in the face. If he was at all intimidated, if he feared death in the least, he certainly didn't show it. In fact, he wasn't looking at the weapon at all. Instead, he was staring squarely into Krut's eyes, as if trying to get a measure of Krut as an individual, as to just how likely the green man was to squeeze the trigger and blast Calhoun's innards all over the wall.

"Impressively quick, wouldn't you say?" Krut asked cheerfully. "Observe." He slid the gun into his holster and then pulled it out again, the movement such a blur that it seemed as if the weapon literally leaped from the holster into his hand of its own accord. "One more time?"

"You've made your point," Calhoun said quietly. "Are you going to shoot now?"

"Cut you down with no warning, as you did Krassus?" Krut looked almost disappointed at the notion. "No, no . . . this is where we get to discover which is worse, Calhoun. The moment of death . . . or the anticipation. You will have the rest of this day, this evening, and much of tomorrow morning to think about what's going to happen. And at noon tomorrow, you will meet me out on the street, and there we will have a little duel. At which point, I will draw my weapon, far faster than you will be able to pull out yours, and shoot you down." He smiled, clearly taken with the mental image. "I will send you to the afterlife, where you and Krassus will be able to continue your disagreements throughout eternity. You could, of course, go on the run. If you do that, rest assured I will hunt you down, kill you, take your head and bring it here to display, so that all the residents of this little city that you wish to protect will know their protector for the coward that he is. I trust we understand each other."

"Perfectly," said Calhoun.

"Until tomorrow, then," said Krut. He bowed slightly and then exited the tavern, keeping his gun leveled on Calhoun, backing up so that his eyes never left him. Calhoun kept a level gaze fixed upon him, even staring at the door long after Krut had departed through it.

"You sure tricked him, Majister!" Moke said, breaking the silence that followed.

There were puzzled looks at the boy from all around. He looked at the confused adults, not remotely understanding why they were failing to grasp the obvious. "The Majister drew his gun slow so that the green man would think the Majister wasn't as quick! But tomorrow, you're going to see something! Right, Majister?"

His voice was filled with boundless enthusiasm . . . which was curbed slightly when Calhoun, even though saying, "Right," allowed something to peer through his eyes that Moke recognized instantly, and which froze his thoughts. That something peering through was concern. Genuine concern.

The green man *was* faster. Much faster.

And the lawman known as Mackenzie Calhoun clearly didn't have the faintest idea how to deal with it.

# GARBECK & SHELBY

IT WAS SOME HOURS LATER, long after the two fleets had returned to their respective worlds, when Shelby found Garbeck, exactly where she thought she was going to find her: down in the Ten-Forward Lounge. Just walking into the place reminded Shelby of the fact that, on the *Excalibur,* many people referred to the equivalent spot as the Team Room; a name picked up from the old space program. It was a term that, for some reason, Calhoun had preferred.

Garbeck was staring at the empty glass, looking rather dismal as she did so. Shelby sat down at the table without being invited. "So, how drunk are you?" she inquired.

"Depends. Are my eyes open?" asked Garbeck thickly.

"Yes."

"Then the answer to your question is, 'Not enough.'" She signaled for the waitress to bring over another shot of whatever the hell she was having. Since she was off duty, Shelby didn't feel the need to remonstrate with her for straying from the more accepted synthehol. The waitress brought the drink, but rather than ask what it was, Shelby picked it up before Garbeck could down it. Garbeck didn't appear to have enough energy left to complain; she just stared blankly at Shelby, as if the captain had suddenly appeared in a burst of light, like a member of the Q continuum.

Shelby sniffed the drink and gasped. "My God! What did they do, drain this from a warp core? You could power a starship with this."

"Private stock." She snapped her fingers to gain the waitress' attention and, once she had it, made a tilting motion with her arm that signaled she wanted an entire bottle brought to the table. The waitress complied, bringing a bottle about half-filled with the potent liquor.

Shelby read the label. "Big Bang?" Garbeck nodded, a bit too enthusiastically, and she almost slammed her head on the table before Shelby caught her by the shoulder to prevent her from doing so. "Where'd you get this stuff? Romulan space?"

"Pocatello, Idaho."

"I hear they're very similar." She put the bottle down gingerly, not wanting to jostle the contents lest she accidentally cause the thing to explode somehow. "Thank you for interceding, by the way, when that scientist endeavored to rearrange my face."

"Not a problem," Garbeck told her. She was trying to lean on her elbow, but it was wobbling viciously. She tried to solve the problem by steadying the table, which actually hadn't been moving at all.

"Just out of curiosity," Shelby said, encompassing both Garbeck and the bottle with a gesture, "may I ask . . . why?"

"Because you're my captain. I figured it was in my job description somewhere . . ."

"No, I meant, why are you crawling inside a bottle?"

"I resent that characterization, Captain," Garbeck said in a very arch tone. "I am not crawling. Babies crawl. I am an adult. Adults walk. I am walking inside a bottle."

She rolled her eyes. "Garbeck . . ."

"The whole way," Garbeck said suddenly, and she leaned forward, clutching the bottleneck as if it were the sole object that was preventing her from falling and thudding her chin on the tabletop. "The whole way, down to the transporter, they begged me. Begged me and begged me and begged me. Begged begged begged beg—"

"I get the picture, Garbeck," Shelby interrupted her. "They begged. And you found that upsetting."

"Of course I found it upsetting! Wouldn't you?"

"Yes. But if I had found it upsetting . . . wouldn't you then think that I was deficient somehow in terms of personal strength?"

Garbeck didn't answer immediately. As a matter of fact, she didn't answer at all. She simply stared off into space, and for a long moment Shelby thought she had fallen asleep. She leaned forward, put her fingers in front of Garbeck's face, and snapped them a couple of times. This, apparently, was enough to rouse Garbeck back to full concentration, and she looked a bit accusingly at Shelby, as if annoyed that Shelby had dared to disturb her rest.

Shelby ordered, and got, some synthehol for herself. She felt like keeping her faculties focused.

"I should have been stronger," Garbeck said suddenly, and there was something in the increasing strength in her voice that caught Shelby's attention. "I knew what I was doing was right . . . what you were having me do was right. You had no choice, really. And they *did* do what they were accused of doing. They're not denying that . . . well, they are, but it's a bit too late. The problem is that their leader . . . and Shuffer's brother . . . is not being held to account for his actions."

"Unless you count for the fact that he basically had to give up his own brother."

"I don't know that we count that at all. For all we know, they never got along. He might have been glad to see his brother depart." Garbeck shook her head in disgust. "I should be . . . immune to it, wouldn't you think? But I'm not, apparently. I'm furious over the fact that the Ferghut is getting away with this."

"The Ferghut isn't exactly 'getting away' with anything," Shelby reminded her. "His world is still being crushed by overpopulation. And the Makkusians are no doubt watching every single move, trust having been replaced by vigilance." She took a sip of her drink, but then put it down, preferring to nurse it. Garbeck, on the other hand, simply threw back another shot.

"I have a hollow leg," Garbeck told her, but considering the way Garbeck was going through the bottle, Shelby had a sneaking suspicion that everything from the neck down was, in fact, hollow. It seemed the only way she could possibly contain that much liquor.

"Tell me," Shelby said abruptly, as if she were changing subjects. "What if we encountered a world that had a newly minted, planet-wide disaster. And let's say that I suggested to you that we slingshot back through time, go to a point before the disaster, and head it off. What would you say to me?"

Garbeck didn't even have to give it a moment's thought. "I would say that if you attempted to utilize the *Exeter* in such a blatantly inappropriate manner, against all temporal regulations of Starfleet, then I would personally do everything I could to relieve you of command." Then she blinked in surprise, and actually looked pleased with herself. "How about that! That sounded like the old me! I was getting worried!"

"Yes, that was certainly a close one," Shelby said dryly. "And once upon a time . . . I would have, one hundred percent, had the exact same reaction. But when it actually happened, well . . ." She shrugged.

Garbeck looked at her in amazement, even through the drunken haze hanging over her. "When it . . . happened? You mean, you . . . ?" And then she realized. "Calhoun."

"Thaaaat's right," said Shelby. "If he'd tried it when I first came on as his second-in-command, I would have been all over the ship trying to get everyone and his brother to help me stop him from doing something completely insane."

"But when he did do it . . . ? Did you . . . ?"

"Stop him?" She laughed softly. "In a lot of ways, Garbeck, Calhoun was more like a force of nature than a starship captain. Trying to stop him was like trying to throw yourself in the path of a tidal wave. Most of the time, you just wound up looking all wet."

Garbeck regarded her commander with quiet amusement. "And you want to be like that, don't you?"

"My, my. The drink is making you remarkably insightful today."

"It's so much more exciting to be a force of nature than to be a regulation-bound pencil pusher, right, Captain?"

"I never particularly thought about it in those terms."

"Maybe not consciously. But unconsciously . . ."

"I think the unconscious gets an unfair rap," remarked Shelby. "It takes more blame for negative outcomes than God."

"It's true, isn't it, though? Someone like Calhoun, he's more exciting to watch in action than a captain who does everything right."

"Right? Is that what it comes down to, Garbeck? Right and wrong?" She shook her head. "What are rules, in the end? They're things people come up with to guide them through those things that they know. The problem with space exploration is that, over and over again, you come up against those things that you *don't* know. That no one knows, or has any experience with."

"And because of that, rules should go out the window? Izzat what you're saying, Captain Shebly?"

Shelby smiled. "Shelby. It's Shelby."

"Where?" Garbeck turned and looked over her shoulder.

"No, I mean . . ." She waved it off. "Never mind."

But Garbeck fought through the confusion in her addled brain and realized. "Oh. I said 'Shebly.' Sorry." She licked her lips. "I think my tongue's swollen to twice its normal size."

"In some situations, that could make you very popular," said Shelby with wry amusement.

"The point is," Garbeck said with renewed emphasis, thumping her hand on the table, "Without rules, we're . . . we're all Calhouns. Running around, doing whatever the hell we want. It's anarchy. It's chaos. It's not a smoothly run organization at all, and most of all . . . there's no sense of responsibility. No one would have to answer to anyone else. Actions must have consequences."

"I agree."

"There, y'see?"

"But you're presenting only two extremes. There has to be a middle ground, Garbeck. And I wish I could tell you that I knew what it was, but . . ." She sighed. "I don't. But part of me wonders whether—by this point—I've become too much like Mackenzie Calhoun."

"Captain Shebly," Garbeck said with effort, "we may have had our differences, but I can assure that—no matter how extreme our disagreements may have become, and no matter how much I think you're mucking things up—you are not, and never will be, anything like Mackenzie Calhoun. And, if I have anything to say about it, neither will I."

"You're certainly right about the latter, in any event."

"Thank you," she said proudly.

"For one thing, Calhoun could hold his liquor."

"I can hold my liquor!" Garbeck said indignantly. She picked up the bottle and cradled it, a bit unsteadily, in both hands. "See?"

Shelby laughed. "I'm very proud of you, Commander. Very proud."

"Thank you." And then her mouth drew taut, and Shelby was certain that Garbeck was fighting back tears. "I'm always going to hear them, you know. Those poor bastards. Set up by their leader . . . one of them by his own brother. Crying for mercy. Begging, pleading. Three of them told me they had children, did you know that? Wanted to go back to them. I had to ignore them, ignore it. But it was a clear Prime-Directive situation, you know. Textbook. Absolute textbook."

"I know. It was," agreed Shelby. "And when you led them away, I heard the begging, too."

"They were only following orders."

"Yes."

"Just like we do."

"Yes."

"They didn't deserve what happened to them."

"But they performed certain destructive actions. Actions, so I'm told, have to have consequences, lest we descend into anarchy."

Garbeck looked up at her in confusion. "Who said that?"

"You did. Five minutes ago."

"Oh." She shrugged. "Well . . . what do I know?"

"About as much as any of us knows, Number One. About as much as any of us knows. And somehow . . . it's never enough."

They sat there and stared into the bottle as the long evening hours stretched on, waiting for the screams and pleadings for mercy to die in their heads. And it never quite happened.

# *RHEELA*

THE TIMING OF THE ARRIVAL of the Circuit Judiciary couldn't have been better . . . or, at least, so it seemed. With Krut having issued his challenge, and the distinct possibility that, as of the morrow, there might not be a Majister, at least the pending case of Kusack could be attended to.

The Judiciary—who, by startling coincidence, had arrived mere hours after Krut's ultimatum—was an unassuming but learned individual. Word of his arrival had spread quickly. Rheela was on her way into town anyway, because Moke had bolted home after witnessing the confrontation between Calhoun and Krut, and she had felt the need to go to him, to see if she could offer any aid or encouragement. It was a nonsensical thing to contemplate, really. What could she do? What could she truly hope to accomplish? Just make a damned fool of herself, most likely, but that still wasn't going to stop her from making her best effort.

But when she had arrived in town, she had discovered people crowding into the central meeting hall, almost tripping over one another in their anxiousness to cram inside. Rheela had pretty much figured it out before she even got near. There had been no meeting scheduled, no natural disaster had occurred that she, at least, could discern. Thinking about what could possibly have incited such reactions, she quickly came to the (very correct) conclusion that the Circuit Judiciary had finally made his presence known to the small city once again.

She managed to ease her way in through two rather heavyset individuals, gliding adroitly between them while they were hesitating and trying to figure out which of them was going to give way so that the other could pass through (since their walking in side by side was unworkable). She managed to find a seat at the far end of one bench. No one glanced her way, even though she recognized a couple of them from the crews who had been coming to restore her house. She tried to figure out whether being cold-shouldered was a good thing or not.

There was the Circuit Judiciary; a reedy man who was learned about everything, except about not acting insufferably pleased that he was learned. The Praestor was in the process of informing the Judiciary just exactly what had happened to land Kusack in gaol, and the further circumstances surrounding the death of the previous Majister, Fairax. Kusack stood before the Judiciary, his hands securely tied, his head hung so that he didn't have to look the Judiciary in the eye. Calhoun was seated in a single, freestanding chair nearby. Rheela immediately noticed something different in Calhoun's expression, as opposed to everyone else's. Calhoun was watching the Circuit Judiciary very carefully, as if he was waiting for the Judiciary to say something important. But there was something in Calhoun's face, something about his expression that gave Rheela pause. It made her wonder what he knew that no one else in the room did.

The Judiciary was silent for some moments after Milos stopped talking. He was tilted back in his chair, his eyes gazing at the ceiling as if he was going to find his decision written there in letters three feet high. Then he moved his chair forward, his gaze seeming capable of dissecting Milos to his core.

"Is this," he said slowly, "the only case of significance you have to bring before me?"

Something in his voice alerted Rheela—and, to varying degrees, those around her—that there was a problem. Milos, however, looked confusedly blank. "Yes, sir," he replied.

The Circuit Judiciary made a contemptuous snorting noise, as if the matter that he had been called upon to decide was not remotely worth his time or consideration. He had a large book open before him, presumably one of law. He slammed it closed with a thud that made everyone in the room, except Calhoun, jump slightly. "Then you have wasted my time," he growled. "The defendant is free to go."

The cry of outrage was deafening, everyone shouting at once . . . once again, everyone except Calhoun, who was simply shaking his head slightly from side to side. Kusack was grinning broadly, obviously pleased with the result.

Milos' voice managed to tower above everyone else's. "Sir!" he cried out. "This man . . . he murdered a man, Turkin, who played with him in a game of cards . . . and his brothers killed our beloved Majister . . . !"

"We speak of matters of life and death here, Praestor. If Kusack were responsible for a murder, such an act carries penalties that have a definite air of finality about them. So certainty is required. What you have told me here does not begin to approach that certainty." Voices began to rise once more in protest, but the Judiciary outshouted them. "In regards to the death of Majister Fairax . . . well, I regret it as much as you. He was a decent and honorable man. But Kusack was merely present at that incident. No one is claiming that he himself pulled the trigger. In fact, he was behind gaol bars at the time. You have tried to paint him as some sort of accomplice, but your description of the events simply do not fit the requirements of law that define an accomplice." When he spoke of law, his fingers caressed the book with cool satisfaction. "As for this Turkin fellow . . . where are your witnesses? The other cardplayers, for example . . ."

"Two of them were Kusack's own brothers," admitted the Praestor. "Two others were . . . well . . . hired guns. They were not permanent residents of the city and have moved on . . ."

"And the remaining witness was the arresting officer himself, Majister Fairax, who is now, regrettably, deceased," said the Judiciary. "If you had brought Kusack's brothers to me and they had admitted to their brother's act, that would carry weight. Yet they are not here, nor has your present Majister made any effort to hunt them down."

There was a dead silence, almost challenging. Calhoun said quietly, "I am one person. I cannot cover the entirety of the planet single-handedly. If I had a squadron of men at my disposal, I would not know which direction to send them in pursuit. If I had some form of instantaneous communication with other towns . . ."

Despite the seriousness of the situation, there was chortling from around him. " 'Instantaneous communication'?" said the Judiciary incredulously. "What sort?"

Calhoun shrugged slightly. "You could string wires—cables—between cities. Communicate in that way."

The chortling turned into outright derisive laughter. The Judiciary looked at the Praestor as if to say, *This is the madman you've installed as the agent of law in this city?* "The transmission of voices over wires or cables," the Judiciary said patiently, "is physically impossible."

"Far be it from me," Calhoun said with a faintly mocking tone, "to challenge one whose scientific knowledge so outstrips my own."

The Judiciary heard the challenge in Calhoun's voice, but chose to ignore him. Instead, he rose from behind the table, tucking the book under his arm. "With the witnesses either unavailable or dead, we have only secondhand information on which to base the prosecution of this man. It is insufficient. Why are you still here, Kusack? I have told you you are free to go. Go."

With a triumphant whoop that pierced the sudden stillness of the meetinghouse, Kusack bounded out the door. His laughter floated behind him.

The Maestress was now on her feet, and she pointed a bony and wavering hand at the Judiciary. "A grave miscarriage of justice has occurred here today, sir," she told him. For once, Rheela found herself in agreement with the little wretch.

"I do not adjudicate in matters of justice, Maestress . . . only law," the Judiciary informed her. "Now, if there is nothing else . . ."

"There is, actually," Calhoun said. He had risen as well, and he had a satchel slung over his shoulder. "A child's toy. I devised it for a young man of my acquaintance. I was hoping you could help me test it."

The Judiciary stared uncomprehendingly at Calhoun. "What . . . ?" he managed to get out.

Calhoun was not affording him the slightest bit of attention. Instead, he was busy pulling out two cups, joined by a string affixed at the base of each. He proferred one of the cups to the Judiciary and said, "If you wouldn't mind . . . ?"

The Judiciary slowly took the cup, turning it over and over in his hand, as if trying to figure out what trick was hidden within.

"Now, back up," Calhoun said pleasantly, "until the string draws taut."

The Judiciary looked around in confusion, saw the blank stares of those around him. Caught up in the moment, he walked backward until the string between the two cups was tight.

"Now, hold it to your ear," Calhoun told him.

Eyes narrowed in suspicion, the Judiciary nevertheless held the cup to his ear. Calhoun then whispered something into his cup so softly that no one could hear what he had said.

But the Judiciary's eyes widened, and his face went pale with shock as the cup slipped out of his hand and fell to the floor. Whatever Calhoun had said, the Judiciary had obviously heard it. And whatever he had heard apparently wasn't very calming or flattering. Clutching his book of law tightly to him, he pivoted on his heel and bolted out the door, nearly stumbling as he did so.

Everyone was staring at Calhoun as he calmly picked up the fallen cup and placed the makeshift device back into his satchel. Then he glanced around at the other townspeople once more before walking out of the meeting hall. The silence extended for long moments after his departure, and then the Praestor loudly cleared his throat. "Well," he said, "I suppose that you can all return to your homes. There's nothing more to see h—"

"Wait!" Rheela was on her feet, her mouth moving before she even realized she was going to speak. "Wait . . . what about the duel? This . . . this Krut person! What are we going to do to help him—?"

There were blank stares from all around her. One would have thought she was speaking in a foreign language.

"Do?" It was the Maestress who had spoken, her voice dripping with derision.

"It is a personal matter," Milos said. "We all heard it . . ."

"Personal matter! He is our Majister! Our defender of law!" Every eye was upon her, judging her, and she could practically feel the contempt radiating from them. But she ignored it, pushing on, determined. "You stood here and witnessed a man go free who was partly to blame for the death of our previous Majister, a man beloved by all. Will you stand by and see another good man be killed while trying to do what's right?"

"Will we sacrifice ourselves to save him?" Spangler called from the back.

"Why shouldn't we?" she replied with grim amusement. "After all, Spangler . . . wouldn't that make a better story? That's all you're interested in, anyway: stories. Not about affecting the outcome; just about standing by and watching it all happen. And then you tell other people about it in your newspaper, so they can shake their heads and talk about what a dangerous place the world is, and aren't they fortunate to have avoided any such unpleasantness themselves. Well, you should not be avoiding this upcoming 'unpleasantness'! You should be getting your hands dirty trying to stop it! You all should!"

"Perhaps," the Maestress said coolly, "we should vote on it."

Immediately there were shouts of "Yes! Let's vote!"

The vote was fairly quickly attended to. After all, when only one person raises her hand to vote "Aye," an exact count of the "Nays" isn't really all that necessary.

\* \* \*

It was extremely quiet around the dinner table that evening. Over the past weeks, as they had become increasingly comfortable with one another, there had been something that had been extremely rare around the household: laughter. They had basked in each other's company, and for what had seemed all too brief a time, Rheela had occasionally entertained fantasies of what it would be like if it could be this way always.

But this evening, it was different. Silence lay shrouded around them, and finally Rheela put down her utensils a bit too loudly. The loud *clink* of the utensils naturally got Calhoun's and Moke's full attention.

"I'm tired of everyone trying not to make eye contact with each other," she said. She looked from one to the other, her gaze settling on Calhoun. "Is he really that fast? This Krut? As fast as Moke told me?"

"He's very fast," Calhoun admitted.

"Faster than you?"

"I don't know. I think so, yes."

"How can you just sit there and make such a calm assessment of it?"

"No matter how fast or how skilled a person is, there's always going to be someone who's faster or more skilled," Calhoun said, also putting down his eating utensils. The food lay largely untouched on his plate. "There's no point in getting upset about it."

"There is if it means your death!"

"I'd rather die fighting than of old age," said Calhoun thoughtfully. "But don't worry. I've no intention of dying tomorrow."

"But you think he's a faster draw than you."

"Yes."

"Then you're going to die!"

He started to reply, but then caught Moke's expression out the corner of his eye. He spoke in a low tone, even though the boy could easily hear it. "You're upsetting the boy."

*Why shouldn't he be upset along with me!* Rheela wanted to howl. But she literally bit her tongue. Instead, she got up from the table so forcefully that she banged her knees on the underside of it, sending some of the food tumbling. Reflexively, she started to reach for it, but then caught herself and turned and dashed out into the unseasonably cool evening air. She heard voices floating behind her, heard Moke saying, "Why is she so upset? He's not going to kill you, is he?" and Calhoun, damn him, saying, "No, of course not. I'll be fine." Her fury grew upon hearing that, because she didn't want him lying to the boy. But what, really, was he supposed to say? "Yes, son, he's going to kill me. You're talking to a dead man."

The tears welled up in her eyes, and then he was behind her, a hand resting on her shoulder. She whirled and held him tightly, and marveled at how solid his body was. She knew at that moment just how much she wanted him.

"We'll run away," she whispered.

Her voice must have been muffled against him, but he was still able to hear her well enough. "Run away?"

She pulled her face away from him and nodded fervently. "We can. We can do it. You, me, Moke . . . we'll pack up, steal away into the night . . ."

"Wouldn't do any good," he said. "I know the type of 'man' Krut is. Now that he knows I'm here, he'll track me down. And then he'll try to kill not only me, but also you and Moke. Besides . . . I was never much for running."

"And how are you for dying?" she demanded bitterly. She was crying again. She hated that, hated the crying. She had thought herself all cried-out years ago . . . back when the stranger had left. The stranger who had put Moke into her body and departed as mysteriously as he had come. "Have a lot of experience dying, do you?"

"Dying, yes. Never quite gotten to 'dead.' But I've done the dying part enough not to be intimidated by it."

"Well, I am. I am incredibly intimidated by it, and I don't want to lose you! I don't want you to go away!"

He took her firmly by the shoulders and the scar on his tanned cheek was bright crimson against it. "You knew I would go away, sooner or later. I've never been anything other than honest with you about that. I'm just—"

"Passing through, I know, I know. But it's not fair! I don't want you passing through! I want you to stay here, and grow old with me, and Moke, and there's no violence, no hatred . . ."

"It sounds wonderful. It does. But I—"

She kissed him then. She gave him no choice, really. Her lips were hungry against his, as if she was trying to draw strength directly through the contact. Her face was slick with tears, and she didn't know where to put her hands, on the back of his head or on his back. They just roamed aimlessly over his body. . . .

And then she released him. She looked deeply into those purple eyes that she felt she could swim in endlessly, and she whispered, "She must be quite a woman . . . this whoever-it-is you're thinking of when I hold you. The one I'm not." She paused, and then said softly, "I'm not stupid, you know. Somehow I always knew you were from . . ." She glanced heavenward. "From up there. Like Kolk'r, descended from on high . . ."

"I'm no deity, I assure you," he said with a faint smile. But there were no pretensions between them either, no pretending that he was simply a native of Yakaba who just looked odd. The pleasant fiction that allowed the more mundane, more foolish members of her race to get through the day in the serene belief that they were the premiere creatures of the galaxy.

"And she's from out there, isn't she? Wherever you come from, that's where she is, too."

"Yes."

"And she holds your heart."

"Yes. I didn't realize how much until I was truly faced with the prospect of never seeing her again."

"I envy her. Envy her a great deal. And . . . you might never see her again."

"That's possible," he admitted.

"Yet you would be loyal to her, even though you might never see her again."

"I wasn't thinking about being loyal to her," admitted Calhoun. "But I've found that I can't be . . . disloyal."

She looked down. "Do me one favor, Calhoun."

"Anything that I possibly can."

"Don't . . . stay here tonight. Because I think this may be your last night on this world, and knowing that you were down the hall, and I could not go to you, could not touch you or love you . . . I don't think I could stand that. I think that would be very cruel, and I very much doubt you have any desire to be cruel to me."

He nodded slightly. "As you wish."

He tipped his hat to her, and then walked slowly toward his luukab. She said nothing as he approached it, but simply stood there, her legs trembling, feeling as if she was going to collapse from grief any moment. But she refused to do so. She was determined to stay on her own two feet and not give in to weakness. And as he climbed atop the luukab, she called to him, "I won't come into the city tomorrow. I won't be there to watch you die."

"I don't blame you," he said without turning to look at her. "I wouldn't come to watch me die either."

And on that, their last night together, he rode off into the darkness.

# LEFLER

ROBIN LEFLER, FORMERLY OF THE starship *Excalibur,* stopped dead in her tracks in the lobby of the El Dorado resort and rubbed her eyes. She couldn't quite believe who she saw coming toward her.

"Commander?!?" In terms of disbelief, she also couldn't quite comprehend why she sounded, and felt, so overjoyed to see the first officer of the *Excalibur* coming toward her. And, even more astounding than that, Shelby actually seemed pleased to see her. Lefler had always had the opinion that Shelby felt a bit impatient with her. As if somehow Lefler wasn't measuring up to what Shelby felt an officer should be. Then her fingers flew to her lips in chagrin. "Oh, I'm sorry! Captain, I should be saying, right?"

"We'll let it go this time," Shelby said with mock gravity as she took Lefler's hand in her own and shook it warmly. "It's good to see you, Robin."

"You, too, Captain. You're looking good. Command suits you, I think."

"That's what I keep telling myself. It's been . . ." She gave a small smile, and Robin might have imagined it, but there seemed to be pain in the smile. "It's been an interesting few months. The first month or so was the hardest."

"Why? What happened the first month?"

"Oh, the usual . . . averted a war, condemned some people to death. Standard stuff." She tried to sound jesting about it, but it certainly didn't come out that way. Realizing that dwelling on it might not be the best tack to take, Lefler quickly—and wisely—changed the subject.

"Are you here on Risa for shore leave?"

"Actually, no." They sauntered over to a nicely cushioned couch situated near a splashing waterfall. Shelby glanced at the waterfall and chuckled.

"I know, I know, it's a bit much," said Robin. "But believe it or not, you get used to it. So," and they sat on the couch, "if not shore leave, why are you here?"

"Well, there's a ceremony coming up that you've been invited to, but you haven't been responding to Starfleet communiqués about it."

"Ohhh," moaned Lefler. "I'm so sorry about that. We had some, uhm . . . unpleasantness here on Risa Major . . . unpleasantness. It knocked out systems for quite a while. In fact, we're still doing repair work on it. This entire lobby," and she indicated the space around them, "was nothing short of a disaster area. Took ages to get it back into shape. In any event, our communications grid has been spotty. A lot of transmissions have been lost. But hey . . . at least I knew to inform Starfleet of where I was heading off to, so they'd know to send you here. I assume that's what happened."

Shelby nodded. "And since our schedule called for us to come through here, I didn't mind stopping off to be the one to tell you the news."

"What news?"

"They're relaunching *Excalibur.*"

Lefler's eyes glittered with excitement. "Really?"

"Really. From the outside, it looks like a standard *Galaxy*-class, but inside . . . well, do you know what the ancient term "hot rod" means? And she's been commissioned with the name of our old ship. Not only that, but there's going to be a launching and christening ceremony."

"Where?"

"Well, final dry runs were held at the drydock at Starbase Eight. That's where the ceremony's going to be held. Invitations have been sent out to the command crew, and everyone's going to be there. Even Jean-Luc Picard. He was, after all, the one who was responsible for getting Mac to join Starfleet, so obviously he felt it would only be right. And who would gainsay him, right? The only outstanding invitation was to you."

"Of course I'll come! When is it?"

"In a week. Actually, we're on our way there now. My orders are simply to bring you along if you're interested."

"We? You mean your ship? The *Exeter?* You came here in your ship?"

Shelby smirked. "It certainly seemed easier than walking here."

"Yes, of course," laughed Lefler, thwapping her own forehead in chagrin. "I'm sorry, it's just . . ." Her hands fluttered. "I feel like . . . there's all sorts of emotions just kind of running around inside me. I feel like I don't know where to look first, you know?"

"Believe me, I know. I do know. Oh, and your mother is naturally also welcome to come. She's here with you, I take it." And when Lefler nodded, she added, "Also, I was wondering if you know the whereabouts of Si Cwan and Kalinda. Wouldn't quite be the same without our unofficial ambassador and his sister along. They're the only other ones who haven't responded . . ."

She saw the expression on Lefler's face then . . . something that was a cross between anger and pain.

"Robin," she said slowly, "what happened?"

Lefler turned away. "Just . . . some problems here on Risa."

"What . . . kind of problems?"

"Oh, the people-getting-killed, screaming-disaster kind of problems. You know. Typical." She was trying to sound flip, but she wasn't remotely succeeding.

"I think," Shelby said, "you'd better tell me what happened."

"Captain, that isn't necessary—"

"Lefler," said Shelby sternly, "you're still in Starfleet, even if you have holed up on a resort planet. I still outrank you. Tell me. What. Happened."

Lefler took a deep breath and let it out slowly. "All right . . . look, Captain. If I tell you . . . then let me just tell you, okay? Don't stop me or ask me questions or anything. Let me just get through it. Fair enough?"

"Fair enough. Shall we go somewhere to—?"

Lefler shrugged. "Here is as good as anywhere else. Okay, so . . . where to start . . ." She rubbed the bridge of her nose. "Where to start . . ."

Shelby, as per their agreement, waited silently.

"All right," said Lefler after a long moment's pause. "Mother and I decided . . . well, Mother decided, really, and I just came along because, you know, go stop my mother when she gets something into her head . . . that we would go on vacation here, to Risa . . . to this hotel, called the El Dorado. We met some . . . interesting people here. One of them was a genuine relic: a man named Montgomery Scott, also known as Scotty, who used to be chief engineer under the command of Captain Kirk. He was time-displaced, for reasons too complicated to go into. Annnnnyway, he was working here at the El Dorado—having initially come to work on straightening out the resort's computer system, and staying on as a sort of 'greeter' in a customized pub called the Engine Room. He took an immediate shine to my mother . . . but she, in turn, became interested in a man named Rafe Viola.

"I, meantime, decided to do some exploring. I wound up falling through a weak part of the ground and encountered a subterranean creature that was some kind of huge, gelatinous mass that was extremely nasty and very hungry. I wound up being saved at the last moment by, of all people, Nikolas Viola . . . the son, of course, of Rafe. We became . . . a bit involved. It's . . . not really relevant.

"Except . . . things weren't remotely what they appeared to be. It turned out that Rafe Viola was actually a fabricated name . . . that his true name was Sientor Olivan. And Olivan had quite a track record. For one thing . . . he created the computer virus that was responsible for setting the events in motion that blew up the *Excalibur.*"

"Oh, my God," breathed Shelby. "I had received word that an individual purportedly responsible for it had been identified, but the details were sketchy."

"Well, I'll fill them in for you . . . except, you know, you promised . . ."

"Not to interrupt. My apologies."

"It's all right. In any event, the night that everything went insane, Mother and I were having dinner with Olivan and his . . . Nik . . . in a restaurant here called the Shakespeare Tavern. What we *didn't* know was that Olivan had tapped into the El Dorado computer as well . . . not with the intention of destroying it, but instead of enriching himself. He was using it to access not only the accounts of the resort, but the personal accounts of every single visitor here, past and present, with the intention of siphoning all their funds into a hidden account of his own. Scotty and the resort's manager, Mr. Quincy, discovered it while working in the resort's computer core. Unfortunately for them, Nik discovered them as well. Nik killed Quincy with his bare hands, and then tried to get Scotty . . . who leaped into the pit of the computer core in order to get away.

"All of this, we didn't know. We just thought we were having dinner . . . except something in Olivan's attitude tipped off my mother. And that's when Si Cwan and Kalinda showed up . . ."

"Showed up here?" asked Shelby, and then realizing, she said, "Sorry."

"Yes. Showed up here. You see, they'd been tracking down Olivan, because Olivan had killed a beloved teacher of Si Cwan's . . . a man named Jereme, who had also been a teacher of Olivan's. Except there was some confusion, because Kalinda claimed that it had been Nik who had killed Jereme, not Olivan himself. In any event, it didn't matter to Si Cwan, because he was ready to take out both of them, he was so furious over the death of his teacher.

"But Olivan, he didn't seem the least bit bothered. In fact, he seemed incredibly confident, and seconds later, we found out why. I'll never forget. He said that even though he hadn't been ex-pecting any sort of trouble, he had prepared for it nevertheless. And he said, 'I introduced a virus into the central computer of the El Dorado, which I've just triggered,' and he tapped his belt buckle, 'with this. Within two minutes, this entire resort will be-come one gargantuan death trap. I am the only one who can stop it. If you kill me, Si Cwan . . . even if you manage to do so, which I very much doubt . . . then you will be dooming everyone you see in this room to a very violent death. Your choice, Si Cwan. For the sake of everyone here . . . I hope you choose correctly.'

"And that's when things got really interesting . . ."

# *TAPINZA*

"WHAT THE HELL DO YOU MEAN, you promised Krut first shot? *We* should have first shot!"

Temo was bristling with fury as he stood in the middle of Tapinza's office. Seated in chairs nearby were his brothers, the newly freed Kusack and the less-than-talkative Qinos. Tapinza, behind his desk, was the picture of calm.

"Krut came an awful long way to kill Calhoun," Tapinza said coolly. "And his grudge goes back a bit further. So I felt it the least I could do to accommodate him. Granted, he didn't know initially that Calhoun was the one who had slain his business partner, but now that he does know . . ."

"This is intolerable!" Temo raged.

Harshly, Tapinza said, "You *will* tolerate it. I've already endeavored to make your life easier. Or did you think the Judiciary let your brother free because of Kusack's charming personality?"

Temo made a dismissive noise. "You're now claiming credit for a decision of law that went in our brother's favor? What sort of arrogant—?"

Tapinza slapped his hands together so forcefully that it made the three brothers jump. A door opened at the far end of the room, and two men walked in. They were two of a kind, both grizzled and low to the ground, eyes glowing with a sullen malevolence. Kusack's eyes widened as he recognized them immediately.

"Solly . . . Bartog . . . you remember Kusack," Tapinza said cheerfully. "Kusack, say hello to—"

"You were at the game!" Kusack said in alarm. He turned to Temo as if his brother hadn't heard and said again, "They were at the game! The card game! The one where I—"

"We all know what you did, Kusack," interrupted Tapinza. "Calm down. You are among friends here. Well . . . if not friends . . . certainly not enemies, in any event. Solly and Bartog are in my employ."

"It was a setup," Qinos said hollowly.

"No, not a setup," Tapinza told him, shaking his head vigorously. "Purest happenstance. But one becomes successful by seeing where the opportunities lie."

"They owe me money," Kusack said sullenly.

"Indeed they do. And if I had chosen to produce them, they could have testified against you, providing sufficient eyewitness testimony to send you to a very deep hole, Kusack. So I strongly advise that, rather than complain or otherwise be belligerent, you keep in mind just who your friends are." He surveyed the occupants of the room balefully. "Now . . . you will do exactly as I say, exactly when I say it. Temo, Qinos, Kusack, You'll station yourselves at key points around the city, waiting in ambush. Krut will have his opportunity at Calhoun. If something goes wrong, then . . . only then . . . will you take your turn at him. If you do as I say, then we have potential for a rather impressive alliance. If you do not do as I say, then I will put an end to you. Don't think that I can't. People become extremely dead underestimating me. Are we all clear on this?"

Qinos and Kusack both looked to Temo, as they customarily did. Temo did not look away from Tapinza for a long moment, and then finally he nodded, his face unreadable.

"Good," said Tapinza, and he clapped his hands and rubbed them together briskly. "Okay, then! The show should be starting quite soon! Let's get into position . . . and enjoy the day."

# LEFLER'S STORY

*I STOOD THERE, not knowing where to look first.* Si Cwan was facing the man he'd called Sientor Olivan, and whom I'd known until recently as Rafe Viola. Next to him was his son, or at least the man whom I'd believed to be his son . . . except that, at that moment, I had no idea who anyone was anymore. I barely knew who I was.

It was like the air between Olivan and Si Cwan could be cut with a sword, it was so thick with tension. And Si Cwan certainly had the sword, all right. But whatever anger he was feeling, whatever emotions were being tossed around inside him, he didn't let any of it show. Instead, he just stood there, like a big Thallonian statue.

"I can shut it down with this remote, Cwan," said Olivan, tapping his belt buckle again. "But I'll only do it once Nik and I are gone. And since it's at least a ninety-second dash to our ship, which is out in the main landing area, I suggest you get out of our way, because you're running out of time to have me shut down the death-trap scenario."

"We've no way of knowing if he's lying . . . or even if he will shut it down once he's gone," Kalinda said to her brother.

Si Cwan certainly knew that . . . but apparently he also knew that he couldn't take the risk. He stepped to one side, but his gaze never left Olivan's face. "This isn't over," he growled. "I tracked you here. I can follow you anywhere."

Olivan didn't bother to respond. Instead, he just started to head out. Nik cast one look in my direction, and I have no idea what was going through his mind. Regret? Smug triumph? I've no idea. His face was just . . . just blank. Which was fine, I guess, because at that moment I had absolutely no idea what to think about anything, so I guess I was something of a blank myself.

They headed for the door . . . and suddenly there was this . . . there's no other way to put it, a battle cry. And charging in through the door, bellowing like a lunatic, was Montgomery Scott.

Now you've got to understand: Olivan is an incredible hand-to-hand fighter. It's one of the things he learned from Jereme. He's on Si Cwan's level. Hell, he's *above* Si Cwan's level. And Scotty is . . . well, not exactly in shape, let's put it that way. Under ordinary circumstances, Scotty doesn't even get within two feet of him before Olivan puts him down. But these weren't ordinary circumstances. Because Scotty was coming in just as Olivan was going out, so it was totally unexpected. And not only that, but Olivan thought that Scotty was dead. So, for just a second, Olivan was frozen in place in confusion and surprise. As it turned out, that was all that was needed.

Scotty plowed into him like a rhino, shouting out stuff in Scots that I couldn't even begin to understand, though I doubt any of it was especially flattering. Scotty managed to get a grip on Olivan's shoulder and upper arm, and then Scotty's weight and momentum were enough to send both of them crashing to the floor.

Everybody in the tavern was shouting at once, but it all blended together so that nobody really understood anything that anybody else was saying. Even with everything he had going for him, Scotty didn't last for more than a few seconds, as Nik stepped in behind and yanked him off his father. He whipped Scotty around, and Scotty saw him and shouted, "And you! You were the one who killed Quincy!" and he tried to lunge at him. But Nik was more than ready for him, and he moved so fast that he was practically a blur as he sent Scotty tumbling to the floor.

"Get away from him!" shouted my mom as she charged forward.

Nik did step away, but only after he kicked Scotty in the gut. Scotty let out a yelp, but by that point Nik was already helping his father to his feet. "You said he was dead!" shouted Olivan.

"I thought he was! I saw him jump!" said Nik defensively. He turned to Scotty and yelled at him, "How can you still be alive? How?"

Mom was crouched next to Scotty, trying to get him not to move, but Scotty fought his way up to a half-sitting position, and he had this look of grim satisfaction on his face. "It's like ah told Quincy, before ye murdered him, ye bloodthirsty Saracen. Ah prepare for everything. And if ah have to be crawlin' around a computer core shaft with a sheer drop, ah make sure to have antigrav boots on in case ah make a misstep. They make 'em smaller and more elegant in this century than in muh own, and they get th' job done."

"Very foresighted. Very clever," Olivan said. Then he saw that Nik was staring at him. "What's wron—"

Then he looked down at where Nik was looking. He looked down at his belt buckle. The one that had the device in it that was going to be able to shut down the whole "death-trap" thing.

It was busted. When Scotty had knocked him to the floor, it had shattered.

"Oh, no," Olivan said. He didn't look quite as confident as he had a moment before.

"This could be a problem," Mother said.

Scotty was looking around in confusion. "What's wrong? What happen—?"

That was when we started hearing the rumbling. It was very distant, but it sounded as if it was getting closer and closer with every passing second. People in the tavern were all babbling, looking around, trying to figure out what was going on.

It was Scotty, naturally, who figured it out first. "The wave generator!" he said. "At the beach front! It's out of control! What caused th—?" But then he answered his own question as he looked at Olivan. "You! You rigged the computer somehow! That's why your son was rootin' around there!"

"This is a fine time to blame me, engineer," snarled Olivan. "Everything would have been fine if you hadn't—"

And then he spun around. How he knew the attack was coming, I've no idea, but he just knew, that's all. Si Cwan was coming right at him with the sword he'd taken off the wall. Olivan moved so quickly that even now, no matter how many times I run the scene back in my mind, I still can't actually see him, you know? He was under the sword so fast, just so fast, and then he was behind Si Cwan, his arms around and through, and his hands were on the back of Si Cwan's neck. I swear to God, just within that period of no more than two seconds, he had outmaneuvered Cwan and was about to break his neck.

It was Kalinda who saved him. She let out a screech and jumped at him, grabbing him by the back of the head. It didn't take Olivan more than a second to deal with her, lashing out with a leg and sweeping her feet out from under her. But it was the momentary distraction that Si Cwan needed. Somehow, I don't know how, he slipped between Olivan's arms, and then he whipped the sword around and sliced Olivan on the leg. Olivan let out a yell of fury and clutched at it, blood seeping between his fingers. But his shout was drowned out by the yells of alarm from the other people in the tavern as the ground began to rumble even more. And we could hear the onrush of water, like someone had left a faucet running. A really, really, really big faucet. People were trampling over each other to get out.

But for all that they heard anyone else, Si Cwan and Olivan could have been alone in a desert. They faced each other—Si Cwan poised with the sword in a striking position, Olivan staring at him balefully. "You've gotten faster in your old age, Cwan."

"And you've just gotten older," Cwan shot back. "You had no intention of shutting down the 'self-destruct' program, even if you'd made it to your ship."

"As soon as I knew you were here? Of course not. I'd flood a planet to get rid of you, Cwan."

Nice guy.

Scotty was looking off in the direction from which the rumbling was coming. I could practically see him running calculations in his head. It was clear that he had absolutely no intention of wasting time asking for Olivan's help, even though Olivan was responsible for it in the first place. If nothing else, he likely didn't trust him to be cooperative, and besides—in retrospect, it was probably a matter of pride. He was going to be damned if he admitted that there was something one person had done to a computer that he couldn't undo. "We've got t'shut down th'wave machine b'fore ev'ry man, woman and child in the place drowns! I can do it down in th'computer core. It's a two-man job—"

"I'll help," my mother said immediately.

It's taking me so long to tell you this, I can't really impart the sense of urgency that was going on. People weren't just talking, like I am to you now. They were shouting, or speaking over each other. Everything was heightened, everything was happening so fast . . .

And that was when an arm grabbed me from behind. Not coincidentally, there was a person attached to it . . . that person being Nik.

"Don't move," he said harshly in my ear. "I don't want to have to kill you." Which suited me just fine, since I didn't want to have to die.

My mother yelled out my name even as Nik shouted, "Step back from my father, Cwan! Step back or your little friend here dies! You, too, Scotsman! Everyone! Back, or she dies! I mean it!"

I tried to get a word out, tried to shout that they shouldn't worry about me. But he had one hand on my throat, choking off anything I might try to say. I struggled against him, but I couldn't do anything. I felt in him the strength that enabled him to kill people with his bare hands. I had taken such comfort from the power in his arms, and the rest of his body, days earlier, when he and I had been . . .

Uhm . . .

Well . . . let's just say that, when he'd first held me, it had been under somewhat different circumstances. And that which I had taken such comfort in earlier was now terrifying me. Trust turned inside out. Not a pleasant feeling.

I tend to think any other mother would have been reduced to begging, pleading, howling for her daughter's life to be spared. Not mine, no. She just studied the situation as coolly as you please. Then, without batting an eye, she turned to Scotty and said, "Let's go."

Scotty was dumbfounded, even though water was already starting to splash around his feet. "Wh-wha'? But . . . but they have—"

"They're going to have a soggy corpse—and lots of company to go with it—unless we do something quickly, Scotsman," she said brusquely. "They're not going to harm Robin because they want her for a hostage, a shield against Si Cwan and Kalinda. I give it about nine minutes, eighteen seconds before this place is underwater unless we do something about it, and wringing our hands over a hostage situation isn't what I consider 'something' . . . no offense, sweetheart."

I grunted, since air was still not forthcoming to my lungs, and flashed her what amounted to a "high sign." What else could I do? The thing was, she was right. My mother was someone who knew exactly what had to be done, and when it had to be done, and she wasn't about to let her personal concern over her daughter get in the way of her ability to prioritize.

"Let's go. Hurry. Hurry!" she said with greater urgency to Scotty, snapping him from the trance that had momentarily seized him. With a final backward glance at me, my mother and Scotty splashed out the door.

Olivan, showing only the slightest limp, circled around and came up next to us. Nik shook me slightly, like a warning that I shouldn't try to break free or otherwise provide him any sort of inconvenience. But, very softly, he whispered into my ear, "Don't fight me and you'll get out of this alive."

I didn't have a particular interest in arguing the point.

Si Cwan wasn't taking his eyes off Olivan, as if expecting him to make some sort of move. He kept the sword at the ready and glanced, with obvious satisfaction, at the spreading red stain on Olivan's leg from where he'd slashed him. "Why?" he demanded. "Why did you feel the need to kill Jereme?"

"It wasn't me, actually. It was him," Olivan said, nodding a head toward his son and looking rather proud as he did so. "Nik."

"But he did so at your instruction."

"Yes."

"Why?" Si Cwan was totally focused on Olivan. I wasn't even sure if he knew I was still there.

"What do you want, Si Cwan? A long, elaborate explanation of why I do what I do? I did it because it was time to do it. And Nik did it because he had no choice in the matter. That's all the explanation I have any intention of giving you . . . and, truthfully, all you really deserve. And now," and he bowed deeply, "it is time for us to leave. If you want the young woman to die, by all means, follow us."

My last sight of Si Cwan was him and Kalinda, rooted to the spot, water splashing up around their ankles, and the distant rumble indicating that more was on the way.

# RHEELA

SHE HAD TOLD HERSELF she wasn't going to go.

She had promised herself, sworn it to herself. As the sun had come up, had climbed higher into the sky, over and over she kept saying, "I won't do it. I won't." And she had kept right on saying it, up until the point where Moke had told her in no uncertain terms that he was going. "Mac needs us," he said, with clear conviction.

She tried to figure out some way to tell the child, to make clear to him the magnitude of the disaster that was likely going to occur, and finally there was no other way for her to say it. "Moke . . . he may very well die," she told him.

"He's our friend. We're his friends. I love him, Ma."

"So do I. But . . ."

"No." He shook his head vigorously. "No, no 'but.' If you love somebody, there's no 'but.' "

She tried to come up with some sort of response to that, but nothing readily presented itself . . . perhaps because she knew it to be true. And so she and Moke hastened to the town. All the way in, she prayed that she would not wind up seeing what she was positive she was going to see: the death of a man who had come to mean a lot to her.

As the luukab's back swayed gently, Rheela instinctively held Moke closer . . . so much so that he let out a small squeal of complaint. She let up on him then, but was no less concerned about the gravity of the situation.

It seemed to her that the town was exceptionally quiet. Normally, when she came into the city, there were people bustling about, the general noise of conversation, laughter from the tavern, arguments, raised voices, crying children—the usual range and assortment of interactions that were normal for large groups of individuals cohabiting in a relatively small area. But there was none of that this time. Instead there was a deathly silence hanging over the entire area, like a funeral shroud.

The luukab, under Rheela's guidance, lumbered down the main street, and she guided him toward the Majister's office. It was disconcerting to her that the only sound to be heard was the steady *thwump thwump* of the luukab's padded feet. She thought she saw, out of the corner of her eye, people glancing out at her from windows or around doors, but every time she looked in one direction or the other, anyone observing her would vanish.

She drew the luukab up just outside the Majister's office and slid off in one direction, Moke dismounting on the other. If the silence that surrounded them registered on the boy, he gave no indication of it. Instead, he seemed much more interested in the sky. He was sniffing it, his nostrils flaring slightly, and he said, "Ma . . . I think there might be a storm."

She looked upward as well, but saw nothing. That was odd; usually she was attuned to such things. Then again, she thought grimly, it was likely that Moke was reacting not to the actual weather but to the mood of the town around him. He didn't understand why, of course. He was still a child, after all. There was so much he didn't understand. . . .

If only Calhoun could have remained around to explain it to him.

She scolded herself immediately. Was she already going to be thinking of Calhoun as one gone? Was she to write him off that coldly and dismissively? Certainly he had some sort of chance . . .

. . . didn't he?

She took a deep breath, the hot air feeling particularly scalding in her lungs, and then turned to Moke. He was still staring at the sky. "Moke," she said crisply, and Moke turned to her, looking momentarily puzzled, as if he'd forgotten where he was or whom he was with. Then he shook it off and smiled wanly. She reached out, took his hand, and together they walked into the Majister's office.

Calhoun was sitting in his chair, his feet up on the desk, looking utterly relaxed. He was twirling some sort of small silver cylinder in his hand, and he looked up at them as they walked in. This did not seem, to her, to be a man who was especially concerned about the prospect of his imminent demise.

"Hello," he said pleasantly. Those eyes, those incredible eyes held her gaze. She tried to imagine them closed in death, or staring lifelessly at the skies, and she couldn't even begin to do so. He just seemed too full of vitality to fall prey to something as mundane as being killed. "Come by to chat for a bit?"

"Hey, Mac!" said Moke with abundant cheer. Calhoun reached out a hand and Moke gripped it firmly, grinning lopsidedly. The small, silver object that Calhoun had been fidgeting with immediately caught his attention. "What's that thing?" he asked.

"This? Oh . . . just a good luck charm."

"Ahhh. Okay. I'm glad you got something like that."

"You are?"

"Yeah, 'cause if you have something to help you with luck, that's good, 'cause Ma's worried about you."

"Is she?" Calhoun looked flattered. "Why should she be worried?"

"She thinks you're gonna die."

"Moke!" Her face colored at the child's unabashed candor.

"Does she now?" Calhoun didn't seem the least bit bothered by the pronouncement. "Well . . . I suspect she's right." But then he added quickly, "However, there's nothing to say that it's going to be today."

She felt as if her heart was being pulled from her chest, and the words came out all in a rush. "Calhoun, there must be some other way," she said, silently scolding herself for the desperation in her voice, but unable to help herself. "There must be something other than fighting."

He raised a skeptical eyebrow. "Such as . . . ?"

"I don't know!" she said in exasperation. "Something! Anything! You're a smart man!"

"And if I were so smart, I wouldn't have allowed myself to get pulled into this situation?"

"Yes. That's exactly right."

Suddenly a rough voice sounded from outside. "Calhoun!" it bellowed. "Calhoun! Coward! Fool! I'm calling you! Unless you want me to come into your hidey-hole, I suggest you come out and face me."

He looked to Rheela with an air of resignation and spread his hands, palms up, in a manner that seemed to say, *What else can I do?*

Unable to believe that she was doing it even as she did it, Rheela started pushing on Calhoun's shoulder as he rose from behind the desk. "Get going. Out the back."

He laughed. It wasn't in a derisive way. He seemed amused, even a bit charmed by the urgency in her tone. "Out the back?"

"Yes. Hurry. I'll stall him."

"Unless you're planning to run into the middle of the street and do a striptease, I somehow doubt that you're going to capture his attention for very long."

"Do a what?" she asked in confusion.

He seemed about to explain, but then thought better of it. "Trust me," he said gently, putting his hands on her shoulders and moving her to one side. "This is just something that I'm going to have to take care of."

"And if you die?"

"Then I die."

"But I couldn't stand it if you did! I—!"

She felt ashamed, humiliated that there, in front of her son, the emotions that she'd kept in check for so long were hemorrhaging from her. And yet, for all the shame and mortification she felt over leaving herself so exposed, it was also the best that she had felt in years.

Calhoun put a finger gently to her lips and said softly, "Later. After."

"There may not be an after!"

"There always is," Calhoun told her. "It's just not always where we think it's going to be."

*"Calhoun!"* bellowed the challenging voice once more. Rheela's heart was thudding wildly. It was clear from the sound of that—that whatever-it-was—that it was not going to be patient for much longer. Not that it had displayed much in the way of patience thus far.

"That is not the sound of a happy person," Calhoun understated. "Let's go out and see if I can rearrange that frown into a smile."

He sounded almost chipper about it. So much at ease that the entire thing had taken on an air of unreality. She simply couldn't believe that he was smilingly about to go out there and die. "Mac—" she said with growing urgency, and she knew—beyond question, right then—that if there was any way she could just knock him out, sling him over her shoulder, and make a break for it, she would do it.

With quiet confidence, he said, "Not now. Later. Later would be better."

Without another word, he squared his shoulders and walked to the door and out.

Moke immediately went to the door to watch. "Moke, come away from there!" she ordered, but he stayed right where he was. After a moment, rather than make an issue of it, she joined him, watching fearfully.

She couldn't believe the creature that was waiting for him. He looked like a monster—tall and green, powerfully built, with arms the size of thick cacti. The expression on his face was a fearsome thing, one that she was sure she would take with her to her grave. He was watching Calhoun like a predator eyeing its prey. The creature—Krut was its name, she believed he had said—simply stood there, its hands hovering in a leisurely manner near the butts of the twin weapons it had strapped to either hip.

Calhoun was walking with measured stride, but he wasn't approaching the creature directly. Instead, he seemed to be drifting to one side, moving directly across the creature's path. Krut was standing there, watching him with keen interest. Mockingly, he started to move in the same manner as Calhoun, with that same stride that seemed so casual in Calhoun and so contemptuous in Krut. In fact, he exaggerated Calhoun's movements, swaying back and forth, thrusting out one hip and then the other. If any of the mocking aspects of his attitude were bothering Calhoun, one couldn't discern it from the Majister's calm demeanor.

And now Rheela was starting to see her fellow townspeople more clearly. They were daring to peer out windows and not look away, or position themselves just inside their doors, so they could have a clear view but not be in any danger themselves. Their cowardice was so appalling to Rheela that she could practically taste bile rising in her mouth.

"Keep moving, Calhoun. That's right," sneered Krut. "Keep right on moving. That's what you do best, isn't it? Kill someone, then disappear. No place to run this time, Calhoun, no matter how much you dance about."

Calhoun continued to move, undeterred by anything that Krut was saying to him. Krut kept on circling, moving this way and that, his hands still at the ready to respond to any sudden movement Calhoun might make toward his weapons. Calhoun wasn't looking at Krut's guns, however, nor his hands, but instead directly and unwaveringly into Krut's eyes. There was absolutely no fear in Calhoun's face. None. It seemed unlikely that he was ready to die, nor was he resigned to it. But it was quite clear that he was not the least bit afraid of it.

"You can stop this, you know."

The voice had been soft and almost directly in her ear, the words audible only to her. She jumped slightly and looked to her left. Tapinza was standing there. There was a craftiness in his eyes that she found most unappetizing.

"Oh, can I, Maester?" she replied, making no attempt to hide her skepticism.

He barely glanced toward the drama that was unfolding in the street. Instead, he nodded ever so slightly. "You can end this . . . by asking me to end this."

"And how do you propose to do that?"

He shrugged noncommittally. "Creatures such as this Krut are fairly predictable. He doesn't care for honor so much as he does wealth. I am a wealthy man, Rheela. If I offer Krut some of that wealth in exchange for sparing the Majister's life, I have no doubt whatsoever that he will be more than happy to walk away from this potential disaster."

She couldn't quite believe it. It couldn't possibly be that simple. "You would do that?" she asked.

"For you? Of course." But then he paused and added, "Of course, naturally . . . if I am expending money, I expect a return on that expenditure. It would be poor business otherwise. You . . ." He let the word hang there a moment, clearly relishing it. "You . . . would serve as a very sound return. On my investment, that is."

They were speaking so softly that Moke hadn't even realized at first that they were conversing. But he noticed now, and looked from one to the other quizzically, trying to understand what was going on.

Rheela comprehended, though, all too well. The only thing that was amazing to her was that it took her as long as it did to see where he was going with it. "You want me to be in business with you. To charge the people of Yakaba for my weather abilities."

"Once upon a time, yes. But the stakes have risen to the level of life and death," he said, nodding his head in the direction of the face-off in the street. "Now, my dear Rheela, I want more than that. I want you yourself. In my life. In my bed. I will have you to wife, my dear Rheela, and all that you have will be mine. That is the price of saving your precious Calhoun."

"You bastard!" she whispered hoarsely. "How could you put me in such a position?"

Moke's head was snapping back and forth so quickly that it looked as if his head was going to fall off. "Ma . . . ?" he said, his tone low in automatic imitation of the adults. "Ma, what's he saying? What's wrong? What's—"

Then Rheela's eyes widened. It was as if blinders had been removed from her eyes, and she could only be angry with herself that she had taken so long to figure out that which was so obvious. "*You* brought him here! The huge green monster! You brought him to our world! You set this up! Set up all of it! All to maneuver me into this position!"

Moke understood that all too well. He looked from Tapinza to Krut and back again. There was a look of stricken betrayal on his face. "You brought him here?" he demanded to know, his childish voice rising in agitation.

"How Krut got here isn't really relevant," Tapinza said easily. "What matters is what's going to happen to Calhoun . . . oh, just about any time now. And what matters is whether you, Rheela, are going to do anything about it before it's too late."

Not discerning the nature of Tapinza's terms, Moke said urgently, "Do it, Ma! Save Mac! If you can, you gotta!"

Never had Rheela felt more helpless. She was completely boxed in. And every fiber of her being screamed at her to reject the "offer" flat. To make it clear to this . . . this vomitous excuse for a living being that she would have none of it. That Rheela was not going to knuckle under to pressure, no matter what the odds, simply to save the life of one man who had gotten himself into this situation and refused even to try and find some way out of it.

All that went through her head in an instant, and she opened her mouth to say all that to Tapinza, and a hell of a lot more besides. But at the last instant, just before she spoke, she saw Calhoun still moving warily, still facing off against a behemoth who was very likely going to cut him down any second. And in that instant, every single thing she was going to say to Tapinza disappeared, to be replaced by a simple, "All right."

Tapinza looked as if he could scarce believe it. "Did . . . you say . . . ?"

"I said all right," she told him angrily. "You win. Happy? Satisfied? But none of it will happen unless you put an end to this, before he puts an end to Calhoun."

With a lopsided and confident grin, Tapinza called in a loud voice, "Excuse me! Sir! My name is Tapinza, and I am a Maester of this city. I was hoping to speak to you for a moment . . ."

"Later," Krut said, never taking his eyes from Calhoun. "I have someone to kill."

Since she knew beyond doubt now that Tapinza had arranged this entire thing, Rheela's lips twisted in contempt as she listened to the exchange between Tapinza and Krut. It was so obviously staged, so clearly a "prewritten" conversation that they were now acting out—badly—for the benefit of the townspeople.

Continuing to play his part, Tapinza said, in a manner suggesting utter confidence, "That may not be necessary, sir. I believe we can come to an arrangement that will spare the life of our—"

Krut fixed a deadly gaze on him. "I said, 'later.' "

Rheela felt a small bit of alarm at the base of her skull. Something about the way Tapinza was looking seemed to indicate to her that that wasn't the reply he'd been anticipating. "You don't understand, sir. I have—"

"I don't care *what* you have," Krut said. "This man is going to die, and there's nothing in all this world that you can say or do that will stop that."

"But . . . we had—" The Maester almost literally bit his tongue. Rheela, of course, knew roughly what he'd been about to say. They'd had a deal? A bargain? An understanding? Any or all of those. Whatever it was they'd had, however, it was clear that it meant nothing to Krut.

"He . . . is going . . . to die," Krut said very slowly, almost patronizingly, as if reciting the realities of the situation for the benefit of an infant. "Here. Now. At my hand. I don't like his actions, or his moving about, or his attitude, or his fancy scar, or purple eyes. I don't like him, and I'm going to kill him."

Tapinza wasn't able to say anything. It wasn't as if he couldn't think of anything to say, but he was stammering so fiercely that he couldn't get the words out.

Calhoun abruptly said, "If my moving about bothers you . . . very well. I'll stand right here." Sure enough, Calhoun planted himself stock-still. Krut naturally stopped exactly where he was to face him.

"Tired of running? Wear yourself out?"

"Something like that," said Calhoun, still not showing the slightest fear. In the brightness of the noonday sun, she could see the small good luck charm glinting in his hand. Whatever properties the charm might have, she doubted that it was going to save him from this.

"I'll tell you what, Calhoun. I will be fair to you . . . which is more than you've been for others," said Krut. "I will give you . . . the chance to draw first."

"Krut!" called Tapinza, still trying to insert himself into the proceedings, apparently not fully grasping that matters had moved beyond his control. "This isn't necessary—!"

"Oh, yes it is," Krut told him flatly, "and unless you shut up right now, killing you is going to become just as necessary as killing him."

Tapinza choked, as if his entire throat had constricted. His hands moved in helpless little circles.

Rheela wanted to shout out to Calhoun, to beg him, to tell him once and for all how she felt about him . . . something, anything. But she was afraid to, for she was worried that to do so would be to distract him at a crucial moment. And so she kept her silence. Moke, however, started to move, and she saw it at just the last instant. She grabbed him by the arm, yanked him back, and clamped a hand over his mouth to stop him from shouting Calhoun's name and drawing his focus away from where it had to be at this critical moment.

"So, Calhoun!" Krut said, as if there was no one else in the street. It seemed to her that Calhoun was separated from her by a gulf hundreds of feet wide, even though he was standing mere yards away in the street. "Do you wish to take me up on my offer of trying to draw first? Or are you going to simply stand there like the coward you are and make no effort at all to defend yourself?"

"Are you sure about this?" Calhoun inquired, his voice steady. "You're willing to let me have my turn first?"

"Absolutely," said Krut. "You may have the opportunity to go for your weapon. And I assure you that before it's even cleared your holster, I will draw mine and shoot you down. But it will not be a killing shot, Calhoun, oh, no. Not a quick kill, that is. I'm going to shoot you in the stomach, Calhoun. Have you ever seen a man die of a stomach wound?"

As if speaking from a land of utter darkness, Calhoun replied, "I've seen men die in just about every way that you can imagine."

"Good. Then you know the fate that awaits you. At least, you think you do. But as you're lying there in the street, clutching at the blood spreading across your belly, trying to reinsert the innards that are leaking out . . . perhaps I will walk over to you and have mercy on you." He grinned in anticipation of the moment. "Will you beg me at that point, Calhoun? Will you beg me to end your misery? Will you pray to me or curse me, I wonder. And what will I do, what will I do? You know . . . I'm not quite certain I know myself. I might indeed spare you continued misery by ending your worthless life right then and there. Or I may stand there and watch you suffer. Could be a long, drawn-out process, though. Could take you a couple of days to die. I'm not entirely sure whether I'm really willing to stand there for all that time just for the pleasure of watching the light flicker from your eyes. Then again . . . perhaps it might just be worth it. For to see you suffer from the continued agonies of—"

He was still talking when the explosion erupted under his feet.

It was deafening. Windows shattered up and down the street, people crying out and clapping their hands over their ears. The air was charged with the aroma of something burning, and there was a wave of heat so powerful that Rheela felt as if it was going to burn her eyeballs right out of their sockets. And then . . . came the sounds. The sounds of large, green body parts descending from where they had been propelled, high into the sky. An arm plopped into a water trough. Despite the seriousness of the situation, Rheela groaned. The trough was one of just a small number of water storage locations around the city, and now it was contaminated. What a hideous waste.

A boot thudded to the ground, wisps of smoke still trailing from the end. And then the majority of Krut landed. Head, torso, an arm, his thighs. Where the rest of him was, it was impossible to say. What was not impossible to determine, however, was that Krut was unquestionably not in a position to cause any more problems.

Calhoun walked with measured stride to Krut's still-smoldering corpse, or at least what was left of it. He stared down at him blandly. "Your turn," said Calhoun.

It was Moke who broke the stunned silence that followed, and there was nothing but pure joy in his voice. "That was spectacular!" he shouted. "What did you do?"

"Moke!" said Rheela, trying to sound scolding, but, truthfully, the relief flooding over her was so overwhelming that she could barely get the word out.

In response to Moke's question, Calhoun held up the silver cylinder. "Remember that little excursion we went on, Moke? Those things we found called 'mines.' I planted them in the street hours ago as a present for him. This detonated them." He tossed the cylinder to Moke, who caught it effortlessly.

"And that's why you kept moving. To get him in position so he'd be standing on them!"

"You—" Surprisingly, it was Tapinza who had the nerve to voice a protest. "You cheated! What sort of Majister cheats?"

"The smart kind," replied Calhoun easily. "Given the choice, I'll take living over dying anytime."

And suddenly, in response to absolutely nothing that Rheela could discern, Calhoun suddenly seemed to be reacting with alarm. His body appearing to move before his mind had even processed the information, Calhoun lunged to one side. The instant he did so, a plaser bolt sizzled through the air and scorched the ground where he'd just been standing.

Calhoun rolled to his feet and ran. His reflexes started to take him toward the office of the Majister, but then he looked straight at Rheela and, apparently deciding that to keep heading toward them would put them at risk, he bolted in the other direction.

There was a screeching of delirious triumph, voices she didn't know, but it was obviously the men who were shooting at Calhoun. They were shooting from cover, wherever they were, trying to pick off Calhoun without presenting themselves as targets. But Calhoun was not about to make it easy on them. He moved so incredibly quickly that Rheela could barely track him. It was as if he had an inkling of where plaser bolts were going to hit before they struck. At one point he actually skidded to a halt and backpedaled, avoiding a blast by the narrowest of margins.

He swept the plaser through the air, firing off a steady array of blasts, not aiming so much as just trying to create some sort of cover for himself to retreat. Rheela heard screaming and realized that it was her own voice, and Moke was struggling in her grasp, trying to run to Calhoun and help him in some manner. The notion was insanity, of course. One young boy couldn't do anything.

She glanced around desperately for help, and saw more of the townspeople watching, just watching. Not saying anything, nor doing anything. Just silent spectators to a sequence of events that they were making no effort whatsoever to prevent.

He could have taken refuge in any of the buildings, but once again, his concern for the others in the town was of paramount importance to him. Obviously he was concerned about a shootout occurring in whatever building he sought refuge within, and he had no desire to endanger the lives of anyone else. He looked around desperately, spotted the luukab peacefully tied at the hitching post, and bolted toward it.

For a moment, she thought he was going to hide behind the great beast. That would only last for a few moments, as his attack-

ers would doubtlessly use their plasers to cut the luukab to rib-
bons where it stood. She momentarily mourned the imminent
demise of the creature, and then discarded any such absurd notions. It was Calhoun's survival, and only his, that mattered to her.

As it turned out, however, even the life of a luukab was important to Calhoun. Before his attackers could fully draw a bead on
him, he leaped forward, a vault of such height and elegance as
Rheela had never seen. He hit the back of the luukab, which let out
a startled grunt in response, and then he was up and over, jumping
to the roof of the building next to the luukab. He barely caught the
edge of the roof by his fingertips, and Rheela was sure he was
going to fall off. But, in an amazing display of dexterity and upper-
body strength, Calhoun hauled himself up. One blast nearly tagged
him, scorching his left thigh just before he hauled it up and out of
the way. There was an impressive array of stone and sculpture
work lining the top of the roof, and it provided him cover, as long
as he kept low. He crouched behind one of the statues as plaser
bolts chipped off pieces from it. Wherever his assailants were, they
obviously weren't able to get a clear shot at him.

*Oh, Kolk'r, let him be safe,* Rheela kept thinking.

Calhoun did nothing at first; merely crouched there while the
plaser bolts continued to strike all around him. Rheela realized
what he was doing: He wasn't wasting time, energy, or ammo. Instead, he was studying where the bolts were originating from, so
as to get a bead on his assailants.

And still no one did anything to help him.

Perhaps it was unreasonable of her to believe that someone
should be helping. She knew that, intellectually. But even so, she
knew that a few of the citizens were armed. They could have
pitched in to help. They could have emerged from hiding, tried to
sight where the attackers were, pick them off themselves. But no.
They were hiding. They were afraid.

A cold fury boiled up in Rheela. She thought about all the effort
she had put into trying to connect with the people, to get them to
like her, to help them. Help them to prosper, to grow . . . and even

more, to grow up. She felt as if some mission had been imparted to her. Whether it was from Kolk'r or wherever, she had no idea. But it had been her mission just the same.

However, she was rapidly coming to the conclusion that it had been entirely in her imagination. They had attacked her, they had scorned her, they had assaulted her home . . . and yet somehow this, this display of cowardice, rankled her like none other, and brought her flowering ire to full blossom.

"Bastards," she breathed. "Bloody bastards."

Tapinza looked at her, as did Moke, temporarily distracted from his struggles by the intensity and fury now evident in his mother. And then, suddenly, there was a scream.

Across the way, on another rooftop, there was a man staggering, clutching his chest. Rheela recognized him instantly, for she had seen him not that long ago . . . standing trial. It was Kusack, and when last she'd seen him, he'd been walking out of the meetinghouse with a smug expression on his face. The expression was now gone, permanently, along with his continued existence. Smoke was rising from a burn on his chest, left there by the plaser bolt that Calhoun had just fired. His screech ended with a choked, burbling noise, and then Kusack pitched forward off the roof and hit the ground. Rheela winced inwardly at the noise he made when he hit, but at the same time felt a grim sort of satisfaction.

And from across the way there was a howl of such fury that it practically marked the location of the one who vocalized it. Calhoun didn't hesitate, but fired at the source. The screech was oddly truncated then, and Rheela looked in the general direction that it had come from. As much as she had felt a grim moment of victory before, now a wave of nausea swept over her. She saw a man in a window across the way—or, at least, she assumed it to be a man. It was actually mostly the upper torso, half slumped out the window. There was a plaser in his hand that, at that moment, was tumbling from his lifeless fingers. The head was unrecognizable as a head, completely ruined by the bolt that had drilled right through it. Whoever it had been, he had obviously been someone who felt close to Kusack, and had reflexively cried out in anger even as he tried to nail Calhoun. But Calhoun had obviously discerned the general area of his location, and his cry of protest had helped to bring Calhoun's attention right to him.

And then all was silent.

Calhoun stayed perched upon the roof, looking around carefully. He was studying the area, trying to discern where any other possible threats might be.

*He made it . . . oh, my Kolk'r, he made it,* Rheela breathed, unable to believe it. And out loud she whispered, "He made it . . ."

And as her heart fluttered with relief, that was the moment that Moke pulled clear of her. Crying out with relief and exultation, Moke barreled into the street, shouting, "You made it! You *made it,* Mac!! *Woooohoooo!! You made it!!"*

"Moke, get back!" shouted Calhoun from above, "there's still danger—!"

The words sent alarm racing through Rheela's veins, but they were completely lost on the enthused child, who just kept repeating, "You made it! You made it! Ma says you made it! You—"

He ran past the water trough, which still had the severed body part from the green man named Krut floating in it. And suddenly there was a great splashing of water, sending the precious commodity spilling to the ground as it slopped over the sides. Moke barely had time to turn, and then a large, sopping arm was wrapped around his throat, the other around his chest, and Moke was being hoisted into the air, pressed against the chest of the man who had just emerged from the trough. A straw fell away, obviously what he'd been using to enable him to breathe while he lay under the water, waiting in ambush as a last resort.

From high above, Calhoun shouted, "Put him down, Temo!"

The man called Temo clutched the struggling Moke more tightly. "Make a clear shot of yourself, Calhoun! That's all I want! Y'hear? One clear shot's all I want! S'all I need!"

"You don't want to hurt him," Calhoun called.

And still all the people of the town were hiding, quavering in their hidey-holes, afraid or uninvolved or just plain disinterested. With a piteous wail that might have been pulled from a dying beast, Rheela cried out, "Let him go! For Kolk'r's sake, let him go!"

"Shut up!" shouted Temo. "That bastard killed my brothers, and he's gonna die! And you, Tapinza," he continued as Tapinza opened his mouth to speak, "one word out of you, and I'll shoot you where you stand!"

Tapinza had never seemed quite so small to Rheela as he did at that moment. Small and pathetic and powerless.

But Rheela was not powerless. She was fueled by righteous indignation and the white-hot heat of a mother's love, and spurred by this, she started toward Temo. "Let him go!" she cried out. "You have no right to manhandle him! To hurt him! To terrorize him! If your fight's with Calhoun, then have it be man to man, but leave the child out of this!"

"Rheela, get back!" shouted Calhoun. "Temo . . . all right! Here!" He stood, raising himself from behind the statue, putting his hands over his head.

But Temo wasn't looking at him. Instead, his eyes narrowed in recognition as Rheela approached. "Ahhh . . . the weather witch. And our Majister's beloved."

*I wish I was,* she thought, but all she could say, driven by the fury of the moment, was, "Let my son go!"

"Temo! Up here! Rheela, back away! Tapinza, do something!" Calhoun was shouting orders, but the people in the street were beyond hearing, beyond caring.

*"I want my son!"* howled Rheela.

"You can have him in hell," replied Temo, and he swung the plaser around and fired once.

Rheela never even saw the blast. All she knew was that, suddenly, there was a massive pressure on her breast, like a gargantuan hammer blow, that lifted her clean off her feet and sent her sailing through the air. She landed hard, several feet away, flat on her back, suddenly unable to get any air into her chest. She smelled burning flesh right under her nose, but didn't yet associate it as being her own. Moke was howling, wailing at the top of his lungs. She had completely lost control of her body. It was as if she could not get her head to connect with anything below her neck. Now there were voices shouting from all around her, but she couldn't sort one from the other. Somehow—she had no idea how—she managed to flop her body over like a great, dead sack of flesh, and she found herself looking up into Moke's eyes. His voice was unrecognizable, racked with pain and terror. He was still being held by Temo, who was shouting something to Calhoun, and Calhoun was shouting back, and Tapinza was shouting, and the noise blurred into one great roaring rush. It was only at that point that she came to the realization that she had been shot, and following that realization, she further understood that she was going to die, rather soon. She was so disconnected from the moment that the prospect didn't actually bother her.

*"Maaaaaaa!"* Moke cried out from very far away. She looked to him, looked to her son, this great and mysterious creature who had been part of her life for such a relatively brief time . . . and yet it had seemed as if her life had not truly started until he had entered it.

She saw deep, deeply into his eyes, and noticed something there that she had never noticed before. Something fearful and terrifying; and as Moke's terror turned to blind fury, that which was in his eyes grew in fury as well. It was as dark and as powerful as any storm she had ever summoned, and it was in the control of a child, which meant it was not in any control at all.

And suddenly, just like that, she had a flash of insight about herself that was as pure and clear as she'd ever had in her life. She suddenly understood everything, and, in understanding, was both ashamed and terrified.

*Don't,* she tried to whisper, *don't . . . hurt them . . .*

But it was too late. The storm had come. The darkness was complete.

# LEFLER'S STORY

*I MADE A TOKEN effort to struggle against Nik, but he was simply too strong.* All conversation between the three of us—not that there had been much of a conversation up until that point—had ceased.

We moved through the grand lobby, and there was water everywhere, pouring in through the door, coming in from an overhead balcony. It was about knee-high at that point, getting harder to slog through, and suddenly a new wave hit us. It surged through the door and knocked us flat, jarring me loose of Nik's hold on me. I went under, thrashing about, remembering that it was possible for someone to drown in even an inch of water, and this was a hell of a lot more than an inch.

Someone grabbed me by the back of the neck. I was sure that it was Nik, and I tried to shake free of him. I can only imagine how I must have looked, trying to scramble away under water like some sort of crazed frog. Whatever small bit of air I'd managed to take into my lungs jarred loose in the struggle and, reflexively, I breathed in water. I started to struggle again, but this time in blind panic instead of a desire to get away. Then I was yanked to my feet, coughing water violently out of my mouth and expelling it through my nose.

"You're slowing us down!" Nik shouted in my face.

"You're welcome to let me go if I'm that much of an inconvenience to you!" I snapped back at him.

"Nik! Stop playing around!" shouted Olivan.

We hauled ourselves out through the main doors, and in the distance I saw something horrific. It was, honest to God, a tidal wave, and there seemed to be another one right behind that one. I had no idea where all the water was coming from, but it sure seemed as if it was from everywhere.

Nik looked, to put it mildly, disconcerted. "The way to the field is completely flooded!" he shouted. "We'll never be able to get to our ship in time!"

"I'll bring it to us!" Olivan called back. All around us, we could see people splashing around helplessly, not knowing what to do or where to go. "It'll need five minutes to go through its take-off cycle!"

"We may not have five minutes!"

"Higher ground! We need higher ground!"

"This way!"

Nik shoved me ahead of him. I was soaked to the skin, but he still had no trouble hauling me around as if I was weightless. Considering that days before he had acted as if how much I weighed was a big deal in hauling me up from a dangerous situation, it made me wonder just what else he was capable of.

Nevertheless, even as he pushed me along, he called, "Let's leave the girl! We don't need her anymore!"

"We bring her!"

"But—"

"I said, bring her!"

It was so strange. Nik's reaction wasn't just as if he was having a disagreement with his father. He actually seemed to be trying to . . . to resist him somehow. If that's what he was attempting, however, it didn't work. Instead he just nodded, as if it was his idea to continue to keep me in play as a pawn.

We half-ran, half-swam through the water, and got to an area that was elevated, a mountainous area that led up to camp sites and excavations. We splashed up and out of the water, and I drew a brief sigh of relief, even though I knew this was only a temporary respite. The dirt beneath our feet was already thick with water, co-agulating into mud. We shoved our way up the path anyway.

"How could you have done it?" I managed to say to Nik, who had stopped clamping down on my vocal cords. My voice came out raspy and unpleasant. "Why did you . . . how could you have—?"

"Killed people?" He shrugged. "It's not especially difficult. You don't think of them as people. Just obstacles, or things that you don't want around."

"My God . . . I don't know you at all . . . you're not . . ."

"The man you thought I was?" He laughed bitterly. "No man ever is. The only question is whether the woman figures it out or not. We're none of us what we appear to be."

"Si Cwan is," I said fiercely as I stumbled and slid in the mud. He caught me and pushed me up, over up. "He's exactly what he appears to be. He's noble and true and he's going to hunt you down, no matter what it takes . . ."

He swung me around and stared into my eyes like he was trying to discover something there. He looked like he was about to say something . . .

Suddenly there was a loud, horrific squealing sound, like nothing I'd ever heard. Nik froze where he was, as did I. We looked ahead of us.

There was some sort of crazed, dripping-wet creature ahead of us. It was bristling with fur and teeth, snarling and swaying its massive head back and forth, as if daring us to go past. Even Olivan had frozen where he was, looking properly respectful.

"It's a targ. A Klingon targ," Olivan said slowly.

"Would you mind telling me what the hell a Klingon targ is doing on Risa?" Nik asked, trying to sound calm. It wasn't easy to do. We didn't have weapons and the creature was itself a weapon.

"When our little computer program kicked in, one of the things it did was release the force barriers that kept the animals in the zoo. The targ must be an escapee."

"Great, Father. So . . . now what?"

His father surveyed the situation for a moment. I saw that he was manipulating what appeared to be a chronometer he was wearing on his wrist. But then I realized that it was actually the remote device he was using to summon his ship. If I hadn't been busy imagining how nice it would be to throttle him, I would have been admiring his ability to do more than one thing at a time.

"Throw him the girl," he said.

"What?" said Nik loudly, beating me to the punch by half a heartbeat.

"Targs are very vicious, but not particularly bright," he said, as calmly as if he was discussing the weather. "They're easily distracted. If you push the girl right on top of it, it will be busy savaging her, and in the meantime, we can be on our way."

"No!" He sounded horrified. I couldn't figure him out at all. On the one hand he spoke like a stone-cold killer, but on the other hand there seemed to be things that he was simply unable or unwilling to do.

"Do it!" Olivan shouted, and there was nothing of any willingness to compromise in his voice.

And without hesitation, like a puppet on a string, Nik shoved me right at the targ.

My feet went out from under me, the mud providing no traction at all, and I went down hard. I was practically under the targ's hooves, and the only thing that stopped the beast from trampling me right then and there was the fact that it was surprised. It darted backward, as if suspicious that my presence in front of it was a trick. Its roaring was drowning out what Olivan was saying, but it was probably something like, "Come on, let's go!"

I tried to roll away from it, but Olivan had been right. Once its attention was on me, it wasn't going to be pulled away from me. It let out a roar, its foul breath rolling over me, and I choked. It still had vestiges of whatever the hell it had eaten earlier on its breath. I gagged on it, and then the creature charged me. I had no chance. I threw up my arms to ward it off, as if that was going to help one iota, and then, over the creature's bellowing, I heard Olivan in the distance. I had no idea what he was shouting, and then, suddenly, the targ let out a grunt of surprise.

I was no less surprised than the targ when I saw that Nik had landed on top of the beast. "Go! Go!" he was shouting at me. I stumbled back, confused, trying to figure out what was happening, and then Olivan grabbed me so tightly that I immediately lost all circulation to my forearm.

"Nik! Get away from it! Get away!" Olivan was shouting.

Nik seemed to be fighting for position, even as the targ was doing everything it could to shake him off. It threw itself to one side and then the other, and all the time Nik held on, his face a mask of concentration. He had one arm firmly under the creature's chin, which was how he was managing to hold on at all, and was endeavoring to get leverage with the other arm, as if trying to find just the right spot.

"Nik!" Olivan cried out once more. There was another huge wave of water coming. Within a minute, even the area where we were standing would no longer be safe.

And then Nik seemed to get the angle he wanted. His teeth set, he twisted as hard as he could. There was a crack so loud that it sounded like lightning had struck nearby, and that crack was accompanied by an agonized squeal.

The targ shook violently, and Nik released his hold on it. He rolled out of its path, but it wasn't as if the creature was going to take another run at him. Instead the targ staggered around, its head at an odd angle, clearly not yet aware that it was dead. Then the message finally managed to get to its brain, and the targ stumbled once, twice, and then fell over. It twitched several more times, its cries dying in its throat, and then it lay still.

Olivan looked angrily at his son. "That," he said heatedly, "was not what I told you to do."

"You didn't tell me not to do it."

"Don't play games with me, boy! You know what I—" He shook his head. "This is idiocy. Let's go. Bring the girl; there may be another targ."

"Please, Father . . . enough. Let's let her g—"

But he gave Nik a look that seemed designed to cut him in half. At this point, I had no idea what was going on, or what sort of hold Olivan had on him. But clearly Nik was in no position to fight it, whatever it was. He grabbed my wrist and pulled me behind him, and under his breath he muttered, "Please don't fight me. I don't want to have to hurt you."

It was pure craziness, but somehow I really did believe that this . . . this murderer didn't want to do me harm.

We went higher and higher. From our vantage point, I could see people desperately splashing around in the rising water. Some were belatedly trying to follow in the same path that we'd been taking, but they were having trouble getting to it. And I could also see another wave building up, this one even larger than the one before. I couldn't help but feel that this was going to be the big one, and it would just wipe out everything, including us.

And then I saw it, angling in quickly from the direction of the central landing field. It was a four-man shuttle, moving right toward us, and Olivan was guiding it with confidence. Without even bothering to glance in my direction, Olivan said, "Rip her shirt off and use it to bind her hands. Get ready to bring her on the ship."

"Father!"

"Knock her unconscious, if you prefer. I don't need her resistance . . ."

"But—!"

The ship was getting closer, almost within landing distance. Olivan was clearly becoming angrier and angrier that Nik was giving him problems. "Don't you understand, you young fool? You don't get to say 'but'! You don't get to defy me! I'm your cre—your father, and you will do as I order you!"

But Nik had caught the sudden switch in his father's voice, the blip in his wording. "Dad," he said cautiously, as if he was defusing an explosive. "Dad . . . what's going on?"

The shuttle angled around toward us, settling into a landing position five feet away. Had the situation been less dire, I would have admired his technique.

"We don't have time for this," Olivan said curtly.

"Let's make the time, Father."

The doors to the shuttle dilated open. "Render the woman . . . unconscious . . . and get in the shuttle," Olivan said. His voice was like iron. His full concentration was on Nik. "Do . . . as I say."

Nik was visibly trembling. I'd never seen anything like it. It was as if Olivan's voice was tearing him apart. "I . . ."

"No 'I.' No 'you.' Just me. And you will do as I say. Now." Then, more loudly, he repeated, "Now! *Now! N—*"

And because he was so completely focused on Nik, what happened next caught him completely off guard. There was a sudden rush of air, something hurtling through it. Even with all the distractions, Olivan—as he had before—sensed imminent danger. This time, however, he was a half-second too late.

There was a thudding sound, like a knife being slammed into a melon. Olivan stood there, looking surprised, staring down at his chest and seeing the blade and hilt still quivering. He touched it, as if doing so would be the only way that he could verify that he was, in essence, dead.

Nik was so much in shock that he released me, forgetting about me completely as he took several steps toward his father and then stopped, his attention being caught by the individual standing in the doorway of the craft.

It was Si Cwan. Kalinda was behind him, smiling in grim satisfaction. Cwan was still in a pose like a javelin thrower, at full extension. Slowly, he lowered his arm and nodded approvingly, his expression matching that of his sister.

"You checked . . . the registry . . . of my personal vessel," Olivan said in wonderment. "How very . . . clever of you." He sank to his knees, and there was blood trickling from his mouth.

Stepping out of the vessel, Si Cwan extended a hand to me. "Robin. Quickly. Into the vessel. I," and he looked forcefully at Nik, "will attend to this one."

"I'm not going anywhere, Si Cwan! Not without my mother and Scotty!"

The wave was roaring up from the sea, thundering with such choppy force that we practically had to scream to make ourselves heard.

Nik made a move toward me, but Si Cwan stopped him in his tracks with a contemptuous, "Are you so little of a man that you need to hide behind a woman?"

His face darkening, Nik said, "I didn't have to hide behind anyone to kill Jereme, Thallonian."

"No. You didn't. Now . . . let's see you try to kill me."

"He had no choice."

It was Olivan who had spoken. He was looking at us with such utter contempt, that—had I not been so sick with worry about my mom and Mr. Scott—I would have gone over and kicked his teeth in on general principles alone.

Nik looked at him in confusion. "What . . . what do you mean . . . no choice . . . ?"

Olivan coughed up more blood, and he was looking with hatred at Si Cwan. "You won't kill him, Cwan. I know you. You're too pure, too noble of spirit, just as the girl said. You're going to let him live . . . on general principles . . . because even you wouldn't condemn someone to death who had no choice in their actions . . ."

"What are you talking about?" demanded Si Cwan.

"This . . ." Olivan said, his voice getting weaker, "is . . . not real. Not . . . my son. My . . . my technology . . . created . . . it . . ."

"It?" Nik wasn't faking. He clearly had no idea at all what Olivan was talking about.

"This . . . is no son of mine . . . it is . . . a clone . . . of me . . ."

I felt a distant buzzing in my head, as if my brain was going to start leaking out of my ears. Nik stared at his father—or sire, or whatever—and tried to speak, but his voice choked. Si Cwan was standing a few feet away, still dangerous, but for all the threat Nik posed right then, Cwan might as well have been a million miles away. "What?" he finally managed to whisper . . . which, given the circumstances, is probably all I would have managed to say.

"You heard me . . . clone . . . programmed . . . hardwired into your brain . . . to obey me . . . so you could . . ." He coughed up a larger glob of blood. It was pretty disgusting, really. Part of me just wanted to scream, *My God, die already!* ". . . so you could . . . be me . . . so I would . . . live on . . . you have . . . no free will . . . no nothing . . ."

"I do!" shouted Nik defensively. "I . . . I can think on my own . . . I can . . . !"

"Good . . . here's . . . here's your . . . chance . . . look . . . here . . . here comes . . . the water . . . at least I die . . . knowing that you . . . you . . ."

His voice trailed off, his eyes widening. At first I thought, in the insanity of the moment, that he was seeing some sort of great, final destiny approaching him at a rapid pace. But then I realized what he was looking at.

It was the water.

It was subsiding. The wave generators were working to pull the water in reverse. Not only that, but I could already hear great drains opening up, siphoning off the water that had threatened to overwhelm the entire facility.

"They did it," I whispered, and then, louder, I practically shouted, "They did it!"

Olivan saw it happening, saw it all.

"I . . . hate . . . Scotsmen . . ."

And with those parting words, Olivan let out a raspy sigh that I had heard all too frequently in my life—a death rattle.

I've wondered about him any number of times since then. What it was he saw in Si Cwan that he hated so much. What he saw in Jereme, their mutual teacher. I think that maybe, sometimes, there are people in this world who are just so consumed with fury that if there's anyone out there better than they are, that they just get dragged down by it. There's two different kinds of people in the galaxy: those who see people who are better than they are and are inspired to aspire . . . and those who see people who are better, and only want to tear down the other people in order to make themselves feel better. I think Olivan was one of those.

Either that, or he was just a creep.

I'm not talking about Nik.

I guess that's kind of obvious, isn't it?

Nik stood there, just kind of shaking his head. "He's lying," he whispered. "This . . . this is all crazy . . ."

And suddenly he became aware of Si Cwan advancing on him. So did I. Si Cwan stepped over to his father, yanked the sword out of his chest without giving the body a second look, and turned toward Nik.

Nik started to back away. He stepped to the side of the landed shuttle, moving back farther, even farther, shaking his head.

"Fight me," grated Si Cwan.

"No, I . . . I have to sort this out," said Nik.

"You are a murderer. There's nothing to sort out. You killed Jereme, and the manager of this place, and who knows who else, and you will die for it, here and now."

"Si Cwan, no!" I shouted. "You can't!"

He seemed surprised that I would say that, and I realized he was taking it as a question of his ability rather than a moral dilemma. "Yes, I can," he said reasonably.

"He's not fighting back! He's confused, he's—"

"We're not confused," Kalinda said. "We know what has to be done. It is our right, as the aggrieved parties . . . as Thallonian nobles . . ."

"There's no Thallonian Empire anymore, and your whole order of nobility is gone! You have no authority!" I practically shouted.

"I have a sword. That's all the authority I need."

Things were spinning out of control. Nik looked like a lost child. It was hard to believe that, earlier, he had been a ruthless killer; now he seemed completely adrift. His willpower seemed to have died with Olivan. He kept backing away from Si Cwan, farther and farther, his eyes wide, his hands up defensively.

I ran toward Si Cwan and grabbed his free arm. He could have shoved me away, but I could see he had no desire to treat me so roughly. "Robin . . . this is not your affair."

"The hell it's not! He dragged me around like a sack of wheat! But he also saved my life! You bet it's my damned affair! Back off, Si Cwan!"

"No."

I had never heard him like that, the one word just . . . just thudding down on me like an anvil. He was so . . . so alien. So distant from me, in so many ways. It was like . . . like I didn't matter to him. Like nothing mattered to him except killing. I felt as if I didn't know him at all. Like this Si Cwan was a stranger to me.

I pulled on his arm again. "I mean it, Si Cwan!"

There was something in his eyes, then, that was so cold. This teacher, this Jereme, must have meant the world to him, to have unleashed something so terrible, so implacable in him. It was like his eyes were dead. Like shark's eyes.

And that was when we heard a scream.

We turned, and Nik wasn't standing there anymore. Instead, where he had been, there was a hole. When he'd stepped back, the ground had opened up beneath him. And I instantly realized what had happened. He had fallen into one of the subterranean areas similar to what I had tumbled into days ago.

His initial scream had been in startlement from the plunge. But then . . . my God . . . the real screaming started. From below, in the darkness, and I realized what was happening. That . . . that thing, that gelatinous mass of whatever the hell it was, was pouring over him, consuming him, devouring him.

"Si Cwan! We have to help him!" I cried out.

"What's happening?" He genuinely didn't know, although he could certainly tell from the howling beneath that it wasn't anything good.

"There's a thing down there! It's carnivorous! It's killing him!" And now I could hear other things, aside from his shouts . . . a sick sound, like . . . like slurping, like strips of meat being pulled off bone. *"Hurry, hurry, oh, my God, hurry!"*

He just looked at me blandly. "Why?"

"Why? *Why?*" I thought I was losing my mind. "Get a rope! From that craft! There must be something! There must . . ." And then I charged for the hole. "Lower me down, I'll reach him, we'll form a chain, I'll—"

Si Cwan reached out, wrapped his arm around my waist, and for what was certainly not the first time that day, I was hoisted off my feet. Si Cwan's expression never changed. He just carted me away as I struggled, try as I might to resist. I pounded at his chest. I doubt he felt it. I was beginning to wonder if he could feel anything. Kalinda's expression was less cold-blooded. There was a trace, just a trace, of compassion on her face. But she did nothing to come to Nik's aid, nothing at all.

And I protested and shouted, and demanded to know how he could be doing such a thing, and eventually I noticed that Nik's cries had stopped. There was nothing now except a faint slurping from whatever-the-hell that was that lay beneath.

"I can't believe you did that," I kept saying, "I . . . I can't believe it . . ."

"He killed my teacher," Si Cwan said, as if it was the simplest thing in the world. "The only thing I regret is that I did not take his life with my own hand."

"But what if he truly didn't have free will! What if . . . what if—"

He seemed about a hundred feet tall as he looked down at me. "I do not deal in 'what if.' I deal in 'what is.' "

He gave a disdainful glance at Olivan's shuttle, which he had used as a Trojan horse to get the drop on his opponent, and started down the hill. Kalinda lagged behind and, to my surprise, she took my hand and looked at me with what appeared to be understanding.

"I'm sorry," she said in a low voice.

But I don't entirely think that she was. And I know that Si Cwan wasn't.

And the thing I keep coming back to is that, in many ways, Nik—whatever he was—came across, in the end, as only a child, swept up in events that were more terrifying than he could possibly comprehend. There is nothing so sad in this universe as a lost child, I think.

# *MOKE*

EVERYTHING HAD SEEMED TO HAPPEN in slow motion. One moment, his mother was running toward him, but so slowly, as if the ground was moving under her feet, forcing her to keep her distance. And then there was a roar, an explosion from just behind his ear, and suddenly his mother was sailing through the air, like a bird, or an angel. And then she was on the ground, with a hideous black scorch mark across her chest, and an expression on her face that would have been comical if it hadn't been so horrific.

He cried out to her over and over again, and the man who was holding him was laughing. Laughing at her. Laughing at him.

And then the laughter began to diminish, drowned out as it was by a steadily increasing pounding. The pounding got louder and louder, and it was the rumbling of thunder. And there was a flashing of light behind his eyes. His mother had always taught him to count between the blaze of lightning and the crack of thunder, and in that difference lay the distance between the two. But the thunder in his head and the explosion of lightning in his eyes was simultaneous, and the storm was right there in his head.

He tore his gaze away from his mother and looked up at the man who was holding him. The man, Temo, was laughing contemptuously, and then he looked at the boy, and was so startled that he lost his grip on him. At that moment, Moke could have torn away from him, could have run. But he did not. Instead he turned and faced him, and whatever the man was seeing in his eyes, it was so frightening that the man fell to the ground as if the strength had gone completely out of his legs, the gun in his hand forgotten.

*I must be terrible indeed,* thought Moke, as if his mind was outside his body, and then he added with satisfaction, *Good. That's good.*

The people of the town were starting to emerge. They thought that the danger was over. Idiots. Idiots. All of them. There was that old woman, the Maestress, who was always saying bad things about his mother, and there was the Praestor, and the writing man, and the one who took care of people when they died, and all the others, one by one coming out to see what had happened. Or else to see for themselves that his mother was really, truly going . . . going away . . .

*Dying . . . you can say it . . . your mother is dying . . .*

He could not see his own eyes, of course, but if he had, he would have seen the blackness that was seething within. Blackness that was matched by the skies above. The people of the town were pointing, murmuring in confusion and fear. Good. Let them be afraid. Let them know. Let them know what was going to happen, because it was all their fault, all their fault . . .

His terrified child-mind cried out, *Maaa . . . I want to come with you.*

And with perfect clarity, he was certain he heard his mother's voice in his head, with the reply, *No, my love . . . you have to stay here . . .*

Stay here? With them?

Them . . . and this man . . . Temo . . . and the other man, Tapinza. His ma had said that he was responsible for all this, too. They were to blame, everyone in the town was to blame . . .

Except Mac. He wouldn't be punished. He had tried to help. He had even saved his mother once. He was not Moke's father, but that was okay, he was close, and he deserved not to be punished . . .

. . . but the others were going to be.

Until that moment, Moke had had no concept of death. He had just somehow assumed, deep down, as was typical for children, that his mother was always going to be there. But he was not stupid. He saw it in her eyes, in the trembling of her body, in the hole in the upper portion of her ruined body . . . she was going to be leaving him. He imagined that such a journey, such a happenstance, was a lonely and frightening thing. If that was the case . . . then he was going to make certain that his mother did not make that journey alone.

If she was going away . . . she was going to have company.

Lots of company.

The thunderheads rolled in with staggering ferocity. The roiling of the sky matched the fearsome blackness in Moke's eyes, and the wind began to howl with a noise that sounded eerily like it was issuing from a living throat.

He saw the stunned looks on the faces of Tapinza and the townspeople. They were looking at the unmoving body of his mother, stupidly trying to figure out how in the world she was doing all this. One final gesture of contempt for the woman they had tormented for so many years. But, obviously, they didn't realize, hadn't realized, ever . . .

But Moke had known. In his subconscious mind, in his inner resources . . . he had known. Known that whatever power his mother might or might not have had . . . it paled in comparison to his own. But he had never been willing or desirous of utilizing it because, on some level, he needed to feel that his mother was the powerful one. That she was in charge. That was simply the way of the world, the way things were supposed to be, and Moke didn't want to think that he was more formidable than his mom.

Except that he was.

He was not operating on conscious thought. It was purely the unfettered agony of a child who had inhabited the local weather patterns and unleashed a storm front of epic proportions. There was a chance that, if left untampered with, the weather might have brought a storm into the region on its own. But Moke was not about to leave matters to chance—oh, no. Because his mother was going away, and he couldn't go with her, and he was going to make sure that when she went wherever she did, all the people who had been cruel to her and hurt her were going to be right there alongside her. And they would have to explain to Kolk'r why they had done the things they had done, and he hoped that Kolk'r would send them to a bad place for a very, very long time, maybe forever. But the first order of business was making sure they were there to be sent, and that, at least, was something Moke could attend to.

Seconds earlier the skies had been clear, although thick clouds had been on the horizon. Now there was such blackness that it was hard to believe there had ever once been a sun beaming down upon the world, or that the sun would ever come again. The townspeople sensed great disaster at hand, sensed that this storm was unlike any they had ever known. Here there would be no dancing in the streets, no laughter, no heads tilted back in supplication and thanks as big, warm rain droplets cascaded from on high, bringing life and joy to a grateful populace. No, this was a pure elemental display of a child mad with grief. The people did not yet fully understand what was happening, and as was so often the case, that which they did not understand, they feared. However, as it so happened, this was one of those instances where the fear was well placed.

Moke looked upward, his arms outstretched, as if welcoming the gathering storm. Day had been transformed into night, and on a world that had known only heat for the most part, there was a frightening chill in the air. The townspeople tried to run, but now the winds had come. It battered them, keeping them from getting indoors, battering at them like so many invisible rams. They cried out, they screamed, they protested, but all such noises were carried away by the winds, drowned out by howls like a million damned souls that would soon be adding still more to their number.

Temo, released from the nearly hypnotic spell of those darksome eyes, shook himself out of his momentary stupor. He looked down, saw the gun that had slipped from his nerveless fingers, and—grabbing it up—aimed it squarely at Moke. But Moke's attention whipped around, centering completely on Temo. Moke was the eye of the storm, the center of concentrated calm in the midst of a whirling mass of destructive force. But Temo was just on the outside of the eye, part of the chaos, and very vulnerable.

Temo was fast, but he was not faster than light. A crack rent the air, as if splitting it in two, and a lightning bolt lanced down from a cloud black as pitch. It slammed through Temo, and for a moment it actually looked as if it had impaled him. The force of the electricity lifted Temo off the ground, tossing him through the air in much the same way as his plaser blast had sent Rheela tumbling down the first steps into oblivion. For one horrific moment, he actually danced in midair, convulsed by the force of the electricity that fried every molecule in his body. Finally it released him, allowing him to crash to the ground and lie there twitching for some minutes thereafter, even though his blackened and smoking body was already lifeless.

The people had seen what had happened, and realized that they were next. They redoubled their efforts, trying to run. Had they thought to converge on Moke simultaneously, they might actually have succeeded in stopping him. He was, after all, still a child, heir to the frailties of the average living creature. But they were too caught up in their screeching panic to want anything other than to run for their lives. Instead, the wind scattered them like tenpins.

Praestor Milo staggered to his feet, trying to find some order in the chaos, and then something hit him from on high. It struck just above his forehead, knocking him to the ground and leaving a large welt of swelling blood. He looked down in confusion at the thing that had just flattened him. He had never, in his life, seen a hailstone. Nor had anyone else in the town. But they were about to see more than enough for a lifetime, as more began to fall.

The stones pounded down upon the helpless citizens, and they tried to run, but could not—there was nowhere to go. The hailstones crashed through the roofs of their dwellings, smashing through them like falling anvils, blasting apart windows. People were struck, bruised, battered.

Tapinza—he who had instigated all of this, he who had had designs on Moke's mother, who had brought the green monster that had tried to kill Calhoun, who was in league with all of it—he, Tapinza, tried to run.

But he had caught Moke's attention, and Moke—once he had noticed something—did not allow it to go.

The wind had become far more fierce, if such a thing was possible, and now it converged around Tapinza. He clawed at the air, trying to batter it back, but there was nothing for him to push away, even though it was solid enough to do him damage. He cried out Moke's name, but as with all other protests, it was carried up and away . . . and so was Tapinza. It started slowly at first, but then increased in speed as the whirling vortex lifted Tapinza. He tried to apologize, he tried to beg for mercy, he tried promises of wealth and grandeur, of fame and fortune. He even tried to claim that he was Moke's father, which was not remotely true— although, at that moment, it wouldn't have mattered even if it were.

Higher and higher still went Tapinza, so fast that, in no more than an eyeblink, he went from being on the ground to a couple hundred feet above it. Then, like a cat moving on to more interesting prey, the wind released him, and Tapinza fell.

Exactly one person noticed—the Maestress. It was hard for her not to; Tapinza was falling right toward her. Obviously, the Maestress Cawfiel was caught between warring emotions. On the one hand, she knew that attempting to catch the falling Maester would be suicide; on the other hand, she couldn't bring herself to clear out of his way and thus abandon him at his time of greatest need. And so she stood there, transfixed, unable to decide what to do. Then, at the last moment, as she saw the velocity with which the body was falling, she realized that her death was upon her, and the thought terrified her—which was interesting, considering she had spent a long time thinking that nothing terrified her anymore.

She let out a screech of protest and fright that was, of course, drowned out by all that was around her, and then a large hand grabbed her by the back of her dress and yanked her out of the way as Tapinza hit the ground. He did so with such force that blood spattered everywhere, including all over the Maestress. She stood there, paralyzed, decorated with bits of Tapinza's body. She didn't even look to see who it was that had saved her life. Instead, she was focused only on the unmoving sack of meat and bones that had once been the only creature who walked the planet who had stirred anything akin to emotion in her withered soul.

The howling of the wind was mirrored in the howling torn from Moke's throat, and the storm grew greater, and the hailstones fell with greater ferocity, and there was lightning all around, and the town was being smashed to pieces, and the rest of the people were going to die, that was all, just die, die, death everywhere, a great sea of death, for Moke had never known death before, but now that he grasped the concept, he was going to visit it on all of them, everyone who had ever hurt his mother or him or—

"Enough."

Over all the desperate and terrified cries, over all the yelling, over all the insanity that was around them, the voice of Mackenzie Calhoun carried. He was standing barely two feet away from Moke, and it was clear from the look in his eye that he was going to accept no excuses, no protests of innocence, no further battering of people or property. Mere seconds before, he had pulled the Maestress out of the way of a very ugly death. Now, he put his own life on the line, standing before a child insane with grief, and he said again, in a tone that made it clear that this was an order, "Enough, I said."

"But they—"

"Moke," and this time there was an implied menace, "enough. Your mother wouldn't want this. Neither should you." Then, his voice suddenly getting softer, more compassionate, he said, "Go to her. She needs you now."

Moke hadn't even realized that there was life left within his mother. Immediately, the town forgotten, spared by the mercurial nature of a child's attention span, Moke ran to his mother. He collapsed at her side, staring down into eyes that saw him only with love.

"You made . . . quite a mess . . ." she managed to say.

"They hurt you . . ."

"I know. But they can't hurt me . . . anymore . . ." She was speaking as if from very far away. There was, amazingly, a sound of mild relief in her voice.

"Ma . . ." he said urgently, but was too overwhelmed at first to continue.

Calhoun knelt beside her. At first, she looked at him blankly, as if aware that she knew him from somewhere, but couldn't quite place where that might be. Then she realized. As if reading his mind, she whispered, "It's . . . all right . . . not your fault . . ."

"Just rest," said Calhoun.

She clearly tried to shake her head. "Plenty of time . . . for that . . ."

The winds were dying down, and only a last few hailstones were trickling from the sky. The moans and cries of the people were starting to become audible.

Her voice became even more hoarse, a bare shadow of itself. He had to strain to hear her. "I understand now . . . never had power . . . until Moke was born . . . my mother had it . . . not me . . . then, when Moke was born . . . got power . . . didn't realize . . . I never had it . . . he did . . . I'm a . . . a catalyst . . . there's something in me . . . that triggers ability . . . in my family . . . that's why . . . I couldn't make rain . . . when Moke was around . . . because of me, my mother had it . . . because of me . . . so did Moke . . . never on my own . . . and Moke, on his own . . . won't . . ."

"I don't wanna be on my own," Moke wailed.

"You won't be . . ." she said softly, and she looked to Calhoun. "Will he?"

Calhoun slowly shook his head and there was a sad smile on his face. "Never."

She tried to lift her arm, but it wouldn't respond. With infinite gentleness, Calhoun raised her hand up and put it against his face, on the side opposite the scar.

"Whoever she is . . ." Rheela managed to get out, ". . . the woman who . . . holds your heart . . . she's . . . she's very lucky . . . tell her . . . I said she is . . . you will . . . tell her . . ." He nodded.

"Moke . . . honey . . . Mommy loves you . . . always . . . you can make the clouds go away now . . . have it stop being . . . so dark . . ."

"I have, Ma. Look . . ."

Above them, the clouds had indeed parted, and now, from on high, a single stream of light enveloped them, as if the eyes of the gods on high were staring straight down upon them.

"Much . . . better . . ." she whispered. "Just let me . . . enjoy the light here . . . for a few moments . . ."

And Moke held her close until she was gone.

# SHELBY

SHELBY DIDN'T SAY ANYTHING for some time after Robin Lefler finished speaking. When she did, it was simply, "Then what?"

Lefler shrugged, as if nothing much mattered after that. "Well . . . Si Cwan and Kalinda left not too long after that. I'm not too sure where they went. Although . . . believe me, Captain, I know them. If there's a relaunch of the *Excalibur,* they'll know about it, and will probably show up."

"And what will you say to him? To Si Cwan, I mean."

"I know who you meant. I just . . ." She shook her head. "I don't know." Then, as if to try and change the mood through sheer force of will, she slapped her thighs and said, "My mom and Scotty have been working day and night since then, overseeing repairs and such. The owners of the place want to put Scotty in charge of the joint as manager. He keeps saying he's not interested, although Mom keeps telling him just to think of it as a really big pub."

Shelby laughed at that. Then she said, "Do you think your mother will want to come along to the christening?"

"Oh, I doubt she'd miss it. By the way . . . you haven't told me. Who's captaining it?"

Shelby smiled.

At first Lefler didn't understand the silent grin, but then she got it. "You? *You?* But . . . but you just got the *Exeter!*"

"I know. But when the *Excalibur* came open, well . . ."

"You applied for it?"

"Actually . . . no. No, I was asked if I was interested. At first I said no, but then, on reflection—the reflection coming about a minute later, you understand—I agreed to it. I had some trepidation, I fully admit that. But somehow . . . I thought that—well—"

"He would have wanted it that way?"

She nodded. "Exactly."

"Who asked you if you were interested?"

"Actually . . . you won't believe it . . . but it was Jellico."

Lefler's jaw dropped. "No!"

"Yes. I know, I know, it's . . . kind of hard to believe. Every so often, he'll say or do something that surprises the hell out of me."

"Me, too," said Lefler wonderingly. "What about the rest of your command crew? Do they mind making the transfer?"

"Well . . ." Shelby cleared her throat. "They're . . . not making the transfer, actually."

Lefler blinked. "They're not?"

"No. There have been some . . . well, some personality conflicts. Things haven't gone quite as smoothly as I'd hoped. I suppose, in a number of respects, it wasn't fair to them."

"Fair to them? In what way?"

Shelby looked at her levelly. "I was asking them to live up to the standard set by one of the best crews it's ever been my privilege to work with. A crew that—frankly—I've come to miss the hell out of. And a crew that I'm hoping I can reassemble to be under me on the *Excalibur.*"

Lefler's lower lip trembled. "I . . . I think I'm going to cry . . ."

"That won't be necessary. A simple 'Yes, Captain' will suffice," said Shelby, taking great pains to ignore that she was getting a touch misty-eyed herself.

Lefler drew herself up and, tilting her chin proudly, said, "Yes, Captain. It will be an honor to serve under you again." Then she laughed and shook her head. "I still can't believe that, for once, Admiral Jellico did something just to be decent."

"Well . . . he may have had some mild degree of superstitious self-interest in mind."

"What?" Lefler had no clue what she was talking about.

"Well," said Shelby, clearly amused at the prospect, "he also said something about not putting it past Calhoun to find a way to come back from the dead and haunt him if anyone except either him or me was in charge of the new *Excalibur.*"

"You know what? I wouldn't put it past him either."

# CALHOUN

IT DIDN'T TAKE CALHOUN LONG to locate Krut's vessel. Unlike his own shuttle, which had been more or less destroyed in the landing, Krut's ship was giving off energy emissions as its onboard circuitry went about its automated business. Utilizing the tricorder, Calhoun found the ship in short order. He looked at it grimly, not the least bit amused to see the nature of the ship. It was a Federation runabout. There was no telling where Krut had gotten it from, but it was likely that either he'd stolen it, or somehow hijacked it after killing whoever it was who had previously been in it. Certainly such a vehicle allowed him to travel around with relative impunity. Furthermore, as he studied the ship's controls, he found a variety of holo comm disguise programs built in. In essence, if someone chose to make visual contact with the runabout, the runabout would send back a customized image, depending upon who was doing the hailing. A Vulcan ship would see a Vulcan in command of the runabout; a Rigelian would be talking to a Rigelian, and so on. It was possible for a sustained scan and double-check to penetrate the disguise, but for casual encounters, it was more than sufficient to allay suspicions.

Moke had been silent since his mother's passing. Calhoun had considered Moke and himself lucky that they'd gotten out of the city when they did, and with as much ease. The townspeople, after all, did not realize that Moke was about as dangerous as the average small boy was now that his mother was gone. The unusual bond, the link that they had shared that had enabled him to wield his weather powers so forcefully, was gone. If they'd understood that he was no longer a threat, they would have torn him apart, and very likely Calhoun along with him, if he'd tried to defend the boy. Fortunately enough, the people were so terrified that they simply stood (or lay) there as Calhoun and Moke left the town, riding on the back of the luukab, which—astonishingly—had weathered the storm with such equanimity that one would have thought it no more hazardous than a light shower.

They had also brought the body of Moke's mother. It was not a pleasant notion, but Calhoun would be damned if he left Rheela's body behind. Who knew what they would do to it? But although he was worried about Moke's reaction to his mother's corpse accompanying them for the ride, he needn't have been concerned. Moke didn't seem to pay any attention to their "cargo" at all. Calhoun had a feeling as to why: as far as Moke was concerned, his mother was gone. The brutalized shell that remained behind was no more his mother than an empty boot was the sum and substance of the foot that had once occupied it.

Calhoun, though, was loath simply to bury her, since he didn't trust the townspeople—once their terror had dissipated, to be replaced by outrage over what had occurred—not to seek out her grave and defile it. The solution was presented to him when, guided by the tricorder, he located Krut's ship, situated in a secluded area not far from town. Upon entering, he discovered assorted weaponry, including a standard issue Starfleet phaser. A natural enough item for a runabout to have, although once again he thought bleakly about where Krut had come across it; he'd probably taken it off the body of a Starfleet officer.

When he emerged from the ship, holding the phaser, he slid Rheela's body off the luukab and placed it on the ground as delicately as he could. It was more for the boy's benefit than anything else, since obviously Rheela couldn't feel anything anymore. Moke watched the entire thing with calm, almost distant eyes.

Calhoun took several steps back, and then turned to Moke and said gently, "You can say good-bye if you wish."

"I already did," he said, looking much older than he had when Calhoun first met him, months ago.

He nodded, then thumbed the phaser to "disintegrate," and fired once. The beam struck her and, in a haze of light, she discorporated.

Moke looked with wonder at the phaser, and then to Calhoun. He pointed to the weapon and said, "Is she in there now?"

Calhoun suppressed the urge to laugh. This was, after all, a sad moment, not one that suggested levity, no matter how unintentionally funny the boy's question had been. "No, Moke . . . she's not in here. She's . . ." He paused and then said, "She's with Kolk'r now."

He mulled this over and said nothing. Calhoun hoped that he would understand, although the truth was that Calhoun was much older than Moke and there were still quite a few things that he himself didn't understand . . . and quite likely never would. Then, tentatively, and even a little fearfully, Moke asked, "Are you going to use that . . . to send me to be with Kolk'r and Ma, too?"

Calhoun couldn't help but think it was the saddest question he had ever heard anyone pose in his entire life. He shook his head. "No, Moke. No, hopefully it's going to be a long, long time before you go visit with, uhm . . . Kolk'r."

"So what's going to happen to me?"

"Well . . ." Calhoun took a deep breath. "I figured you would come with me. I'll take you home. My home."

Moke looked skyward. "Is it . . . up there?" When Calhoun nodded, Moke asked, "Is it scary?"

"It can be," Calhoun said honestly. "But then again, there's scary things everywhere. And it can be very exciting as well. I think you'll like it."

For a very, very long time, Moke stared at him . . . so long that Calhoun started to wonder if something was wrong. And finally, Moke said to him, "Are you my father?"

And Calhoun gave the only response that he could:

"I am now."

He considered that a moment, and then nodded. "Can I call you 'Dad'?" he asked.

"If you would like to. Would you like to?" Moke nodded. "All right. That would be fine."

"Dad . . . ?"

"Yes, Moke."

"Did you love Ma?"

He smiled sadly. "I could have, given time . . . and different circumstances. Yes, I could have loved her very much. But I do love someone . . . who is very much like her. Come. I'll take you to meet her."

And moments later, the runabout lifted off the surface of Yakaba, never to return, while the stray atoms of Moke's mother flitted about, forever a part of the atmosphere that she had once joyfully manipulated.

# EXCALIBUR

THE OFFICIAL TRANSFER of the captaincy of the *Exeter* from Shelby to Garbeck went smoothly enough. On the bridge of that ship, Shelby said—as the rest of the crew looked on—"I'm officially turning her over to you, Captain. Good luck to you."

"Thank you, Captain," replied Garbeck and—in one of the very, very few instances in Starfleet where it was still customary—she saluted. Shelby snapped off a sharp return of the salute, which was fairly impressive, considering how rarely she made one. Then Shelby went down to the transporter room, where Ensign Chris Kennedy waited to beam her over to her new command.

When she arrived on *Excalibur,* they were all waiting for her.

There, in the main reception hall, the entire crew had assembled. Burgoyne and Selar were there, and to Shelby's complete astonishment, their infant son, Xyon, was already standing and clutching his mother's pant leg. Burgoyne was looking on proudly. Soleta was also there, looking a bit more—haggard, somehow, although Shelby might have been imagining it. Zak Kebron was there, and Shelby had forgotten how incredibly massive the Brikar was. Nearby was Mark McHenry, engaged in a relaxed chat with Robin Lefler. Again, it might have been Shelby's imagination, but she felt as if Kebron was—every so often—casting suspicious glances in McHenry's direction. She had no idea why that would be the case, though. Morgan Lefler was there as well, chatting with Jean-Luc Picard and Admiral Jellico. Picard was just staring at her, in what could only be considered polite frustration, as if he knew her from someplace but couldn't quite figure out where that might be. Also present were Si Cwan and Kalinda. Apparently, Lefler had it pegged exactly right. They had found out, and they had come on their own. She watched as Si Cwan walked straight up to Kebron. The two of them had historically had very little patience with one another, but this time, when Cwan tapped his heart and head in sequence and bowed slightly—a traditional Thallonian greeting of respect—Kebron actually returned the gesture in as polite a manner as he could. It almost gave Shelby hope for the future.

A future . . . without Calhoun.

God, she hoped she wasn't making a mistake.

"You're not."

She turned and saw Kat Mueller standing there, hands draped behind her back. Mueller, former head of the *Excalibur*'s night-side, was a statuesque German woman with a gravely humorous attitude and a fencing scar that somehow, comfortingly, reminded Shelby of Mac.

"I'm not what?" inquired Shelby.

"Not making a mistake."

Shelby blinked in surprise. "How the hell did you know I was thinking that?"

"That's my job as first officer of the *Excalibur*. To know what you're thinking, and then tell you when you're wrong."

"How about when I'm right?"

"If you need me to tell you that, you've no business being captain."

Shelby grinned. "You know what, Kat? I think making you my first officer is one of the best decisions I've ever made."

"You see? You don't need me to tell you you're right about that."

Picard approached Shelby then and said softly, "I don't mean to intrude on a captain's privilege, Captain Shelby . . . but we might want to consider moving to the bridge to begin the actual ceremony."

"An excellent idea, Captain."

"And, if I may say so . . . I still believe you're making a mistake," Picard informed her. "If anyone is to speak on behalf of Calhoun and dedicate this ship to him and his spirt, it should be you."

"Perhaps. But you've got the better speaking voice."

Picard smiled. "How can I argue with that?"

On the way up to the bridge, walking the halls, Shelby saw familiar face after familiar face. Each person smiled and greeted her with a respectful, pleasant, "Captain." She sighed inwardly and couldn't get away from thinking, *If only Mac had lived to see this.*

Shelby was the first to step out of the turbolift. She looked around the bridge in wonder. Even though she had never set foot on it before, somehow—amazingly—she felt as if she'd come home. The others stepped out behind her, or came in a subsequent lift. Even though she had been speaking to all of them downstairs, she still greeted them by name. Finally, when they were all assembled, she said, "Well . . . here we are again." This drew a polite laugh, and then she continued, "It's good to see you all. Very good. The last time we were together, we were in a bar, where I was busy telling you that doing what we're about to do was an extremely bad idea . . . because we couldn't possibly re-create the atmosphere and sense of family that Mackenzie Calhoun created for this vessel. Since then, well . . . it's been a busy few months for me. And for Lieutenant Lefler, as I'm sure you've all heard by now." There were nods from all around. "And I'm sure the rest of you have likewise had very busy, interesting, and even exciting experiences in the intervening months."

The other members of the command crew looked around at one another.

"Nope. Been pretty quiet," said Burgoyne.

"Nothing extraordinary," affirmed Doctor Selar.

Soleta, her face a mask, said, "It was . . . actually quite dull."

"I don't even remember what I did," said McHenry.

"I slept," Kebron said.

Slowly, she looked around at them, and then said, "Well . . . I'm sure that you could all remember if you put your minds to it. But right now, I think we'd . . . like to work on remembering something—or should I say, someone—else. Captain Picard?"

"Well . . . Captain Shelby," Picard smiled affably, straightening his jacket as he stepped to the center of the bridge. He placed his hands on the back of the command chair. "I thought you were doing fine, to be honest, but if you really want me to speak, well . . . who am I to refuse a fellow captain's request?" He cleared his throat.

"I suppose Captain Shelby asked me to speak . . . to handle the dedication . . . because I 'discovered' Mackenzie Calhoun, as it were. I would like to tell you that I knew he was destined for greatness in Starfleet the first time I saw him, but that would be far from the truth. What I saw was a young, raw, untrained talent. What I sensed . . . what I hoped . . . was that he would go places, given the opportunities. And he did.

"But the thing that was most remarkable about Mac . . . as we liked to call him . . . was not simply that he was given opportunities, but he also took them. And not just took them, either. He practically grabbed them between his teeth and held onto them, savoring every opportunity as if it was his last.

"There are so many positive things to say about Mac. To speak of his bravery . . . his innovation . . . his leadership . . . his grace under pressure . . . his ability to make us think, to question, and even . . . dare I say it . . . to get under our skin from time to time."

"Hear, hear," said Shelby, and there was gentle laughter, but she felt her eyes misting up, and she quickly wiped it away.

"There was so much that he wanted to accomplish, and it is nothing short of tragic that his life was cut short the way it was. But the manner in which he died . . . was the manner in which he lived. Sacrificing himself, saving his crew, putting consideration for everyone else ahead of himself. And attaining superhuman achievement in doing so. In five minutes . . . five minutes . . . he managed to get the entire crew into escape pods. It's phenomenal, almost supernatural."

Shelby noticed, out of the corner of her eye, McHenry shifting his feet, looking slightly uncomfortable. She wondered if he needed new boots.

"The point is . . . where Mackenzie Calhoun was concerned, nothing was impossible. And it is that spirit of daring . . . of determination . . . of a willingness to defy all odds to get the job done . . . that we dedicate this ship, this fine crew . . . and this command."

There was a round of applause from everyone there as Picard, standing behind the command chair, swiveled it around to face Shelby, so that she could take her seat.

And then the door to the captain's ready room hissed open. Shelby's back was to it, but she saw the look of pure shock in Picard's eyes, and before she could turn, she heard a familiar voice say in a slow drawl . . .

"All right, Picard. Take your damned hands off my chair."

# CALHOUN

MOKE RUBBED HIS EYES as he emerged from the sleeping area in the back of the runabout. He didn't even give the stars out the viewport a glance. Calhoun considered this a bit amusing. When they had first launched, the boy had been practically glued to the front viewport, amazed at the sights, gasping at the view. "So many," he'd kept whispering. Seeing the glories of outer space through the eyes of a child served to remind Calhoun of just how truly wondrous a place the void could be.

But by this point in the journey back to Federation space, Moke had become so accustomed to the view that he barely noticed it anymore. Grozit, *the kid's adaptable,* Calhoun thought.

What Moke did notice was a small twinkle of excitement in Calhoun's eye. "What's happened, Dad?" he asked.

"How do you know something's 'happened'?"

"I don't, for sure. But you just kinda look . . . I dunno . . . like you heard something funny."

"Amazingly perceptive for one so young," Calhoun admitted. "Moke . . . remember how I said that, before I came to your world . . . I lived in another place . . ."

"A ship. Like this one, only much, much bigger," Moke said quickly. The lad was quick, Calhoun had to give him that. He had been uncertain about trying to explain the world—the universe—in which he resided to a boy who came from a planet that had little to no concept of such things. But the boy had comprehended everything Calhoun had told him, or at least had been able to distill it to enough of an essence that he could follow and accept it.

"Yes, that's right. And do you remember the ship's name?"

"*Excalber . . .*"

"Close. Ex-cal-uh-bur," he said, one syllable at a time, and Moke mouthed each with him.

"And the *Ex . . . calibur* blowed up . . . ?"

"Oh, yes. It blowed up rather impressively. The thing is, Moke, I've just picked up over general news broadcasts on the ether . . . they've built a new one. Or, at least, they've taken a ship that they were close to completing already and given it the name of my ship. And here's the great thing: They're going to be officially christening it in a Starfleet drydock in about two days."

"Why is that a great thing?"

"Because," Calhoun said with puckish satisfaction, "I think it would only be polite of me to stop by and say hello."

"But you said that everybody thought you were dead."

"That's right," nodded Calhoun. A glint of wicked amusement shone in his purple eyes. "Remind me, Moke, when we have a free moment, to give you a copy of a story written many, many years ago. It's called *Tom Sawyer . . .*"

# EXCALIBUR

"*I KNEW IT!*" SAID JELLICO in wonderment.

Shelby felt as if the muscles had gone dead in her legs. Her gaze was riveted on the man who was standing in the door of the ready room. He had a scraggly beard reaching around the edges of his chin, there were a few more streaks of gray in his hair, and his skin was darker than she remembered. He wasn't wearing a Starfleet uniform, but instead some sort of . . . of getup that looked more appropriate to a primitive society. Most bizarre of all, there was a small boy standing behind him, dressed in similar garb.

He couldn't be here . . . looking like that . . . in this place, at this time . . . it simply wasn't possible . . .

Except, there he was . . .

No one said anything after Jellico's stunned outburst. Every eye was on Shelby, who was as shocked as anyone else. Slowly she walked toward him, amazed that she was able to get her legs to function at all. She drew to within a foot of him, afraid to say anything, afraid of breaking the moment, afraid of it all popping like a soap bubble.

He spoke to her.

"Marry me," he said.

She drew back a fist and hit him so hard in the face that it almost knocked him off his feet. He staggered against the door frame, holding his chin in surprise.

*"Who the hell are you,"* she demanded irately, *"and what have you done with Mackenzie Calhoun?!?"* She stared at the boy behind him, and pointed. *"And who the hell is that?!"*

Intimidated but undaunted, the boy said quietly, "I'm Moke. I'm his son."

Dead silence. Finally, it was Kebron who spoke.

"Busy six months," he said.

There had been questions, of course, dozens of questions, flying at him from all sides. There had been medical probes and careful examinations. He had been subjected to a truth scan, and even more questions, and finally . . . finally . . .

It came down to the two of them.

Calhoun and Shelby, in sickbay, of all places, while he pulled on his shirt after what had seemed the umpteenth examination. He had that same damned smile on his face, undimmed by all that had happened. "Do you like the beard?" he asked, stroking it.

She stared at him. Just stared at him.

"Do I take that as a no?"

"You're here." She said it in wonderment. "You're . . . really here."

"Yes. I really am."

"How the hell did you get into the ready room? How did you get aboard the ship at all, and get all the way up there, all without anyone seeing you?"

"A stolen ship with a personal transporter and a rather innovative disguise program to deceive sensors. I've already turned it over to Starfleet R&D. They were most interested in it, as you can well imagine."

She was shaking her head. "You couldn't let me do it, could you? Couldn't let me take over the *Excalibur.* After all the resistance to the idea, after all the complaining about coming back . . . you still had to be in charge of this ship."

"What can I say? Picard was right. It gets in your blood."

"It's my ship now."

"I want it back," he said simply.

She laughed at that. "And what am I supposed to do? Go back to being first officer, after being a captain? Take a step back in rank?"

"Is that what you're concerned about?" Calhoun, who was usually the most unflappable of men, looked and sounded surprised. "Your career?"

"I don't know, Mac! I mean . . . I'd barely adjusted to you being dead, and you're back! And you're asking me to marry you! How the hell am I supposed to react to that?"

"I can't tell you how to react. I can only ask you."

"You just asked me to be dramatic."

"No. I asked you because I almost died . . . and because I spent the past months with a good, honest, and loving woman, and an entire life that I could have embraced wholeheartedly, but didn't, because all I could think about was you. And because I've come to the realization that dying doesn't particularly frighten me. I've lived with death, seen so much of it, that it holds no terror for me. I won't embrace it, but I won't fear it. But the only thing I'm afraid of is living without making a commitment to you for everyone to see. So that everyone—including you and I—know that, wherever we go, whatever happens . . . we'll have each other to come back to. You see, Eppy? That's all it'll take. We just have to make a solemn promise always to come back to each other, and if we do that, we can live forever, because neither of us would break a solemn promise."

"You're insane."

"No. I'm in love." He took her by the shoulders. "And you are, too. You say you want a command, Eppy? Jellico's already told me there's one available for you. The *Trident*. Perhaps we can pull a string or two and have both ships assigned to Thallonian space. After all, it's the new frontier. More than enough to keep two ships busy at this point. And I suspect, at this point, Jellico will agree to just about anything, just to get me away from him."

"Two ships."

"Yes."

"And we're each captain of one of them."

"Plenty of good officers out there for two ships–including, I'm told, two who served under Kirk and are back on active duty. They should be—"

"And if we're married and captains on different ships, when would we be together?"

"Eppy . . . I crossed half a galaxy and came back from the dead to be with you. A little thing like two different ships isn't going to stop us from being together if we want to be. So."

"So what?"

"So . . . will you marry me, Eppy?"

She stared at him for a long time. "If I do, will you stop calling me Eppy?"

"No."

"Can I keep your sword?"

"No. I want that back."

She stared into those purple eyes that she had known for a fact she would never see again.

"Oh, the hell with it. I'll marry you anyway."

The wedding took place on the bridge of the new *Excalibur,* with Moke acting as ring bearer, and was conducted by Captain Jean-Luc Picard, who wished the record to note—in no uncertain terms—that Mackenzie Calhoun, despite whatever nice things Picard had said during the ship-christening ceremony, was the single most frustrating individual he'd ever met.

Calhoun chose to take that as a compliment.

As did his wife.

# *THE STAR TREK: NEW FRONTIER MINIPEDIA*

## by David Mack

### Adis

A highly placed member of the Romulan political hierarchy, a rich and powerful politician who is said to be a member of the Praetor's inner circle. Tall and aristocratic-looking.

Came to the Titan colony to assassinate Rajari because Rajari's smuggling had interfered with Adis' private arms sales to the Cardassians.

### Adulux

Litenite who sought the help of Zak Kebron and Mark McHenry in the search for his abducted wife, Zanka. Adulux' brow is slightly distended, and he has thick, black hair. Though he claimed to love his wife, he treated her poorly, and after her rescue from her abductor, she eventually left him.

### Ahmista

Desolate, ash-covered world on which Tarella Lee lived with a Promethean weapon, which sustained her and destroyed all other sentient and semi-intelligent life-forms on the planet. The planet was rumored to be a place where the Prometheans could be found. It is the third and outermost planet in its star system.

### *Alas, poor Yorick!*

Famous quotation from William Shakespeare's play, *Hamlet*. Spoken facetiously by Hamlet when a grave-digger hands him an unearthed skull. Yorick was the court jester during Hamlet's boyhood. The full quotation is, "Alas, poor Yorick! I knew him, Horatio!"

### *Aldrin, U.S.S.*

A Starfleet vessel, registry number not established. It put an end to the piracy and smuggling of Rajari, a Romulan fugitive, who was later determined to be the biological father of Starfleet Lieutenant Soleta.

### Alice in Wonderland
Common misquote of the title of Lewis Carroll's book *Alice's Adventures in Wonderland*, a satire of the 19th-century British government whose plot focuses on a young girl who tumbles through a rabbit hole into a fantastical realm where nothing makes sense. It is often confused with its sequel, *Through the Looking Glass.*

### Alora
Planet that deported its unwanted members to the colony planet of Enev.

### Alpha Carinae Central Hall of Worship
The primary temple of Xantism on Alpha Carinae, and residence of that world's High Priest of Xant.

### Alphans
Humanoid species indigenous to Alpha Carinae. Large, muscled, relatively savage of mien. They converted to Xantism in the 24th century for a brief time. They soon rebelled against and killed the High Priest of Alpha Carinae, releasing a virulent pathogen that exterminated their species and every plant and animal life-form on the planet.

### Ap'Boylan, Laura
Ship's counselor aboard the *U.S.S. Exeter,* under the command of Captain Elizabeth Shelby. A Betazoid woman with large, limpid eyes and blond hair.

### Arango
Son of Tara of Rolisa. In a parallel reality's future, he begat Izzo, who begat Faicco the Small, a great thinker. In this reality, Arango died during birth, when Rolisa was devoured by the Black Mass.

### Arbora the Unseen
Leader of an Unglza clan from the eastern territories of Zondar.

### Argelius II
Pleasure planet. According to Morgan Lefler, "So hedonistic that it makes Risa look like kindergarten."

### Arthurian
Adjective meaning "related to or derived from the mythology of King Arthur," a legendary British monarch who was renowned for his Knights of the Round Table, castle Camelot, queen Guinevere and his sword, Excalibur.

### Atik
A Dog of War who had the darkest, blackest fur of any of the Dogs. The only Dog who carried weapons, a pair of razor-edged swords captured during a

foray. Always considered himself a "Dog of Destiny," one upon whom Fate often smiled.

**Atlantis**
Mythological lost civilization on Earth. Legends say the island of Atlantis was destroyed in a cataclysm and swallowed by the sea.

**Atol**
A henchman of Zoran.

**Augustine, Lieutenant Toreen**
Junior officer aboard the *U.S.S. Exeter* under the command of Captain Elizabeth Shelby. Served a residency in xeno-studies as part of a NonObservable Team assigned to Makkus ten years prior to its invitation to Federation membership. Was recommended by *Exeter* first officer Garbeck for an away mission to Makkus.

**Awakening, Time of The**
Period in Vulcan history associated with Surak, the father of Vulcan's logical philosophy.

**Ayre, Lieutenant Kristian**
A conn officer aboard the *U.S.S. Enterprise* 1701-E.

**Azizi**
Replaced Celter as provisional governor of Nelkar, following a popular uprising sparked by the heavy-handed tactics of Laheera.

**Aztecs**
Ancient society of Native Americans who resided in Central America until the arrival of European explorers, whose foreign disease vectors infected and rapidly wiped out the native population.

**Bard, The**
Nickname for William Shakespeare, a late 16th-century Earth playwright.

**Bairns**
Scottish word for "children."

**Barsamis**
Friend of Mackenzie Calhoun, who was murdered by an Orion trader named Krassus. Barsamis' death was avenged by Calhoun.

**Barspens (planet)**
A relatively barbaric world, its most popular form of entertainment is public

executions. Xyon of Calhoun was scheduled to be the main attraction at one such execution, but he narrowly escaped.

### Barspens (species)
Race native to their eponymous homeworld, they make a squishing sound when they shift side-to-side on their tentacles. Moving on their tentacles, they seem to glide.

### Bartog
A wandering Yakaban gunman who was a player in the card game that ended in Kusack's murder of Turkin of Narrin.

### Basner, Lieutenant Naomi
Former chief security officer of the *U.S.S. Exeter*, under the command of Captain Shelby. Was a fan of 20th-century comic books. Underwent physical therapy after a shooting incident on Zeron III. Killed in the *Exeter* holodeck after disengaging the safety protocols for a training simulation.

### Battle of Condacin
A conflict the Danteri High Command assumed would be the "preeminent military strike of the century" against the Xenexians, but which ended with a Danteri defeat at the hands of rebels led by M'k'n'zy of Calhoun. The brother of Danteri officer Delina was killed in this battle.

### Bearclaw
A very tasty, fluffy pastry popularized on Earth in the 20th century. Reputed to be very popular aboard the rechristened *U.S.S. Excalibur*, under the command of Captain Mackenzie Calhoun.

### Beth, Ensign Ronni
A member of Burgoyne 172's engineering crew aboard the *U.S.S. Excalibur*. Fairly slim and athletic, with a round face, large eyes, and shoulder-length curly hair. An avid skier. Was romantically involved with fellow engineer Ensign Christiano, but their relationship ended badly.

### Beyond Gate, The
Black hole in the Tulaan system, through which Xant, deity of the Redeemers, is said to have "gone on" to the next plane of being. The Redeemers believe He will re-emerge from the Beyond Gate at the time of the Second Coming of Xant.

The *Excalibur* crew lured the Black Mass into the Beyond Gate to destroy it and prevent the destruction of Tulaan IV, much to the chagrin of the ungrateful Redeemers, who considered that solution a defilement of a place they hold sacred.

**Bibbyte**
A young, determined Makkusian who served aboard Hauman's flagship during the Makkusians' retaliatory strike against Corinder.

**Big Bang**
A potent liquor from Pocatello, Idaho, Earth. Commander Alexandra Garbeck kept a bottle of the stuff in her "private stock" aboard the *U.S.S. Exeter.*

**Black Hole Ride**
Amusement park simulator ride visited by Robin Lefler with her friend, Nik. The ride was closed for repair at the time of their visit.

**Black Mass, The**
The Black Mass was a swarm of wormlike creatures that boiled out of the Hunger Zone at varying intervals, devoured entire worlds and suns, then returned to the Hunger Zone to digest its meal, transforming it into energy plasma.

It was capable of existing in and traversing deep space. It propelled itself across interstellar distances by discharging energy plasma and, at a high but space-normal velocity, slingshotting around a pulsar or neutron star within the Hunger Zone to achieve warp speed. Its motion during migration had the effect of severely disrupting space-time. After devouring a world and/or its sun, it again discharged energy plasma until it encountered another pulsar or other superdense stellar entity, then slingshotted around it to resume warp speed back to the Hunger Zone.

Individual Black Mass entities resembled the remora, a wormlike fish on Earth; one end of a Black Mass entity's body was a toothless mouth that occasionally flutters closed, but reopens soon after. They intertwined themselves so closely it was difficult to ascertain their numbers.

**Blaymore**
In a parallel reality's future, gifted daughter of Rolisan philosopher Faicco the Small. Does not exist in this reality, because her ancestors and their world were destroyed by the Black Mass.

**Boragi**
Indigenous inhabitants of Boragi III. Aggressively neutral, and noted for their ability to stir up problems without becoming specifically involved themselves. Then, when things fall apart, the Boragi come in to pick through the wreckage.

The Boragi secret is that they are skilled manipulators of humanoid emotions, stirring up love, hate, and everything in between. They foment wars in a variety of ways, from causing planetary leaders to hate each other at a gut level to prompting a leader to have an affair with the wife of an opposing world's leader.

**Boragi III**
Homeworld of the neutrally meddlesome Boragi.

**Boretskee & Cary**
A husband-and-wife pair of representatives for a group of Thallonian refugees rescued by Captain Hufmin and, in turn, the *U.S.S. Excalibur.* They were called upon to attest to Laheera of Nelkar that they had been treated well by the *Excalibur* crew, and that the Starfleet ship was not, in fact, an aggressor, but rather a rescuer.

**Boyajian, Mr.**
*U.S.S. Excalibur* officer who filled in for Zak Kebron while the security chief was off-ship with Si Cwan, searching for Si Cwan's sister, Kalinda, and also for ops officer Robin Lefler, while she was on an away mission to the planet Nelkar. He was described as a tall, dark-haired tactical specialist.

**Bragonier**
A member of the Royal House of Danteri, who participated in negotiations with the Xenexians that were moderated by Captain Jean-Luc Picard of the *U.S.S. Stargazer.*

**Brandi**
A short Makkusian woman, aide-de-camp to Hauman, the Makkusian leader.

**Braxton, Captain**
Commanding officer of the Federation Timeship *Relativity.* Asked Commander Shelby to relieve Captain Calhoun of duty after Calhoun transported the *U.S.S. Excalibur* back in time by four days to rescue a world that Braxton said was fated for destruction.

**Brikar**
A high-density species with dark-bronze-colored skin, three-fingered hands, and thick, tough hides. They possess only small earholes and vertical slits for noses. They can withstand phaser blasts that might kill several humans. In order to function in Earth-normal gravity, they require special gravity compensators. Once so equipped, they are extremely strong and surprisingly nimble for their size.

**Burgoyne 172**
Chief engineer of the *U.S.S. Excalibur* under the command of Captain Mackenzie Calhoun. Burgoyne, a Hermat, is something of an anomaly among hir people: extremely outgoing, playful, and pleased with hirself whenever s/he manages to solve some sort of problem or difficulty.

Enjoyed a brief romantic dalliance with Mark McHenry. Burgoyne described their association as "friendship with fringe benefits."

Burgoyne sired one offspring with Dr. Selar. They named the child Xyon, in honor of the son of Mackenzie Calhoun, who appeared to have been killed defending Tulaan IV from the Black Mass.

When Dr. Selar insisted on raising Xyon as a Vulcan citizen, Burgoyne sought legal remedy from the Hermat Directorate, but was refused. S/he was forced to plead hir case for parental rights before the Vulcan Judgment Council, in opposition to Selar. The two parents eventually reached a mutually agreeable settlement.

### Byrillium
Compound alloy capable of withstanding low-intensity phaser blasts by absorbing the beam's energy and redistributing it, diminishing its force. Romulans use it to make body armor.

### Calhoun, Captain Mackenzie
Captain Mackenzie Calhoun was well known as the leader of the planetary revolution that freed the planet Xenex from Danteri control before he entered Starfleet Academy.

During Calhoun's tenure in the Academy, he earned a reputation for being high-energy and quick with his fists, and for never backing down from any confrontation.

Captain Calhoun's given name on his homeworld of Xenex was M'k'n'zy. When he joined Starfleet, he changed it to Mackenzie, the closest Terran-language equivalent, and adopted the name of his home city, Calhoun, as his surname.

Calhoun has an older brother, D'ndai, who conspired with Thallonian Chancellor Yoz to overthrow the Thallonian royal family.

With Catrina of Calhoun, M'k'n'zy fathered a son, Xyon of Calhoun, during the Xenexian uprising against the Danteri. He met his adult son for the first time in Thallonian space, but regarded him as little more than a friendly stranger.

While marooned for six months on the planet Yakaba, after the destruction of the Starship *Excalibur,* Calhoun befriended Rheela, a young single mother, and her young son, Moke. When Rheela was murdered and it became clear that her orphaned son would be in grave danger if left behind, Calhoun adopted the boy and returned with him to Federation space.

Calhoun married his former first officer, Elizabeth Paula Shelby, six months after he was believed killed during the destruction of the refitted *Ambassador*-class Starship *Excalibur,* and shortly after the christening of the new, *Galaxy*-class Starship *Excalibur,* whose launch ceremony he crashed in his usual, highly dramatic fashion.

### Calhoun, City of
The home city of M'k'n'zy, later known as Captain Mackenzie Calhoun.

### Cambon

A freighter ship piloted by a man named Hufmin. The *Cambon*'s comfortable passenger complement was 29, but when it was rescued by the *U.S.S. Excalibur,* it was carrying 47 refugee passengers.

### Captain's Table, The

A popular captains-only club and bar in San Francisco, on Earth. More exclusive than the highly popular Strange New Worlds officers' club and bar, also located in San Francisco.

### Capulets

One of the two fictional feuding families in William Shakespeare's play, *Romeo and Juliet.* The Capulets' daughter, Juliet, falls in love with Romeo, son of their rivals, the Montagues.

### Carroll, Ensign Charles

Starfleet special services officer aboard the *U.S.S. Exeter,* under the command of Captain Elizabeth Shelby. An old poker buddy of *Exeter* first officer Garbeck, who helped arrange his transfer to the *Exeter.*

### Catalina City

Main entry port of the Titan colony. Reportedly named after the wife of one of the colony's founders. The city's economy is based primarily on tourism. The city has decayed badly in recent decades and is now marred by a pervasive, garish seediness.

### Catrina

A woman on Calhoun whose husband was slain in battle against the Danteri before she had borne an heir. Because tribal chief D'ndai was not available to provide her with an heir under the terms of Xenexian custom, that responsibility fell to D'ndai's brother, the warlord M'k'n'zy, who was ten years Catrina's junior. Their union—M'k'n'zy's first—produced a son, Xyon of Calhoun.

### Cawfiel, Maestress

"Spiritual mother" and political prime mover in the city of Narrin, on Yakaba. Said to be "older than dirt," she is half a head shorter than the second-shortest adult in town, and has skin that is pale almost to the point of translucence. She has short, green hair. She bore a deep grudge against Rheela, and conspired unsuccessfully against her.

### Celter

Governor of the city of Selinium on Nelkar. Celter extended asylum to the Thallonian refugees rescued by Hufmin and the *U.S.S. Excalibur.*

**Central Design**
Branch of Starfleet that handles new starship design and construction.

**Chapel, Christine**
Nurse aboard the original Starship *Enterprise* during the command of Captain James T. Kirk. Nearly a century later, former *Enterprise* chief engineer Montgomery Scott claimed Morgan Primus bore an "uncanny" resemblance to Nurse Chapel.

**Cheshire Cat, The**
A character in the Lewis Carroll book, *Alice's Adventures in Wonderland.* The Cheshire Cat could slowly turn its body invisible, until all that remained was its enormous grin. Robin Lefler's mother, Morgan Lefler, nicknamed her "Cheshire," because of Robin's constant efforts to bolster her mother's spirits.

**Christiano, Ensign**
Member of Burgoyne 172's engineering crew aboard the *U.S.S Excalibur.* Was romantically involved with Ensign Ronni Beth, but left her for another woman. Killed during an incident in engineering when the Tentacle, a.k.a. "Sparky," pulled him into the warp core. Ensign Ronni Beth tried to save him, but failed.

**Circuit Judiciary**
A judge on Yakaba who roams from city to city, adjudicating criminal and civil cases. The Circuit Judiciary, or "C.J.," visits the same locality roughly every six months. The Circuit Judiciary who heard Kusack's case was, in Calhoun's estimation, "an unassuming but learned individual."

**City of The Dead, The**
A vast graveyard and collection of tombs, crypts, and mausoleums in the capital city of Romulus, where it is known as the Rikolet.

**Clark, Engineer's Mate First Class Kate**
Crewman aboard the *U.S.S. Exeter,* under the command of Captain Elizabeth Shelby. An old poker buddy of *Exeter* first officer Garbeck, who helped arrange her transfer to the *Exeter.*

**Collie**
A long-haired breed of dog native to Earth. The breed is renowned for its human-friendly disposition and loyalty.

**Comar IV**
A planet on the outer rim of the former Thallonian Empire.

**Corinder**
Neighbor world to Makkus.

### Corinderians

Native inhabitants of Corinder. They were longtime allies of the Makkusians, but when the Makkusians began considering accepting membership in the Federation, the Corinderians engineered a lethal virus and spread it to the population of Makkus, using insects native to that planet. Makkusian scientists exposed the treachery after the initial insect threat was dealt with by Captain Shelby and the crew of the *U.S.S. Exeter.*

### Cudsuttle

The Momidiums' head of extraterrestrial relations. Brokered the deal with Captain Calhoun of the *U.S.S. Excalibur* for the release of Morgan Primus, a.k.a. Morgan Lefler.

### Cwan, Sedi

Uncle of deposed Thallonian prince-turned-Federation-ambassador, Si Cwan. Failed to stop the Black Mass from devouring Rolisa, a Thallonian-controlled planet.

### Cwan, Si

Formerly a popular prince of a royal family in the Thallonian empire whose family was overthrown. Si Cwan actually was liked by the people; nonetheless, those around him were hated and reviled, which was one of the reasons that the Thallonian empire crumbled. Si Cwan and the survivors of the coup sought refuge in the Federation. Cwan, however, now returns to the Thallonian empire to prove that the family is willing to work with the Federation and "by extension" the people of the Thallonian sector, in order to achieve peace.

After a lengthy search, Si Cwan located his missing sister, Kalinda, who had been abducted by Zoran Si Verdin. Later, Si Cwan undertook a new quest to avenge the murder of his mentor, Jereme, who was killed by Nikolas Viola, son of Si Cwan's longtime rival, Sientor Olivan.

### Dackow

A henchman of Zoran, Dackow was an irrepressible "yes-man."

### Danter

Homeworld of the Danteri, in Sector 221-G.

### Danteri

A humanoid species with dark-bronze-colored skin who pride themselves on being prepared for all situations. They occupied the planet Xenex for more than 300 years, until they were overthrown by a grassroots rebellion led by M'k'n'zy of Calhoun.

### Danteri Empire, The

A strategically situated group of worlds located in Sector 221-G that became members of the Federation following their troops' ouster from the planet Xenex. The Danteri Empire is located in close proximity to the fallen Thallonian Empire, and may have been involved in that government's collapse. Regardless, the Danteri have designs on the acquisition of former Thallonian territories.

### Darkshade

The most mysterious sector of Thallonian space. No ship that has ventured into the area has ever returned. The more scientifically minded believe that it is some sort of gateway, possibly to another time, possibly to another dimension. It is believed by some of the more fanciful that it is the source of all evil.

### Delina

Aide to Falkar. Delina sacrificed his life to save Falkar from a falling boulder pushed by M'k'n'zy of Calhoun.

### Dissuaders, The

An Unglza offshoot clan from the northern territory of Zondar. Considered by their fellow Zondarians to be an arbitrarily negative group.

### D'ndai

Mackenzie Calhoun's older brother, who conspired with Thallonian Chancellor Yoz to overthrow the Thallonian royal family and participated in the plot to assassinate deposed prince, Si Cwan.

### Dogs of War, The

The Dogs of War are one of the few groups from Thallonian space who have actually made incursions into Federation space. There are only about a hundred of them, ferocious living weapons, a genetic breeding experiment gone awry. They are vicious, feral and extremely devastating fighters, with thick fur, claws and teeth.

After they were defeated in a battle with the Brikar more than ten years ago, the Dogs retreated to their home system to lick their wounds. After a recuperation period, the Dogs spent some time marauding on the outer edges of Federation territory, then relocated to the edge of Thallonian space. They later sought out The Quiet Place, and many died in the attempt to reach it.

### Dorado, Laurence

Founder of the El Dorado luxury hotel on Risa.

### Dunn, Lieutenant Commander Christopher James

Chief engineer of the *U.S.S. Exeter*, under the command of Captain Shelby. Nicknamed "C.J." His favorite phrase, when acknowledging orders, is "Done and Dunn," much to his shipmates' chagrin. Also prone to thinking aloud and rambling profusely.

**Eenza**
An ethnic group on the planet Zondar that waged a centuries-long civil conflict with its neighbors, the Unglza. The eventual outcome of their conflict was predicted by the Zondarian prophet Ontear.

**El Dorado**
Terran literary/historical reference: A legendary "City of Gold" in South America on Earth, spoken of by the Aztecs to the Spanish explorers who arrived in the 15th century.

In the 24th century, El Dorado is a well-known luxury hotel on Risa, named with tongue-in-cheek aplomb by its founder, L. (Laurence) Dorado. Hotel manager Theodore Quincy hired former Starfleet engineer Montgomery Scott to iron out problems with the resort's state-of-the-art computer core. Scott ended up staying on staff as a "greeter" for the hotel's bar, The Engineering Room, before returning to Starfleet to head up the Starfleet Corps of Engineers.

Morgan Primus and her daughter, Robin Lefler, were visiting the hotel in the 24th century when a man named Rafe and his son, Nik Viola, sabotaged the resort's central computer and murdered Quincy.

**Enev**
Colony world located near the planet Haresh. Colonized by the planet Alora with the dregs of its society. When Enev was threatened by a vicious magnetic storm, the *Starship Excalibur,* under the command of Captain Mackenzie Calhoun, answered its distress call and rescued its colonists in the nick of time. However, this rescue mission delayed the *Excalibur* from reaching the planet Haresh in time to prevent its entire population from being slain by the Redeemer virus.

**Enevian Empire**
Enormously powerful political entity of the 39th century. It came to dominate what was once known as Thallonian space, and forced many worlds and species into servitude. Its leader, Shad Tiempor, predicted its eventual domination of the Milky Way Galaxy.

**Enevians**
Colonists of the planet Enev.

**Engineering Room, The**
Bar in the El Dorado hotel where people, after a few drinks, are known to "act on impulse" or become "totally warped." The bar's "greeter" was, for a time, Montgomery Scott, former chief engineer of the original *Starship Enterprise* under the command of Captain James T. Kirk.

***Excalibur, U.S.S.***
Starfleet Registry number NCC-26517. The *U.S.S. Excalibur* was a

newly refitted *Ambassador*-class starship under the command of Captain Calhoun. Her last assignment was to monitor the collapse of the Thallonian Empire in Sector 221-G, render aid, and keep the peace when necessary.

The ship exploded shortly after rescuing the Redeemer homeworld Tulaan IV from The Black Mass.

A new *Excalibur* was commissioned several months later. This new *Excalibur*, a *Galaxy*-class starship, was christened and launched, in a formal ceremony, from Starbase 8.

### *Exeter, U.S.S.*

Starfleet vessel. Former *Excalibur* first officer Elizabeth Paula Shelby's first command as a captain.

### *Faicco the Small*

In a parallel reality, a Rolisan philosopher, one of the greatest thinkers in galactic history. Son of Izzo; father of a son, Milenko, and a daughter, Blaymore, who shared his intellectual gifts. Does not exist in this reality, because his ancestors and their world were destroyed by the Black Mass.

### Fairax, Majister

Yakaban law-enforcement officer in the city of Narrin. Served under a four-year contract. Wasn't very fond of most of the people under his jurisdiction, except for Rheela. At her request, he placed the ailing and incoherent marooned Captain Calhoun in "gaol," or jail.

### Falkar

A Danteri commander of the House of Edins who pursued the teen-aged rebel M'k'n'zy of Calhoun during the Danteri occupation of the planet Xenex. Falkar and a squad of troops under his command, including his second-in-command, Delina, were killed by M'k'n'zy when they pursued him into a region of Xenex known as The Pit. Falkar's son, Ryjaan, would later grow up to become a Danteri representative.

### Fenner

A Class-M world with an early level of spaceflight technology and a recently united world government. Selected for conversion by the Redeemers, who sent a High Priest of Xant to the planet.

### Fennerian jungle

Hiding place of the High Priest of Xant, who was dispatched to convert Fenner to Xantism. The High Priest was found and captured, unharmed, by Starfleet security officer Ensign Janos. The jungle of Fenner is renowned for its beautiful sunsets.

### Ferghut, The

Leader of the Corinderian people, chosen by an artificial intelligence that scans the populace for suitable candidates. The office of the Ferghut is an anonymous position that is conferred for life. The decision to make the ruler anonymous was rooted in the belief that it would help shield the leader's family from retribution or scrutiny, and that it would make each new leader a "blank slate" upon whom the future of Corinder could be written.

### Fermit, Subminister

Hareshi politician, and primary political rival of Haresh's appointed leader, Minister Rizpak, who is also Fermit's brother-in-law. Fermit was a physically formidable individual.

### Final Challenge

Under Danteri Law, the family of a murder victim can opt for a Final Challenge, in which a family member fights the accused to the death. If the accused wins the conflict, he is allowed to go free. If he loses, however, death can be drawn out over any period desired. Any manner of killing one's opponent in a Final Challenge is considered acceptable.

### Finnegan, Cadet

A rambunctious Starfleet cadet who pushed the young Cadet Selar into the Academy pool when she showed reluctance to dive in. This cadet is not to be confused with the Cadet Finnegan who tormented a young James T. Kirk many decades before, although the two cadets' behaviors bear an uncanny similarity.

### Fireworld

One of the major tourist attractions of Thallonian Space, the Fireworld remains a major mystery. It has a surface of constant, unending fire that burns and burns without apparently having any source. No one is quite certain whether the fire is limited to the surface, or whether the entire planet, right down to its core, is one gigantic ball of flame.

### Fista

A Dog of War, litter brother to Krul. Lean and hungry looking, with mottled gray fur.

### Flamebird of Ricca 4

A beast to which Soleta compared the Great Bird of The Galaxy.

### *Flutzed*

Hermat slang term, made official by the Hermat Language Council, meaning "messed up; not performing as expected due to error."

**Fogelson, Ensign Scott**
*U.S.S. Excalibur* bridge officer who filled in at ops for Lieutenant Robin Lefler.

**Foutz**
Barspens prison guard of average height who tormented Xyon of Calhoun. Xyon later slew Foutz by breaking his neck.

**Fr'Col**
Sole surviving member of the Ruling Council of Montos City. An elderly man, with graying whiskers sticking out from his chin at odd angles. Walks with a bowlegged shuffle. Carries a triangular stone in one hand as a symbol of authority, and uses it as a gavel.

**Freenaux the Undesirable**
Leader of an Unglza clan from the eastern territories of Zondar.

**Furn**
Domesticated, benign-looking farm animal indigenous to Liten. Large and slow-moving, and not very smart, even for an animal. If fed and cared for properly, it will provide liquid sustenance on a daily basis. If knocked on its side, it is unable to right itself, and will die if not assisted back to an upright position.

**Gamma Hydrinae system**
Home of the Momidium species.

**Gaol**
Yakaban word for jail.

**Garbeck, Commander Alexandra**
First officer of the *U.S.S. Exeter,* under the command of Captain Elizabeth Shelby. Slim, bordering on diminutive, but possessing an air of quiet authority. Her hair is long, knotted in an efficient bun, and her chin comes to a point that is perpetually upthrust, ever so slightly.

**Gauntlet, The**
A region in the Lemax system, between two warring planets in the former Thallonian Empire. The area was infamous as a battlefield, but was silent for centuries after the Thallonians ended the conflict. After the fall of the Thallonian Empire, fighting resumed almost immediately, and the *Cambon,* a noncombatant vessel transporting Thallonian refugees, became caught in the crossfire.

**Kolk'r**
Yakaban supreme deity.

### *Gi'jan*
Hermat word for a quest of a personal nature.

### Giniv
Vulcan woman with a saturnine face and slightly stocky build. A close, personal friend of Doctor Selar since their childhood. Stood with Selar before the Judgment Council during the adjudication of Selar's parental rights regarding her offspring with Burgoyne 172.

### Goddard, Commander Seth
An officer at Starfleet Command who reactivated Lieutenant Soleta's commission to active duty, and posted her to serve as science officer aboard the *U.S.S. Excalibur* under Captain Calhoun.

### Gold, Lieutenant
A smug and aloof conn officer who serves on the night watch aboard the *U.S.S. Excalibur.* He is a tall, lean, and very handsome man of mixed African ancestry.

### Golden Gate Bridge
One of the largest suspension bridges on Earth, constructed in the 20th century. Located in San Francisco, and prominently visible from much of the Starfleet Academy campus.

### Gothil
A late member of the Ruling Council of Montos City, he requested a visit from the officers of the *U.S.S. Excalibur* shortly before his demise.

### Great Bird of the Galaxy
A creature once considered mythological, its existence was finally confirmed when it "hatched" from the planet Thallon, destroying that world entirely.

Subsequent investigation was correlated with the beast's mythology, and led to the conclusion that, when the Great Bird ended its last life-cycle, it imparted its "essence" to the world of Thallon, which accounted for the unique attributes of that world's mineral-rich surface. After a period of many centuries, that mineral bounty was reabsorbed as the creature's new incarnation gestated, and it was then reborn, destroying its temporary planetary "nest."

### Great Chair
The throne of The Overlord, leader of the Redeemers of Tulaan IV. The Great Chair is located in, of course, the Great Hall.

### Great Hall
The central gathering place and seat of power of the Redeemers, located on Tulaan IV. It is the single most impressive structure on the planet, with tall

spires and a large number of statues, including one at the top of the hall that absorbs the scant light of the Tulaan moons for use as energy.

**Great Machines, The**
Devices used by the Thallonians to tap into the vast mineral wealth of their planet's surface.

**Great Sea**
Water mass separating the main continent of Zondar from the neighboring continent of Kartoof.

**Great Square**
A public square in the city of Thal on the planet Thallon, now disintegrated.

*Grozit*
A profane Xenexian expletive.

**Hammons syndrome**
An incurable, degenerative bone disorder. Known to plague Romulans, it might affect other species, as well.

**Haresh**
A planet in Sector 221-G. Its culture has a long and proud tradition of formal dueling to resolve disputes of various kinds.

Haresh's entire population was slain by the Redeemer virus after they killed a Redeemer High Priest. Captain Calhoun of the *U.S.S. Excalibur* wanted to intervene earlier as a moderator, but was unable to reach the planet in time to prevent the tragedy.

Calhoun responded to this failure by breaking several dozen Starfleet regulations and slingshotting the *Excalibur* around the Haresh sun, traveling back in time by four days so that he would be able to intervene before the Redeemer virus was unleashed.

**Hauman**
The Makkusian leader who accepted the Federation's offer of membership from Captain Shelby of the *U.S.S. Exeter*. Hauman is a tall man, nearly seven feet tall, with long brown hair and an aura of peace that many humans find quite relaxing.

**He Who Had Gone On**
A phrase used by Redeemers to refer to their deity, Xant. Usually followed immediately by the phrase "He Who Would Return."

**He Who Would Return**
A phrase used by Redeemers to refer to their deity, Xant. Usually preceded immediately by the phrase "He Who Had Gone On."

### Hecht
Male security guard aboard the *U.S.S. Excalibur.* The first *Excalibur* crewman killed under the command of Captain Mackenzie Calhoun.

### Hermat Directorate
The primary governing agency of the Hermat species, presided over by the Hermat Elders.

### Hermat Elders
Shapers of the Hermat civilization, they control the Hermat Directorate, set official policy, and interpret the species' canon of laws.

### Hermat Embassy
On Earth, the Hermat Embassy is based in New York City. It is presided over by Tanzi 419, the Hermat ambassador to Earth.

### Hermat Language Council
Hermat Organization composed of linguists and scholars that meets annually and examines usage of the Hermat language by Hermats among themselves and in dealings with other species. Recent decrees mandated the use of new pronouns to reduce confusion during dealings with other species. The council also approves the adoption of words into the Hermat language that have worked their way into the common vernacular.

### Hermats
An hermaphroditic species, i.e., one that possesses fully functional gender organs of both male and female sexes. Not psychologically inclined toward long-term relationships or monogamy, they prefer to mate with several partners during their fertile years.

In addition, the Hermats possess razor-sharp canine teeth, and they have developed a unique set of pronouns to accommodate their dual-sex status.

Hermats, as a race, tend to keep to themselves. Their tendency toward segregation from the rest of the Federation is well known. While Hermats are not necessarily xenophobic, they have some difficulty relating effectively to members of other species. They are renowned for their versatility and ingenuity.

The Hermat Directorate does not officially recognize half-breeds as Hermat citizens, deserving of protection under Hermat law, despite a previous notable exception to the policy that was made on behalf of the half-breed offspring of Lebroq, a Hermat Elder.

### Herz
A Thallonian guard who was dismissed from the royal service for allowing Soleta and Ambassador Spock to escape Thallonian custody. He later allied himself with the rebellion, and took pleasure in lording it over the deposed prince, Si Cwan, when the former royal was returned to Thallon to face "justice."

### Hierarchy, The
The rigidly delineated chain of seniority and authority observed by the Redeemers.

### High Priest of Alpha Carinae, The
A High Priest of Xant, outgoing and actively evangelical, who was killed by the local population. His murder released a virulent pathogen that spread rapidly across the planet, killing every living thing, plant and animal alike, on the surface and in the oceans in just under 72 hours.

### High Priests of Xant
Missionaries of the Redeemers. One High Priest is sent to each world selected to be converted to Xantism. Violence against High Priests is discouraged by the presence of a lethal pathogen stored within their bodies, which is released in the event of their unnatural death. Killing a High Priest of Xant effectively unleashes a planetary death sentence, as the residents of Alpha Carinae unfortunately discovered.

### Hodgkis
A farmer in Narrin, on Yakaba. The biggest, most physically intimidating man in town, Hodgkis kept mostly to himself. When he appeared at town meetings, he was generally silent. Tended to be present at any major town event. After Rheela was attacked by a mob and her house burned down, Calhoun made an example of Hodgkis and coerced the man, and the other strong-bodied men of the town, to rebuild Rheela's home.

### Hodgkiss, Captain
Former commanding officer of the Federation starship *Exeter.* Was promoted to a higher position at Starfleet Command, paving the way for Elizabeth Shelby to receive her own first command.

### Houle, Lieutenant j.g. Michael
Tall, handsome shuttlebay officer aboard the starship *Excalibur,* under the command of Captain Calhoun. Was newly promoted to junior lieutenant when Morgan Lefler overpowered him and attempted to steal a shuttle from the *U.S.S. Excalibur* shuttlebay. Houle came to in the nick of time to prevent her escape and save the life of Ambassador Si Cwan.

### Howzer
Yakaban man. A preening, self-satisfied mortician, and an elder of the city of Narrin.

### Hufmin, Captain
Captain of the freighter *Cambon,* veteran star pilot, and occasional smuggler from Comar IV. His ship was disabled in The Gauntlet while transporting

Thallonian refugees to Sigma Tau Ceti, and was later rescued by the *U.S.S. Excalibur.* He was killed by Laheera of Nelkar.

### Hunger Zone, The

Origin point of the Black Mass, which remained in the zone until its hunger became overwhelming. The Black Mass was able to migrate out of the zone in any one of an infinite number of directions. The intervals between migrations were unpredictable, but were theorized to be related to how much matter the Black Mass consumed on each migration. Its three last forays were roughly 50, 10 and 90 years apart.

### Intempho

A trickster god in ancient Thallonian mythology, always pictured wearing a distinctive medallion. Hated the other gods, and strove to do away with them, but could not strike directly. Stole fire from the gods and gave it to the Thallonian people, who used it to create great works. According to legend, when the gods demanded that the Thallonians give back the secret of fire, the Thallonians set fire to the gods' Great Temple, ushering in their world's age of reason. Si Cwan read of this tale in an ancient book that was part of his sister Kalinda's library.

### Izzo

In a parallel reality's future, a Rolisan citizen, son of Arango and father of Faicco the Small. Does not exist in this reality, because his ancestors and their world were destroyed by the Black Mass.

### Janos, Ensign

Mugato security officer aboard *U.S.S. Excalibur.* Has thick white fur, a forehead horn, and fangs. Incredibly strong and highly intelligent; has a remarkable pain threshold and exceptional olfactory senses, as well as 300-degree vision, thanks to a flexible neck. Incapable of facial expressions other than rage or a grimace. Works the graveyard shift by popular demand. Eschews contact with other Mugato, not very sociable with regard to other crewmembers, endures a state of self-imposed, permanent celibacy.

### Jeet

A young Montosian man, whom Riella regarded as "gawky," but suspected might mature into a handsome man, given enough time.

### Jellico, Admiral Edward

A former, temporary captain of the *U.S.S. Enterprise* 1701-D, who clashed with Commander Riker and other members of the *Enterprise* crew. Jellico now serves as an admiral and oversees fleet operations in Sector 221-G.

### J'e'n't

Three-headed Xenexian god of lightning.

**Jereme**
Member of a species known as the Kotati. Quite short compared to Thallonians. A self-defense teacher, his students included Si Cwan and Kalinda. He was the only non-Thallonian individual who ever acted in a teaching capacity for the Thallonian royal family.

Considered one of the greatest self-defense experts in the history of Thallonian space, he came and went from Thallon as he wished, and maintained teaching facilities in several locations.

**Jeweled Sceptre of Tybirus, The**
Name given by the Barspens leaders to an artifact they stole from the people of Ysonte.

**Joining Place, The**
A special room held for generations by the family of Voltak of Vulcan, reserved for the formal Joining Ceremony of mates and the consummation of the *Pon farr* ritual.

**Judgment Council**
Primary judicial body of the planet Vulcan. Selar and Burgoyne argued their respective cases for parental rights of their offspring, Xyon, before the Council. Burgoyne was forced to claim the right of *Ku'nit Ka'fa'ar* to settle the dispute.

**Juif**
A henchman of Zoran.

**Jutkiewicz, Kyle**
Weapons officer aboard the *U.S.S. Exeter,* under the command of Captain Elizabeth Shelby. An old poker buddy of *Exeter* first officer Garbeck, who helped arrange his transfer to the *Exeter.*

**Kahn, Lieutenant Karen**
Chief security officer of the *U.S.S. Exeter,* under the command of Captain Shelby. Kahn is of mixed Asian ancestry, and is lightning-fast in a variety of martial arts. As deputy chief of security, she filled in for Lt. Basner during her period of physical therapy, shortly after Captain Shelby assumed command of the *Exeter.* Promoted to chief of security after Basner was killed in a holodeck accident caused by deactivating the security protocols.

**Kalinda**
Former princess of Thallonia and sister of deposed Thallonian prince Si Cwan, who calls her by her nickname, "Kally."

Abducted by Zoran to the planet Montos; there she was surgically altered to appear as a Montosian, and brainwashed into believing her name was Riella and that a Montosian woman named Malia was her mother. Zoran did this so that he could take advantage of Kalinda's Summons to locate The Quiet Place.

Kalinda escaped Montos with the aid of Xyon of Calhoun, with whom she had a short-lived romantic relationship aboard the *U.S.S. Excalibur.* Subsequent to her return from The Quiet Place, Kalinda's psychic connection with the recently demised has become strong.

### Kartoof

Continent on the planet Zondar where the prophet Ontear correctly predicted a devastating earthquake would strike.

### Katha Legend, The

A seminal work of Vulcan folklore that predates the species' era of logical philosophy.

### *Kayven Ryin*

A science and research vessel that sent the *U.S.S. Excalibur* an S.O.S. and a passenger manifest, which included the name of Si Cwan's missing sister, Kalinda. The listing of Kalinda later proved to be a ruse by Zoran to lure Si Cwan into a trap.

### Kebron, Zak

Chief of security aboard the *U.S.S. Excalibur,* under the command of Captain Mackenzie Calhoun. Kebron is a member of the high-density race called the Brikar, and must wear a small gravity compensator on his belt at all times. If he does not, his more-than-earth-normal mass makes it impossible for him to move.

He is capable of enduring phaser blasts that would kill a normal humanoid, and he is a skilled player of three-dimensional chess.

With Mark McHenry, he put a stop to a series of harrassing incidents and abductions on Liten. During that mission, Kebron witnessed a confrontation in which Q insinuated that Mark McHenry is not what he appears to be, and might be considerably more than just a preternaturally gifted human. Because Kebron and McHenry have been friends since their Academy days, Kebron has not decided who or what to believe, and is keeping his own counsel until he has more information.

### Killick

The Unglza chief delegate to the Zondarian pilgrimage, which was sent to greet Captain Mackenzie Calhoun and escort the the *U.S.S. Excalibur* to Zondar. He shared this responsibility with Ramed.

### Kondolf Academy

One of the foremost private universities in the Alpha Quadrant. Housed within an enormous satellite. Capable of providing top-notch education to the best and brightest of Federation society. Known for its difficult course work, grueling schedule and rigorous discipline.

### *Ko'norr'k'aree*
Legendary lost civilization on Vulcan.

### Korsmo, Captain
The now-deceased and highly regarded former captain of the Starfleet vessel *U.S.S. Excalibur.* He was Captain Mackenzie Calhoun's immediate predecessor, and was killed during the second Borg assault on Earth. His final actions as captain preserved the ship and saved many members of his crew.

### Kosa, Dr. Daniel, M.D.
Chief medical officer of the *U.S.S. Exeter,* under the command of Captain Shelby. A pure-blooded Sioux, jowly and gray-haired. Notorious for muttering "no respect" while giving physical examinations and treating illnesses and injuries.

### Kotati
Humanoid species, with skin tones similar to those of humans. Their hair is white and adorns the head in the shape of a ring. Males are known to sport long mustaches. They have fins at the sides of the head, and their eyes are an intense red.

### Krakis
Romulan soldier with a prominent facial scar. Ordered by Adis to kill Rajari, he was stopped by Starfleet Lieutenant Soleta.

### Krassus
An Orion slave trader who murdered Barsamis, a friend of Mackenzie Calhoun, over a commercial dispute regarding an Orion slave-girl named Zina, who subsequently became Krassus' mate. Krassus was killed when he foolishly attempted to ambush Calhoun with a knife.

### Krave
Adolescent Andorian male, student at the Kondolf Academy. Scion of one of the most influential families in the Federation. Arrested on Liten by Starfleet officers Mark McHenry and Zak Kebron for terrorizing the local populace.

### Krod
Mythical, semireligious place in Rolisan mythology. Often mentioned in expletive form, such as, "What in Krod is that?"

### Krul
A Dog of War. Not much of a warrior. Incapacitated by Xyon of Calhoun during the Dogs' attack on Barspens.

### Krusea the Black
Zondarian ruler whose rise to power was foretold by the prophet Ontear. Father of Otton the Unready.

### Krut
An Orion thug hired by Tapinza to come to Narrin Province on Yakaba and help eliminate Mackenzie Calhoun. Challenged Calhoun to a high-noon showdown on the main street of Narrin. Things did not go as well as Krut had expected.

### *Ku'nit Ka'fa'ar*
Ancient, nigh-obsolete Vulcan ritual; the term's literal translation is "The Struggle for the Way." It dates to the schism that occurred when the philosophy of logic was first espoused on Vulcan by Surak, leading to strife between those who chose logic and those who sought to retain the old, more violently passionate ways. Parents who held differing opinions fought for the right to impart their philosophy to their offspring. This schism led to the eventual exodus from Vulcan of the distant ancestors of the Romulans.

### *Ku'Net Kal'fiore*
Vulcan term of endearment; roughly translated, "one for whom you have use."

### Kurdwurble
Momidium captor-cum-companion to Morgan Lefler, a.k.a. Morgan Primus, during her five-year incarceration, for trespassing, in the Gamma Hydrinae system.

### Kurdziel, Dr. Karen
Member of the *U.S.S Excalibur* medical staff. A trim woman with blue hair and a great deal of patience.

### Kusack
Yakaban man, imprisoned by Majister Fairax at the same time as the marooned Captain Calhoun.

Kusack was a broadly built and imposing man. He was imprisoned for killing another man, Turkin, during a game of cards, in the presence of Majister Fairax.

### Laheera of Nelkar
Female commanding officer of an unnamed Nelkarite starship that attacked the *U.S.S. Excalibur.* She killed Captain Hufmin as part of her threat to extort technology from the *Excalibur,* but her ploy failed, and Captain Calhoun later exposed her actions to her people, who turned on her.

## Lamb, Lieutenant Tim
Geosciences specialist aboard the *U.S.S. Exeter*, under the command of Captain Elizabeth Shelby. An old poker buddy of *Exeter* first officer Garbeck, who helped arrange his transfer to the *Exeter*. He has a receding hairline.

## Lassie
Fictional canine character of a 20th-century Terran book, movie and television series. Lassie was a collie dog.

## Lebroq
Hermat elder who bore a half-breed child. Although half-breeds are not officially recognized as citizens under Hermat law, the offspring of Lebroq received a special exception because of Lebroq's high status among the members of the Hermat Directorate.

## Lee, Allison
Security officer aboard the *U.S.S. Exeter*, under the command of Captain Elizabeth Shelby. A "strapping" young woman, according to Captain Shelby. Accompanied Shelby on her second away mission to Makkus.

## Lee, Tarella
A woman whose favorite color is blue, favorite Earth season is winter, likes white wine but not red, dresses mostly in black, and has a deep laugh. Journeyed with Morgan Lefler into Thallonian space to find the Prometheans. Tracked them to Momidium, where Morgan was captured.

Tarella went on to Ahmista, where she discovered a Promethean weapon, bonded with it, and came to regard it as her lover. The weapon, seeking to protect Tarella, exterminated every other significant life-form on the planet. Tarella, alone on a mountaintop, went mad and spent her days drawing sustenance from the weapon and singing to herself. The weapon was later destroyed by Morgan Lefler.

## Lefler, Morgan
Mother of Starfleet officer Robin Lefler, who was conceived on Morgan's first date with Robin's father. A near-immortal being, Morgan faked her own death in a shuttle accident off the coast of New Jersey, during her daughter Robin's teenage years. Morgan turned up alive ten years later as a prisoner of the Momidiums in the Gamma Hydrinae system, traveling under the *nom du voyage* Morgan Primus. She'd come to Thallonian space with her companion, Tarella Lee, in search of the Prometheans.

## Lefler, Robin
Ops officer aboard the *U.S.S. Excalibur*, under the command of Captain Calhoun. Lefler had previously served as a member of the engineering staff of the *Enterprise* 1701-D. She is renowned for her off-the-cuff recitation of

"Lefler's Laws," pithy observations and comments that mysteriously seem to suit whatever occasion is presented.

A brunette, she stands 5'6" and tells people she weighs 108 pounds, though that's a bit of a fib. She's also a Virgo, likes reading children's poetry, and enjoys taking walks in light rain.

### Lemax system

A populated system of the former Thallonian Empire.

### Lesikor

World on which half the population was killed by the Redeemer virus after attacking their High Priest of Xant. The Redeemers intervened in time to stop the assault on the priest, thereby narrowly sparing the other half of the planet's population.

### Lio

A Makkusian who served as sensor officer aboard Hauman's flagship during the Makkusians' retaliatory strike against Corinder.

### Liten

Technologically unsophisticated world, whose inhabitants were the victims of harassment and practical jokes by a trio of delinquent students from the nearby Kondolf Academy, and by the ever-incorrigible omnipotent meddler, Q.

### Litenite Elders

Leaders of the civilian populace of Liten. Their position on the matter of extraterrestrial visitors to Liten is one of official governmental disbelief. They are effectively uninvolved with the farming territories of Liten, where the farmers tend to handle their own affairs without outside interference.

### Litenites

A slightly diminutive humanoid species, generally slender of build, with skin tinted a soft green. Indigenous to Liten. Among their customs is that of the dying robes, ceremonial garments worn at the expected time of death. The robes are handed down within families.

Litenite farmers are a hardy folk, rugged individualists who pay little heed to the Liten Elders and choose instead to follow their own ways and solve their own problems.

### Lost City of Malcour

A circular empty area four miles in circumference on the otherwise completely populated planet Malcour. Legend has it that it was once populated by a race of angels, who shunned contact with the immorality they saw around them, and eventually found a way to remove their city from the Malcourian people's contaminating influence. Archaeological investigations have been unable to confirm or refute the legend. The Lost City is a major tourist attraction on the planet, as such an empty space exists nowhere else on Malcour.

### Luukab

Riding animal used by Yakaban farmers. Large, hairy, and four-legged, with rocklike skin beneath thick hair, and a large tusk that is handy for a rider to hold on to. Require little in the way of nourishment, and seem to thrive on Yakaban cacti. Not well-suited to extreme heat, so it is often used for riding only very early or late in the day, or at night.

### Lyla

The dynamically capable, female-persona synthetic consciousness that guides Xyon of Calhoun's small starship, also named *Lyla*. The ship possesses a cloaking device and a wide variety of armaments. Lyla's personality engrams were taken from her previous incarnation as a humanoid and imprinted into the ship's computer, as part of an experiment by the scientists of the Daystrom Insititute.

### MacGibbon, Lieutenant Matthew

Conn officer of the *U.S.S. Exeter* under the command of Captain Shelby. Tall and well-muscled, with thick, red hair. Works very well in tandem with Lt. Althea McMurrian. Together with McMurrian, answers to the combined nickname "McMac."

### Maester/Maestress

A civic title employed by Yakabans to denote people of considerable influence.

### *Magellan,* shuttlecraft

Simulated vessel in the Black Hole thrill ride, located in the El Dorado resort hotel on Risa.

### Maja, Battle of

Skirmish in the Xenexian rebellion against Danteri oppression, in which M'k'n'zy of Calhoun fought and reputedly saw a vision of "colors."

### Majister

A Yakaban law-enforcement officer who serves under contract, usually for four-year terms.

### Makkus

World on the outer edge of Sector 47-B. After a period of rapid technological advancement, the Federation made first contact with Makkus, and began considering it for Federation membership. The invitation to membership was delivered by Captain Elizabeth Shelby of the *U.S.S. Exeter,* and was rejected by the Makkusian leader, Hauman. The planet has an official policy of pacifism. One of its prominent landmarks is a monument to peace constructed entirely of neutralized weapons.

### Makkusians

Indigenous people of the planet Makkus. Pacifists. They still have some ships capable of interplanetary and limited interstellar travel, but disdain most space ventures except those undertaken for humanitarian purposes. The Starfleet advance report on Makkusians' attitudes toward technology and exploration described the species as "disinterested with a passion." They adhere to a strict policy of political neutrality.

### Malia

Montosian woman, claimed to be the mother of Riella. Conspired with Zoran, also known as the Red Man, to hold Riella prisoner on Montos until the young woman experienced a vision of The Quiet Place.

### Mandylor 5

A planet of the Thallonian Empire on which a rebellion against the ruling class was suppressed.

### Mankowski

Transporter officer aboard the *U.S.S. Exeter,* under the command of Captain Elizabeth Shelby.

### Maro the Questioner

Leader of an Eenza clan from the western tropical region of Zondar.

### *Marquand II,* runabout

Replacement for the original, destroyed runabout *Marquand.* The *Marquand II* also was destroyed, by the Dogs of War, shortly after entering service.

### *Marquand,* runabout

A runabout assigned to the *U.S.S. Excalibur.* Si Cwan and Zak Kebron traveled aboard the *Marquand* to a rendezvous with the *Kayven Ryin* while the *Excalibur* was busy with another rescue. The rescue mission turned out to be a trap, and the *Marquand* was destroyed by Zoran, an enemy of Si Cwan. Si Cwan and Zak Kebron escaped by transporting to the *Kayven Ryin.*

### Maxwell, Dr.

A physician on the staff of Dr. Selar, aboard the *U.S.S. Excalibur.* Maxwell's passing resemblance to Dr. Selar's late husband, Voltak, initially led Selar to take a dislike to him, but the difficulties were quickly resolved.

### McHenry, Mark
Conn officer aboard the *U.S.S. Excalibur,* under the command of Captain Mackenzie Calhoun. McHenry is a brilliant navigator, capable of performing calculations faster than the ship's computer. And while he's doing that, he can also be calculating pi to the fiftieth decimal place.

He has short-cropped red hair, blue eyes, and freckles.

During a confrontation witnessed by Zak Kebron, Q suggested that McHenry is not what he appears to be, and might be considerably more than just a gifted human. McHenry denies Q's insinuation, but Kebron is uncertain what to believe or whether to share his thoughts on the subject with others.

### McMurrian, Lieutenant Althea
Ops officer of the *U.S.S. Exeter,* under the command of Captain Shelby. Has red hair that matches Lieutenant MacGibbon's in shade. McMurrian rarely smiles, her mouth perpetually drawn in a tight pucker. Together with MacGibbon, answers to the combined nickname "McMac."

### Medita
The primary population center of Tulaan IV and home of The Redeemers. An inhospitable region, where the temperature rarely rises above freezing, the nights are long, and the weather is harsh. Very little vegetation grows there.

### Meggan
A young girl, one of the refugees rescued by Captain Hufmin and later held hostage by Laheera of Nelkar. Meggan was rescued from captivity by the timely action of the crew of the *U.S.S. Excalibur.*

### Mekari
Romulan soldier who fatally shot Rajari on Titan colony. Starfleet Lieutenant Soleta shot off Mekari's hand with a phaser.

### Melkor, House of
Family name of the expatriate Romulan criminal Rajari.

### Meyer, Security Officer
A security officer aboard the *U.S.S. Excalibur* who beamed down to the planet Nelkar with Lieutenant Robin Lefler. Meyer is a slim and wiry man with blue eyes, and has a reputation as having the fastest quick-draw with a phaser on the ship.

### M'Gewn
Star sector in which the Redeemers attempted to impose their religion on the native inhabitants. The *U.S.S. Excalibur* took action to thwart the Redeemers' efforts there.

### M'Gewns

A warlike race that chose to challenge the Redeemers, ended up in over their heads, and requested aid from the Federation, which refused to become involved in a situation the M'Gewns had instigated.

### Milenko

In a parallel reality's future, son of Rolisan philosopher Faicco the Small. Does not exist in this reality, because his ancestors and their world were destroyed by the Black Mass.

### Milos, Praestor

Political leader of the city of Narrin. Duly elected for ten years in a row.

### Mitchell, Lieutenant Craig

Second-in-command of engineering aboard *U.S.S. Excalibur,* under Burgoyne 172. Handles direct reports from engineering staff, including ensigns Beth, Torelli and Yates. Heavyset, with brownish-black hair and a thick beard. Has recently lost some weight, and plans to lose more. Known for cracking the worst jokes on the ship.

### M'k'n'zy of Calhoun

The original, Xenexian given name of Mackenzie Calhoun, captain of the Federation *Starship Excalibur.*

### Mojov Station

An independent starport facility that serves as a convenient way station to several nearby frontiers and borders.

### Moke

Son of Rheela. An impetuous young boy who idolized Tapinza, to his mother's great concern. Encountered the marooned Captain Calhoun in the Yakaban desert, and led him back to Rheela. Was later revealed to be the true source of Rheela's weather-affecting talents; members of their family act as catalysts for one another, and are powerless when alone.

After his mother's murder, he was adopted by Captain Mackenzie Calhoun, who returned with the boy to Federation space.

### Momidiums

Humanoid species with a strong resemblance to slugs; indigenous to the Gamma Hydrinae system. Pale complexions that show the veins under the skin. They move in an undulating fashion that makes them appear to "ooze." Much stronger than they appear; faces are generally round, eyes are uniformly orange, noses are horizontal slits, mouths are narrow. They consider laughing out loud to be poor manners, and are not a very spiritual species. They held Morgan Lefler, a.k.a. Morgan Primus, as a prisoner for roughly five years, and traded her back to the *U.S.S. Excalibur* in exchange for agricultural technology and needed vaccines.

**Montagues**
One of the two fictional, feuding families in William Shakespeare's play, *Romeo and Juliet.* The Montagues' son, Romeo, falls in love with Juliet, daughter of their rivals, the Capulets.

**Montos**
World off the beaten path of Thallonian space. It has two moons. Not very advanced, with minimal space travel technology. Place to which Thallonian princess Kalinda was abducted by Zoran, and placed in the custody of a woman named Malia.

**Montos City**
Capital of the planet Montos. The land just beyond the city is not very inviting. Farther away are some small mountains and caves, which Montosian children are warned to avoid.

**Montos City, Ruling Council of**
Chief governmental body of Montos. Consists of one member, Fr'Col.

**Montosians**
Pale-skinned species indigenous to Montos.

**Mook**
Slightly stoop-shouldered species with compound eyes and mandibles that click during speech.

***Mra'he'nod***
Romulan word analogous to "armageddon," a day on which the skies of Romulus will blacken forever, and the dead will rise and rampage through the cities, taking all who lived with them into the abyss for eternity. Romulans tell their children that this day will eventually come, and for that reason it is important to remain in the good graces of departed relatives.

**Mueller, Commander Katerina**
Executive officer of the *U.S.S. Excalibur,* equal in rank to the first officer. Mueller commands the ship during night watch. Trim, tall, hard-bodied and athletic, dark blond hair in a severe knot, cobalt-blue eyes; a terrific rocketball player. Sports a thin scar on her left cheek, which she got while learning fencing in Heidelberg. Had a romantic relationship with Mackenzie Calhoun years prior to their assignment on *Excalibur,* while they served together aboard the *U.S.S. Grissom.*

**Muton**
Name of a conquerer in the eastern province of the planet Zondar, whose birth was foretold by the prophet Ontear. The prediction resulted in thousands of children born in that province being named Muton, a consequence that led critics to accuse Ontear of crafting a self-fulfilling prophecy.

**Naldacor**
Refuge of the Dogs of War.

**Narrin**
A township within the province of the same name on Yakaba. None of its buildings are higher than two stories, and are, for the most part, rather ramshackle.

**Narrin Province**
A geographic and political jurisdiction on the planet Yakaba. Was home to Rheela, Moke and Tapinza.

**Nelkar**
Homeworld of the Nelkarites, located within the former Thallonian Empire.

**Nelkarites**
The Nelkarites are a humanoid species with golden skin and no apparent hair. Their voices have a musical sort of vibrato, and some consider their appearance "angelic."

As a species they generally are regarded as fairly harmless, having never started any conflicts and willingly submitting to Thallonian rule. However, the Nelkarites are a scavenger race, pilfering abandoned alien technology and cobbling together their space vessels from various foreign parts, even though they don't always understand those technologies.

**Noble House, The**
A peculiar and ancient gathering place for some of the richest and most powerful members of the Romulan Empire, it consisted of several impressive towers topped by gleaming golden domes, atop which were poised statues of great winged creatures of prey. It was located north of the Romulan capital city and Rikolet, and was said to be the true seat of Romulan political power, until Rajari, acting posthumously through Starfleet officer Soleta as his unwitting accomplice, blew it up in the late 24th century with a device triggered from the Rikolet.

**NonObservable Team**
Standard part of UFP procedure for determining a planet's development and whether its population is ready to be approached for Federation membership. NOT teams watch the natives from hidden outposts, or, in some cases, disguise

themselves as residents of the world and mingle to get a reading of how socially advanced the culture is.

### Norpin V Colony
Wiped out in the early 24th century by unforeseen planetary hurricanes of tremendous intensity.

### NOT
Acronym for "NonObservable Team."

### Nyx
Adolescent Tellarite male, student at the Kondolf Academy. Scion of one of the most influential families in the Federation. Arrested on Liten by Starfleet officers Mark McHenry and Zak Kebron for terrorizing the local populace.

### Okur
One of two guards who protected Laheera of Nelkar. Okur also was Laheera's lover. He died defending her during a popular uprising.

### Olivan, Sientor
Former disciple of self-defense master Jereme. Human orphan; a childhood illness left him with minor physical tics. Considered the closest in ability to Jereme himself, he was being groomed to take over the school until he developed a streak of cruelty that prompted Jereme to expel him.

Later traveled under the alias Rafe Viola. Thallonian ambassador Si Cwan accused Olivan/Rafe of murdering Jereme after Si Cwan's sister, Kalinda, claimed to have witnessed the crime in a psychic vision. She later recanted, instead accusing Olivan's son, Nikolas Viola.

Olivan took credit for the creation of a computer virus that threatened the Federation during the "Double Helix situation" and subsequently destroyed the *Starship Excalibur.*

### Omon
A Dog of War, with meticulously kept dusky-red fur. Moved with assurance and swagger, and his mannerisms were big and full of confidence.

### Ontear
A prophet and seer on the planet Zondar. He predicted a victor in a civil war between two Zondarian ethnic groups, resulting in the breakdown of ongoing peace talks and several decades of additional bloodshed.

### Ontear's Realm
A "sacred land" on the planet Zondar. Some residents of that world believe the prophet Ontear continues to reside there, even after not having been seen for centuries.

**Ookla the Mook**
A student of Jereme, at the teacher's school on Pulva. He greeted Si Cwan and Kalinda upon their arrival.

**Otton the Unready**
Son of Krusea the Black. A Zondarian ruler whose defeat was predicted by the prophet Ontear.

**Overlord, The**
Leader of the Redeemers of Tulaan IV. Typically the tallest and largest of the Redeemers. Has the ability to use as weapons words that, according to Redeemer dogma, "tap into primal truths of the universe," truths the Redeemers claim they instinctively grasp and other species instinctively reject.

**Oxon Three**
World on which all life-forms were exterminated after its occupants killed a Redeemer missionary High Priest of Xant.

**Padulla Province**
Locality on the planet Yakaba.

**Paige, Lieutenant**
A tactical officer aboard the *U.S.S. Enterprise* 1701-E.

**Party Girl, The**
Nickname given to Robin Lefler by her mother, Morgan Lefler. It referred to the young Robin's constant efforts to cheer up Morgan, who frequently was depressed.

**People's Association for Peace**
A small group of young Alphan males on Alpha Carinae, who led a rebellion against their world's High Priest of Xant. When their de facto leader, Saulcram, killed the high priest, they unleashed the pathogen that killed them and exterminated every living thing on their planet.

**People's Meeting Hall, The**
The name given to the Thallonian Throne Room by Thallonian rebels, following the popular uprising and ouster of the royal family.

**Pit, The**
An area of Xenex roughly thirty miles across, known for its inhospitable clime—"unpredictable weather, dust storms, torrential rain followed by scorching drought, among other horrors"—and its vicious local fauna. The Pit is also regarded by some local dwellers to have supernatural overtones, and it some-

times is referred to as a rift in reality, or as a nexus for parallel realities. Until recently, it was the destination for a Xenexian coming-of-age ritual known as "The Search for Allways."

### Plains of Seanwin
Site of a battle on Xenex, in which rebel forces led by M'k'n'zy of Calhoun defeated a Danteri force led by Falkar.

### Plaser
A crude but effective Yakaban energy weapon that emits a stream of charged plasma along a focused energy beam. Its power source is not compatible with that of Starfleet phasers.

### Platypus
A marsupial, indigenous to Earth, reportedly created by the being known as Q.

### Plexian deities
The mandatorily promoted gods of Plexus IV.

### Plexus IV
Planet where it is a crime for newly arrived visitors to decline to stand and listen to the extremely long-winded proselytizing of the local clergy. A day/night rotation on Plexus IV lasts approximately 47 standard Earth hours.

### Praestor
Yakaban honorific that identifies someone as an elder and senior civic leader.

### Prime One
Second in the Hierarchy of the Redeemers. Answers only to the Overlord.

### Primus, Morgan
A *nom du voyage* of Morgan Lefler.

### Promethean ship
Huge beyond human capacity for measure, it has no solid sides, interior or exterior as understood by the human mind. It appears as waves of shimmering force in all directions, like a Dyson sphere of pure force.

### Promethean Space
Vast and nebulously defined region of space that overlaps Thallonian space by a wide margin. It is populated by a mysterious and advanced race that has a variety of names, but are generally known as the Prometheans.

### Prometheans

Large and powerfully built, this extremely advanced, mysterious race has a philosophy that is the opposite of the Prime Directive. Namely, they believe that it is their obligation to impart knowledge to various races who pass through their section of space. Unfortunately, thus far, the vast majority of races that have tried to use Promethean knowledge have come to untimely and fairly ugly ends. Morgan Lefler described them as "master manipulators."

### Pulva

Remote world in Thallonian space where the self-defense teacher Jereme maintained a school. One of the students at the school on Pulva was Ookla the Mook.

### Qinos

Yakaban man. Brother to Temo, Shadrak and Kusack. Helped Temo attempt to rescue Kusack from jail in the city of Narrin.

### Qontosia

Planet that has mountain ranges with vistas renowned for their breathtaking beauty. Suggested by Robin Lefler to her mother as an alternative vacation destination to Risa.

### Quiet Place, The

The sole planet orbiting Star 7734, at Marks 113–114, in Sector 18M. Pilgrims returning from the Quiet Place are inevitably transformed in some way, although for good or ill is not always easy to discern at first. Some return claiming to have seen the dead, or are able to predict the future, or possess arcane knowledge that they never had before. Some claim to have looked upon the face of God, or gods. Others come back as pale and wretched things, shadows of their former selves who can barely string two sentences together.

Apparently being sought by everyone, from the Thallonians to the Dogs of War to the Redeemers, for a variety of reasons. The planet recently was visited by Zoran Si Verdin, Si Cwan, Kalinda, Zak Kebron, Soleta, Xyon of Calhoun and several Dogs of War. Zoran and the Dogs of War were left stranded on the planet surface.

### Quincy, Theodore

Manager of the El Dorado hotel on Risa. A short, avuncular fellow with thinning hair and a too-eager-to-please manner. Known for being very fidgety with his hands. Murdered by Nikolas Viola, who broke Quincy's neck and threw his body down the hotel's computer core shaft.

### Quinzar the Wicked

Zondarian ruler whose rise to power was correctly predicted by the seer Ontear.

**Quinzix the Unforgiving**
Leader of an Eenza clan from the western tropical region of Zondar.

**Quiv**
Adolescent Tellarite male, student at the Kondolf Academy. Scion of one of the most influential families in the Federation. Arrested on Liten by Starfleet officers Mark McHenry and Zak Kebron for terrorizing the local populace.

**Rab**
Young Zondarian boy, of the Eenza ethnic group. Son of Ramed and Talila.

**Rajari**
Romulan criminal who raped T'Pas. That act produced a daughter, whom T'Pas named Soleta.

After a lengthy term of imprisonment in the Federation, Rajari bought his freedom with information that aided the Federation against the Cardassians in the Dominion War. He was released and set up in a civilian life on the Titan colony, where Soleta confronted him and learned he was terminally ill with Hammons Syndrome.

He subsequently manipulated her into carrying out his vengeance against the Romulan government, by tricking her into journeying to Romulus and triggering an explosion that wiped out a prominent landmark in the capital city, killing many Romulan leaders.

**Ramed**
The Eenza chief delegate to the Zondarian pilgrimage, which was sent to welcome Captain Mackenzie Calhoun and escort the *U.S.S. Excalibur* to Zondar. He shared this responsibility with Killick. After the reception on Zondar, he abducted Calhoun and attempted to kill him. He was stopped by Burgoyne 172.

**Red Gods, The**
Reverential term used by the technologically unsophisticated Rolisans to refer to the Thallonians, who were further described as "they who come from the sky and return to the sky at will."

**Red Man, The**
Riella/Kalinda's nickname for Zoran, whom she occasionally saw visiting her imposter mother, Malia, on Montos.

**Redeemers, The**
Fanatical worshipers of the deity Xant. Their religion is based in the Medita region of Tulaan IV. They proselytize alien species aggressively by sending missionary High Priests of Xant to convert entire worlds to Xantism. Members belong to a rigid structure known as the Hierarchy, at the top of which are the

religion's leaders, known as Prime One and The Overlord. Their skin is obsidian black, and their eyes are a deep glowing red.

The Redeemers were forced to seek the help of the *U.S.S. Excalibur* and its crew when their homeworld was targeted by the Black Mass. Although the rescue mission was ostensibly a success, Xyon of Calhoun released two small Black Mass creatures on the surface of Tulaan IV, undetected. It is possible the two creatures might eventually grow large enough to destroy the planet.

### *Relativity,* timeship

A Federation timeship from the 29th century, commanded by Captain Braxton. Appeared in orbit over the planet Haresh after Captain Calhoun ordered the *U.S.S. Excalibur* on a course that took it back in time by four days to prevent a worldwide catastrophe.

### Respler 4-A

A world of the Thallonian Empire on which dissidents who opposed the royal family were executed.

### Rheela

Female farmer, native to the planet Yakaba. Mother of a young son, Moke. The identity of the boy's father is ambiguous, and Rheela raised the boy alone.

Although Rheela had a reputation among her neighbors for being a rainmaker, a precious thing in a desert region, some of the people of Narrin, such as Maestress Cawfiel, tried to paint her as "evil" or as a "weather witch" because they disapproved of the fact that her son was born out of wedlock, and she either could not or would not name the father.

She was murdered by Temo, a Yakaban criminal.

### Riella

Name given to the kidnapped and brainwashed Thallonian princess Kalinda after her abduction to the planet Montos by Zoran. Despite attempts to cosmetically alter her appearance, her complexion remained too dusky for her to fit in with the pale-skinned Montosians, so she was placed in the custody of Malia, whom Riella was led to believe was her mother. Malia kept Riella under virtual house arrest as much as possible.

### Rier

Leader of the Dogs of War. The group's best fighter and tracker. Led the Dogs to Barspens in search of the rogue Thallonian warrior Sumavar.

### Rikolet, The

"The City of the Dead" located within the capital city on Romulus. Its stone and masonry work is even more magnificent than that of the capital itself. Its innumerable crypts spread out from the gated entrance, across the landscape as far as the eye can see. Interment in the Rikolet is reserved for the rich and powerful, nobility, senators and praetors. The House of Melkor's tomb is located down and to the left of the entrance.

**Rizpak, Minister**
Leader of Haresh.

**Rojam**
A henchman of Zoran.

**Rolisa**
In the future of a parallel quantum reality in which the Black Mass does not exist, this is the "greatest world in all the known galaxy." Though neither strategically located nor possessing valuable resources, it became a model for civilization, populated by great thinkers, and its guidance ushered in an era of peace, prosperity and evolution beyond the need for physical bodies. In the universe known by Captain Calhoun and the *U.S.S. Excalibur*, Rolisa was devoured by the Black Mass just less than twenty years prior to the fall of the Thallonian Empire.

**Rolisans**
Inhabitants of Rolisa. In one reality, they became great thinkers and leaders of a new galactic civilization. In this reality, they were a snack for the Black Mass.

**Ronk**
Impatient and perpetually cranky dirt farmer from the southern district of Yakaba. Now resides in Narrin, where he is particularly outspoken during the monthly town meetings.

**Rules of Vulcan Discipline, The**
Starfleet Lieutenant Soleta told her associate, Sharky, that the first three Rules are:
1) Know yourself completely.
2) Rule One is impossible.
3) To know oneself completely is to know that the impossible is illogical.
Soleta claims there are Vulcan masters who have spent lifetimes studying the ramifications of the first three rules. She also told Sharky the 5th Rule is "Ignore the previous three rules." The veracity of Soleta's account of the Rules to Sharky is unknown.

**Ryjaan**
A Danteri representative who opposed direct Federation involvement in Sector 221-G following the collapse of the Thallonian Empire. His father, Falkar of the House of Edins, was a Danteri military commander who was killed while attempting to hunt down M'k'n'zy of Calhoun.

### Sanf
Thallonian communications officer aboard the imperial flagship, under the command of Sedi Cwan.

### Saulcram
Young male resident of Alpha Carinae. During the rebellion against Redeemer control, he struck the killing blow against the High Priest of Alpha Carinae, releasing the pathogen that annihilated all life-forms on the planet.

### Scannell
Male security guard aboard the *U.S.S. Excalibur.* His mind was destroyed by hostile forces in the line of duty. He was the second *Excalibur* officer killed in the line of duty under the command of Captain Calhoun.

### Search For Allways, The
A coming-of-age ritual for adolescent Xenexians that entails traveling into the dangerous region of Xenex known as The Pit, and wandering its wastes until one experiences visions of one's future and discerns one's true purpose in life. The ritual of The Search vanished from modern Xenexian traditions as its death toll mounted, but it continues as an underground challenge or dare, a test of bravery and ego.

### Seclor, Doctor
Vulcan physician whose duties Selar assumed while Seclor recovered from a bout of xenopolycythemia. Selar was on Vulcan at the time, while caring for her newborn child, Xyon.

### Second Coming of Xant, The
An event foretold in Xantism, the religion of the Redeemers. The dogma of Xantism declares that Xant journeyed into another plane of existence by entering the Beyond Gate, and that in the future he will return through the Beyond Gate.

### Section AZ83 (read "Alpha Zed 83")
Sector of Thallonian space in which the Hunger Zone lies. All efforts to explore there have been unsuccessful. Probes launched into the Hunger Zone have been eaten.

### Sector 18M
Location of The Quiet Place, at Marks 113–114, in orbit of Star 7734.

### Sector 221-G
Location of the now-collapsed Thallonian Empire.

**Sector 47-B**
Region of the Alpha Quadrant to which the *U.S.S. Exeter* was assigned after the installment of Captain Elizabeth Shelby as its commanding officer.

**Seidman, U.S.S.**
Starfleet transport vessel, sent to pick up security officers Hecht and Scannell, the first two *Excalibur* crewmen killed under the command of Mackenzie Calhoun.

**Seklar**
Vulcan male patient of Doctor Seclor. Seklar had been having aches in his joints for close to a year before seeking treatment. He was attended to by Dr. Selar.

**Selar, Dr.**
Chief medical officer of the *Starship Excalibur,* under the command of Captain Calhoun. An accomplished physician who trained under Dr. Beverly Crusher of the *Starship Enterprise,* Selar has been accused of lacking bedside manner.

One of the most important moments in Selar's life was the death of her mate, Voltak, during the early moments of their *Pon Farr* joining. This premature disruption of the Vulcan mating ritual resulted in a delayed-reaction mating urge, which forced Selar to resume *Pon Farr* less than three years after the death of Voltak.

Although Selar initially selected Captain Calhoun to act as her mate during her unexpected *Pon Farr,* she ultimately mated with Burgoyne 172. She subsequently became pregnant, and named the child Xyon, in honor of Xyon of Calhoun, the ostensibly late son of Captain Mackenzie Calhoun.

**Selective Branching, Theory of**
Enevian precept of advanced temporal mechanics, developed in full by the 39th century, that is based on the highly fluid nature of time. The theory resolves many of the paradoxes that plagued early temporal theories.

**Selinium**
Capital city of the planet Nelkar.

**Sentries, The**
Law-enforcement officers on Liten.

**Shadrak**
Yakaban man. Brother to Temo, Qinos, and Kusack. Helped Temo attempt to rescue Kusack from jail in the city of Narrin.

**Shakespeare's Tavern**
Elizabethan-style tavern restaurant on Risa. Waitstaff wear period costumes,

and the decor includes such touches as manuscripts of Shakespearean plays in both English and the "original Klingon."

### Sharky

A heavyset, dyspeptic human with hair whose thinness is matched only by his temper. Has a paranoid, obsessive attachment to his freighter, and won't leave it except under the most dire of circumstances.

A fairly experienced smuggler, his life was saved by Soleta during her wandering years. He repaid his life-debt to her by helping her sneak onto the surface of Romulus and subsequently escape back to Federation space.

### Shelby, Captain

Commanding officer of Starfleet vessel *U.S.S. Sutherland*. No relation to Starfleet officer Elizabeth Paula Shelby.

### Shelby, Elizabeth Paula

Shelby was part of an elite unit assigned to assess weaknesses in the Borg during the Federation's early confrontations with that species. She served briefly as first officer of the *U.S.S. Enterprise*, under the command of Commander William Riker, following the abduction of Captain Jean-Luc Picard by the Borg. After helping rescue Picard, Shelby graciously relinquished her post as *Enterprise* first officer to Riker, who, though he often found Shelby to be frustrating, commended her as a highly skilled officer.

Shelby is a tough-as-nails officer who makes no secret of her ambitions. She was a top candidate for the captain's chair aboard the *Excalibur*, until the post was given to her ex-fiancé, Captain Mackenzie Calhoun. Shelby was assigned as Calhoun's first officer in hopes that she could keep him in line, but she soon established a *modus vivendi* with Calhoun, and served as his first officer with great distinction.

After the destruction of the *Ambassador*-class *U.S.S. Excalibur*, Shelby was promoted to captain of the *U.S.S. Exeter*. She later transferred off the *Exeter*, citing personality differences with her senior staff. She was offered, and accepted, command of the new, *Galaxy*-class *Excalibur*, and reassembled the crew from the prior *Excalibur*.

At the christening and launch ceremony for the new starship, Mackenzie Calhoun dramatically interrupted the proceedings to let it be known that reports of his demise were greatly exaggerated, and to propose marriage to Shelby. She accepted, and was married to Captain Mackenzie Calhoun on the bridge of the newly christened *Starship Excalibur*. Captain Jean-Luc Picard performed the ceremony.

### Sh'nab

A tribal elder of Calhoun during the early days of M'k'n'zy's tenure as warlord in the Xenexian uprising against the Danteri.

**Shuffer**
Head of the Corinder Science Council. Bears a slight resemblance to his brother, the Corinderian Ferghut, who implicated him and four other senior members of the Science Council for hatching a conspiracy to commit genocide against the Makkusian race.

**Shukko**
A Dog of War slain by Xyon of Calhoun for his skin, which was used as a disguise to fool Vacu.

**Sigma Tau Ceti**
Intended destination of the freighter *Cambon* before it was disabled by a crossfire in a region of the Lemax system known as The Gauntlet.

**Six-Card Warhoon**
A card game, similar to poker, and very popular on Mojov Station.

**Skarm**
A henchman of Zoran.

**Slon**
Younger brother of Dr. Selar, and a high-ranking member of the Vulcan Diplomatic Corps. Stands a head taller than Selar, and has a very triangular face and exceedingly curved eyebrows that give his face a look of perpetual disdain.

Slon posesses a far more wry outlook on life than do most Vulcans. He has no children, has never experienced *Pon farr,* and, according to Selar, never will, because of his "special friendship" with a Vulcan male named Sotok.

Acted as a liaison with the Hermat Directorate during Burgoyne's petition for parental rights regarding Xyon, Burgoyne and Selar's half-breed offspring.

**Soleta**
Science officer aboard the *U.S.S. Excalibur.* Her previous experience in Thallonian space made her uniquely qualified for service on the *Excalibur,* which was assigned to Thallonian space.

Early in her Starfleet career, during a visit to Plexus IV, she was detained for roughly 94 hours for failing, upon her arrival, to stand and listen to the local clergy extol the virtues of the Plexian deities.

During her first mission in Thallonian space, she was captured on the planet Thallon while conducting geological research. She was rescued from a Thallonian prison by Spock, who was disguised as a Thallonian. On their way to safety they were intercepted by Thallonian prince Si Cwan—later known as Federation ambassador Si Cwan—who chose to facilitate their escape rather than sound the alarm. Si Cwan later asked Soleta to repay this favor by smuggling him aboard the *Excalibur.*

Because her natural father was a Romulan, Soleta has occasional difficulty controlling her emotions. Soleta was raised by her mother, T'Pas, and adoptive father, Volak.

Soleta first confronted Rajari, the Romulan criminal who raped her mother, while she was serving aboard the starship *Aldrin*. Years later, she tracked the terminally ill Rajari to the Titan Colony, following his release from a Federation prison. He duped her into traveling to Romulus on his behalf and triggering an explosion that killed several Romulan leaders and leveled a prominent landmark in the capital city.

### Solly
A wandering Yakaban gunman who was a player in the card game that ended with Kusack's murder of Turkin.

### Sotok
Vulcan male who is the "special friend" of Selar's brother, Slon.

### Space Station K-19
Starport where Ensign Ronni Beth purchased a ring that she gave to Ensign Christiano as a gift.

### Spangler
Yakaban man. Runs the local newspaper in Narrin. Can be annoyingly earnest.

### Sparky
Nickname given by Burgoyne 172 to the Tentacle, a creature of energy plasma that attempted to hatch from the *U.S.S. Excalibur*'s warp core. Later protected the ship from being destroyed by the energy field of a Promethean vessel.

### SPIT
An acronym for a Short-range Portable Individual Transport device. Designed purely to allow the more affluent members of a society to travel privately, rather than by using a transport center as the "lower classes" are obliged to do.

### Staiteium
A really dense, tough metal.

### Star 7734
Location of The Quiet Place, in Sector 18M, Marks 113–114.

### Strange New Worlds
Popular officers' club and bar in San Francisco, puckishly named for the

Starfleet motto. The bar's motto is, "Explore Us!" Less exclusive than the popular, ship-captains-only San Francisco bar known as The Captain's Table.

### Sulimin the Planner
Leader of an Unglza clan from the eastern territories of Zondar.

### Sumavar
Once one of the premier warriors of the Thallonian Empire, he was well past his prime when he was hunted down on the planet Barspens by the Dogs of War, who sought from him the location of The Quiet Place. He died without giving it to them.

### Summons, The
In every third or fourth generation of the Thallonian imperial family, a princess of the line, upon reaching a certain age, receives the Summons. There is never advance warning, the princess simply disappears one night, sometimes to return, sometimes never to be seen again. If the princess returns, she never speaks of what she witnessed, except in the vaguest of terms. Kalinda was the last Thallonian princess to receive the Summons.

### Suti
A friendly nickname for Suti-Lon-sondon, used only by the Zondarian prophet Ontear.

### Suti-Lon-sondon
One of the oldest acolytes of Zondarian seer Ontear. Sometimes referred to by Ontear simply as Suti.

### Takahashi, Lieutenant
Night watch ops officer aboard the *Excalibur.* Also known as "Hash." An Asian man of youthful mien, with ostensibly naturally blond hair.

### Talila
A Zondarian woman, of the Eenza ethnic group; wife of Ramed; mother of Rab.

### Tanzi 419
Hermat ambassador to Earth. Long, silver hair. An old friend of Burgoyne 172, Tanzi attempted to intercede on Burgoyne's behalf with the Hermat Directorate, which refused to entertain Burgoyne's petition for official Hermat intervention in his custody battle with Selar over their offspring, Xyon.

### Tapinza, Maester
Male Yakaban, neighbor of Rheela. Was the most successful businessman in Yakaba's three major provinces, and an expert at piloting landskippers and

other forms of desert transportation. Had a fierce scar that ran from the top of his forehead to just under his nose. His brow was a bit sloped, his eyebrows thick and green, and his overall effect was that of a primitive. He was, however, quite astute, and saw in technology a potential that many of his fellow Yakabans do not see. He was killed by Moke, as revenge for his role in the death of Moke's mother, Rheela.

### Tara
Rolisan woman. In a parallel reality, a distant ancestor of Faicco the Small, one of the greatest thinkers in the known galaxy. In this reality, she died during childbirth when the Black Mass devoured Rolisa.

### Team Room, the
The main crew lounge aboard the *U.S.S. Excalibur,* located on Deck 7 in the rear of the saucer section. Its name was a holdover from a term used in the early days of space exploration.

### Temo
Yakaban man. Brother to Kusack. Came to Narrin with his two brothers, Qinos and Shadrak, to rescue his other brother, Kusack, from Majister Fairax's gaol. In the attempt, Temo murdered Majister Fairax. Temo and his brother Qinos later attempted to ambush Calhoun during a duel with Krut. Their scheme did not go as planned. The ambush went awry, Temo murdered Rheela during the altercation, and was killed in turn by Rheela's son, Moke.

### Tentacle, The
Aptly descriptive name given to a creature composed of energy plasma that "hatched" from the warp core of the *U.S.S. Excalibur,* killing Ensign Christiano. Research by Lt. Soleta indicated the Tentacle was likely related to the Great Bird of The Galaxy, which destroyed Thallon.

### T'Fil
Vulcan female. Nursemaid to Selar's child, Xyon.

### Thal
The capital city of the now-destroyed planet Thallon.

### Thallon
A disintegrated pile of rubble that was once the capital planet of the Thallonian Empire. It was never harmless.

### Thallonian Empire, The
A wide-ranging autocratic empire that controlled most of the star systems in Sector 221-G, until its recent collapse.

**T'han**
A large, agrarian animal on Xenex.

**T'hanchips**
Xenexian profanity that refers to the fecal products of a *t'han*. Can be used as a synonym for "nonsense."

**Tharns**
Xenexian animal held in low regard. Typically referenced in the Xenexian epithet, "son of a tharn."

**Thul, Gerrid**
"Madman" who created a computer virus that came close to wiping out the Federation. His allies, who included Rafe Viola (a.k.a. Sientor Olivan), introduced a delayed-reaction computer virus into the *Excalibur* that destroyed it. That virus was an artifact of the incident the Federation called the "Double Helix situation." The same virus was later introduced by Nik Viola into the central computer of the El Dorado hotel on Risa.

**Tiempor, Shad**
Ruler of the Enevian Empire in the 39th century. Placed the *Excalibur* and the planet Haresh under retroactive Enevian protection in the 24th century, thwarting a Redeemer assault on the planet and preventing the Federation timeship *Relativity* from destroying the *Excalibur*, which tried to protect Haresh from the Redeemers.

**Titan Colony**
One of the first extraterrestrial colonies founded by Earth's fledgling space program. By the 24th century, the colony was in serious disrepair and was generally neglected by the Federation. Its main entry port is Catalina City. Local authorities enforce strict laws against the possession and use of energy weapons.

**Torelli, Engineer's Mate**
An engineering crewman, working under Chief Engineer Burgoyne 172, aboard the *U.S.S. Excalibur.*

**Toth**
Tactical officer aboard the Thallonian flagship under the command of Sedi Cwan.

**T'Pas**
Mother of Starfleet officer Soleta. Raped by a Romulan criminal named Rajari on a remote world. The rape produced Soleta, whom T'Pas and her mate, Volak, raised as their own child. T'Pas died unexpectedly, at a young age for a Vulcan, the victim of a rare virus.

### T'Pau

Ancient Vulcan female adjudicator. Presided over Burgoyne 172's petition for parental rights to Xyon, whom he sired with Selar. T'Pau upheld Burgoyne's parental right to demand the ritual of *Ku'nit Ka'fa'ar.*

### Tulaan IV

A planet of varied climates, its lush agrarian centers are sparsely populated and tended by robots. The Redeemers congregate in a harshly cold and inhospitable region known as Medita.

### Tulaman the Misbegotten

Leader of an Eenza clan from the western tropical region of Zondar.

### Tulleah, Mount

A high elevation located in the Gondi Desert on Vulcan. Selar ascended Mount Tulleah many times during her youth, finding it a source of peace and contemplation. It is faithfully represented in at least one holodeck simulation aboard the *U.S.S. Excalibur.*

### Tulley, Lieutenant Commander Chris

Science officer of the *U.S.S. Exeter,* under the command of Captain Shelby. Slim and waspish. Graduated from Starfleet Academy two years early.

### Turkin

A Yakaban man who was murdered by Kusack following a disagreement over the outcome of a card game.

### Unblinking Eye of Mynos, The

Name given by the Barspens leaders to an artifact they stole from the people of Ysonte.

### Unglza

An ethnic group on the planet Zondar that engaged in a protracted civil war against its neighbors, the Eenza. The eventual outcome of their conflict was predicted by the Zondarian prophet Ontear.

### Vacu

The most massive of the Dogs of War, a full head and a half taller than Rier, the leader. Not very bright. Was deceived by Xyon of Calhoun, who slipped past Vacu to use the Dogs' own command ship to destroy their other vessels.

### Verdin, Zoran Si

A Thallonian agitator, a best friend turned worst enemy of deposed prince Si Cwan. Si Cwan described Zoran as being "almost insane in his hatred."

Zoran laid a trap for Si Cwan aboard the science vessel *Kayven Ryin* by placing the name of Si Cwan's sister, Kalinda, on the ship's passenger manifest. Zoran later confessed to having murdered Kalinda, but subsequently recanted the statement. In truth, he abducted Kalinda to the planet Montos, where he brainwashed her into believing she was a Montosian, the daughter of a woman named Malia. Verdin visited occasionally to keep tabs on Kalinda, so that he might follow her when she received The Summons, to locate The Quiet Place.

### Viola, Nikolas

Son of Rafe Viola. A young man, commonly goes by the diminutive "Nik." Handsome, with strong, chiseled features, eyes of ocean blue, thick eyebrows. His nose is slightly large. His hair is blond, combed tightly back, with a perfectly pointed widow's peak.

Rescued Robin Lefler from a tight spot while spelunking on Risa. Later murdered Quincy, manager of the El Dorado hotel, and attempted to kill engineer Montgomery Scott, who escaped attack by leaping—apparently to his own death—down a deep computer core shaft. Nik was in the computer core area to plant a virus in the El Dorado's central computer on behalf of his father, Rafe, who might have been manipulating him through mind control.

Nik was killed on Risa by a subterranean, gelatinous carnivore.

### Viola, Rafe

An alias of Sientor Olivan, a human male whom Si Cwan accused of murdering Si Cwan's teacher, Jereme, based on the account of a dream experienced by Si Cwan's sister, Kalinda.

A tall and distinguished-looking man, Rafe was handsome, and his hair was carefully cropped and shaped, with crests of gray on either side.

Rafe Viola/Sientor Olivan was instrumental in creating and delivering a computer virus that destroyed the Federation *Starship Excalibur*. He planted a similar virus in the central computer of the El Dorado hotel on Risa.

### Volak

Mate of T'Pas and nonbiological father of Starfleet officer Soleta. Tall, distinguished, with eyes glittering with quiet intelligence.

### Voltak

A Vulcan archaeologist who was the husband and mate of Dr. Selar. He died of a coronary failure while consummating the *Pon farr* ritual with Selar.

### Vonce of the Many Fortunes

Leader of an Eenza clan from the western tropical region of Zondar.

### *vrass*

A Vulcan vegetable soup that simmers for a long time before being served.

**Wagner, Lieutenant Glen Scott**
Deputy chief of security aboard the *U.S.S. Exeter,* under the command of Captain Elizabeth Shelby. Wagner reports directly to Lt. Kahn, *Exeter* chief of security.

**Walking Grin, The**
Nickname given to Robin Lefler by her mother, Morgan Lefler. It referred to the young Robin's constant efforts to cheer up Morgan, who frequently was depressed.

**Watson, Polly**
A transporter officer aboard the *U.S.S. Excalibur.*

**Widow Splean**
Feisty Litenite woman farmer who was assaulted by delinquent students of the Kondolf Academy. The two Tellarites and their Andorian accomplice threatened to knock over the Widow Splean's harmless furn.

**Williams, Commander Holly Beth**
Starfleet officer assigned to the command offices on Vulcan. Friendly, casual, insists on being called "H.B.," and won't answer to "Holly." Speaks with a slow drawl, has a round face, seen-it-all eyes, and short brown hair. Provided clandestine, unofficial help to Soleta in locating the released prisoner Rajari.

**Wynants, Medical Technician Patty**
Member of Dr. Kosa's staff aboard the *U.S.S. Exeter.* Twin sister of Sali Wynants, who serves aboard the *Exeter* in the same capacity. The twins are known to speak in sync with one another, and to sometimes finish each other's sentences.

**Wynants, Medical Technician Sali**
Member of Dr. Kosa's staff aboard the *U.S.S. Exeter.* Twin sister of Patty Wynants, who serves aboard the *Exeter* in the same capacity. The twins are known to speak in sync with one another, and to sometimes finish each other's sentences.

**'Xana**
Woman to whom Morgan Primus addressed a personal letter. Although the exact identity of the addressee is unclear, there is some evidence to suggest the letter was intended for Lwaxana Troi of Betazed.

**Xant**
Deity of the Redeemers of Tulaan IV, who refer to Him as "He Who Had Gone On" and "He Who Would Return." Redeemer mythology holds that Xant

passed through the Beyond Gate into another plane of existence, and that He will return through the Beyond Gate at the time of the Second Coming of Xant.

### Xantism
The religion of the Redeemers, who worship the "great god Xant."

### Xenex
A Class-M world located near the border of the Thallonian Empire in Sector 221-G. It is the homeworld of the Xenexians, and of Starfleet Captain Mackenzie Calhoun, a.k.a. M'k'n'zy of Calhoun, who in his youth led a revolt that ended the 300-year-long occupation and oppression of Xenex by the Danteri.

### Xenexians
Indigenous inhabitants of the planet Xenex.

### Xyon
The half-Vulcan, half-Hermat offspring of Burgoyne 172 and Dr. Selar. Named in honor of Xyon of Calhoun.

Although predominantly Vulcan in appearance, Xyon displayed such Hermat traits as early maturation of physical skills and a mode of locomotion that involves traveling on all fours rather than fully upright.

### Xyon of Calhoun
Son of M'k'n'zy and Catrina of Calhoun. Captain of the *Lyla*. Born during the Xenexian uprising against the Danteri. Possesses low-level, instinctual psionic abilities that proved sufficient to fool the Redeemer Overlord into believing Xyon was dead. Later faked his own death during the *Excalibur*'s rescue of Tulaan IV from the Black Mass, by slipping away during a crisis using his ship's cloaking device.

### Yakaba
A harsh planet with large swaths of barren terrain and desert. Its city communities tend to be fairly insular in nature. Communication and contact between localities is discouraged.

### Yakaban
Humanoid species indigenous to Yakaba. Typically pale in complexion.

### Yates, Ensign
An engineering crewman, working under Chief Engineer Burgoyne 172, aboard the *U.S.S. Excalibur.*

### Yorick
Fictional character: the late lamented court jester of Shakespeare's play, *Hamlet.*

### Yoz, Thallonian Chancellor

A leader of Thallonia who attempted to apprehend Soleta for trespassing. Soleta managed to embarrass Yoz while she resisted arrest, eventually trapping him under his own mount. Yoz later helped the people of Thallonia overthrow the ruling class, including High Lord Si Cwan and his family.

### Ysonte

Technologically inferior world, from which such priceless treasures as centuries-old, elaborately carved gems and statues were stolen by Barspens leaders, who presented them to the Barspens people as "sacred artifacts."

### Ysontians

Native inhabitants of Ysonte. Little technology, not much in the way of weaponry. Excellent artisans and sculptors. They hired Xyon of Calhoun to recover their stolen artifacts from the Barspens.

### Yukka Chips

Small, greenish, curved waferlike Thallonian delicacy.

### Zanka

Litenite female, the beautiful wife of Adulux. She was abducted for several days, or possibly longer, by Q. After her rescue from captivity by Adulux, Mark McHenry and Zak Kebron—upon whom she developed an unrequited crush—she soon left Adulux for another man.

### Zantos

This world produces what is regarded as the best ale in the quadrant, better even than Romulan Ale and twice as difficult to obtain. A Starfleet survey team was captured on Zantos by local inhabitants, and the leader was subjected to harsh punitive measures. Allegedly, Starfleet Captain Mackenzie Calhoun snuck onto the planet's surface and absconded with a case of Zantos Ale, with the Zantosian fleet in hot pursuit.

### Zina

An Orion slave-girl who belonged to an Orion trader named Krassus. She originally was meant to be sold by Krassus to a buyer named Barsamis, but Krassus reneged on the deal and murdered Barsamis when he filed a protest. Krassus later lost Zina to Mackenzie Calhoun in a game of Six-Card Warhoon, but the loss turned out to be a ruse to allow Zina to distract Calhoun with her feminine charms while Krassus attempted to stab Calhoun from behind. Their plan failed. Miserably.

### Zondar

Planet wracked by a bloody civil war between the Unglza and Eenza that was halted by the Thallonians, who were under the command of a distant ancestor of Lord Si Cwan. The Thallonian fleet ended the conflict by destroying the eastern seaboard of a major Zondarian continent, killing 500,000.

### Zondarians

Natives of Zondar. They have leathery skin that glistens, making it appear always wet. They are all bald, devoid of body hair, and have clear eyelids that make clicking sounds when they blink. They are highly insular by nature and resentful of outsiders; their social structure is based around clans. They possess limited transporter technology that can beam materials to and from fixed transmat pads, but they lack the capture-and-receive technology possessed by the Federation and other, more advanced major Alpha Quadrant species.

Ever wonder what to serve at a
Klingon Day of Ascension?

Just can't remember if you bring a gift
to a *Rumarie* celebration?

You know that Damok was on the
ocean, but you can't recall just what
that means?

Have no fear! Finally you too
can come prepared to any
celebration held anywhere in
Federation space.

Laying out many of the complex and compelling rituals
of *Star Trek*'s varied cultures, this clear and handy guide
will let you walk into any celebration with assurance.
*Plus*: in a special section are the celebrations that have
become part of the traditions of Starfleet.

From shipboard promotion to the Klingon coming-of-age
to the joyous exchange of marriage vows, you can be a
part of it all with

# STAR TREK®
## Celebrations

Pocket Books
A VIACOM COMPANY

3116